Praise for Sherrilyn Kenyon

"Kenyon's writing is brisk, ironic, sexy, and relentlessly imaginative." —*Boston Globe*

"The most in-demand and prolific author in America these days." —*Publishers Weekly*

"[Kenyon] sucks you into [her] world and keeps you there from the first page until the last." —*Midwest Book Review*

"Kenyon delivers the goods readers have come to expect, and more." —*Booklist*

BORN OF VENGEANCE

SHERRILYN KENYON

St. Martin's Paperbacks

This is a work of fiction. All of the characters, organizations, and events portrayed in this novel are either products of the author's imagination or are used fictitiously.

BORN OF VENGEANCE

Copyright © 2017 by Sherrilyn Kenyon.

For information address St. Martin's Press, 175 Fifth Avenue, New York, NY 10010.

ISBN: 978-1-250-08279-4

Our books may be purchased in bulk for promotional, educational, or business use. Please contact your local bookseller or the Macmillan Corporate and Premium Sales Department at 1-800-221-7945, ext. 5442, or by e-mail at MacmillanSpecialMarkets@macmillan.com.

Printed in the United States of America

St. Martin's Press hardcover edition / February 2017
St. Martin's Paperbacks edition / January 2018

St. Martin's Paperbacks are published by St. Martin's Press, 175 Fifth Avenue, New York, NY 10010.

10 9 8 7 6 5 4 3 2 1

For my older brother, who gave me the love of all things space related and who first introduced me to science fiction. And to my sons, who are starting their own SF novels, as well as my hubby for all the SF conventions he's indulged me with for all these decades. To my readers, especially those who began The League adventures with me back in the early 1990s when the first novel was published—my goodness, how far we've come! And to all those who continue to look to the skies and think, what if?

And for my incredible team at SMP for all they do, especially Monique, Erica, Brant, Jennifer, Alex, and John, who do so much on my behalf. They are my silent heroes. And Ervin for the incredible covers he produces! And of course, Robert and Mark for being my champions in all things and for all the countless hours of hard work you put in. You guys rock!

ACKNOWLEDGMENTS

I'd like to take a special moment to acknowledge my grandfather, the Rev. O. C. Allred, who, when a little girl asked, "Grandpa, do you think there's intelligent life on other planets?" he answered with a profound statement that forever changed my life: "Well, Sherri, the Bible doesn't say that the good Lord only created one Heaven and one Earth. So it's quite possible that there could be millions of other worlds out there that He made. As for intelligence, I certainly hope so. 'Cause Heaven knows it's a struggle some days just to find a little bit of it here on Earth."

PROLOGUE

"Go ahead and court-martial me. I'm not about to baby-sit some pampered little bastard because he's bored with cocktail parties!" Major Ember Wyldestarrin glared at the colonel who'd just dropped a serious bombshell in her lap. The smug wanker walked beside her as if he were enjoying the fact she'd been assigned watch duty for some aristocratic playboy whose reputation for hedonism must have set untold intergalactic records.

And if not, *that* was truly a crime. Surely no one had ever been born with a larger sense of entitlement or ego than the infamous Bastien Cabarro. She couldn't pick up an e-mag or news feed that wasn't laced with his latest exploit or misadventure. The only thing larger than his list of paternity suits was the bill for his average dinner party.

Yeah, *that* was just what she wanted for a wingman.

Never.

Colonel Werrin smirked. "Technically he's a very large pampered bastard. Or pain in the ass. At least for me. Which is why he's being assigned to *you*. My least favorite pain in the ass. After *your* last stunt, I can't think of a better punishment."

She scoffed indignantly. "Stunt? I saved twenty-two soldiers! Anyone else would have been given a medal."

"Yes, had you not brought down half the station in the process of it. And torched Colonel Dayan's prized fighter."

"Technically *that* wasn't an accident." She used his words against him to point out the fact that she'd quite intentionally set fire to Syrin's fighter. After she'd caught the worthless prick cheating on her.

In her own bed.

With her youngest sister.

It'd been a moral imperative. Besides, they should all be grateful she'd only assaulted his ship, given what she'd really wanted to destroy. In fact, it was still a daily struggle not to murder that prick where he stood.

And her sister, to boot.

"Which is why you're being assigned a new wingman. And you're lucky. General Dayan wanted me to bust your rank down to private and make you a member of the rank-bust club along with Cabarro, who just went from major to captain two weeks ago after *his* last stunt—and that by order of his own uncle."

Note to self, never ever *date a man whose father outranks me.*

Yet another reason why she wanted to stay far away from Cabarro. His uncle didn't just outrank her—that bastard *was* their military. Commander general of the Gyron Force she was a part of, Barnabas Cabarro was also the prime commander for the entire Kirovarian armed services. You crossed him and he could not only bust your rank, he could end your life and no one would question it. The fact he could take his own pampered nephew's rank without sanction said it all.

No one questioned Barnabas Cabarro when it came to

the Kirovarian military. Not even the pampered visir asshole.

But that was neither here nor there. Rolling her eyes, she wanted to scream in frustration. It galled her through and through to be in this mess because of a conscience-less prick who couldn't keep it in his pants.

Then again, it wasn't completely Syrin's fault, really. It was mostly because of her temper that knew no boundaries and her baby sister who had no morals.

I will not be that stupid again.

Next time I'll murder the bastard and hide his body where they will never find it.

And she couldn't imagine anything worse than to be saddled with a womanizing pig prince for a wingman. He'd be like a kid in a candy store with her all-female family. Never mind what Alura would do if she ever saw him . . .

Yeah, this had all the makings of hell for her.

As they approached the training field, she swept her gaze over the soldiers there. Two dozen were running maneuvers.

Well, almost two dozen . . . one who should be among them stood off to the side with a cocksure grin as he made time with a corporal.

Oh, let me guess. . . .

That had to be Cabarro. He fit what she was expecting to a T. Tall, gorgeous, and more than aware of it. What a scabbing piece of work.

She felt sick just to be *this* close to him, and he was across the quad. Last thing she wanted was to be near enough to look into what would no doubt be a pair of smug aristo eyes. "Please, Colonel. I'll do *anything* to get out of this."

"Beg all you want. Cabarro is yours till the binary suns of Ritadaria freeze over."

Of course he was.

Just as she started to curse her CO out loud and get that court-martial so that she wouldn't have to worry about this, she heard a high-pitched squeal. At first, she thought it her imagination.

Until it came closer.

Louder.

"Incoming!" she shouted a few seconds before a bomb struck home. And this wasn't a drill. It hit the building to the east with such force that the percussion and aftershock knocked her from her feet. Fire and shrapnel exploded as the bomb disintegrated the north arsenal and set off every piece of ordnance kept inside its facility—causing even more damage and mayhem.

The playboy cried out and dashed off to hide.

Of course he did.

The aristos would *never* sully their hands with helping the wounded. Or trying to dig out survivors.

Furious, she ran to the training field, where a number of their younger soldiers had been injured. As quickly as she could, she checked on them and assisted the medics.

Until a frantic cry drew her attention toward the offices on her left that had partially collapsed during the aftershocks. "Lieutenant Wyldestarrin? Can you hear me?"

No . . . please God, no!

Her heart stopped as she realized one of her younger sisters was inside that building. A building that was about to come down completely, which would probably render a rescue impossible.

Then she heard the voice beneath the rubble that begged for help. One that cried out for their mother and father.

Tears welled in her eyes. "Alura!" She ran toward the rescue workers with everything she had as she forgot all about the fact that minutes ago she'd wanted her sister dead. That Alura had betrayed her. All that mattered right now was that her sister needed her and that she couldn't let her baby sister die.

That was her blood in that hole.

And she was the big sister Alura relied on.

By the time Ember reached them, she saw there were several soldiers trying to dig Alura out of the rubble.

One in particular stood over the tenuous remains with calm confidence as he secured a line to the ground. "Listen to my voice, Lieutenant, and breathe. I'll get you out in a few minutes. You with me?"

Alura answered with pain-filled whimpers.

Ember scowled as she saw what the tallest soldier there was planning to do. Dressed in a drab olive-chip battlesuit that kept his features completely hidden, the captain intended to rappel to her sister's side in the hole where she was trapped. "You can't reach her like that."

The captain scoffed at her concern. "'Course I can, Major. Been climbing and rappelling my whole life. Certified for rescue. Now, stand back. We don't need anything else falling in on the lieutenant. Especially not her older sister."

And with that he literally jumped straight down into the hole at an extremely reckless pace.

Convinced he was going to land squarely on top of her sister and kill her, Ember bit back a scream. But with expert skill, he stopped his descent a few inches from Alura's position and then, in a most amazing feat, flipped himself upside down so that he could begin shifting debris from Alura's body.

"Hey gorgeous," he said teasingly as he huffed to dislodge a beam. "Come here often?"

"Are you insane?" Alura snarled at him.

"Yeah. Good thing for you, too, otherwise I wouldn't be here right now. I'd be off somewhere where it's safe."

Alura laughed, then groaned in absolute misery.

Terrified and shaking, and mad at herself because there was nothing more helpful she could do, Ember tried to see what he was doing, but it was extremely difficult. Instead, she heard the steady, patient tone of his voice as he explained to Alura what he was doing while teasing her with light banter in spite of the danger.

"Now, hold your breath. This is going to pinch a bit. But as soon as it's moved, we can get you out of here."

"We?"

"Yeah, me and the strident voices in my head that are calling me even more names than you are. Much ruder ones, too. 'Cause let's face it, there are much better places to be this time of year. Ever been to North Beach?"

"No." Alura sniffed back her tears.

"Well, you stay with me and don't let anything happen to yourself, and I promise I'll take you and your husband or boyfriend. Pet gopher. Whatever tickles your fancy. We'll all go for a nice, long vacation after this."

Alura cried out in sudden agony.

"What happened?" Ember shouted before she could stop herself.

"It's fine," he said in that same calm, even tone. "I got her free and—" His voice broke off as he tilted his head to listen to something. "What's that sound?"

It took her a heartbeat to hear it.

"Shit!" Ember studied the sky for what she heard. "It's another run!"

His expletive was much more colorful and vulgar.

Worse? The rope holding them slipped from the additional weight of her sister's body as he lifted her free and began climbing for the surface. The anchor holding it in the ground started to come loose.

Ember grabbed it and held fast. "I'm pulling!"

He didn't speak. Rather, he moved faster as he struggled to get himself and Alura out of the hole as quickly as possible.

The rope slipped even more, threatening to send them both even deeper into the wreckage.

"Help!" Ember shouted for assistance with the rope and anchor. But with the new run headed for them, everyone was fleeing to save their own asses.

No one cared that she was in the open or that her sister and her rescuer would die when additional bombs fell.

The anchor slipped more.

As if he knew intuitively what the others were doing and that there was no help to be had, the captain shot out another line from his belt. "Get your sister up. She's a lot lighter. Easier for you to pull free."

"What about you?"

"Don't worry about me. Get her to safety, Major! Move!"

Ember let go of his rope to pull at Alura's. He was right. It was much easier to lift her sister up without his extreme muscled weight added to it.

Moving as fast as she could, she got Alura out of that hole and helped her off to the side where the medics had set up a makeshift triage. Without hesitating, she started back for their rescuer. But she'd barely taken a step before the second round of bombs hit.

The ground shook even more than it had during the first run. Alura screamed from behind her as part of the triage came down around them.

Ignoring her sister's panic and shaken by the day's events, Ember pushed herself to her feet and ran back to the hole to help their blessed benefactor.

It was too late.

Nothing remained of where he'd been.

Nothing. Only flaming rubble.

No! Sick to her stomach, she stared at the smoldering remains. That last run had completely obliterated the opening. Flaming chunks of building had crashed down over it. There was no sign whatsoever of the captain.

Not even his helmet. And no way to reach him without heavy equipment or an exosuit.

For a moment, she feared she'd vomit as she remembered the kindness of the unknown man who'd saved Alura's life.

And hers. She didn't even know his name. Why hadn't she thought to ask so that she could at least notify his parents personally? Offer up a prayer for his kind soul?

Had he not sacrificed himself, she'd have been right there when that building came down. Alura, too. How in the name of the gods could this have been his fate for such a noble and decent act?

How?

Someone coughed and wheezed behind her as if trying to clear the smoke from his lungs. "Please don't tell me there's someone else we have to dig out of there. 'Cause really, I don't think I have another good deed in me. At least not today."

Gaping, she turned to find the captain standing behind her. Granted, he was bleeding and roughed up by the experience. But that tall, gargantuan beast was alive against all odds. Against all belief.

"How?" She scowled at him.

Pulling his helmet off to show her a bruised, yet ruggedly handsome face, he flashed a charming grin at her. "Hard to kill. God knows, my sister's been trying to do it since birth. Lucky for me, I don't go down easy."

"Cabarro! Answer your damn link! Your ødara's going wild and blowing up command because she can't make contact! She wants to make sure we haven't killed you. Yet!"

Ember glanced around for the prince.

To her shock, the captain in front of her tapped his ear and adjusted the piece through the blood that was oozing from his injuries before he spoke. "Hey, Øda. . . . Yeah, I'm good. Just lollygagging about as usual. Chasing after hot women and cold drinks." He paused to grimace and drop his helmet on the ground. "Um, can I call you back in a bit? There's something I need to see to. Don't worry. Nothing bad. Love you."

No sooner had he disconnected the call than his legs buckled.

Ember's breath left her with a rush as she saw the huge red stain that was spreading over his side from where he'd been wounded. "Medics!" she shouted, running to him. She wrapped her arms around his shoulders to help him lie back, and was momentarily stunned to discover just how ripped he was beneath that suit.

His breathing ragged, he met her gaze as she worked to staunch the blood from the worst gash in his side. "Did the lieutenant make it out?"

"She did. Thank you."

The med team swarmed him and forced her away so that they could inspect his injuries.

An involuntary gasp left her lips as they cut open his reinforced armored suit and she saw the jagged wound where shrapnel had caught him across his abdomen. More than that, he was covered in scars. This wasn't some leisurely prince who sat around with servants fetching for him. Or lollygagged as he'd told his mother.

Those scars were from battle wounds.

He shoved at the medic as he tried to cover his face with an oxygen mask. "Hey, Major?"

Stunned that he remembered her, she stepped forward. "Yeah?"

He held his link out to her. "Keep me posted about your zusa. I have a promise to keep. This link will get you through to me."

"Latenn, we have to get you out of here."

Bastien rolled his eyes at the group fussing around him. "I only need one MT. For God's sake, we got wounded all over the place. Would you bastards tend someone else? Or I swear I'm getting up and walking home. Then you'll all have shit to deal with when my ødara finds out."

They scrambled away from him as if he were on fire, except for an older MT who shook his head at Bastien.

"Mask now, Latenn?"

Grimacing, Bastien returned it to his face. Then he gestured at Ember with their military signs that said he'd be back in action ASAP.

The MT lifted him up onto an air-gurney, and saw him off to the nearest ambulance.

Unsure of what to think of her new wingman, Ember opened his link. He'd not only unsecured the biolock before he'd handed it to her, he'd left her a message.

> *If you can possibly look past my obvious birth defect of a royal disorder, Major Wildstar, I'd love to have dinner with you. Or at least promise me that you'll come on that trip to North Beach? Double date? Your zusa and her boyfriend as chaperones? And don't worry. Pretty sure I left my balls in that hole, so you're safe from my nefarious playboy ways.*
> *~Bas*

Laughing in spite of it all, Ember slid his link into her pocket and went to check on the other survivors. But as she continued to help with the rescues, her thoughts kept drifting back to Bastien Cabarro and those ruggedly sculpted, perfect male features. In that regard, he was exactly what she'd imagined their youngest visir to be. Handsome beyond belief. Charming.

Heroic, however, was a new concept. And completely unexpected.

As was his nonchalance about his injuries with his mother. And the regard he'd shown for those around him.

Yeah, she couldn't reconcile the rumors she'd heard with the man who'd risked one hell of a charmed life to jump into that deadly hole and calmly rescue her sister. She'd been expecting the kind of spoiled shit who whined over a hangnail and demanded three days of leave until it healed.

She was still contemplating that thought five hours later when she finally made it to the hospital to check on Alura.

Their other four sisters were already there, hovering and gossiping outside the room while their parents visited inside.

"So . . . you met the visir. . . ." Ashley's voice was grating in its probing, teasing tone. Much taller than her, Ash had their mother's light brown hair and vibrant blue eyes.

Ember growled at her. "What do you know?"

"Is that Ember?"

She peeked through the cracked door to see Alura sitting up in the bed. "Yeah, babe, it's me."

Even though it was against hospital regulations, Alura waved her in so that she could take her hand. Her dark blond hair was covered with a bandage, and her face was a bit scuffed, but only Alura could look that attractive in a surgical headdress and wearing bruises.

"Did you get *his* number?" she asked excitedly.

Wow . . . can't even ask if I'm okay after I saved your worthless ass . . .

Thanks, sis. Love you, too.

Ember scowled at her sister and her weird concern given the near-death experience they'd just gone through. Given the number of casualties they'd lost in the bombing. She, alone, would be attending the funerals of seven good friends. Two of them had been school and playmates both she and Alura had known the whole of their childhoods. "His?"

"The visir! Didn't you hear what he said? He invited me to his palace at North Beach!"

Ember choked as she passed an annoyed smirk to their parents. "That's not exactly what the man said. The invitation was for you and your boyfriend."

"I don't have a boyfriend. . . ." She gave their mother a sneaky, calculated wink. "Yet."

And the self-serving harita was off and running . . .

Fury cut through Ember so fast that she was grateful her sister was in a hospital bed. It was the only thing that saved Alura, since Ember was still raw over the fact that Alura had been the one her ex had been in her bed with when she'd come home from maneuvers.

That betrayal and rage still burned her to the bone.

And Alura's excuse? That she'd done it for Ember's own good. After all, Ember didn't need to be with someone who would cheat on her with her own sister.

Yeah . . . Let's hear it for Alura logic.

Ember crossed her arms over her chest. "Don't get too excited. He's already asked me out and I accepted." A slight lie, but she fully intended to accept his offer now.

Just for spite.

Alura's jaw dropped. "*You*? Don't be silly, Lu-Lu. You know as well as I do that he didn't mean it. Besides, I'm going to marry the visir. You'll see."

Oh, yeah . . . her sister's ego was second only to Bastien's. And she'd had enough of Alura thinking she owned the universe and could take anything she wanted. She wasn't all that and a bag of friggles.

Ember cleared her throat. "I think Bastien has something to say about that."

"Ember." Her mother's tone was sharp with warning. "We almost lost Alura today. Why don't you go outside and wait with your sisters?"

"Fine." Take her side. Her mom was good at that. Her father, too. It was what had made Alura so hard to deal with. If ever someone had been born more spoiled than Bastien—Alura would be her name. Why their parents had chosen to dote on that brat, no one knew.

Of course, their parents denied it. They didn't see it. Laughably, they thought themselves fair and impartial.

Yeah, right. As if.

The rest of them had always known that in any dispute Alura won and they had to apologize and give the baby what she wanted. It was sickening, but there was nothing she could do. So she headed for the hallway and the sanity of her sisters who knew the bitter truth.

But before Ember could evac the room, Alura was already off and running with her plans for how she intended to rope the unsuspecting prince in for a wedding.

Wanting to sock her where she lay, Ember entered the hallway and almost walked into her eldest sister, Kindel.

Her sister tsked at her fury as she tucked a strand of her riotous, dark curly hair behind her ear. "Simmer down,

Em. Not like the playboy's going to settle down with anyone, anytime soon."

She growled at the patronizing tone. "Aren't all of you sick of her doing this?"

With a shrug, Brandy snorted. "What difference does it make? Not like you're going to date him, anyway. You already told me how much you hate the aristos."

Before Ember could respond, Bastien's link rang in her pocket, as if he had a sixth sense that he was their topic of conversation and sought to interrupt them.

Without a word to her sisters, she stepped away and answered it. "Major Wyldestarrin."

"Hey, Major, this is Cabarro. Wanted to check in and see how you're doing. Make sure you weren't hurt in the additional runs. And that your sister pulled through. Is the rest of your family safe? You need anything?"

It was a sad state of affairs when an aristo had better manners and heart than her useless sister. "All good. You?"

"Bored out of my mind."

She found that hard to believe. "What? No adoring fans?"

Laughing at her question, he sent over a request for a video feed.

Ember accepted, expecting to find him with a packed ward full of admirers. To her shock, he scanned the sterile hospital room to show her that he was there all alone.

Not even a guard kept him company.

"I can tell by your expression, not what you were expecting." Bastien turned the camera back on his features, which were scraped and bruised from his injuries, but still stunning. Even more so because he'd gotten them while doing her a favor. "You should probably never gamble with no better poker face than that, Major. Your opponent would clean house."

She felt heat sting her cheeks at his teasing. "Sorry. I just assumed you'd be surrounded by groupies and family."

"Yeah . . . no. My sa's giving an address to the people after the bombing to reassure them and allay their fears, while the rest of my family is running around tonight stomping out other fires over it. And my øda's at a rally for the families of the soldiers we lost to raise funds and aid for them—which is where I'd be if the damn doctor would release me. Or I'd be at the barracks."

She scoffed before she could stop herself.

"Hey, now!" he said, offended. "Believe it or not, I spend most of my nights in the barracks with my squadron. You can check my tracer logs and see. The vast majority of those stories you hear about me in the news feeds are complete fiction. A handful of the wilder ones notwithstanding—and those I proudly own up to, and will be more than happy to tell you all about. And show you the pictures that are too risqué for prime time." He rubbed at his eyebrow. "Anyway, so what about that dinner?"

Leaning against the wall, Ember scowled as she tried to understand this strange enigma who was talking to her for reasons she couldn't even begin to fathom. While she wasn't a ghastly goat of a human being, she was a far cry from Alura's great statuesque beauty and she knew it.

At five-six, she was average height for a Kirovarian woman. And many a potential dating prospect had commented on the fact that she was a bit more muscular than she ought to be and tended to walk like she was going to war, armed for the Andarion Ring. Her only remarkable feature came from her father—a pair of sharp, penetrating green eyes. Sadly, most guys never noticed those. Except to say that the intensity of her gaze made their nuts and guts shrivel.

Though to be honest, she doubted if anyone or anything

could ever intimidate Bastien. Indeed, he seemed to have an ego smelted from titanium.

"Why are you asking me out, Cabarro?"

That devilish grin warmed her a lot more than she wanted it to. There was something about this man that was way too delectable. She could easily see him charming her pants right off her. "You think I'm a spoiled asshole. I strangely find that admirable in a woman. Shows you're a good judge of character. I like that even more."

She laughed. "You're ridiculous."

"Ah c'mon," he teased. "You're Gyron Force . . . I'm Gyron Force. We both think I'm ridiculous. We got so much in common already."

Scoffing, she shook her head at him. "We are nothing alike, Your *High*ness."

"Fine, Major. Have it your way. But my sa's about three and a half seconds from declaring war on a neighboring empire. What if this is the end of our world as we know it? What if everything you cherish perishes tomorrow? Wouldn't you like to say that you got to date a visir, just once, before it all goes to hell?"

Damn, he was a lot more endearing than he needed to be. And it wasn't because he had a title. He was just an affable ass. That alone would serve to get him into all kinds of trouble. Along with those incredibly handsome features and that edible physique. It was the most dangerous combination ever created and she could see herself getting into all kinds of trouble.

Every instinct she possessed told her to run as fast as she could in the opposite direction.

Then she made the mistake of looking at his sweet face.

Yeah, he was lethal.

And she was done for.

"Fine. *One* date. But only because of your saðir and his war."

He winked at her. "Hey, I'll take that yes any way I can get it. Just don't break my heart, Major. It's a terribly fragile thing."

Ember snorted at the very idea of that. "I find that hard to believe."

"Don't. I might be spoiled with sociopathic tendencies, but I'm never insincere." And with that, he signed off.

Ember froze as she realized that all four of her sisters were gaping at her. Worse? They'd heard every single word of her exchange with Bastien.

That sobered her humor fast. "What?"

Ashley scoffed. "What do you think you're doing? You can't even be contemplating a date with *him*. Are you out of your mind? Alura will kill you!"

"Why did you say yes to going out with that reprobate?" Brandy stood with arms akimbo.

Ember's gaze went back to where Alura sat laughing with their parents, and an image of her in bed with Syrin went through her mind. In that moment, she knew exactly why she'd accepted his invitation.

"Simple. This is war."

CHAPTER 1

ONE YEAR LATER

"Are you going to tell Bastien?"

Ember paused at Kindel's question that would have ruined her appetite for the lunch they were supposed to be having had Bastien's father not already done so an hour ago.

Her throat tightened as she blinked back tears she didn't want her sister to see, lest she be motivated to do something that could get them both arrested. "No, definitely not, and the last thing I could ever tell him is that his father's threatening to disinherit him."

"Why not?"

"First, it'd kill him to know that. He loves and respects his father. Second, you know the man. Bas would go off, half-cocked and confront his father, then all hell would unleash and who knows how that would play out." She envisioned everything from Bastien shooting his father to him eloping with her and then growing to hate her years from now once he realized what all he'd given up to marry her.

No matter the scenario, they all ended with them

miserable. And with Bastien hating her for coming between him and his family.

"I don't know what to do."

"Do you love him?"

"More than my life." Ember bit her lip as a single tear slid past her control. Gah! This would be so easy if she was the gold-digging bitch his family thought she was.

Then she could let go and not look back. Or marry him and not give a single shit what they thought. Because what his father didn't know was that Bastien had already told her how much money he'd inherit on his wedding day. He didn't need his father's inheritance. Or approval. His grandparents had all left him with a staggering amount of property and creds. The unbelievable mass of wealth stymied her best mathematical abilities to comprehend.

But the money didn't matter to her any more than it did to Bastien. Since she'd never had that kind of wealth, she couldn't wrap her head around it.

Besides, it was his, not hers. All she cared about was Bastien. Not his titles. And no amount of cred could replace his thoughtfulness or unique views. The way he could brighten her day by simply entering a room. Make her smile with nothing more than a wink and that devilish grin that made her want to rip his clothes off and hold him for eternity.

How could she give that up?

Angry that she couldn't stop her stupid, useless emotions, she wiped the tear away and drew a ragged breath. "Love can't survive bitterness, zusi. You know that better than anyone."

It was why Kindel was single. The love of her life had given up a command position to stay with her. Three years later, he'd been so angry over it as he never had another opportunity for advancement, that it'd torn their relationship apart. To this day, Justiss wouldn't even look at Kindel.

Ember didn't want that to be Bastien. The thought of his hating her . . .

That was the only thing unbearable.

"What am I going to do?"

Kindel took her hand and smiled sadly. "I don't know, Em. I screwed up my life. Last thing I want to do is screw up yours."

She snorted. "Not helpful."

Her link buzzed.

Ember started to ignore it, until she saw Bastien's avatar. That goofy photo he'd made as a joke and programmed into her link a few weeks ago.

This way everyone will know what a total jack-off you date and a reminder to you that no one else will have me and my weirdness. So you never have to worry about me cheating or straying. I know the best when I see it and no one's better than my girl.

Trying not to laugh at the memory, she picked it up and answered.

"Hey, lovely."

Ember scowled as she heard something that sounded like blaster fire in the background. "Where are you?"

"Um . . . nowhere. Just wanted to say that I love you."

"Are you under attack?"

He hissed in her ear, then made a noise that sounded like he was straining.

"Bas?"

"Yeah . . . sorry. I, uh, I'm having a little trouble hearing you."

Over blaster fire! "Oh my God! You're in a firefight?"

"Little bit."

"Are you pinned?"

The longest pause of her life crackled in her ear before he finally answered. "Don't worry, Em. I'll be home tonight. Just wanted to hear your voice."

Her heart sank as she saw the news on a nearby monitor. It showed the attack he was in. The royal envoy his father was supposed to be in had come under Eudoran fire. But at the last minute his father had sent Bastien and Quin instead.

At the last minute . . .

"Bastien," she breathed. "I love you. No matter what happens, please don't ever forget that."

"I won't." He cut the line.

Ember's hand shook as his father's words echoed in her mind. No . . . it wasn't possible.

"Em? What is it?"

Swallowing her panic, she jerked her chin toward the monitor. "That's Bastien in that mess."

Kindel cursed. "You want to scramble?"

Yes, but she had more to think about at the moment and she knew for a fact that Bastien could hold his own. "Kin? Can I ask you something?"

She sat back down with a frown. "Sure."

Ember took a moment to gather her swirling thoughts before she spoke the horror that she struggled to comprehend. "Bastien's father intimated that he'd rather see Bastien dead than married to a pleb." She cut another terrified glance to the monitor. "You don't think he would have done that today on purpose, do you?"

Kindel was now as pale as she was. "Oh God, Em . . . I don't know. I'd like to think no parent could even contemplate such a thing."

"But?"

"They're aristos and not us."

And that was what she was afraid of. His father had

warned her that Bastien intended to propose, and that if he did so, there would be consequences most dire. Consequences that would guarantee her no happy ending.

The only way she wouldn't be happy was if something happened to Bastien.

Like death.

She finally breathed again as Bastien and his brother emerged from the building on the monitor. Their clothes were ruffled and Bastien had dirt smeared across one cheek, but his hazel eyes were light as he assured the reporters they were fine.

This time.

"I can't marry him, Kindel." Not if it meant his life.

"He won't give up without a fight."

"I know," she choked. "But I'd rather he learn to hate me than know that I selfishly cost him his life or his family."

"Em—"

"Don't," she said, cutting Kindel off before she could talk her out of this. "It's what has to be done. Not just for him, but for all of us. At least he gave me a part of himself he's never given anyone else." Something his family couldn't take from her. Especially since they didn't know about it.

Yet even the very thought of being without him tore her apart.

At least he's alive this way.

Better he live with someone else than marry her and die because of it.

That's the lie I'm going to force myself to live with.

"What the minsid hell is this?" Bastien stared at the transfer orders on his link in total disbelief.

Blocking his access to the barracks where up until an

hour ago he'd lived with Ember, the lance corporal turned bright red as she cleared her throat. The petite brunette handed him his tactical bag that someone else had packed with his uniforms, Gyron Force axe, and other personal items he didn't want to think about. "Sorry, Captain. Thought you knew. Orders came through first thing this morning while you were out on PT. You've been reassigned to Bletch Division."

You've got to be kidding me . . .

Gaping at the bullshit, he moved his gaze from her to the two MPs behind her as if she needed backup. Like he'd ever take his frustration out on a lower-ranking soldier.

That wasn't his style. If he was going to assault anyone, it would be someone who had the authority and means to fight back, and stand a good chance at kicking his ass.

Someone like his sister whom he suspected of having done this shit to get even with him for proposing to Ember last night. And why not? Lil had been furious that he'd asked their mother for their grandmother's ring. Furious that he'd dared to even contemplate placing such a precious Kirovarian heirloom on the hand of a lowborn pleb. Lillian had been shrieking at him for days over it.

No doubt, it would thrill Lil to no end when she learned that Ember had coldly refused the ring.

And him.

That she'd left him kneeling in the restaurant like an idiot, begging for one single kind word from her.

I don't need this dritvík right now, Lil.

Bastien was still reeling from Ember's rejection. She hadn't just ripped his heart out. She'd publicly gutted him. Worse, she hadn't even bothered to return to their barracks last night. Rather, she'd gone over to her parents' house and left him alone in their bed to wallow in the misery of knowing he'd screwed up somehow.

He just didn't know what he'd done wrong.

Why he wasn't good enough for her to marry when she was everything to him.

Sick to his stomach, he took his pack from the corporal, knowing he'd have to report for his patrol soon. "Under whose command?"

"Major Cabarro."

Of course. Just as he suspected. "My *yokken* zusa." The profanity was out of his mouth before he could stop it.

She turned an even brighter shade of pink. "Yes, *styrrah.*"

A tic started in his jaw. If Lil had really done this to get back at him for proposing to Ember last night, he'd murder her for it. In her sleep. So help him!

"Who authorized it?" It better not have been his brother.

Or his uncle.

She stammered a bit before she pulled it up on her own link. "M-m-major Wyldestarrin."

No dritvíkken way . . . Bastien's breath left him in a rush as his brain struggled to grasp a reality he didn't want to face.

Ember had done this to him. Intentionally. Without a single word. Without mercy or regard? She'd transferred him over to his sister's division when she knew how much he hated being under Lil's thumb. His sister treated him like a socially-stunted toddler and lived to embarrass him in front of everyone. She went out of her way to set him up for ridicule. He'd rather slit his own wrist than be near Lil in uniform.

Or out of uniform, either, for that matter.

Damn, that was even colder than the way Ember had left him hanging last night after the proposal.

Why not just castrate me and be done with it? Why go to such extremes to punish me?

What the hell did I do to you?

Trying to salvage whatever was left of his shattered dignity for the second time in a handful of hours, he nodded. "Thank you, Corporal."

As he turned to find a transport to his new base, he slung the pack over his shoulder and tried to put it out of his mind.

Bastien couldn't. It was impossible when his entire world had crashed down on him. *I didn't do anything.*

Unwilling to let it go, he pulled his link out and hailed Ember.

It rolled to her voicemail in such a way as to let him know that she'd done it herself the moment she saw it was him calling for her.

With an irritated sigh, he waited for the buzz. "Hey, Em, it's me. I just got my orders and I'm heading to my new barracks. I know you said you needed some time to decide about the marriage, but I didn't think that meant that you were expelling me from your life entirely. You could have given me some warning." He paused as he realized anger and accusation had crept into his tone.

He wasn't really angry at her. Truth was, he was hurt. Kicked in the stones and bleeding internally.

Worse? He had no one to turn to for this. His drinking buddies wouldn't understand. They'd tell him to go nail someone else and get her out of his system. His family would think him an idiot for sulking over a pleb.

Fain Hauk wouldn't want to hear it since he was still raw about his own wife and what had happened there.

And his best friend wasn't talking to him. She was rolling his calls to voicemail.

Honestly, Bastien didn't want to yell at her. He just wanted her back. It was why he'd proposed. He didn't want to live his life without her in it.

So he gentled his tone and spoke from his heart. "I miss you, Em. Love you even more. Call me." He cut the line before he gave in to the tears that were choking him. Gave in to the misery that was about to send him to his knees.

Clearing his throat, he took a deep breath and tried to get his bearings.

"Bastien?"

He winced at the sound of Alura's voice as she came skipping over toward him. That was all he needed right now.

Like another hole in his heart.

With a ragged breath, he braced himself to face her. "Yeah?"

"You okay?" She slowed down as she neared him.

"Fine."

With a sympathetic frown, she placed a comforting hand on his arm. "Brandy told me about last night. You want me to give you a ride to your new post?"

Yeah, right. Ember would have a seizure on them both. While she might be pissed for the moment over some imagined slight, she'd hopefully calm down in a few days and get over it. But if she saw him with Alura that would guarantee that she'd never speak to him again. "It's okay. My sister's waiting."

She nodded. "I'm sorry, Bastien. I just wanted you to know that if you need a friend, I'm here. Anytime." She kissed his cheek.

Mumbling an insincere thanks, he quickly grabbed a

transport and put as much distance between them as he could. One thing about Alura . . . she had a nasty habit of chasing after her sisters' boyfriends for reasons only Alura knew. All of them wanted her head for it.

And he had enough problems with the world gossiping about his behavior. Be damned if he'd fuel *that* fire. There wasn't enough alcohol in the entire Kirovarian Empire and all her territories to make Alura appealing to him. Not enough alcohol in all the Nine Worlds for that matter.

I just need some time, Bas . . .

His gut tightened as he heard Ember's voice from last night in his head again. It didn't make sense. Everything had been golden between them. They'd been dating for a year and never had he been more sure of anything. They rarely fought, and never over anything major. Day and night, they were together and she'd seemed as eager for his company as he was for hers.

Until this.

Just trust in her. She'll come around. You know she will. She loves you. You love her. Love wins over everything else.

As stupid as it sounded, he really believed that. Most of all, he really believed in her.

Few days and everything would be back to normal. She'd get over whatever was bugging her and they'd be planning their wedding.

All he had to do was be patient . . .

ALMOST TWO MONTHS LATER

"You unbelievable bastard!"

Bastien had barely stepped off the ladder of his fighter

when he turned to find Ember in the hangar bay. Her cheeks flushed, she glared at him with fury in her eyes, making them all the greener. Honestly, he was so happy to see her here that he didn't even mind the fact that she'd insulted him.

At least not until a second later when she unexpectedly kneed him straight in the groin.

Pain exploded through him as he dropped his helmet and doubled over, fighting against the sudden wave of nausea that threatened to send him to ground.

"You went out with my zusa?" She ground those words out from between her teeth in an effort to keep the fight between them. But it was too late. Half the bay had seen her assault and stood frozen in curiosity.

"Not what you think," he managed to choke out past the pain.

"No?" She shoved a photo into his face that Alura had posted of them in the restaurant. One that had been picked up by a number of news agencies and broadcast all over. Ironic really that it had more coverage than the assassin's attack on his mother two days ago, or the near miss he'd had himself just yesterday. "Guess I'm hallucinating, then."

Cursing his stupidity, he righted himself even though all he really wanted to do was find an ice pack and a bed. "Why are you so mad anyway? I asked you before I did it."

And that was definitely the wrong thing to say as it sent her off into a round of incoherent sputtering that resulted in the only recognizable words being pieces of vulgar profanity that would have gotten slapped had he let them fly.

But at least it got her talking to him again. This was the longest conversation they'd had since the night he asked her to marry him.

With one last choice insult for his manhood, she started off.

Bastien took her arm and gently pulled her to a stop. "Em—"

"Don't you dare!" She jerked free of his grasp and raked a scathing glare over him. "You knew how much this would hurt me and yet you did it anyway. How could you?"

That question left a bleeding welt on his soul. And the answer was so simple that he couldn't understand how she missed it.

Because he'd wanted her to tell him not to go. To say that she wanted him back. That she still loved him and there was some hope left for him to hold on to.

She'd cut him off completely and he'd been beyond desperate. *That* was why he'd done it.

Instead, she'd told him that she didn't care what he did. To go out with Alura.

But her fury now gave him the very hope that he'd been praying for. "It was only dinner. I took her straight home. Nothing happened between us."

"You think I believe you? That I'd *ever* believe you after this?"

She should. He'd never been on a worse date in his life.

"What's going on here?"

Bastien went cold at the sound of his older brother's voice intruding on their fight. *Dritvík!* That was the last thing he needed.

Disgusted, he watched as Quin joined them. Almost even in height to him, his brother had wavy brown hair that was two shades darker than his, and hazel blue eyes. Eyes that he focused on Bastien with a condemning stare. But that didn't faze Bastien at all. He was too used to it. Too used to Quin judging him as lacking in all things.

Since the day Bastien was born, his older brother had

been jealous of the attention their mother had given him. Jealous of the fact that Bastien had the privileges of being a visir without having all the hassles of training to run the empire. It ate at Quin and made him a snotty, acerbic shit most days.

And today he was in a particularly bad mood. He curled his lip at Bastien. "Must you sully our good name every chance you get? Don't you have more important things to worry about than chasing after another piece of tail? Like finding the bastard who tried to kill our mother?"

"Stay out of this."

But it was too late. Ember was already leaving.

"Em!" Bastien started after her.

"Go to hell, Cabarro!"

Quin jerked him to a stop. "Show some dignity, damn you! You're a visir of this empire! We don't chase after common filth!"

Growling, Bastien slugged his brother. "You're not fit to speak of her and don't you dare insult her again!"

"I'll have you whipped for this!"

"Go for it, *theren*. I dare you." Bastien laughed in his face at the mere thought of what their mother would do if Quin even attempted to have him harmed.

Wiping the blood from his lips, Quin curled his lip. "One day, Bas, I hope you get what you deserve."

"And what's that?"

"A lesson in who your real family is and what hanging out with trash like that gets you."

FIVE WEEKS LATER

All his life, Bastien Aros Cabarro had stupidly thought the most frightening three-word phrase in the entire

Kirovarian language was his full name when spoken by his mother in that nut-shriveling tone she had whenever he did something that displeased her.

He was wrong.

Truly the most frightening three words? Bar none? Those sons of bitches had just flown out of the mouth of his ex's baby sister. In a crowded room of people his parents would murder him over scandalizing.

"Bastien, I'm pregnant."

Stunned by this unbelievably cruel hatchet of fate, he stared blankly at Alura as if Ember had cold-cocked him again, and honestly, it was what this news felt like.

This could *not* be happening.

Not now. Not tonight in the middle of my parents' thirty-third anniversary party.

Not with Alura . . .

Dear God, what have I done?

Unfortunately, he had an iron-clad answer for that last query. At least on a biological level. On a moral one? He'd seriously SCUBARed his life—screwed it up beyond all recovery. That painful bastard stepchild of being FUBARed—which he also was. Or would be once Ember learned about this.

If she didn't know already.

He'd be lucky if she *only* shot him in the heart. Or head . . .

And not the one that rested on his shoulders.

"Did you hear me?"

Needing a moment to catch his bearings, Bastien drained the glass of whisky in his hand before he stuttered for the first time since he'd learned to speak. "Uh . . . yeah."

That deceptively nonchalant tone got him a vicious slap from the stunning long-legged blonde in front of him.

Not that he blamed her. He wanted to slap himself, too.

He held his hand up to stay the royal security guards as they moved in to take Alura into custody. Last thing he needed was an even bigger scene during his parents' anniversary party that Alura had crashed so that she could ensure she had a large audience for the verbal bomb she'd just detonated on top of him.

But then, she was good at such spectacles and he had to give her credit—unlike Ember, Alura was always one for a great performance. The more attention on her at any given time, the better.

Positive. Negative. Alura didn't care, so long as she was at the center of it. Which was no doubt why she'd come here in full military regalia, with her accommodation ribbons clearly visible so as to garner as much sympathy as she could. Let everyone know that she was a decorated war hero from the most prominent military family Kirovar had ever bred.

And that he was nothing more than the *knættr* who'd wronged her.

Yeah, that about summed it up.

"Bas?"

Even better . . . there was that infamous tone that said he was in trouble with his family. Only instead of coming from his mother, it was his older sister using it. "All's well, Lil. I've got this."

Moving to stand by his side, his ever graceful sister, Lillian, swept a condemning stare over him and then down Alura's body, taking in her ACU battlesuit that clashed greatly with the formal wear everyone else had donned for the black-tie event.

Yeah, he could have done without the condemnation and resentful disdain in Lil's green eyes.

It was matched only by the searing sneer Quin had pinned on him from the other side of the room.

With as much dignity as he could muster, Bastien set his empty glass down on the windowsill right as his father stepped into the fray with that hostile grimace that was nowhere near as effective at quelling his actions as his mother's tsking. Strange whenever Bastien thought about it. Even at sixty, his father was a huge beast of a man who wasn't known for compassion or diplomacy, yet he'd never once intimidated Bastien.

At all.

Something that had made his father insane from the moment Bastien had first opened his eyes seconds after birth and, according to his grandmother, pinned an insolent stare on the monidar. Then yawned and reached for his mother, who had petted him every day since.

Aside from a few well-noted ass-kickings, anyway. For all her doting and loving, his mother wasn't a pushover—especially not when it came to her kids.

Alura, on the other hand, tucked her chin to her chest and shrank back at his father's approach. A bad move, as the one thing his father despised in all creatures was a weak spine.

With one made of absolute iron, Bastien put himself between them so that his father couldn't reach Alura without stepping past him. "Sorry we disturbed the party, *Saðir.*"

"What have I told you about bringing your—"

"Careful what words you choose, *Alvaldr,*" Bastien said sharply, cutting him off with his royal address to remind his father of their audience before his father made the situation worse for them all. The man had obviously missed Alura's stunning declaration on her arrival to the room.

And since everyone in the gargantuan crowd was holding their communal breath to catch every single word of the scandal, they had yet to repeat the news for the emperor's hearing.

Like that would last.

Clearing his throat, Bastien turned and gently took Alura's arm. He pulled her forward to meet his father.

When he spoke, it was loud enough for everyone around them to hear his words without mistaking them. "You'll have to forgive my fiancée, Sa. We were planning to tell you and Ødara the good news later, after the party, but Alura's dress didn't make it to the palace from the delivery service I ordered for her . . . she was late getting in from her patrol and didn't have time to pick up another change of clothes, and you know how pregnancy hormones play havoc with a woman's sensibilities. Rather than show her the proper sympathy for her predicament, leave it to me to always say the wrong thing at the wrong time. I'm told I inherited that gene from you, *Alvaldr*."

The last bit caused a round of laughter to echo in the room from their guests.

And it served to do just what Bastien had intended. It set his father back on his heels as he digested those words with the same expression Bastien was sure had been on his own face a few minutes ago.

"Pardon?"

Bastien inclined his head to his father. "May I present my fiancée and the future *ødara* of my child, Lieutenant Aurora Wyldestarrin, or Alura, as her family and friends call her."

His father came as close to stuttering as Bastien had ever seen him. "Wyldestarrin?"

Bastien didn't miss the shock underlying his father's question. And before he could answer, the rumors took off through the room like wildfire, echoing and slapping him even harder than Alura had.

"Did I hear that correctly? He traded one zusa for another?"

"She doesn't look like the other one. What was that pleb's name, again? Flame or something silly like that?"

"Well, I'm not surprised. It was just a matter of time before he knocked up another pleb. Who didn't see *that* coming?"

"No wonder she broke it off with him. Can you imagine finding your zusa in bed with your boyfriend? I'd have shot them both!"

Bastien ground his teeth as pain tore through him over their cruelty. More than that, he resented them speculating about his life and motives when they knew nothing about the details of the event.

Knew nothing about him, personally.

Sorry, worthless bastards and their biting tongues they thought so much of. But that was the problem in life—everyone wanted to be a know-it-all expert, and act like they had all the facts and answers when they knew absolutely nothing whatsoever about the matter at hand. Just a handful of unrelated details they put together from half truths and outright lies, using their own petty minds and base thoughts to fill in the gaps. The accusations they made against him spoke more about them than it did him. Because in the end, those false assumptions and allegations came from inside their own corrupt souls that they exposed to the light by their words and deeds. They unknowingly accused him of what *they'd* do and not of what he'd actually done.

"The careless mouth oft betrays the truth of the heart." His paternal grandfather's words rang in his ears. The old man had been right. *"Great minds talk about philosophy and ideas. Small minds talk about people."*

Truer words had never been spoken.

Little did the *jikkas* know they were quickly telling him which side of that equation they fell on. And it wasn't good for them. For the one thing about a Cabarro, they never forgot a slight of any kind. Their unofficial family motto was that winning wasn't everything. Rubbing it in the face of your enemy was also important.

And the only ones worse about that than the Cabarros were the Triosans—his mother's family. Which meant he had a double dose of it hard-wired into his DNA.

As if she sensed the turmoil inside him, his mother appeared at his back and placed a gentle hand to his shoulder. "Congratulations to you both." She kissed his cheek. "Alura? If you'd like to follow me, I'll have my secretary attend your needs so that you won't feel out of place."

The party slowly resumed, but Bastien's mood was ruined. As was his life.

Especially when Lil returned to his side and shook her head. "Couldn't keep it in your pants for five minutes, could you, *blyt theren*?"

No one could make the affectionate Kirovarian term for *little brother* sound more patronizing than his sister.

Wanting to punch her like he'd done when he was five and she'd stolen all his toys to show him who was the bigger and stronger sibling, Bastien excused himself. He'd deal with Lillian's insanity later. Right now he needed to resume his discussion with Alura and figure out what had happened to cause this.

Well, he knew the mechanics. Sort of. But that night they'd spent together was still really fuzzy in his head. Honestly, he barely recalled anything after he'd left Quin in the landing bay and had gone straightaway to get loaded. Upset over his encounter with Ember, he'd been so effing drunk that he could barely stand when Alura had shown up unexpectedly at the bar where he'd plowed through so much Tondarion Fire, it was a wonder he still had functioning kidneys.

Damn it!

Not that he blamed the alcohol. He was the moron who'd gone out with Alura before that. But Bastien hadn't considered their dinner anything more than one revenge meal to stab at Ember.

It's what I deserve for being a bastard.

Clearly, as Lil had said, this was his fault. He owned every bit of it. He was the one who'd accepted Alura's dinner invitation.

The one who'd gone drinking alone and been so irresponsible that the last thing he remembered was blacking out in the bar, then waking up naked in Alura's bed.

He just wished he could undo the last few months. How could anyone fuck up their life so bad, so fast?

His stomach drew so tight that for a moment, he feared he'd vomit. He'd never meant for any of this to happen.

It's what you get for being a jackass. The only reason he'd ever accepted Alura's invitation to dinner had been to make Ember crazy. To hurt her as much as she'd cut him.

Yeah, and how's that working for you, champ?

Bastien cursed himself silently for this blunder. To this day, he didn't know what he'd done to piss off Ember so completely. Everything had been going great between them.

Until he'd ruined it all by proposing. *That* horrific memory was still enough to shrivel his gut with horror and degradation.

It'd been the most perfect night when he'd taken Ember to her favorite dance club. Had paid an exorbitant amount to have the rooftop decorated like it was free-floating in space—a fantasy she'd once confided to him that she'd carried since childhood. And there, while her favorite song had played, he'd held out his grandmother's ring and asked her to marry him.

He'd expected an enthusiastic yes.

Instead, she'd stared at the ring as if it had poisonous fangs and was coiled to strike at her. It'd been the longest pause of his life, while half the club looked on and he knelt, waiting . . . and waiting.

Finally, she'd stepped back and swallowed hard. "Bas . . . I . . ."

His stomach had hit the ground as he dreaded for her to finish that sentence. "You, what?"

"I'm not ready to settle down yet. And I know you're not. I think we should take a break first, and *really* consider this."

Nothing had ever gutted him like those words. She might as well have cut out his heart and shoved it down his throat. Especially when she turned on her heel and left him there like a complete and utter dumbass.

Which was nothing compared to the next morning when he'd met the lance corporal holding his gear and warning him about his new orders.

And squad.

Yeah, that still stung him to the core of his being. In part because Lil continued to treat him like her personal bitch. Every day since then, his sister had made his life a living hell. Mostly because Lil thought it was hilarious that he'd had his nuts handed to him by a mere pleb. She thought it was what he deserved for dating outside their elite aristocratic circle.

But social standing had never mattered to him. Nor had rank. All he'd seen in Ember was the courageous woman he'd die for.

The woman he'd wanted to spend the rest of his life

worshiping and making happy. So the ruthless banishment from her life had come as the worst sort of agony.

Weeks had turned into months as he waited desperately for her to change her mind. She'd barely spoken to him. Every time he attempted contact, she cut him off with bitter barbs and ire.

Now . . .

Ember would hate him forever.

It wouldn't matter that he'd asked her permission to have dinner with Alura before he'd ever accepted her sister's invitation.

Everything would be his fault. And it was.

I should have gelded myself.

Because he had royally screwed up this time. And the look on his mother's beautiful face as he entered her private chambers said that she was in complete and total agreement. Yet only someone who knew her as well as Bastien did would see her disappointed irritation in those regal green eyes. That strategically poised ethereal beauty that never betrayed a single emotion of any kind. One thing about his maternal unit—she was forever elegant. Forever composed. Not one pale blond hair was out of place. Not one vibrant green fiber of her gown was mushed or crinkled.

And only Lia Triosan ydyra Cabarro could pull off a smile that was both warm and chilling at the same time.

"There you are, *minn s'enn.* Alura was just telling me that she's Ember's younger *zusa?*"

"She is." He glanced around the room. "Where is she?"

His mother jerked her chin toward her bedroom. "Changing." Then she lowered her voice to a barely audible whisper. "What were you thinking?"

"That I wanted Ember and she wouldn't have me."

His mother scowled at him. "You loved her that much?"

He gaped at the question. How could she have doubted it? Was she totally blind?

Shaking her head, she pressed her gloved hand to her brow. "I'll never understand you, Bastien, and this strange penchant you have for picking up strays. Aros and your saðir are right. I coddled you too much when you were a boy."

He snorted at her words. "Uncle Aros is in no position to give anyone parenting advice. At least I'm still speaking to my parents. Jullien barely tolerates being in the same room with him. As for Sa . . . I've always said that my only goal in life was to be his burden and to give the two of you something scandalous to talk about at cocktail parties." He glanced to the closed doors. "Mission accomplished . . . with panache."

"Not the time to be flippant."

"Certainly not the time for sobriety. Am thinking I need to get hammered. Sooner rather than later."

She let out a puff of irritated breath. "Bastien Aros Cabarro!"

"Øda!"

With an irritated sigh, she patted at her hair—as if any strand would dare defy her.

Unlike her youngest child. He could practically hear her shrieking at his father in her elegant head—*You just had to have that extra spare for your throne, didn't you? This is all* your *fault, Newie!*

Luckily, her composure never wavered. She merely cleared her throat in that delicate, regal way only his mother could manage. "Well, as mad as I am at you, at least you stepped up and didn't leave her and your child abandoned. I can't fault you there. But I don't envy you the bed you've made for yourself. Her family—and in particular, her zusa—will not be so receptive of you, nor will they view this kindly. More than that, we're at war and no one knows how this is going to turn out, especially with the recent attemps that have been made on all our lives. Bad timing, svenn . . . bad, bad timing."

"What do you expect from the child who crashed a dinner party on arrival? I've been nothing but a pain in your bacrat since the day I ruined your favorite dress and upholstery with my inconsiderate birth during the second course."

Reaching up with a quick smirk, she tugged playfully at his ear. "And yet you've always been my favorite. What does that say about me?"

"You're a glutton for punishment and that *Miksa* didn't beat you enough when you were a girl."

That finally wrung a laugh from her. "No. Never. Just an easy mark for that beautiful smile of yours. I've never been able to deny you anything. You know that." She brushed gently at his hair. "I just wish you wouldn't put yourself in such horrible situations."

"I know. I should be more like Quin."

"I've *never* said that. While I love your theren . . . and your zusa, they lack your resilience and charm. Your quick thinking. Pity, that. It's why I want Quin to make you his chancellor."

Bastien laughed. "That'll never happen. He has no respect for my opinion and even less for my politics."

As she drew a breath to respond, the doors opened to show Alura in one of his mother's older gowns.

And by older, it was one his mother had worn earlier in the year. The vibrant blue set off Alura's coloring to perfection.

Yet it left him cold. Because in his heart, it was Ember he wanted to see here, by his side.

It's not meant to be.

Especially not after this.

He could bemoan it all he wanted, but it would change nothing. Ember was gone forever now. He'd slammed that door and bolted it shut. And he had no one else to blame.

Alura was his future now.

Come hell or high water, he'd make the best of it. As his mother had said, he'd do his best by her. While he'd been drunker than Bob's cat when he'd gone to bed with her and couldn't even recall getting to her condo, never mind sleeping with her, he wouldn't deny waking up naked the next morning by her side. With a hangover that would rival the power of a League strike force.

As for the baby, it would be tested as soon as it was born, as a matter of course. All royal children were required to be scanned for their DNA. Not just to ensure lineage, but to screen for any birth defects or possible health concerns, and to have a sample on file should the child ever be kidnapped.

Or executed.

Alura knew that as well as he did, so there was no need to question the father of the baby, since she knew the truth would come out if she were lying.

I always wanted to be a father.

Just not with Alura as the mother.

Yet since she was, and he couldn't change it, he would show her nothing save devotion and respect. That was the least he could do.

Forcing a smile for her, he held his arm out so that he could escort her back to the party. "Shall we?"

Her triumphant grin was dazzling as she tucked her hand into the crook of his elbow. "Thank you, Bastien."

"For what?"

"Not denouncing me."

"Cabarros don't denounce their own."

She pressed herself against his arm and leaned against him. An act that left him even colder as it reminded him of how Ember used to hold him.

His mother was right. This would kill Ember when she heard it. For that alone, he wanted to cut his own throat. And he'd never forgive himself for doing this to her.

Digusted with himself, he led Alura back to the party where everyone waited for more juicy bits that he refused to give them. Let them speculate. They'd make up whatever truth they wanted, anyway. Wouldn't matter what he said. Or what the real facts were. They'd lie regardless.

The news agencies would be even worse. In their rush to beat out their competition, they'd fictionalize half of the story, and distort and slant the rest to the point it wouldn't even be recognizable. They couldn't bother to get the counties they were reporting from right most of the time, and that included the ones they broadcasted in. Sad really . . .

Alura excused herself from him so that she could go network with the others she was hoping would accept her as a future visira of the empire.

Bastien made straight for another round of whisky while dodging his older brother. One word from Quin and he would knock the bastard out again.

And that was the last lecture he wanted his mother to repeat tonight. He knew Cabarros didn't fight amongst themselves. They weren't Andarion eton Anatoles. Backbiting to that level wasn't part of their court. Cabarros guarded each other's backs.

Family first. Family above all.

"So . . . that's how it's done, eh?"

Alura paused at the rich, deep voice in her ear as she reached for a glass of champagne. She cut a sideways glance to see Barnabas Cabarro there.

Bastien's uncle Barnabas bore a striking resemblance to his older brother, the emperor. Only he wasn't as tall.

Or nearly as frightening.

At least not in appearance. Alura, however, knew exactly what kind of treacherous beast the leader of their military really was. She'd known it since the night he'd come to her and hand-selected her for this mission that stuck in the craw of her throat.

But she had no choice.

If she didn't do it, hers would be the first head he'd take.

"I thought you weren't going to speak to me in public. Isn't that what you said?"

Barnabas grunted at her as he pulled the glass from her hand, then drained it. "You're pregnant, love. Can't be seen drinking in your *delicate* condition."

Alura bit back a fierce groan at the reminder. "We both know that's a lie. So have you figured out the workaround?"

"I've got someone lined up who will give you everything you need, including a sympathetic shoulder when you miscarry in a few months."

"What if I really do conceive by then?"

Barnabas's dark eyes turned chilling as he met her gaze. "Then you and your brat will be joining Bastien and the rest of my brother's family in their graves."

CHAPTER 2

Bastien tensed as Ember approached him. Instinctively, he cupped himself in expectation of what she was about to do. Not that he really needed to. Of their own accord, his balls had shriveled and jumped straight back inside his body as soon as he saw her coming.

To his instant relief, she paused in front of him and crossed her arms over her chest. "Congratulations, Captain. Welcome to the Wyldestarrin family."

Those cordial, formal words with their undercurrent of leashed venom sent a chill down his spine. It was the first time she'd spoken to him since Alura had crashed the palace party and announced her pregnancy.

As if on cue, Alura came dashing up to his side to take his arm. The hem of her voluminous pale green wedding gown swept against his legs, then pooled around her feet. "Emmy! I'm so glad you came, after all. I thought you were planning to boycott my wedding."

Ember raked a cold look over him that said she was gutting him slowly with her thoughts.

With a rusted-out spork.

She smiled at Alura. "Why should I lose a zusa over the actions of an inconsiderate asshole?"

A tic started in Bastien's jaw. "Pardon? You broke up with me, not the other way around. You're the one who wouldn't even return my messages or acknowledge me!"

Ember held her hand up to silence him. "Just stay away from me, Bastien. I've nothing to say to you ever again." And with that, she turned and walked over to where their sisters had congregated.

Bastien glared in furious indignation. How dare she! This wouldn't have happened had she not challenged him to date her sister. It wasn't like she hadn't known how he'd react to her caustic response to his question. How he'd react to a direct challenge.

He was a surly, cantankerous ass and Ember knew it better than anyone!

"Don't worry about it, baby. You'll always have me." Alura kissed his cheek, then went to join a group of her friends.

Was it just him or was there irony that as soon as Alura had said that, she skipped off and abandoned him?

Just like everyone else.

Yeah, he was a total outcast at his own wedding reception. This was a far cry from the wedded bliss he'd imagined the night he proposed to Ember.

Right family.

Wrong bride.

Worse, he'd overheard Ember throwing up earlier as he walked past the bathroom, and she still looked pale and wane.

Not even his own family would deign to speak to him. His mother, father, and siblings were in a corner with Alura's parents on the opposite side of the room. None of his so-called friends would come near him because it was obvious his parents were taking issue with his actions and his peers lacked the balls to risk displeasing their ruling monarchs in the name of friendship. Or their future ones—which would be his older brother and sister, both of whom were already married. So the odds of Bastien ever sitting on the throne were slim to none. Which was fine by him. Last thing he wanted was to occupy the throne, since the only way to get it would be over the dead bodies of his loved ones.

Though tonight, he wasn't feeling much love from them.

Open hostility?

Big affirmative there.

And because he had no chance of inheriting, no one else would dare risk displeasing anyone else in his family. *That, folks, is why I've always been such an unreasonable ass.*

Since the day he was born, he'd never held any delusions about the people around him. They were his friends only so long as they could use him to get close to his brother, sister, or parents. He was a means to an end. It was why he'd loved Ember so much. She, alone, hadn't sought to use him for rank or privelage. In fact, she'd avoided his family and everything to do with royal obligation and ceremony, preferring instead to just spend time alone with him.

And he'd cherished every last moment of it.

But those days were gone. Alura adored her new position in his family. She was lapping up her role as visira like a starving cat in a creamery.

Dear gods, what have I unleashed?

Sighing, Bastien wished Fain Hauk was here. His Andarion drinking buddy wouldn't give two flips about what the royal family thought. Or anyone else.

Unfortunately, the Andarion War Hauks had a bad history with the eton Anatoles. And the ruling eton Anatoles were Bastien's cousins through his maternal uncle's spawning twin sons with the Andarion heiress. So while Bastien was a loyal friend to Fain Hauk, Bastien's cousin Jullien eton Anatole had taken preference for the wedding invite.

Besides, he liked Jullien.

"Wow. Someone who's a bigger leper than I am. Never thought I'd live to see the day. I am impressed, Bas. Truly an incredible feat for Bastien Aros Cabarro, handsome baby boy genius."

Speak of the devil. . . .

Igorning Jullien's use of the irksome nickname Bastien's mother had given him in childhood, he turned to find his half-Andarion cousin standing behind him. Damn, for such a humongous bastard Jullien could move even more silently than the best-trained League assassin. It was a most unnerving trait.

But at least one person wasn't shunning him. Mostly because Jullien, being half human and half Andarion, was used to everyone fleeing at his approach. As if he'd had a choice in his birthright. He couldn't help his mixed heritage, any more than Jullien was responsible for the fact that humans and Andarions had been at war for most of their history. Yet both races held it against the prince as if he was personally responsible for all their sins.

Bastien had always felt bad for his cousin over the way he was treated. Had always gone out of his way to be nice to him. 'Cause if the truth were known, he preferred Jullien over his own siblings most days. While Jullien could be a bit standoffish and blunt, he was highly intelligent and had an honest, offbeat sense of humor that Bastien appreciated. It was a breath of fresh air amidst the courtiers who practiced duplicity and lies in all things.

At least with his cousin, he always knew where he stood and what Jullien thought.

"Good to see you, Julie."

Jullien snorted before he made a grand gesture of fluffing the lace at his left cuff. "Appreciate that bald lie when we both know I'm as welcome here as a lethal STD in a whorehouse."

Which was exactly how Bastien felt at present. He laughed at the perfect description for the two of them.

Jullien stumbled a bit and Bastien sighed at his poor cousin. Even with those dark red glasses covering half his face, it was obvious Jullien was flying high on something that was most likely illegal in every known system. He probably wouldn't even remember being here, and that broke Bastien's heart for him. As Jullien had said, he was ever a leper, and most of their family cursed his name the moment they saw him approaching.

It was so bad and frequent that Jullien often introduced himself as "Dammit Jullien" to people as a joke.

But Bastien didn't see a hybrid human-Andarion bastard in front of him. All he saw was family.

So what if Julie had a set of fangs and human eyes with Andarion features. That had never mattered to him. He didn't judge folks on their looks.

Only on their actions.

He arched a brow as Jullien grabbed a glass of Tondarion Grade-A Hellfire from the tray of a passing server. "Should you be drinking *that* in your current condition?" Depending on what the boy had taken, it could prove lethal.

Jullien knocked it back in a single gulp. "Why not? It's a celebration, right? If the family's lucky, they could get a twofer out of this. Your wedding. My funeral."

Okay, then . . .

Jullien's human bodyguards retreated into the crowd as his father approached them. Similar in looks to Bastien's mother, Aros Triosan was the same height as his son, but lacked Jullien's massive Andarion size.

And that regal pissed-off aura of rebellion that was only undercut by an overt ennui that said Jullien was resigned to his unwanted place in the universe.

Aros grabbed Jullien's arm in a grip so tight that Bastien winced from the bruise he was sure Jullien would have over it. "Shouldn't you be heading home now?"

With a fierce grimace that exposed his fangs, Jullien jerked out of his father's grasp. "Don't worry, Paka. I shall take my inebriated ass out of here before I intentionally expose it and further embarrass you. Besides, my jailors won't like it if I fail to report back by curfew."

When Jullien started to leave, Aros splayed his hand across Jullien's chest to stop his retreat. "For the love of God, could you sober up? Just once?"

Jullien snorted derisively. "And deal with all of you without the benefits of being chemically numb? Are you out of your minsid mind?"

With a smug sneer directly in his father's face, Jullien flipped his hair back with an affected bored nonchalance that was no doubt designed to piss his father off.

And judging by Aros's features, it succeeded.

"But no fears, Paka. I shan't urinate in Bastien's pool tonight. My fury isn't for him." Jullien tucked his cane under his arm before he turned back to Bastien. "Word to the wise, kyzi. Take your bride and get as far away from the family as you can." He jerked his chin at Aros.

"They're treacherous bastards. The whole lot of them. Never trust them at your back. Triosan or Cabarro. They're all selfish to the bitter end. Trust me. Sooner or later, one of them will find the nerve to come for your ass and take you down. Birth order doesn't matter. We eat our own. One child at a time. It's just a matter of time, *drey*."

And with that, Jullien left.

Aros let out an audible sigh of relief. "Sorry about that, Bastien. I don't even know why he came."

"I invited him."

Aros scowled. "Why would you?"

Wow . . . no wonder Jullien was so cynical. But then he'd once had a twin brother who'd died when they were children—some claimed in a fire set in his school at their own grandmother's orders—as Jullien had stated, his mother's entire family had murdered themselves down to only her and her sister, with his grandmother serving as the Andarion queen only after slaughtering her own husband. The Andarions were a brutal, bloody race.

Thank the gods, his own family wasn't like that. And it was why Bastien refused to be a shit to Jullien. The boy needed compassion from someone. He certainly wasn't getting any from his parents.

"He's my cousin."

Aros let out a scoffing laugh. "You heard his parting words about family. He is his grandmother's child. Treacherous to the core of his brutal Andarion soul. Cares for nothing and no one, except himself. I tried so hard to save him from that when he was a boy, and every time I did, he insulted me and refused to do anything I asked of him."

Bastien arched a brow at that recitation of facts. Strange, that wasn't how he remembered their childhood. "All I recall, Uncle Aros, was Jullien trying to keep his head down and getting his ass kicked every time he dared to look up."

"You weren't there for his tantrums and lies. Believe me, you can't trust anything Jullien says. He's the real snake in the grass." He paused to shake his head. "You know, I once had an innocent boy arrested because of a lie Jullien told when he was in school. Poor kid would have gone to prison for something he didn't do had Dancer Hauk—Jullien's best friend—not had the temerity to come forward and tell me the truth about the matter."

"Which was?"

"Jullien was jealous because the other student had scored higher on a test. So he said the boy had stolen his signet ring, which Jullien had hidden to get the kid in trouble. I could have killed him when I found it in the exact place Dancer had said it would be. To my eternal shame, I almost did. Then to get back at Dancer, Jullien schemed with his Andarion cousins to have Dancer's older brother disinherited from their family and Dancer permanently disfigured. When that wasn't good enough, he had Dancer thrown out of the military. I'm telling you, he's evil to his core. Has no concept of loyalty whatsoever. You'd do well to stay as far away from him as you can."

Bastien took a slow drink as he ran that information through his mind. "I never saw that side of him, Uncle. So you'll have to forgive me if I choose not to believe it until I know all the facts of the situation. Jullien was never anything but nice to me. I only judge people by what I see firsthand. Not what others tell me about them. I refuse to render a verdict against anyone based on partial facts that are hand-fed to me for maximum prejudice."

"I hope you never live to regret that naïve loyalty." And with that, Aros wandered off.

Maybe he was naïve. Yet the one thing he'd learned

was that people tended to have their own agendas. And that context colored everything. Things seen in daylight looked very different than they did when seen through a shaded windowscreen. It was too easy to misjudge someone's motivations. Or the facts when you only had a piece of them. To put your own spin on what they were thinking and their reasons for certain actions. He preferred to give people the benefit of the doubt.

Case in point, he could easily call Aros an ass for the way he treated Jullien. And he'd certainly witnessed some stellar acts of parental neglect and abuse when it came to Aros's interactions with his son. But since Bastien wasn't around during their private conversations, he wouldn't hold Aros's hostility against him. After all, Aros had always been nice to him. A perfect, loving uncle.

In fact, he had a hard time reconciling those two sides of the man. Because the funny and loving uncle he knew was a far cry from the suspicious and cold man Jullien called Father. Just as Jullien wasn't the cruel, vicious bastard they all labeled him. While he'd gotten into a few noteworthy brawls with Quin over his older brother's mouthy insults, Jullien had never once taken a swing at either Lil or Bastien—not that Bastien had ever given him a reason to. But Lil had certainly let fly some personal barbs that even Bastien would have been hard-pressed as a boy to let slide without some physical contact between them.

Yet Jullien had never once struck out at her. Because he was so much larger physically than either Lil or Bastien, Jullien always kept his temper leashed around them. The rest of the family . . .

Well, Bastien understood why some of them might not have a favorable opinion of his cousin.

And Bastien definitely wasn't the heartless bastard

everyone at this reception thought he was for betraying Ember. Last thing he'd ever wanted was to cause her a single tear.

The road to hell is paved with good intentions. . . .

And he'd certainly paved his route with a certain misery named Alura.

God have mercy on my soul.

'Cause nobody in this room was ever going to spare him a single drop.

Ember turned her shoulder so that she wouldn't accidentally glimpse Bastien while she talked to her sisters. Every time he came into her line of sight, it was like a vicious kick to her gut.

She still couldn't believe he'd slept with Alura. Not after she'd confided in him how angry she'd been after her last boyfriend had cheated on her with her sister.

What had he been thinking?

That he wanted to hurt you.

Yeah, that'd be about right. And she'd give him credit for knowing exactly where and how to strike the lowest blow. Why else had he called before he'd done it?

Even now, she could hear his voice in her ear on that fateful day.

"Hey . . . your sister just asked me out. Since you've been dodging my calls—"

"I haven't dodged your anything!" To this day, she didn't know why she'd snapped at him in anger. Something about his accusation had fired her temper. But she'd known at the time that it was the worst reaction she could have had with Bastien. He never reacted well to direct confrontation. It invariably caused him to dig his heels in.

And do something rash and stupid.

There was one absolute truth about the captain—he

never backed down. He'd set himself on fire first. For that, she had his mother to thank. That infamous Triosan stubborn streak that was apparently genetic.

"Oh, okay, Major. If *you* say so." Bastien's droll sarcasm had only fueled her fury more.

Wanting to lash out and hurt him as much as he'd stung her, she'd growled low in her throat. "Look, I don't care what or who you do. I'm not your keeper anymore."

"Where did *that* come from?"

"I'm disconnecting now." She'd dropped the signal and forced herself not to throw her link.

Or stomp it.

Instead, she'd called Alura immediately. "You asked out Bastien?" she'd snapped at her sister without preamble. "How could you be such a bitch?"

Alura hadn't shown the least bit of remorse over her actions. And why should she? As the youngest of their family, Alura had always thought herself special and immune from the rules of common courtesy. Of common decency. "You threw him away. Remember? I felt bad for the guy. He's been moping for weeks. Someone needs to have some pity on him. Besides, it's just dinner. Relax."

"Relax? Really?"

"What's your problem, Em?" Alura had dared to use that snotty tone that made Ember want to slap her. "Anyone else would have been on their knees in gratitude to marry a visir, especially one who was so in love with them. Only *you* would turn him down flat, for no good reason."

"Yeah, but you don't have to deal with his ødara looking down her regal nose at you because you're not good enough for her precious little baby. Or worse, his zusa. I swear, every time I get near them, I feel the need to check my shoes."

"Check your shoes?"

"Yeah. Their lips curl like they're both smelling dog shit."

Alura had snorted. "You're ridiculous. No one can make you feel bad unless you allow it."

"Easy for you to say. I don't have your galactic-sized ego."

"And that's why I asked him out. I don't mind dealing with his family. Besides, he looks terrible. You've just about killed him with your callousness."

Like it'd been any easier on her? Truth was, she did want to marry him. Bastien was everything she'd ever wanted in a man.

And more.

But damn his family. They were so irritating and intrusive. Every time she turned around, one of them had been in her face. And since they were royalty, with life-and death-sentencing capabilities over everyone in their empire, she hadn't been able to tell them off.

Worse? His *married* brother had made several inappropriate advances toward her. Then threatened her, her parents, and sisters if she breathed a word about it to Bastien.

The thought of being tied to *that* for eternity . . .

As much as she loved Bastien, it'd been too terrifying to contemplate.

Now her own sister was being a dirtbag.

Again.

Furious and hurt, Ember growled at Alura. "I'm your cusa! You should be thinking about *me*."

"I am thinking about you. I'm tying him up until you come to your senses. Then I'll hand him back. Simple. When you're ready, I'll hand-deliver him to your door, myself."

Something had told Ember even then that Alura was lying. But like a fool, she hadn't listened. She'd wanted to believe that her own blood wouldn't screw her over again. Not with another man. And not with one she loved as much as she loved Bastien.

She should have known better.

"You okay?"

Blinking at the question that snapped her out of her memories and brought her back to Alura's wedding reception, she nodded at her sister Cinder.

Next to the oldest, Cinder was the tallest of her siblings and almost a full head taller than Ember whenever they were barefoot. She'd always envied her sister for that statuesque beauty. As well as her gorgeous reddish-brown hair that cascaded over her shoulders in lush waves and amber eyes Ember would have killed for.

But the best part about Cin was her kind heart and the compassion she'd always held for everyone around her. No matter what, they could count on her for sympathy and hugs.

"I'm good."

Brand laughed in Ember's ear as she joined them. "No, she's not. She's been sick all day. And right now, she's thinking of marching over there and snatching out every last bit of Alura's hair. Want me to help?"

And that was why Ember loved her younger sister Brandiwyn, or Brand as they often called her, always spoke her mind without a filter. Better yet, she usually spoke the minds of whoever was around her without a filter. And if you needed help hiding a body, she would always be there to lend an eager hand, and would die before she ratted you out.

Nothing could break Brand. Not even their mother's glower. Or their father's threats.

Steadfast and loyal, Brand was ever above reproach. It was her temper, daring, and mouth that got her into trouble. She gave as good as she got and refused to back down from anything, or anyone. In that regard, she was an awful lot like Bastien.

"It's okay, Brand, but thank you for the offer."

"Fine, but if you change your mind, you know where I live."

Kindel laughed at her. "And now you know why I had to pat her down before I let her leave the house this morning. I was terrified what she might do to Bastien—or Alura—on your behalf."

Brand reached for another glass of champagne. "Yeah, well, it's time Alura learned to keep her hands off our men."

Ember didn't comment on Brand's bitter words. Like her, she'd lost her last boyfriend to Alura's machinations. "How am I supposed to have another happy family holiday after this?"

Kindel hugged her. "Don't think about it. We're always here for you."

"And if it helps, remember that Bastien asked *you* to marry him. His honor forced him to marry Alura."

Brand was right. But Ember couldn't quite give her the whole victory. "Yeah, but it was his wandering prick that got him into this."

Cinder draped herself against Ember's back so that she could laugh and whisper in her ear. "*That* we can fix, *blyta zusa*. Give me a knife and five seconds."

Leaning back into her arms, Ember smiled up at her. "Love you."

"You, too." Cinder kissed her cheek.

"So what mischief are my girls plotting? And don't say nothing. I know that evil twinkle in those devious eyes."

Ember wrinkled her nose at her mother. Though she had dark curly hair like Kindel's, her mother's features were closer to Cinder's and Ashley's. "They were thinking up ways to ensure that Alura's child was an only."

Their mother tsked at them, but then that was what Charlotte Wyldestarrin did best. As a decorated colonel for the Kirovarian Gyron Force—their elite fighter corps—she often said she could wrangle a platoon of soldiers easier than her six unruly daughters. "Well, if you do decide to make a move, don't get any blood on those dresses. Your aunt Tish wants you to wear them for her daughter's wedding next year."

"Yes, ma'am," Kindel said with a sharp salute. "I shall keep our troops in line."

"See that you do, Major." With an adorable wink, their mother headed back to where their father waited.

Then Ember made the mistake of catching Bastien's gaze.

And the hunger in those hazel eyes scorched her. A hunger he quickly squelched and blinked away as if he realized how obvious and inappropriate it was.

Her stomach hit the floor. And she hated how much she wanted to be the bride beside him. Damn, he looked edible in those elegant clothes that fit his lean, ripped body in a way that should be outlawed. There was no sign of the incredibly powerful and capable soldier she knew him to be. He was all regal visir tonight.

Except he lacked his brother's overt haughty snobbery. With Bastien, his patrician bearing was casual and innate. Good-natured and inviting.

While his siblings refused standard military housing, citing a special need for privacy, Bastien insisted on it. If it was good enough for his people, then he deemed it more than appropriate for himself. He never tried to wiggle past curfew. Never used his regal standing to eat in the better mess halls or to leave base for his food.

She'd only seen him pull rank when someone was abusing their own authority over someone else. Then it was on, and he was quick to slap them down and defend the underdog.

He was wonderful that way.

And the bitter longing in those hazel eyes as he tried not to watch her burned her to the core of her soul. Like Cinder had said, he wasn't getting married tonight out of choice.

But that didn't take the sting out of his betrayal.

You'll get through this, old girl.

She didn't know how. But she would.

Bastien scowled as he saw his uncle leaving the balcony where Alura had gone a few minutes ago for some fresh air. He didn't know why, but something about that bothered him.

Curious, he went to check on his "wife."

No sooner had that title gone through his head than his stomach heaved involuntarily, threatening to undignify him. God, would his body ever stop doing that? What kind of marriage were they going to have if every time he thought about her as his spouse he had a spontaneous need to vomit?

Not wanting to think about it, he stepped outside to find Alura in the moonlight. She was beautiful, he'd give her that much. Hell, physically she might even be the most attractive of the Wyldestarrin brood, but she wasn't the one who made his heart race.

The one who made him feel alive. It wasn't her smile that hardened him to the point of madness. For all her beauty, she left him strangely numb.

"You okay?"

She smiled up at him as she stepped closer and placed her hand to his chest. "Of course. Why do you ask?"

He gestured over his shoulder toward the direction where his uncle had gone. "Barnabas is an acquired taste. I'm told my sa once left him tied to a tree out in the woods to die when they were kids because he couldn't keep his mouth shut and kept aggravating him. Bastard unfortunately survived."

She laughed. "You don't mean that."

Bastien rubbed at his jaw as he considered it. "I don't know. Even my ødara tried to kill him once."

"No! Did she really?"

He smiled at the memory. "Oh yeah. It was a summer when I was six or seven. My dad had sent me and my siblings and cousin Jullien out to train with him for camp. Poor Julie couldn't keep up."

"Julie?"

"The Andarion who was here earlier."

"Oh. I wondered who'd invited that big fat thing to my wedding."

Bastien stiffened at her disdain. "He takes enough shit from people over his heritage. He doesn't need it from family, too."

"Sorry."

It took him a minute to calm down from her having insulted his family. Especially one of his favorite members.

Bastien finally cleared his throat and resumed the story. "Anyway, he has a hard time breathing in our atmosphere. It's a different mixture than what they have on Andaria and his anatomy's not quite the same either. So there he was, wheezing, green, yacking everywhere, and about to pass out. Barnabas wasn't taking a bit of mercy on him and neither was Lil or Quin. They were screaming and shoving at him. Telling him to move his fat ass. I'd never heard so many insults screamed at one person in my life. And I'd had enough of it."

"What did you do?"

"Was my usual charming self. Yanked my helmet off, laid down on the ground, and told them I was done for the day. That *my* ass was too precious for that amount of abuse. And that I was ready for my nap. To call a transport."

She arched a brow at him. "I imagine that didn't go over well with your uncle."

"Like a labor strike with my sa. He set my precious ass on fire, but it got the attention off Jullien and they finally gave him some peace. So, in my opinion, worth it. And when I got home and my øda found out and took a blaster to my uncle . . . totally worth it. Kept me out of those miserable summer treks in hell until well after I hit puberty. And even then, I got to go with a security detail that threatened the life of anyone who sought to harm me."

"Is that why he's so skittish of you?"

"Probably. My øda's a little overprotective. In case you haven't noticed."

"Oh, I noticed. Hard to miss." She walked into his arms. "She already threatened to have me killed if I break your heart."

Bastien didn't comment as Alura rose up on her tiptoes to kiss him. Mostly because she'd already broken his heart. She'd done that the moment she'd forced him into a marriage he didn't want.

But he wasn't cruel enough to tell his mother, because there was no telling what she'd do to rectify it. As they'd both noted, his mom could be a bit psychotic and overzealous whenever it came to him.

When Alura pulled away, her blue eyes were filled with warmth. "Love you. And one day, I'm going to make you love me, too."

"Alura—"

She placed her fingers over his lips to stop his protest. "It's okay, Bastien. I know I'm not your first choice. But I can guarantee you that you'll never want another woman after me. *That* I promise you."

For some reason, those words left him with a cold feeling in the pit of his stomach.

He watched as she left to rejoin the party.

It wasn't until he was alone that he realized she'd never answered his question about why Barnabas had come out here with her.

Whatever. His uncle was probably grilling her like he did everyone else.

Sighing, Bastien decided he'd had enough of this fiasco. Not like anyone here could hate him any more than they already did.

"Cald mitta," he breathed under his breath, using the Andarion words for goodnight.

"Later, bitches" might be a bit more apropos for how he felt.

Peeling off his suit jacket, he draped it over the balcony, rolled the cuffs back on his shirt, then did something he hadn't done since he was a kid skipping out past curfew—he climbed down his mother's prized foliage and snuck across the lawn, taking care to dodge sentries, guard dogs, and cameras.

By the time he made it to the road, he almost felt like himself again.

He crossed the busy intersection on foot, to his private storage unit no one knew about, where he kept a couple of his treasured airbikes his mother would have apoplexy over should she ever discover them. In fact, she'd torched the only one he'd made the mistake of allowing her to see when he'd been sixteen and had been dumb enough to drive it home from the dealership.

Lesson learned.

Never let his mother know about his addiction to extreme speed.

Bastien shrugged his Armstitch jacket on and reached for a helmet. He swapped his shoes for a pair of reinforced boots before he settled himself onto the bike and started it. The engine roared to life with a guttural sound that caused the bike to vibrate through him. Yeah, this was what he needed to clear his head—warp speed and some gravity-defying flips.

Pulling the helmet on, he took a second to scan through frequencies, looking for some raucous music to accompany his mood.

His family had always despised his taste in music—to the point his father had once confiscated every playing device Bastien owned. Since then, Bastien had learned to tune in to the unlicensed pirate stations transmitting from Kirovarian outposts. They alone played the songs his father's committee had banned from their commercial networks. Music deemed too "corrupt" or "dangerous" for the masses.

He actually owed Jullien for this particular skill—his cousin had taught him one summer when they'd been kids, and Bastien had been particularly bored while Jullien had been visiting.

As usual, Quin had ratted Bastien out for violating their father's music policy and gotten him grounded and his room searched. Feeling sorry for him, Jullien had snuck into his room, past their security guards, to cheer him up.

"Don't tell them I showed you this, but . . ." Jullien had

taken apart the intercom in Bastien's room that his parents and security used to monitor his every move, then taught him to rewire it for entertainment. With a wink, Julie had done the same with his video feeds.

"Where did you learn to do this?" Bastien had asked in an awed tone.

"Spend a lot of time alone. Read a ton. Tinker even more. You never know when it's going to come in handy."

Like now.

Bastien paused his own tinkering as he caught the tail end of a private conversation between short-range devices. He wiggled the wires to clarify the signal, thinking he must have been higher than Jullien with what he thought he'd heard a heartbeat ago.

But there was no mistaking it as it came in loud and clear.

"—Base rotates its patrols every four hours, leaving an opening there. The real vulnerability is at the palace. Cabarro refuses to have security in his private chapel when he goes in with his wife for evening prayer at six. You can set a clock by it. Twice a week, at the beginning and end, his eldest joins them. You could wipe out monidar and heir in one fell swoop."

"What of the other two?"

"They patrol together. One good dogfight and we own them."

Bastien's jaw went slack. He was so stunned that by the time he thought to start recording the transmission, they'd stopped talking.

Dammit!

He kicked his bike on and launched it, then headed straight to the palace. His only thought to warn his family, he ignored the traffic and sent it careening. He also forgot about security at the palace.

They opened fire on him.

Luckily, he was used to dodging shit. Though to be fair, it was usually projectiles Quin was hurling at his head out of anger, and not heavy artillery. But his older brother's temper had honed his reflexes to a lethal level.

Bastien didn't stop until he reached the front door, where he was summarily tackled by their guards. "*Oskilir!*" he growled at the security guards on top of him. "It's me!" He jerked his helmet off to show them they'd just assaulted a member of the family they were trying to protect.

That succeeded in making every guard near him shrink back in holy terror. To lay a hostile hand to a member of the royal family was a death sentence.

Especially the adored baby son.

Glaring at them, he shot to his feet and shoved his helmet into the hands of the guard who'd tackled him. "Next time, run the bike's serial number."

"S-s-s-sorry, Latenn."

"No problem. Just be glad it's me and not Quin." Unlike his brother, Bastien wouldn't demand the man's head for this. He was glad they were feral in their duties.

Clapping him on the arm, he cut around the guard and ran for the doors that they opened for him.

He didn't hesitate as he rushed for the ballroom. Nor did he stop until he found his father, who was standing beside his brother, uncle, and new father-in-law.

Newell Cabarro turned toward him with a fierce scowl as he took in Bastien's change of wardrobe. "What in the name of the gods are you wearing?"

"I need to speak with you in private."

"Bastien Aros—"

"Sa! This can't wait! It's important!"

His father let out an exasperated breath. "Everything with you always is."

Brandon Wyldestarrin bit back a smile. "He's young and passionate, Alvaldr."

In that moment, Bastien had a glimmer of hope that Alura's father, unlike his, might actually listen to him and take him seriously. "Commander? I just intercepted some intel from the enemy. I need to file a report. Immediately."

Barnabas quirked a brow at that. "In that case, *I* should probably see to this. It is my job, after all."

His father rolled his eyes. "What could he have possibly intercepted? Especially dressed like *that*?"

Quin laughed while Bastien bristled under the stinging set-down.

To his credit, Brandon kept his face straight.

True to form, Barnabas smirked. "Well, his ødara has always humored him, so I shall keep up the tradition. Come, Bastien. You might as well file it with me, anyway. Not like I don't run the military. Right?"

It was Bastien's turn to smirk as they headed away from his family. "Such wonderful patronization. So glad I almost busted my ass and got shot at to get home to protect everyone. Makes the effort so worthwhile."

With scoffing derision, Barnabas led him toward his father's study. "So what did you hear?"

"It was a report on my father's daily habits and that the enemy knows I'm Lil's wingman."

Closing the door to the study so that they were alone, Barnabas appeared less than impressed with the revelation. "Everyone knows you're Lil's wingman. That's not much of a report, burr."

Crossing his arms over his chest, Bastien gave him a droll *no-shit* glare. "It means there's a spy in our ranks. Someone sending reports to the Eudorans about our routines. I know what I heard."

"Bas . . . you're under a lot of stress."

"What's that supposed to mean?"

"Just that sometimes our minds play tricks on us. Don't you think that if there was an imminent threat to the royal family that I'd be the first in line to nip it before it blossomed into something dangerous?"

Barnabas's calm, reassuring tone began to soothe his ragged nerves. His uncle was right. A large part of his job as the prime commander was keeping up with just such espionage. Especially while they were at war. If a threat were looming, Barnabas would be the first to know.

His uncle patted him on the shoulder. "Now tell me again what happened? Start from the top."

"I was getting on my airbike."

"That your ødara won't allow you to ride?"

"Yeah."

"And what? You were planning to run away from your responsibility?"

That pissy, pithy tone rankled. As did the obvious condescension. Honestly, he was getting really sick of the way his uncle and brother looked down on his every word and deed as if he had a head injury and they had to wipe his ass for him. "Not permanently. I just wanted to clear my thoughts for a few minutes."

"Mmmm. Well, it seems to me that your subconscious picked up on that and ran with it. Probably out of guilt, it concocted this elaborate death plot to make you fear for their safety so that you wouldn't flee, but rather stay here and face what you've done."

Bastien gaped at his censure. He'd taken full responsibility for everything from the beginning. At no time had he denied it or tried in any way to get out of a single bit of this. Hell, he'd even gone alone to the Wyldestarrins and told both Alura's mother and father what had happened and assured them that he wouldn't scandalize their daughter. Whereas Barnabas's sons would have forced an abortion and then exiled Alura out of the empire, he was marrying her and giving both mother and child his full protection.

For that matter, Barnabas had ruined the lives of three different women that Bastien knew of.

So had Bastien's father. Well, not three, but he knew of one in particular the courtiers whispered about whenever they didn't realize he could overhear them. A massive scandal that had almost ended his parents' marriage.

To this day, Barnabas paraded mistresses around his wife and children with no regard for either. So how dare the hypocrite stand there and lecture *him* about morality and responsibility!

"Meaning what, Uncle?"

Barnabas narrowed his gaze on Bastien, but that was the only sign he gave of his anger as he refused to answer the question. "Did you record any of the conversation?"

"No. I didn't think to."

"Then how can you be so sure you heard what you think you heard?"

Because he wasn't an idiot. But he knew that look in Barnabas's eyes. Bastard wasn't listening. And no amount of argument would sway him. Bastien had bashed his head against this wall enough to know the migraine before it began.

Sighing, he backed out with as much dignity as he could. "Maybe you're right."

"Of course I'm right. Now be a good boy and return to your wife. She's been looking for you. Don't you think you should take her home and consummate the wedding?"

Not really. He'd rather set fire to his crotch.

But his uncle was right. This was expected of him.

"Fine. Thank you, Barnie."

There was a subtle yet visible tensing at the nickname Barnabas despised. "Any time, slim."

As Bastien left the room, he passed by his other uncle, Jackson, in the hallway. Much shorter than Bastien, Jax barely reached his shoulders. With brown twinkling eyes, he'd inherited all the humor his other siblings lacked, and was by far Bastien's favorite of his parents' siblings.

They exchanged a subtle head nod before Jax stepped around him and went into the study to see Barnabas.

The moment he did, a peculiar sensation went down Bastien's back like a phantom chill.

Weird. He had no explanation for that. Other than gross paranoia. *Maybe I need to take up Jullien's drug habit.* For the first time in his life, he was beginning to understand why his cousin had the problems he did. 'Cause right now, he didn't want to face any part of this reality.

Barnabas narrowed his gaze on his brother as Jax shut and locked the door. "What are you doing?"

"Wanted to see if you needed any backup with the spoiled little punk."

"No. I've got it." But as soon as his younger brother neared him, Barnabas backhanded him.

Hissing, Jax wiped at the blood on his lips. "What the hell?"

"That *little punk* overheard your report to the Eudorans about his family and their habits and you almost outed us. Are you completely stupid?"

"How did he hear it?"

"Hell if I know. Let this be a warning to you. He's not his sa or Quin. Don't underestimate that little *knættr*. He's smarter than he looks. Our only saving grace is that he's lazier than shit, and more trusting than a newborn babe.

No one takes him seriously. Thank God. If he'd had an ounce of anyone's trust or any concept that someone might actually not like him, they'd be searching for you right now."

"They're not?"

Barnabas shook his head. "I talked him down and put it to rest. Just be more careful and make sure you know where he is before you send any more reports to your contacts. And for the love of the gods, use a secured line next time." He moved to pour himself another drink. "So how did it go?"

"Perfect. They have no problem leaving you in as a governor once we do this. You help them take out Newell and put down any residual rebellion, and the throne's all yours."

"And what about you, theren?"

"What, what about me?"

"Have you a problem with my being on the throne in Newell's place?"

"The only thing I have a problem with is the fact that Newell left me and my platoon for dead before he signed the Eudoran truce. I haven't forgotten that. Payback's a bitch. And this bitch wants to see him and his entire brood in the ground."

CHAPTER 3

Bastien slowed as he neared the cold, sterile room where Alura's family had already gathered. He'd been out on a long patrol with his sister when the emergency call had come in that his wife was in the hospital.

Lil took his hand to let him know she was with him as they entered the herd of stern-faced Wyldestarrins. As typical, Ember ignored him completely. Huddled between her sisters, he couldn't see anything more than the top of her head.

Cinder's wife, Tasi, was the first one to greet him. She stepped forward with a sad smile. "Hey, Bas."

"What happened?"

Tasi glanced to Lil before she met his gaze. Her brown eyes showed the depth of her sympathy. "She went to her doctor's appointment for her checkup and they admitted her."

"Okay . . ." He waited for her to continue.

Brandon came forward. "The doctor wants to speak to you, *burr*."

When Lil started to go with him, Brandon stopped her. "He wanted a private consultation."

"No," she said firmly. "I'm not leaving my *theren* alone for something this important. He needs family with him."

"We're his family."

Lil swept a disdainful grimace around the group. "Tasi I'll grant you. The rest . . . you've treated him like shit and I'm not about to abandon him to your cruelty." She put her arm around Bastien's waist. "He's my *kogur-theren*. I'll personally cut the throat of anyone who hurts him."

Those words brought a lump to his throat. While they might fight ninety percent of the time themselves, he could always count on his brother and sister to be there when he needed them. It was why he loved his family so much.

They were assholes. But they were loyal assholes.

The commander stepped back and allowed him to enter the room with Lil in tow.

Alura sat in the bed with a tear-streaked face. Her mother was at her side, holding her hand. The moment Alura saw him, she burst into tears.

"Wow, Bas, still charming every woman you meet, I see," Lil said under her breath.

He grimaced over his shoulder at his sister's facetious humor. Feeling awkward and unsure, he went to Alura so that he could offer her a hug. "What happened?" he asked her mother.

She didn't answer.

Instead, the doctor came forward. He glanced to Lil. "This is a private family matter."

Lil took on her full regal haughty stature as she raked the doctor with a quelling sneer that would have impressed even their mother. "I am family, Doctor, and unless you wish to spend the rest of your career washing out bedpans, you will take an entirely new tone with me and speak to me only when I allow it and end all such sentences with 'Zyl Latessa.' Understood?"

He swallowed audibly as he realized what he'd just done. And to whom. "Yes, Zyl Latessa."

"Very good. Now, answer my theren's question and remember that he, too, is a crowned member of the royal family."

"Yes, Zyl Latessa." Visibly trembling, the doctor turned toward Bastien, then remembered that he wasn't supposed to have his back to Lil.

Bastien would have been amused if he wasn't concerned about Alura and irritated at Lil for showing her ass right now. "It's fine, Doctor. I'm not one for protocol. I'm just worried about my wife."

"I lost the baby, Bastien." Alura clutched at him and wailed.

The doctor nodded. "I'm so sorry, Latenn. But she should be able to conceive again." And with that, he beat a hasty retreat.

Alura continued to wail in his arms.

"Sh, Alura. It'll be okay."

"No, it won't." Sobs racked her body. "You'll divorce me now. I know you will. You only married me because of the baby!"

His jaw went slack at her accusation. The same one that was mirrored in her mother's gaze. And by the smirk on Lil's face, he could tell that his sister expected him to agree.

But that wasn't him. And he damn sure wasn't about to kick her while she was down.

"No . . . I'm not a cad, Alura. I took a vow to you, before the gods, and I will stand by it." Those words shocked her mother.

And pissed his sister off to no end.

Alura pulled back with a ragged breath so that she could stare up at him to see if he was lying. "You will?"

He wiped at the tears on her beautiful face and nodded. "Of course. I'm not going to leave you in your hour of need. I'm not a total ass. Just a partial one."

That only made her cry harder as she clutched at his uniform.

For the first time since Ember had broken up with him, Charlotte looked at him with something other than contempt. If he didn't know better, he might even think that his mother-in-law finally approved of him again.

Alura trembled and wiped her nose on his shirt. "I love you, Bastien."

"I know." He kissed the top of her head, wishing he felt the same for her. Wishing even more that he could bring himself to lie and say the words back to her like she wanted him to. But no matter how hard he tried, they stuck in his craw.

It was a growing wall between them that he barely touched her. Rarely went home. He still hadn't moved his things from his barracks to the house he'd bought for Alura and the baby. Since he was Gyron Force and they were at war, it was an easy excuse that he was needed for their late-night patrols, and that he was required to stay on base in case they had to scramble for emergency attacks.

He kept telling himself that in time he'd grow to love her. His parents had started out that way—an arranged political marriage between two empires. Now the two of them were best friends and loved each other dearly.

Had he not met Ember, it was what he'd been destined for. His father had been in the middle of negotiations to marry him off to an heiress for the Ritadarion Empire so that Bastien would have been a ruler in his own right. In fact, he would have been married to her by now.

Ember had changed his whole life.

"Bas?"

He met Lil's gaze.

She tapped her wrist, and it was only then that he realized his own arm was buzzing with an alert. "It's a scramble. We have to get back to base."

"Okay." He wiped the remainder of the tears from Alura's cheeks and kissed her lips. "I'll be home as soon as the attack's over to check on you."

"Thank you."

Nodding, he said his good-byes and followed his sister from the room to see that Ember and her sisters had already gone to answer the call. As he and his sister left, Lil cast a censuring glare at him.

"You're really not planning to divorce her now?"

"Don't start on me, Lil."

"C'mon . . . you're putting on a brave face. But even I can tell you're not happy in this marriage. Divorce her already."

"Meant what I said before the priest. Through good times and bad. I'm here for the long haul."

"You're an idiot. And I hope for your sake that she's as loyal to you."

"—Then I overheard Bastien talking to his uncle, Jackson. He had no idea that I could hear them, plotting his parents' murders."

"She's fucking lying!" Bastien shot to his feet, intending to kill his wife. Had he not been in restraints and surrounded by half a dozen armed guards, he would have torn out Alura's treacherous throat with his bare hands.

"Lock him in the box!" Alia Mureaux, the Overseer

of Justice who ran the Trigon Court where Bastien was being tried for the murders of his parents and siblings, came to her feet. Her face was flushed bright red from the anger that made her dark brown eyes protrude. As a long-time friend of both his parents, she was as disgusted and upset by this trial as he was.

And she'd cut him no slack from the beginning. Because, like the rest of the Nine Worlds, she was convinced Bastien was guilty.

Something not helped by the fact that the media continued to run photos of him being arrested while covered in their blood. Worse, Alura kept giving interviews where she cried about how he'd done her wrong, telling everyone she was the victim, and spilling all manner of bullshit lies about him. How anyone could believe her, he had no idea.

Yet they did.

No one remembered a single act of kindness he'd ever done. Her lies and the willingness of fools to believe them overrode all else.

Shaking in rage, Bastien cried out at the injustice as the guards hauled him to the small, enclosed, soundproof cage. He'd had no time to grieve. To process. He hadn't even been allowed to attend the funerals.

Please let me wake up from this nightmare!

But the horror refused to end. All it did was get worse and worse.

The guards shoved him inside, slamming his head against the glass before they shut and locked the door. Unshed tears choked him as he struggled to find his balance and regain his footing while his hands were still shackled behind his back. From his new cage, he could see and hear the trial, but no one could hear him.

Not that it mattered. No one had listened to a single thing he'd had to say.

Even now, he couldn't believe what had happened. One minute, he'd been in the shower at the royal palace, where he'd decided to stay for the night.

Pregnant with her first child, Lil had been too sick to go back to base after dinner with their parents, so as her wingman, Bastien had stayed dutifully by her side—even though she'd been shrieking at him over something he'd done to piss her off. Strange that he couldn't even recall what it was now.

All he remembered were her final words to him.

You're a selfish ass, Bastien! When are you going to grow up?

Furious, he'd gone to shower and relax. Everything had been normal. Just another day. He'd been planning to link up with friends to watch a game in his parents' media room and bet on it.

But before he could finish rinsing out his hair, he'd heard a crash. The kind that left your heart in your throat because you knew it didn't sound right.

Even so, he'd started to ignore it, thinking the guards would check it out, but something had told him to pull his pants on and go investigate it himself.

He'd been headed for Lil's room when he passed by Quin's. The door was partially open—something Quin never did. Since childhood, his brother had always acted as if an open door would make for the manifestation of some hallway monster that would come in and devour them all. It was something they'd fought over repeatedly.

Bastien had seen his sister-in-law's body on the bedroom floor first.

Then his nephew's.

Quin had looked up from where an assassin had him kneeling on the ground to meet Bastien's gaze as Bastien reached for his blaster, only to remember he was unarmed.

"Run!" Quin had shouted an instant before the assassin pulled the trigger.

While Bastien had seen a number of bodies in his career and had been standing next to friends who'd been killed in battle—had taken countless wounds himself—it was not the same as the pain that racked him that night. The pain that went screaming through his soul when he heard that blaster fire and his brother fall silent.

As he turned to run to his room and arm himself, he collided with someone and was knocked unconscious.

When he awoke, he was in a room with Lil and her husband. He was on one side. They were across from him, near the bed. Bound and gagged, he'd struggled as hard as he could to reach them while Lil begged for mercy for her unborn child.

They'd shot her right in front of him.

Bastien had expected them to kill him next.

They didn't.

Instead, they'd released him. Unbound his hands and gag and vanished before he could recover from the horror. When he did, he grabbed the blaster they'd left at his side without thinking and went to find them.

That was when he'd found his parents.

Agony had torn him asunder. He'd dropped to his knees, then crawled to his elegant mother, who was covered in blood. Unable to speak or even process it all, he'd pulled her into his arms to hold her.

"Ødie? Speak to me, please!" Even as he'd said the words, he knew she was gone. But he kept hoping and praying for a miracle that never came.

He'd been cupping her cheek, trying to warm her cold skin, when the League enforcers had stormed in and taken him into custody. Of all the stupidity, he'd thought at first they were there to protect him.

It wasn't until they'd brought him to the Trigon Court headquarters on Gondara and processed him through lockup that he realized he was under arrest for his family's murders.

In an act of complete denial, he'd actually tried to call his father for bail like he always did, thinking that it was some kind of cruel hoax.

Until Barnabas had picked up his father's link to answer it.

Then he knew. His father would have had it on him when they killed him. He was never without it.

Never.

Only his killer would have been able to pry it out of his possession. Only close family would have known where he kept it.

Jullien had been right, after all.

Bastien blinked back tears at the nightmarish memory. As the reality that his uncle had just slaughtered his entire family slowly sank in, he'd stood there in the processing center unable to move or breathe, watching the monitors as the news mercilessly played gory images of his parents' remains without regard for the fact that those were human beings with family members who loved them. That the news agencies were banking ratings off the tragedy of his life.

God, he hated them all for their lack of compassion. Their lack of human decency that they wrapped up in their lies, and masks of moral superiority and hypocrisy as they condemned him for something he hadn't done.

Not a single one of them had bothered to contact him to learn the truth. Yet they all lied, saying they'd tried, when they knew better.

Fucking, feckless pieces of lying shit.

It'd been a full hour later that a cold, heartless

interrogator had gutted him with the news that he was being charged with every one of their deaths.

Bastien had kept waiting for someone to come forward with the truth and spare him his hell. Surely to the gods, someone else had to know better. Had to see what was so obvious!

And yet they didn't. Rather, the blind fools rushed to protect the liar who sought them out and played the victim for them all. They listened to the lies and swallowed them whole, while painting Bastien as the monster he'd never been.

The full reality that they could honestly think for one moment he would be guilty of such savagery hadn't entered the realm of his belief system.

Not until that first interrogator had come in and started torturing him for a confession. A confession he still refused to give them. They could cut all the pieces off his body they wanted, he'd never admit to something he hadn't done.

He was innocent! *He* was the victim and yet those gullible, idiot sharks danced to Barnabas's tune. They all surrounded Bastien, tearing at his flesh to dig the wounds in ever deeper.

No one believed him. Everyone was so convinced of his guilt that no attorney in the Nine Worlds would even agree to representation. Not a single relative would take his calls or speak his name.

Every friend had abandoned him.

Just like now. The hatred in the Overseer's eyes as she glared at him from her seat seared him to the marrow of his bones.

I didn't do this.

But Alura's testimony of lies gave him no reprieve. All it did was solidify his guilt in the minds of everyone who heard her. "I gave a report to his uncle that I thought Bastien might try something. Had I known it would cost Jackson his life, too . . . that Bastien would cut his throat to keep him silent, I would never have said a word."

The prosecutor shook her head. "Were you not afraid for your own life, dear?"

Alura sobbed. "Of course I was! I was petrified every minute I was married to him. It's why I kept a separate residence. Why my zusa refused to marry him when he asked her, and why his own zusa had to be his wingman. No one else could handle him. And you see what it got Lil. He's prone to violent rages. You never know when he's going to explode. Any little thing could set him off!"

Bastien ground his teeth at her utter nonsense. How could anyone believe her?

Yet as he glanced around at the faces in the crowd, he realized he was alone in this. No one was on his side.

No one.

It defied reason that anyone could believe her ridiculous bullshit given what everyone knew about him. Given all he'd done that refuted it. He felt so betrayed by all of them. How could they not see the truth?

Or worse, that they knew the truth and were too cowardly to speak it. Because they feared coming under fire for defending him.

That thought sickened him the most. Because he'd never failed to come to the defense of his friends. His parents had bred him for loyalty. *You stand up for others, especially when they need you.* Friends and family didn't abandon each other.

Yet none of them seemed to have a molecule of it in them.

In the end, he had no choice but to listen to his unwanted wife malign him in front of a universe who knew exactly what kind of liar she was. They had seen it count-less times.

How convenient that in *this* they thought she'd finally found some kind of human decency and conscience when she'd never shown any before.

And three weeks later, after no one, not even his uncle Aros, had come to his defense, he was hauled before the Overseer for the verdict.

Ever elegant and refined, Alia had her gray hair coiled around her head in the kind of intricate style his mother had favored. It made him wonder if the Overseer had done it for that reason. If her intent had been to cut him to the bone with the loss of his family.

"Have you anything to say for yourself, boy?" Her voice was cold and brittle.

"I'm innocent, Your Grace. I could never harm my family. I swear, I didn't do this!"

She rolled her eyes. "Bastien Aros Cabarro, given the amount of evidence presented and the brutality of your actions, and reluctance to show remorse, you are hereby stripped of all title and standing, and found guilty of eight counts of premeditated homicide and sentenced to death. May whatever god or gods you worship have mercy on your rotten soul."

Those words hit him like a sledgehammer to his gut. Never had he felt so alone. Not one single member of his family was here.

Or so he thought.

"Your Grace?"

The Overseer arched a brow at her chancellor. "Yes?"

"I have a petition that came in an hour ago from the Triosan emperor for clemency in sentencing. Would you care to read it?"

Alia grimaced before she gave a curt nod.

The bailiff came forward with an e-tablet.

Bastien's scowl matched hers as he tried to understand why his uncle would speak up on his behalf now when Aros had refused to take any of his calls. Had refused to have any contact with him whatsoever. It seemed incongruous that he'd have sent the letter over while not being here for the hearing.

But after a few minutes, the Overseer took a deep breath. "It appears your uncle still loves you, but I'm disinclined to give you the simple exile for your crimes that he requests. However, I do believe in compromising where I can, and I've no wish to alienate the Triosans. Therefore, I shall commute your sentence from death to make you a Ravin for The League. Should you survive as such for fifteen years, you'll earn a pardon."

He gaped at her ludicrous verdict. Seriously? Ravins were the sentient targets League assassins were given as training assignments to hone their skills. They were implanted with a tracking device and then set free to be hunted down and killed like prey.

Any humanitarian group worth its salt had protested the existence and practice—until their leaders ended up as Ravins themselves for treason against The League.

Bastien scoffed at her *kindness* given the fact that the average life expectancy for a Ravin was six to eight weeks.

For the humanitarian protesters, it'd been a few hours.

But then he wasn't most.

He was a captain first rank, Gyron Force trained, and motivated by a blood lust that ought to terrify everyone in this room.

His fury rising with a heated need for vengeance, Bastien met her gaze. "Oh, I'll survive, my lady. And when I come back, I'll rain down a hell-wrath the likes of which you've never seen, and I promise you that the next time you look upon me, it'll be for the murder of the real killer of my family. And I won't be innocent then as I am today. I will come to you soaked and baptized in the blood of my enemies. You can bank on that."

"Get him out of my court!"

The guards jerked him toward the side door, where, to his instant shock, Ember waited.

Time hung still as he felt a need to embrace her. As all his regret rose to choke him. And hatred, too, if the truth was known.

I wish I'd never met you!

When their gazes met, he saw sympathy. For the merest heartbeat, he thought she'd say something.

But his captors didn't give her the chance. They rushed him past her and threw him into an armored transport, leaving him there to damn her and himself with every breath he took.

Ember started after Bastien, desperate to comfort him and tell him what was going on. But her father caught her arm and kept her by his side.

"You say one word to him and they're liable to indict you as an accomplice."

Grinding her teeth, she wanted to weep in frustration and pain. What had been done to him was all kinds of wrong and she knew it. "He didn't murder his family, Sa. You know that as well as I do. Bastien could *never* hurt them."

"I know."

She met her father's gaze as she sought some kind of sanity in this madness. "Why did Alura lie like that?"

"To protect us from his uncle. You know as well as I do who the real killer was. We have Alura to thank for the fact that we're still standing when so many others have fallen. Don't you dare criticize her."

Ember let out a bitter laugh. The concept of thanking her sister stuck hard in her craw. Unlike her father, she couldn't imagine Alura as an altruist. Not in this.

This bloody coup had torn a hole through their empire. Worse? It'd indicted and torn apart so many of their noble and military families that Ember was terrified to think just how deep the conspiracy against Bastien's family ran. But the one thing she knew for certain, her sister was neck deep in it.

And Alura had worked hard to set Bastien up for his fall.

Tears filled her eyes as bitter anger choked her. Alura had robbed her of her future and then, not content to see her and Bastien suffer, she'd done *this*.

Damn her to hell for it.

"You don't believe that, Sa-sa. Surely. The one man who could have stopped Barnabas has just been handed a brutal death sentence—by his own uncle's hand. How long do you think it'll be before Barnabas silences all of us, too? He knows we know the truth. And worse, *he* knows the truth." She paused as she saw her sister leaving the courtroom with Barnabas and his son.

Disgusted at the sight, she met her father's gaze. "By standing at Alura's side through this, you've just put a snake on the throne and handed victory to our enemies. Barnabas killed his own and framed his noble nephew for their deaths. Do you really think he's going to stand beside a bargain he made to a pleb? And if you do, I have swampland to sell."

"You've gone too far!" he snapped.

Tears filled her eyes as she choked on bile and gall.

"No, Sa-sa. I didn't go far enough. I should have told Bastien the truth when I had the chance." More than that, she should have pulled out Alura's hair and cut her throat when she found out her sister was carrying Bastien's baby. Ember's failure to fight for him then had caused all this now. And never had her future, or that of her loved ones, been more tenuous. "If you'll excuse me, I'm going home to pack and evacuate, because I have no delusions on how this is going to end for us." She jerked her chin toward the direction where Alura had vanished. "Your beloved daughter just signed her name to all our death warrants. And unlike you, I intend to protect my own. *All* of them."

CHAPTER 4

ONE YEAR. TEN MONTHS. THREE WEEKS. SIX DAYS.

"And now *you* know how I've lasted longer than any Ravin in League history." Bastien shot the corpse at his feet in the head one more time before he searched the assassin's body for supplies.

He probably shouldn't have wasted that last charge so cavalierly, but there was something to be said for satisfaction. Even meager outlets, given how rare a commodity it'd become in his life.

"Damn wanker. Couldn't you have a sweet vice? Alcohol? Something?"

He shot him again for being such a stellar, upstanding soldier.

Minsid League dogs. They were wretchedly sober. And this one had feet the size of his sister's. Bastien grimaced as he tossed the boots aside and pulled his worn-out, threadbare pair back on. At least he'd gotten a good coat out of this one. Some fresh ammo and batteries.

Not enough food, though. And they were MREs, which Bastien had been sick of when he was in Gyron Force.

Oh well. He picked the bastard up and carried him to his stripped-out ship, making sure to delete and fry any trace that could lead a search party back here. Then he set the self-destruct sequence and launched it.

Hopefully it wouldn't detonate until it was in the upper atmosphere and it'd burn up completely without raining down debris or leaving anything in space The League might find that they could use to trace him.

You should have buried the body.

But that came with its own risk, in that if someone found a body, they'd start looking for the killer. First lesson he'd learned out here. Launch the bodies into space. Keep the assassins, both alive and dead, as far away from his position as he could.

The only good thing about being stuck here in the Oksanan desert was that it played havoc with all electronic equipment. And while that kept him isolated from the other worlds, it also allowed him to remain breathing.

Bastien picked up the pack of salvaged goods and slung it over his back before he headed toward his burned-out home that had been the former base of one Aksel Bredeh. Scumbag *Knættr* based on the debris Bastien had cleaned out on his arrival.

He didn't know who or what Bredeh had crossed, but someone had taken offense to the man and his troops. There were still bloodstains and blaster marks Bastien couldn't get rid of. Which was probably good since it helped with the illusion that the base remained abandoned should anyone happen upon it.

Not that anyone ever did. Probably why Bredeh had chosen it.

Three hundred years ago, this little rock known as Oksana had been a major player in the politics of the Nine Worlds and had been the home of one of the richest, most revered and prestigious ruling families. In fact, interstellar travel and war had both begun here.

Until the Oksanans had decided to go up against The League and overthrow the one military power that governed them all. The result had been that the once lush, green planet was reduced to the desert hole Bastien now called home.

Probably why the electronics were wonky. No doubt there was enough residual radiation left behind from those bombings even after three hundred years that Bastien would either be sterile or father children with eight legs some day.

He laughed at the thought as he looked up at the bleak, blinding sky. "Least you could do, God . . . make me glow in the dark so I'd save on battery life."

That at least would be helpful.

"Look on the bright side. You only have thirteen and a half more years of this."

Bastien stopped dead in his tracks as that reality hit him harder than a physical blow.

I can't do it.

This last year had almost killed him—and that didn't account for the assassins who were trying to cut his throat. They at least gave him some form of personal interaction. Brief though it was.

And cheap entertainment. The look on their face when he, the lowly Ravin, finished them off was priceless.

No, it was the solitude. The grief that tore him apart. Because here, where there was nothing but his thoughts to keep him company, all he could think about was how different everything would have been had he never met the Wyldestarrins. At all.

How much better off his family would have been had he let Alura die that day, instead of rescuing her. So maybe this fate was justice after all.

I did kill my family.

One act of compassion. Of kindness. By thinking of her life over his, he'd sown the destruction for his own.

No, it shouldn't be that way. She should have been grateful for everything he'd done for her. Should have been loyal.

But people weren't like that. In the end, Jullien had been right about everything. *Put no one at your back unless you want them to drive a knife through it.*

Bastien sank to his knees in the scorching sand. A part of him wanted to lie down and let the hot desert take him and wipe out his existence as easily as the sandstorms did his footsteps. It'd be so much easier. He had nothing to live for. Not really.

That's not true and you know it.

His family had died a hard, brutal death at the hands of his uncle's henchmen. With the help of Alura, Barnabas had gotten away with it. And framed him in the process. If he died, Barnabas would never pay for his crime.

"You promised them."

And a Cabarro *never* broke their oath.

Get on your feet, soldier. Pay that bastard back. Hell. High water. Whatever it took, he wouldn't rest until he stood over his uncle's grave.

He'd made a promise to the Overseer, too.

Hell was coming. And Bastien planned to bring it with both fists.

"How could she do this to us?"

Ember didn't comment on Cin's question as she helped Brand carry their mother's body into the cave they'd found for shelter. "Kindel?"

"I got it. Me and Ash are setting the perimeter charges and monitors."

Brand sank to her knees next to Ember and took their

mother's cold hand. Tears welled in her eyes. "I can't be-lieve she's gone."

Choking on her own tears she didn't dare shed for fear of it incapacitating her, she pulled her sister into her arms and held her. "How's your wound?"

"It pales in comparison to the hole in my heart." Brand had taken three shots as they'd fought their way out of an ambush. An ambush they'd have never survived had their mother not given her life for theirs.

A sob escaped Ember's lips against her will as she struggled to hold back her tears over the memory of her mother falling beneath the barrage of fire. Char Wylde-starrin had always been the strongest, most capable soldier in the universe.

Now . . .

Ember choked. "Has anyone called Sa?"

Cin grew eerily quiet as she secured the opening of their cave so that no one would be able to detect their pres-ence inside it.

At her sister's reluctance to answer, Ember tasted bile in her throat. "What?"

Still she didn't speak. "We need to inventory supplies. They'll be probing for us."

"Cin . . ."

Her eyes swam with tears as she finally looked at Ember and Brand. "He fell with his unit about three hours ago."

Brand stiffened in Ember's arms.

For a moment, she couldn't breathe as her entire world collapsed and she understood exactly how Bastien had felt at the moment he learned about his own parents' deaths. How he'd felt holding his mother's body in his arms.

No, not entirely. She still had her sisters alive and with her. And she wasn't being blamed for their deaths. Nor had she watched them die while being held down, unable to protect them.

Given how capable Bastien was as a soldier, that had to have killed him. She couldn't imagine a worse nightmare for anyone.

Shots rang out.

Brand shot to her feet and drew her weapon. Ember reluctantly left her mother's body to do the same.

Utter silence descended, making her heart race in fear that Kindel and Ashley might have gone down.

Please God, no. . . .

She couldn't handle losing anyone else. Not today. Not like this.

"Em? Cin?"

Her breath came out in an audible gasp as she heard Kindel's voice just outside their cave. "We're here. What happened?"

"Tasi. She's coming in. Don't shoot at her like we did. She's kind of pissed about it."

Cin wiped at her eyes with a nervous laugh as she saw her wife. Ember let out a ragged breath as they embraced and checked each other for injuries. At least one of them had some good news for the day.

"You okay, baby?" Tasi held on to Cin as if terrified of letting her go.

"Yeah. You?"

She nodded. "I was being followed or I'd have been here a lot sooner. I wanted to make sure I didn't bring more trouble to your door."

Ember holstered her blaster as raw panic continued to choke her. "Did you take care of it?"

"I did." Tasi smiled grimly. "Another reason I had to make sure I wasn't followed. Everything's secured. Just like you asked."

Thank the gods. Ember returned to Brand. "So what's going on at home?"

Tasi winced as she saw their mother's body on the ground. "You've all been accused of treason. If they find you, you'll be arrested on sight."

"Alura?" Cin asked before Ember had a chance.

Tasi grew silent.

Ember's stomach grew tight. "Did they kill her?"

She drew Cin into a hug then whispered in a low tone, "No. She's giving statements that have indicted the rest of you."

"How could she?" Brand whispered.

Cin tried to pull away, but Tasi held her fast. "You can't go after her. She's being protected. They're trying to draw you home."

"Good," Cin said firmly. "I'm willing to go."

"But I'm not willing to lose you. Now sit down with your sisters and let's think this through."

Ember was amazed when Cin obeyed her without question. Only Tasi could get Cin to listen. Especially in this mood.

Wiping at her eyes, she struggled to accept this new reality. Her parents were dead. And she and her sisters were wanted outlaws. "I warned Sa-sa. I knew they'd come for us. But Alura . . ."

"I'll kill that bitch!" Brand growled. "Gut her and bathe in her blood!"

At the moment, Ember couldn't agree more. And yet with her world crumbling, what she really wanted was Bastien. She needed him more right now than she ever had before. He'd have a plan to get them out of this. He'd know what to do. This kind of strategic planning was what he did best.

Not to mention scrounging for supplies. It was why

they'd dubbed him Ghost Gadget, or GG, for a call sign. If you gave him a problem, any problem, big or small, he came up with a workable solution. The bastard made it look so easy.

But she had no idea where he was. If he was even alive.

Most likely not. Ravins only survived six to eight weeks. They were long past that now. He'd probably died years ago.

Alone.

That thought almost broke her as she imagined him going down under a barrage of fire as her mother had done. With no one there to care for his body.

No one there to shed a single tear for him.

Her Bas had deserved more than that.

"What are you thinking?" Cin asked. "I see those gears working."

Ember cleared her throat as she blinked back her tears. "Wondering what Bastien would do."

Brand sighed. "You think he's still alive?"

"I don't know." Yet she never failed to pray for him. Even now, he was still a part of her.

"I do," Kindel said as she and Ashley joined them. "He's too ornery to die. That prick will live just to spite them. You'll see. And he'll be back for his vengeance. Just like he said."

Ash laughed. "He always kept his word. No reason to think he wouldn't keep this one."

"Yeah, especially if he felt like I do right now." Kindel took her jacket off and wrapped it around their mother. "They left us for dead."

"And framed us." Ash shook her head. "I want Barnabas's ass in a grinder."

"You'll get it," Brand assured her. "Right after I cut out

Alura's lying tongue and shove it down her treacherous throat."

Yet as Ember sat there, listening to them vent and plot their vengeance, the one thing she knew beyond a doubt was that their lives would never be the same again.

In the blink of an eye, everything had changed.

Everything. And they had no solid ground to stand on. Nothing solid to reach for. Not even their names. Barnabas had taken everything from them.

How could they start over with so little?

And in that heartbeat, she heard Bastien's voice in her head. She saw his handsome, teasing face. *Life tries us all, Em. It's going to kick you in the balls and test every bit of your mettle. The true measure of humanity isn't how you cope when everything's coming your way. It's what you do when you're being pile-driven headfirst into the ground. You can lie down and let them kill you. Or stand up with a fist and a finger and shout out "Is that all you got? 'Cause you ain't gonna take me down, bitches. So bring it with both fists. I'm ready."*

Yeah, Kindel was right. Bastien wouldn't be dead. Not with that ironclad defiance of his. Nothing had ever rattled her baby. You could knock him down for a minute, but you better duck when he stood up.

And Bastien always got up, dusted off the blood, and went for the throat.

How weird that right now all she wanted was to feel his arms around her and to hear his voice in her ear telling her that it would be okay. That she could do it.

Of all the things she missed the most, it was his never-ending optimism. That screwed-up humor he had when everything skidded into a shit pile. His firm belief that she could do anything she set her mind to.

Why hadn't she fought harder for him?

Harder for *them*?

And in that heartbeat, everything broke. Sobbing uncontrollably, she doubled over with the pain of all she'd lost. Brand, Ashley, and Kindel gathered her into their arms while Cin and Tasi placed their hands on her head.

"We've got you," Kindel whispered against her ear. "We will stand together. You know that."

It was what their parents had taught them to do. Why Alura hadn't learned that lesson, she had no idea. But what killed her deep inside her soul was that she hadn't given Bastien the same loyalty.

She'd wanted to go after him to help him after his conviction, and her father had talked her out of it.

Now . . .

I hope wherever you are, Bastien, that you're safe. Happy would be an unreasonable request given the nightmare he'd been through. Alone. And if she could have one wish right now, it would be for Bastien to find someone he could trust.

Someone who would help him.

Why didn't I do something?

He would never have left her and she knew it.

Choking in her grief, she reached for the necklace Bastien had given her that for some reason she'd never taken off. It was a small heart-shaped piece that held a lock of his hair. She couldn't count the times she'd started to jerk it off her neck and toss it in his face. Yet every time she'd considered it, his words had returned to haunt her.

"Keep this snuggled between your breasts, Ember. And whenever I'm not with you, remember that you have a piece of me here. More than that, you carry my heart wherever you go. The universe can take any and every-

thing from you, but no one will ever take my love away. It's yours alone to have and to hold. Forever."

In fact, that last bit was engraved on the back of it.

Yours alone.
To have and to hold.
Forever your Bastien.

And though she might not be with him tonight, she was there in her thoughts.

Someday, if she survived this nightmare, she would find him. And either kick his ass. Or kiss his lips.

CHAPTER 5

THREE YEARS. THREE MONTHS. FIVE WEEKS. SIX DAYS.

Bastien sighed as he marked another day of his fun-filled vacation in hell.

"Not dead yet." Though that wasn't quite as thrilling an accomplishment these days as it'd once been. Because at this point, death might be a welcomed distraction from the boredom.

Suddenly, he heard the rumbling sounds of an engine descending.

That can't be good.

Dumbass! You knew better than to mention boredom . . . be careful what you wish for. You just might get it.

His heart racing, he grabbed his gear and weapons and went to scout out his visitors. *Don't panic, Cabarro. Might be nothing more than another group of Andarions.*

For some reason, those crazy bastards came here a couple of times a year to scale the mountain range. They didn't stay long. Just enough to get to the top and go. He never made contact with them and they assumed the landscape too inhospitable for humans so they didn't look for people out here in the desert.

Occasionally, they left behind some supplies he could salvage.

But as he moved into his sniper position, and focused his distance goggles, he realized this was a different kind of vessel than the shuttlecraft they preferred.

A standard R-class runner by the looks of it. An older one, too, though it'd been meticulously kept up.

He wasn't sure what to make of that. Other than the occupants definitely weren't from The League, either. League military craft were easy to spot and stood out.

No, this style of cargo ship was normally used by merchant shippers or pirates. Sometimes freelance assassins, though that was rare. But then you never knew when a pirate or merchant would hold an assassin's license or when they might be willing to pick up some easy creds by killing a fugitive or Ravin.

Better take a closer look.

Bastien scooted down and stealthily made his way toward them.

Not that he had to go far, as they came off the ship and headed straight for him like he was their target.

Minsid hell. Tavali, by the looks of their impeccable black battlesuits that were marked with gray skulls. Gorturnum Nation would be his guess, given that. Pirate bastards, probably here to scavenge the base. They might have even detected a life form. Though three had left the ship, there could be more onboard.

Bastien took cover.

Two men . . . huge effing bastards at that. One of them could make two of him. Damn! What planet were they from and what the hell had their parents fed them to make sons that tall and muscled?

For that matter, the woman wasn't small. Even she was taller than Bastien. And she was old enough to be their mother. Given their height and the fact that they all had various shades of blond hair, it would be a good bet.

Hmmm . . .

It would also be a good bet that at least one of them carried an assassin's or bounty hunter's license, given the way they walked and the weapons they were packing. These beings were well versed in military-styled weaponry and walked as if they would kill or maim anyone dumb enough to threaten them.

Maybe they're just here to meet a friend. Do some illegal business and leave.

If that was the case, he'd hang back and not expose himself.

But that was getting more difficult to hold to as they got closer and closer to his home.

While he kept the interior of the abandoned base stark and run-down, it wouldn't be that hard to figure out someone lived there.

And if they discovered his stash of weapons or food, he was screwed.

The woman let out a slow whistle as she scanned the damage done to the exterior of Bastien's homebase. "What happened? The League?"

"No. My brother. The mother of his daughter, Driana, was murdered here, and his wife was held hostage. Aksel wanted Nyk to come for a visit. Lucky him. He did."

Bastien scowled at those words and the unexpected emotion they kicked up inside him. He'd assumed the blood he'd cleaned had come from soldiers.

To find out it was a female hostage and someone's mother . . . that hit home and brought an image of his own mother and sister to his mind he could have really done without.

The male in the middle shook his head. "Needless to say, Nyk was a bit perturbed when he arrived. This is a prime example of 'be careful what you wish for.'"

The other man snorted as they picked their way through the debris to enter the rusted-out remains.

Shit! Shit! Shit! Bastien cursed repeatedly as they went in and he tried to decide what to do. He clung to the shadows as he followed them inside his home.

You know what to do. One way or another, they were about to learn he lived here.

He was going to be exposed, that was a given. So he'd best do it on his own terms. Not theirs.

As they started up the rickety stairs that would lead them to where Bastien kept his electronics and what few personal items he'd salvaged, he knew he had no choice whatsoever.

Making sure they couldn't see him, he clicked his weapon from stun to kill and deepened his voice for maximum impact. "Don't."

The bearded man in the middle held his hands up slowly. "We mean you no harm."

Yeah, right . . . Like he was dumb enough to fall for that? "Then why are you here?"

Bastien expected an answer in words. Instead, it came in an invisible wave that knocked the blaster from his hands, lifted him clear off the floor, and pinned him to the rusted-out wall behind him.

Fected hell! *Trisani* . . .

A race that was virtually extinct, which was why the mere idea that these three might be part of that rare breed hadn't entered Bastien's mind. He'd never thought to ever meet one in real life. Possessed of unbelievable psionic powers, they were more myth than reality.

But there was no legend to the fierce power that held him in an iron grip he couldn't escape. Worse? The force on his neck was about to snap it in half.

"Wait!" the bearded Tavali shouted as he held a hand out toward the one who must be holding Bastien up.

"For what?" the Trisani sneered. "A fucking invitation?"

The other Tavali smirked with a reckless disregard for the Trisani's life-and-death abilities. "Set him down."

Growling low in his throat, the Trisani obeyed. "A living enemy makes for a dead you."

Bastien had to agree with that logic as he hit the ground hard enough to rattle his bones and what little sense he'd managed to hang on to.

The Tavali gave the Trisani an amused stare. "I see you've been reading the *Book of Harmony* again."

"Fuck you, Andarion," he snarled under his breath.

Those words stunned Bastien.

Andarion? With blond hair?

How?

Bastien scowled. Every Andarion he'd ever seen had been dark-haired, dark-skinned, with eerie white eyes. And while the woman with them had the traditional Andarion eyes, the bastard standing between them appeared human, except for his enormous size.

Yet unlike the woman, his eyes were covered by dark red-tinted glasses. Bastien had assumed them human in color, not Andarion.

He snorted at the Trisani, who obviously was not his brother, Bastien realized, even though they fought as if they were. "And another lovely quote from your peaceful scripture."

Bastien glanced to the older woman. "Who are you people?"

"We're just passing through." The Andarion shrugged his survival pack off his back. He held it out toward Bastien. "Let us look for what we came after—has nothing to do with you—then you can grab a shower on our ship. I'll leave you with some clothes, food, and water."

In that moment, as their gazes met through those dark glasses the male wore, Bastien had a sneaking suspicion.

No . . .

Couldn't be Jullien.

This Tavali was too fit and trim.

Too sober.

And yet, last Bastien had heard before his own parents had been killed, Jullien had been disinherited by both his mother and father. Thrown out of their empires during a bloody coup on Andaria that preceded the one on Kirovar by only a few months. Jullien's brother, who'd been presumed dead before Bastien's birth, had been found alive, and with his return, Jullien had lost everything.

That had been four years ago.

A lot could happen in four years. He ought to know. His life had skidded to absolute hell in a matter of weeks.

Still, it was hard to think that this might be Julie. Bastien raked him with a suspicious glare. "Why would you help me?"

"Because you look like you could use it."

Yeah, no one else would bother. He'd learned that lesson the hard way. People only helped when they had a reason to.

Bastien narrowed his gaze on those hazel eyes he was now sure belonged to his cousin. "Do I know you?"

"No."

A peculiar expression came over the Trisani's face while he glanced to the woman, then the Andarion. They had to be talking telepathically, which unnerved him, as he'd love to know what they were saying.

If they were planning to attack him.

Bastien tensed the minute those silvery-blue eyes focused on him with a great deal of suspicion.

The Trisani arched a disdainful brow. "You're that Kirovarian prince who slaughtered his whole family?"

Raw unmitigated fury ignited inside Bastien. Before he could catch himself or think better of it, he slammed the pack down and started for the Trisani, only to have the bastard throw him against the wall again with his powers.

"Put him down, Thrāix!"

Aghast, Thrāix glared at the man Bastien was even more convinced was his cousin Jullien. "You would really spare a snake this treacherous?"

"I didn't do it!" Bastien roared, sick of being accused of something so grisly it gave him nightmares every time he closed his eyes.

Thrāix scoffed. "That's what they all say."

Jullien exchanged a glance with the woman, who was remaining oddly stoic and silent through all of this chaos. "I believe him. They never had any real evidence against him, other than the word of his own uncle, who now sits on the throne he inherited after he testified against Bastien. And Bastien's ex-wife, who inherited everything they took from him."

Thrāix laughed bitterly. "Oh, okay, 'cause the younger son *never* murders the older one for a throne."

The expression on the Andarion's face would have made a sane man shrink back in unholy terror.

Obviously Thrāix wasn't sane.

Nor did he value his life or balls.

Jullien curled his lip. "Yeah, and sometimes the second son just makes a ready-made patsy for others to pin their own crimes on. Because everyone *but* that second son is smart enough to figure out that when the entire family dies, he's going to be blamed for it. Funny, he's creative and ambitious enough to remove the direct obstacles to his succession, yet doesn't ever consider that in the obvious chain of suspicion, he's suspect number one and that either jail or death is a much more permanent hurdle against his ruling. Yeah, right. . . . That thought *never* occurs to him, until it's too late. Now, put him down."

Oh yeah, that overly defensive explosion about being a second-born royal son had to be from Jullien. Like Bastien, Jullien had been equally screwed over by his family, because they'd both been misjudged by everyone around them.

Bastien hit the ground with a solid thud that was even more painful than the one before it. Son of a . . . he was going to feel this for the next few days.

"Really?" Jullien said to Thrāix in the same tone an irate parent would use with a petulant toddler.

Thrāix smirked. "You didn't specify 'gentle' as a condition of his release."

Sighing, Jullien growled in the back of his throat while Bastien pushed himself to his feet to confront them. With an agitated grimace, he started back for the stairs. "Aksel's office was on the second floor. What we need, if it's still intact, should be up there." He led them away from Bastien.

Yeah, that's definitely my boy.

And there was one way he knew he could prove that Andarion's real identity.

As they left the room, Bastien called out to him. *"Paktu, mi kyzi."*

"Estra, mi pleti." No sooner had those words been spoken than the Andarion froze as if silently cursing

himself for the automatic response that meant, *Anytime, my blood.*

It was something Jullien had taught him when they were kids and Bastien had been trying to make Jullien feel welcomed and wanted in a palace and family that had made it abundantly clear they all resented his foreign presence there.

Holding the pack that Jullien had given him to his chest, Bastien stayed back from the group as his cousin turned slowly around to face him.

His breathing ragged, Bastien swallowed hard. "Tell me I'm wrong. But it's you, Julie, isn't it?"

He watched an impressive debate play across his cousin's face. Obviously, Jullien was desperate to deny it with everything he had.

Yet after a long pause, he slowly nodded. "Yeah."

Unable to believe that something good had finally happened to either of them, Bastien stared at him as if he were a ghost. Then he laughed and reached out to pull him in for a hug. "Damn, if you don't look good, cousin! Running looks much better on you than it does on me. You wear banishment well."

"You wouldn't have said that two years ago. Trust me."

Clapping him on the back, Bastien released him. "Thanks for not cringing when I touched you. Believe me, I know I'm disgusting and it's more than I deserve."

"It's all good, *m'drey.*"

Bastien knew better. "No, it's not. And for what it's worth, which isn't much, I tried to get my father to harbor you after you were cast out. It sickened me how they did you. I'm really sorry."

Jullien gestured at him. "I'm sorry for *this.* What happened to you after I was exiled?"

That was a long story he didn't want to even begin to

relive. So he shortened it to the pertinent facts only. "League. I'm a Ravin. Been running since Barnabas murdered my family and stole our throne."

Jullien cringed in sympathetic pain. "I figured you were dead by now."

"Same here. Thank the gods for my Gyron Force training." He narrowed his gaze on the new lean and trim Jullien, who looked like he could take the Iron Hammer in a Ring match, instead of his old foppish cousin who'd relied heavily on his servants for every task. Which probably had included wiping his nose and chin.

This was definitely an improved version. "So how the hell have *you* survived?"

To become a Tavali officer, no less. That had to be one hell of a story there.

Jullien smirked. "Thank the gods for Gyron Force training. Had your uncle and father not been such bastards those times I visited, I wouldn't have lasted a week on my own.".

Bastien snorted. "Ain't it a bitch? Barnabas had no idea he was doing us a favor. One I pray I get to return to him by planting my Gyron axe in the center of his skull."

"Gealrewe!" Jullien clapped him on the back as he finally smiled. "Well, since you know who I am, you want me to drop you somewhere? Get you off this rock?"

More than Jullien could imagine. But that was only a pipe dream. Sadly, this was where he was safest.

He let out a long, tired sigh. "Yes—but no. Not unless you know how to pull a League chip out of me."

"No." Jullien glanced at his friends.

"Sorry," the woman said. "Not a clue."

Thrāix shook his head. "Beyond my abilities. I could try to do it with my powers, but it's as likely to explode the chip, which could cause internal damage, and depending on where it's located, that could paralyze or kill him."

Eyes wide at the mere prospect that shriveled his gut, Bastien held his hands up and backed away. "Rather not chance death. My life sucks enough without a maiming or fatality."

Thrāix nodded. "Figured you'd feel that way."

Which made him wonder something about the Trisani . . . "Were you really going to kill me?"

"Had you not been his cousin? Yeah. Still might. If you give me any reason to." Thrāix headed for the stairs with the woman.

"Duly noted." Bastien opened the pack and ripped into one of the meals as he followed after them. "So what brings you here. Really?"

Jullien glanced at him over his shoulder. "Looking for the files Bredeh ran on my family back when he was trying to kill Nyk. I'm hoping I can find something to lead me to my grandmother and the rest of my cousins who've sided with her."

Interesting . . . Nyk, or Nykyrian, was Jullien's twin brother, who was supposed to be dead. From this conversation, Bastien would presume that those old rumors had been right and Grandma must have been the one to put a hit out on Nykyrian all those years ago. Somehow the boy had survived. Made sense, actually. The Andarion queen had killed off most of her family. But why she'd have it in for her own grandkid, he could only imagine.

Then again, she was an Andarion queen. That tended to go with the crown.

"To what end?" he asked Jullien.

"Theirs, I hope."

Bastien chewed, then swallowed the nasty dehydrated

bar as he considered that unexpected declaration. "I thought you and Grandma were always tight?"

Jullien froze and gave him a bone-chilling glare that caused him to take two steps back. Obviously, he'd been wrong about that and had struck one hell of a nerve.

"Sorry," Bastien said quickly. "That's what your father always said whenever he came around. He thought it showed an utter lack of judgment on your part."

"What in the Nine Worlds could *ever* make him think that? I never could stand the old bitch."

Bastien shrugged nonchalantly. "No idea. But he was fully convinced of it."

Jullien snorted. "Anyway, I love my grandmother as much as you do your uncle, for about the same reasons. Had my father ever bothered to have a conversation with me, he'd have known that. And if I don't stop her, she will find some way to kill my mother and brother, and retake her throne. I didn't wipe out an entire portion of my family to put my mother in power to watch that happen."

Bastien scowled at a version of this story he'd never heard before. "No. Wait . . . what?"

"You heard me."

He'd heard him, but that wasn't what he'd been told about the coup on Andaria that had cost Jullien his inheritance. "WAR and your aunt put your mother in power." WAR had been a rebel sect who'd been working actively against Jullien's insane grandmother who'd been a complete tyrant no one had wanted to deal with.

"Yes," Jullien said slowly, "with the information *I* gave them over the years. And particularly at the end. Trust me. No one else could have brought down Eriadne. It's why I'm the only one she put a hit on."

Bastien's jaw went slack at the injustice. And at a fact he hadn't known. Jullien had a League warrant out on him? Damn, that was harsh. Especially if half of what he said was true. And he had no reason to doubt it. "Do *they* know that?"

"They never bothered to ask. But one would think, with their brilliant intellects, they'd have discerned it by now. Again, doesn't take much to figure it out, since I'm the only one from the coup my grandmother has come after with a vengeance. Everyone else was spared her wrath. Kind of makes you wonder why, huh?"

Indeed. 'Cause Eriadne wasn't known for her mercy or forgiveness. That alone told him that Jullien wasn't lying. "Damn, brother. You got screwed."

"Don't we all?"

Bastien nodded in total agreement. "So why you want to help them?"

Jullien shrugged nonchalantly. "Cairie's still my mother. Nyk's still my brother. My grandmother's done them enough harm in their lives. I'm not about to let that bitch do any more. Be damned if I'm going to let her win, after everything else she's done. I'm a bastard that way."

Bastien grinned at something that could easily define them both. "And here all this time, I thought you were nothing but a vindictive asshole."

"Oh, you were *not* wrong about that. I am a vindictive asshole. This is all about payback to the whore. Just the whore, in this case, isn't my mother."

Ouch . . . As they entered the room where he kept the electronics, Bastien sucked his breath in sharply at an insult he'd have *never* leveled at his own mother, and one he'd have killed anyone else for making against her. "That's harsh."

"I am the callous bastard they raised me to be." Jullien scowled at Aksel's system. "It's booby-trapped?"

Bastien stepped around him to enter his password so

that Jullien could use it. "Yeah . . . sorry about that. First thing when I found this place and moved in was secure everything so that if one of the League bastards happened upon it, they couldn't use anything to figure out if it belonged to me or not." He opened the files Jullien was looking for to make it easier for him. "There you go."

Bastien drifted back so that he could eat while Jullien and his crew went through the data in search of something they could use.

And as he watched Jullien searching through Aksel Bredeh's database with an expertise he'd never realized his cousin possessed, he was impressed. This was not the useless piece-of-shit prince his Triosan uncle had railed against. Bastien couldn't count the hours he'd listened to his father and Uncle Aros as they discussed what they needed to do to block Jullien's inheritance.

Had Jullien wanted to, he could have seized the Andarion throne and then taken his father's empire in the blink of an eye. Hell, with the turmoil that rapidly followed on Kirovar, Jullien could have even made a play for theirs, too. Since Bastien's mother was the younger sister of Jullien's father, Jullien had as much blood right to it as Barnabas did.

More so, really.

But that wasn't the cousin Bastien remembered from his childhood. While they hadn't been close, the Jullien he recalled had always tried to stay low and in the shadows. Off everyone's radar. True to Aros's words, his studious and portly Andarion cousin had been sullen and quiet. Extremely reserved, and at times rude. Bastien had assumed it came mostly from the language barrier and Jullien's frustration with their strange "foreign" customs, which were seldom explained to him until after he'd unknowingly violated them and he was mortified and ridiculed when his father or another relative made a grand show of publicly correcting him for it.

It was why Bastien had attempted to learn Andarion. That had given him a whole new appreciation for Jullien's intellect. God knew, Andarion was one screwed-up language. Hard to pronounce and harder still to comprehend if you weren't born to it.

Their grandfather had been even more critical and cold toward the boy. Mostly because he couldn't stand the Andarions, and he'd been infuriated that his grandson and future heir was one of their dreaded breed. Furious at Aros, he'd taken his rage out on Jullien. Every time Jullien came to visit, Quinlan had gone to war on both Aros and Jullien, making both their lives hell until Jullien was returned to Andaria.

Now Bastien shook his head in sympathy as he watched his cousin searching through files.

Yeah, Julie knew an entirely different Triosan grandfather than the doting old man who'd bounced Bastien and his siblings on his knee. And that made him saddest of all. As with his uncle, Bastien had a hard time reconciling how his grandfather could be so kind to him and so hard on Jullien, who'd never deserved such harsh treatment. It'd really screwed with him as a kid to see those different sides of his family.

Made him extremely suspicious of people in general.

Sadly, not suspicious enough. If he'd been a bit more, he might have seen Barnabas's treachery coming before it was too late. But in all the attacks that had come right before his uncle's coup, he'd never once suspected Barnabas.

Or Jackson.

That level of treachery and maliciousness had been beyond his experience or comprehension.

Jullien scooted the chair back from the desk for Thrāix

to lean in. "This is it. But it's not really helpful. Venik has a secured base that's unknown to The Tavali outside of his Nation. He had it built for my cousin as a precaution should something happen to him, so that Malys wouldn't be able to kill Nyran or Parisa in a jealous rage. I will lay odds that's where my grandmother is."

Thräix studied the schematic. "That's so deeply in their territory . . . and Phrixian. We go near that, they'll know."

Jullien raked a frustrated hand through his hair. "We've got to do something. I can't let them kill my family. She's not going to stop trying for my mother's throat."

The woman with him rubbed his shoulder. "At least your immediate family is safe from them."

"That's not good enough."

"You know . . ." Bastien moved forward to access another database of old smuggler routes he'd once used. "There are some ancient trading wormholes that aren't in use anymore in that sector. They don't really appear on most maps." He showed it to Jullien. "I stumbled across this one back when I went through a teenage phase we won't talk about."

Jullien snorted. "I remember that phase."

"We're not talking about it." 'Cause basically, he was lucky he hadn't gone to prison for some of the stunts he'd pulled. It was, however, how he ended up in the military against his mother's protests. His father had insisted on it to keep him out of trouble.

And out of prison.

Bastien pointed to one of the routes that paralleled the station's orbit. "That would drop you in, clear of their surveillance."

Jullien nodded as he studied the map. "Mind if I take a copy?"

"It's all yours."

He quickly downloaded it. *"Thöky."*

Bastien's eyes widened at his use of the Kirovarian term for *thanks*. It'd been way too long since he'd spoken his own language. Even with that Andarion accent, it was a welcomed treat. "Glad I could help."

Jullien jerked his head toward the door. "Want to see about that shower?"

Sadly, he got an actual hard-on at the thought of being clean again from the use of a real shower, with hot running water. "You know I do."

"We can also drop you somewhere else. Really, I don't mind."

How he wished, but Bastien shook his head. "As much as I would, I better stay put. This place plays havoc with League tracking equipment and most electronics. Not sure why Aksel's shit works. But this is the safest place I've found to bed down. While it's not much, it gives me peace of mind at night. I know I don't have to tell *you* what that's worth."

Having been on the run from a League warrant himself, Jullien was the one person who would fully understand the nightmare that was Bastien's life.

Thrāix glanced around Bastien's run-down home. "You want me to make the place a little more hospitable?"

Bastien frowned at the offer, not sure what he meant by it. "How do you mean?"

"I have some skills that can clean this place up and make it more solid and habitable . . . if you want."

Bastien couldn't stop himself from smiling at some of the things he'd kill for. "A solid roof that doesn't leak during the rare rains we have would be incredible. But don't make it too inviting. I don't want it to attract any undue attention. Only things I want crawling in here are the spiders and insects."

"Got it."

With that, Jullien gestured for Bastien and the woman with them to follow him out toward their ship.

As soon as they neared it, Bastien bit back a laugh at the name of Jullien's ship. "*Pet Hate*?"

Jullien grinned as he lowered the ramp. "Seemed fitting for me."

Yeah, given that Jullien had been everyone's pet hate at home, it made sense.

At least he'd managed to keep his sense of humor over it.

Shaking his head, Bastien laughed. "Damn, Julie, you look *so* different from the last time I saw you."

"Yeah, I'm surprised you recognized me."

"I would always know my favorite cousin."

He arched a brow at that. "Not how I remember our relationship."

Bastien grinned as old memories played through his mind. Memories he hadn't thought about in a long, long time. And it was nice to think about something other than the horror that was the last couple of years and basic daily survival. "I will admit that you intimidated me."

Jullien gaped. "What?"

He didn't know why it surprised his cousin so. "Honor to the gods. Yeah. You were massively tall and huge. Twice my size, and you always wore a frowning expression that said you were contemplating the death and dismemberment of the next person who made the mistake of speaking to you."

The woman passed a curious look at Jullien. "Did you?"

"No. Honestly, the frown came from my confusion as I tried to understand what they were saying to me. Triosans speak fast, and their accents are incredibly thick and unlike the language files we were given in school. The court dialect was completely different from what I'd been taught."

Ah, that explained it. And made a lot of sense. "He's right. It took me a few minutes to reacclimate every time I visited. But man, Julie, that's not what it looked like on your face." He laughed at the memory of their childhood. "Your expression was one of perpetual pissed off. Not that I blame you for it. . . . Yet even so, I always looked forward to seeing you."

"Why? You mostly ignored me."

"I always sat by you, if you remember. . . . I just always thought you had some kind of secret knowledge the rest of us lacked. And I wanted to know more about Andarions and if they were as different from us as everyone claimed. Because honestly, you didn't seem like you were all that strange to me."

"Thanks . . . I think."

Bastien winked as the woman laughed before she headed down the hallway that led toward the bridge. Sobering, Bastien narrowed his gaze on Jullien. "In all seriousness, though, you look really good now, and not just more fit and trim. You look happy. Like there's a weight missing from your shoulders. I don't know what happened to you, but I hope it's as good as it seems. You deserve to have some peace from the hell they gave you."

Jullien pulled the glasses down past his eyes so that Bastien could see that they were no longer the hazel green they'd been. Now his eyes were a vibrant red.

A rare color for Andarions, and one Bastien remembered hearing stories about.

"What's the Andarion term for that?"

"Stralen."

"Means you're married, right?"

Jullien nodded as he replaced his glasses. "To an amazing female. Like your Alura."

The mere mention of her name made him fume and pierced his heart with a pain so profound that for a moment, he could barely draw a single breath. Jullien had no idea of the nerve he'd just stomped.

Bastien curled his lip. "For your sake, I pray she's nothing like Alura. That faithless bitch is one of the reasons I'm here."

"I'm sorry, Bas. I didn't know."

"Yeah. Neither did I. Until it was too late." And he cursed himself every day of this wretched existence for being an ass and falling for her lies. Lil had been right. He should have divorced her that day in the hospital and never looked back.

So many regrets. So many things he'd do differently if he could only go back in time.

His gaze filled with sympathy, Jullien took him to his room and showed him where the shower was. He pulled out some of his own clothes for him. "Take whatever you need."

More grateful than mere words could express, Bastien stepped into the bathroom and closed the door so that he could finally have a decent bath again.

The moment the hot, fresh water touched his skin, he wanted to weep. This was what he missed most on his makeshift home.

Well, this and someone to talk to. But the water pumps had burned out completely a long time ago so all he had now was what he'd managed to dig out of the ground as a well for himself. Though he'd tried everything, he had yet to get full running water back in the base.

Closing his eyes, Bastien let the miraculous wetness cascade over him and ease the soreness in his muscles.

And for reasons he couldn't even begin to explain, an image of Ember popped into his head. She'd always loved to share showers. He hadn't thought about that in a long time, either.

Alura had despised it. She thought it was intrusive and gross.

But Ember . . .

She'd lived to corner him right after he'd rinsed the soap off and then give him a whole 'nother reason to have to bathe again. His body went rock hard at the thought of her mouth sliding over his skin until he begged her for mercy.

Desire hit him like an Andarion Ring fighter and left him breathless. Squeezing his eyes shut, he savored the memories of Ember and the way she used to hold him. The way she'd laugh and tease. No one had ever loved him the way she did.

No one had ever hurt him the way she had either.

And that was the double-edged axe that slit him to the core of his soul every time he allowed himself to think about her or to remember his past.

While he wanted to cut the throat of his now ex-wife— Alura had filed for divorce and been granted it by the Trigon Court two weeks after his arrest—he couldn't bring himself to hate Ember.

Even now. Even though he really wanted to at times. Even though a part of him wanted to lay all of this at her feet and blame her.

He couldn't. And for that, he hated himself.

"I just hope you're happy."

Though it killed him to think about it, he prayed that whatever man she'd found to replace him gave her the love she deserved. That the lucky dog treasured her the way he should.

And that thought made his gut tighten. Worse, it churned up bitter emotions and memories.

You faithless, worthless bastard!

He flinched as a memory of one of Alura's more stellar tantrums intruded. She'd been so angry when she found out that he'd been arrested for assaulting Ember's rebound boyfriend. He hadn't meant to.

But there he'd been, back from patrol, when he overheard her sister Cin talking about how upset Ember was that her new guy had stood her up after they'd been dating for a couple of months.

Worse, he'd heard Ember's voice over the link as she cried to her sister. "Why can't anyone love me, Cin? What is so wrong with me?"

Next thing he'd known, he'd tracked the bastard down and had beaten the utter shit out of him.

Yeah, that had bent Alura into all kinds of pissed off.

But he didn't want to think about her right now. He needed to find some way to get free of this death sentence so that he could hand-carry one back to Barnabas.

Finishing up his shower, he left the room just as Jullien returned.

Jullien wore a peculiar expression before he gestured toward the towel Bastien had been molesting on his arrival. Not in a sexual way. But because it'd been so long since he'd last touched anything so soft and good-smelling. "You can have some of the towels, if you want."

Embarrassed that Julie had caught him in a moment of sad weakness, Bastien actually blushed. "Pathetic, right?"

"Not about to judge. You don't want to know how sorry my state was when my wife found me." He handed a tray of food to Bastien.

At first, he tried to eat like a human, but this was real

food. It was warm and delicious. Before he knew it, he was attacking it like a savage and shoving it into his mouth by the handfuls.

Then he made the mistake of glancing to Jullien and realizing that his gluttony, like his towel molestation, had a witness to it.

I am an animal.

Horrified, Bastien wiped his hands off. "Sorry."

"Again, no apologies. Ever. I get it."

Sighing over what a pathetic mess he was, Bastien set the napkin aside. "Who would have ever thought this would be our lives, huh? As a boy, I thought by now I'd be ruling, in complete bliss." That was what his parents had planned for his future. A nice heiress in another empire.

But he'd wrecked that design the moment he met Ember.

"I never thought I'd live long enough to rule. Gods' truth to that. Every day I woke alive in that palace, I counted it a miracle."

Shocked by Jullien's confession, Bastien set the tray aside. "Seriously?"

He nodded. "Once Nykyrian was gone, I figured it was just a matter of time until one of my cousins grew brazen enough to take the fatal shot."

"That's why you wanted to live with your father?"

"Why else?"

Bastien let out a bitter laugh. "Your father thought it was a ruse of your grandmother's so that you could take his throne."

Jullien rolled his eyes. "Of course he did. All he had to do was marry and screw another whore for a son. I wouldn't have cared. I just wanted away from Andaria."

Scowling, Bastien gaped at him. "You know why he never did, right?"

"No idea whatsoever."

"Jullien . . . he loves your mother. I mean, *loves* her. They were supposed to marry. Everything had been arranged, in spite of our grandfather. Uncle Aros was willing to give up his throne for her, then Nykyrian was killed and she went into an institution. After that, his father and the Triosan senate absolutely forbade it. They'd have imprisoned him as a traitor had he married her then."

He gaped as if that was news to him. "What? When was this?"

"Before I was born. But I heard my mother and your father and our grandfather fight about this most of my life. Aros categorically refused to ever take another bride— that was his FU to his father and his people over what they did to him by banning his marriage to Cairistiona. He has been loyal to your mother all these years. Your mother is his heart and soul."

Jullien scowled at him as if he couldn't believe it. "Then why did he allow them to banish me and replace me as heir?"

"Truthfully? Aros thinks you hate him. He says that the first time he picked you up when you were an infant, you screamed like you were being murdered and didn't stop until he put you down. That anytime he tried to touch you, you cringed and recoiled, or ran away to hide. So he learned to leave you alone and focused on Nyk. After Nyk was gone, he didn't know what to do with you." Judgments that had always seemed harsh.

But Bastien also remembered how things were during his childhood. "Every time you visited, you and Aros always ended up in a bitter fight. So he thought it would be best if you stayed on Andaria. It's why he didn't fight them when they removed you from the line of succession. He thought you'd be happier on Andaria. That it would be best for everyone."

Jullien scoffed bitterly. "My father never bothered to get to know me at all."

Fair enough. He'd witnessed enough of their interactions to know that as truth. "I'm sorry, Julie."

"It doesn't matter. My parents orphaned me the day I was born. I never expected much from them, and sadly, they never failed to meet my low expectations." Jullien jerked his chin toward his closet. "Take whatever you need, brother. I'll make sure and bring supplies here whenever I pass through."

Jullien's unexpected charity brought a lump to his throat. God knew that it'd been so seldom given to the man in front of him that Bastien had no idea when or how Jullien would have learned it.

More than that, it'd been so long since anyone had thrown anything other than pain and misery his way that he was finding it difficult to not be suspicious. "Why are you being so kind to me?"

"Because I know what it's like to be left out in the cold. I don't want to do that to you. If I can find a surgeon who can remove your tag, I'll come back with him, too."

Those words almost broke him. Tears welled in Bastien's eyes before he pulled Jullien against him and hugged him. "Even if you leave and never think of me again, the fact that you offered . . . I love you, my cousin."

Jullien pounded him on the back and released him. "I won't forget. I put my hailing numbers in while I ran my searches. If you come under attack, get sick, or need anything, you call me. I mean that. I'll return immediately. Anytime. Don't hesitate."

Bastien wiped at his eyes, despising the weakness he was showing. It really pissed him off that basic decency had come to be such a rare commodity in his life that it left him weeping like a baby.

Yet there you had it. And it'd come from the least likely source of all. His cousin they'd all written off.

Clearing his throat, he followed Jullien to the ramp where Thrāix waited with extra ammunition and weapons.

The sight flabbergasted Bastien. No one gave up weapons without a fight, and this was a lot more than he could have ever hoped for. "I wasn't expecting all this."

Thrāix grimaced. "Yeah, well, I wasn't expecting to let it go, either. But after what I saw in that building . . . I reevaluated my opinion of you. It's not often I'm wrong. But I'm man enough to admit when I make a mistake. I made sure to conceal you, so you should be left alone."

Grateful to a level words couldn't even begin to convey, he inclined his head to them. "Thank you."

The woman whose name he had yet to learn joined them and handed Bastien what appeared to be some kind of prayer book. "I know you probably don't read Andarion, but I want you to have this anyway, for the gods to watch over you and keep you safe."

It was only then that he realized the necklace she wore marked her as a religious leader. Though how Jullien had come to travel with her, he couldn't imagine.

Not that it mattered to Bastien. Only their kindness did. "I will treasure it, High Mother." He paused to meet Jullien's gaze. "Peace be with you, cousin."

"And you."

Suddenly, an alarm sounded.

Jullien scowled as he heard it. "It's Jup. He's under fire."

With no idea who that was, Bastien inclined his head to them. "Go. Help whoever. Thanks again, all of you."

Not wanting to keep them after everything they'd done for him, he sprinted down the ramp and returned to the shadows that had become his home.

From there, he watched as they departed, and whispered a prayer for their protection. While the gods had abandoned him, he hoped they'd stay with Jullien, and it meant a lot to him that he still had one family member who hadn't completely rejected him.

Jullien's presence today had given him something he hadn't had in a while.

Hope.

At least he had one person in the universe who still called *him* family and didn't believe the lies others had spread about him. Sad that his life had come down to this. That something so very little meant so very much.

Yet it did.

Bastien carefully put away his supplies, then thumbed through the prayer book. Thanks to Jullien, he recognized a few words, and through it, he learned the name of the woman, as it was embossed on the cover.

Unira Samari.

She'd also put her digits inside the book, along with a prayer card and a blessed necklace. And a small note for him that she'd written in Universal.

> *The gods have not abandoned you, my son. Though it may seem dark today, there will be a brighter tomorrow. Sometimes it takes a bitter storm to clear the land for a better, more abundant harvest. Should you need anything, even if it's nothing more than a mere friendly voice to keep you company, call me anytime. I promise not to preach, only to listen.*
>
> *May the gods keep you wrapped in their eternal love and protect you always.*
>
> *Unira.*

Bastien clutched her card and pressed it to his chest. Then he tucked it so that it'd stay over his heart and put her necklace on. Such trivial things, really, yet the comfort they gave him were beyond measure.

But they weren't the only gifts that'd been left behind. He didn't discover the rest until he went to shut down his electronics.

Thrāix had been generous, too, and left him a note of his own.

> *Tweaked your system a bit. No one should be without at least one good porn channel, sports feed, and a news feed. And it's locked tight so that no one and nothing will ever detect you. Stay safe, brother. You need anything, call.*
>
> *T.*

Man, Jullien had managed to find himself some decent companions. Far better than the bastards who'd fled from him like rats off a sinking ship.

But that wasn't all. Thrāix had also included tactical scans and intel on Bastien's uncle and his new Kirovarian regime.

"You beautiful Trisani bastard . . . if you were here I'd kiss you."

Because with this he could plan his attack on Barnabas and how he'd take them all down.

Hell's coming, Barnabas. And I'm delivering it personally.

CHAPTER 6

Bastien grabbed his blaster as he heard the sound of an engine. But after his heartbeat quit drowning the sound out, he realized it was Jullien making another supply run to him.

True to his word, he hadn't forgotten him. As often as he could, Jullien popped in with food, medicine, ammo, and weapons.

Thrāix with porn, comedy, and top-notch alcohol Bastien was sure had to be banned in most systems.

And between those unlikely two was always Unira with her calm, mothering nature.

Bastien holstered his weapon as he headed outside to greet them.

As soon as the ramp lowered, Jullien's adopted son Vasili came running down to greet him. The boy was so thrilled to be added to the crew that he didn't even mind whenever Jullien gave him the crap tasks, hoping to make Vas rethink becoming Tavali.

"Bas!"

He embraced the eager teen who was also a blond Fyreblood Andarion like Unira and Jullien's wife, Ushara. "Hey, kid. How you doing?"

"Good."

"Your sisters still making you crazy?"

Vasili screwed his face up as Bastien mentioned the half sisters Jullien had fathered with Vas's mother. "I love them, but . . . yeah. One day you're going to meet them and see what a handful twins are."

Bastien laughed. He'd love nothing more than to meet Jullien's wife and toddler daughters. "And your mom?"

"Having *another* baby."

Bastien arched a brow at the teen's tone. "You okay with that?"

"I'm praying for a brother who can run some interference with the spider twins."

Ruffling his hair and laughing, Bastien stepped away to greet Thrāix, Unira, and Jullien. But the moment he did, he caught the look on their faces that said they were bringing bad news to his door.

"What's going on?"

Jullien handed him a tactical pack. "Have you heard the latest?"

"About . . ."

"The Caronese have declared war on The League, and with them the Triosans, Andarions, Garvons, Gourish, and Exeterians."

"So basically The Sentella started the war and their nations are backing?"

Jullien nodded.

Bastien grimaced at the nightmare that had to be. "And The Tavali?"

"Two of the four Nations have already signed on. So far, the Gorts are not a part of it."

"Because Trajen won't let them fight it," Thrāix said under his breath.

Unira sighed. "For good reason. I'm glad he's keeping

us out of it. I've no wish to start conducting funeral services over those I love."

Yet Bastien knew the gleam in Jullien's eyes that said his cousin had different plans. "Well, let us get to your supplies. I know you've been waiting on some of them."

When Bastien started after them, Thrāix pulled him aside. "Just so you know, your loved ones are safe from the war."

Bastien's blood went cold at his words. "My loved ones are all dead."

Thrāix's eyes lightened to an eerie, indefinable shade of blue. "Not all of them. Trust me. The day will come when you'll reunite. I just thought you should know you're not forgotten and your heart is safe."

Bastien wanted to believe that. Desperately. But he was sure Ember had moved on with her life. He'd long ago reconciled himself with the fact that she was no longer his heart. That what they'd had was over and done with. Nothing more than fading memories that haunted him.

Or worse, tortured him with the vivid memories of a warm body that was far from the cold pile of blankets on the floor that made up his bed nowadays. Still, he couldn't keep his treacherous mind from betraying him. Anymore than his body from craving hers.

Why? He had no idea. It was the worse sort of hell. Maybe that was his real punishment. Knowing she was out there and that he couldn't have her.

Ember cursed as fire rained down on them from League ships. Jay was at the helm and flying like the demonic bitch she was famed for. But their enemy was closing in.

"More fire at click eight!" she shouted into her mic. "Shore it up, ladies!"

The women were eerily silent as they fought. A far cry

from the raucousness of Ember's sisters and the other Gyron Force troops she'd once fought beside. All she heard was the frantic beating of her heart and the recoil of their cannons.

Finally, they heard the sound they'd been waiting for.

"Drive's fixed! Hit it, Captain!"

An instant later, Jay went into hyperdrive, but not before one last volley of fire cut across their ship and sent them skidding sideways.

Ember cursed again as she slammed against the side hard enough to daze herself.

All of a sudden, as everything around her darkened, she was no longer in a space battle. She was home again on Kirovar.

She saw Bastien holding her as he inspected the blow she'd taken that had rung her bell pretty significantly. "Good thing you're hard-headed, huh?" He flashed that charismatic smile that could get him out of any and all trouble.

"You're not funny, Cabarro."

"That's only because you have a head injury. If you were running at your usual speed, then you'd know I'm hilarious."

"Only in your mind."

"And according to you last night, in bed."

She groaned at that. "Don't go there, Captain. I'm in enough pain. Don't need you adding to it."

With a gentle kiss that left her famished and wanting to strip him bare, he let go of her so that he could stand up and use the shadows for cover. Like a phantom wind, he went to the opening of the building they were holed up in. She took a moment to sweep a hungry look down his ripped body, and imagined what he'd look like without that uniform on.

Yeah, she definitely had a head injury. That was the only way to explain why she'd be this horny while they were in this much danger . . .

Bastien scowled. "I'm not detecting any readings. I think we got—" He broke off as someone opened fire on him.

He was back at her side so fast that she hadn't even realized he'd moved. Scooping her up, he carried her and ran with a speed that defied belief.

"Ember?"

Blinking, she realized it was Jalyna Xever standing over her right now and not Bastien. The Fyreblood Andarion captain who ran their Tavali crew.

"Jay?"

"Yeah, Em. Where did you go, girl?"

Home. The word choked her as she remembered that her home no longer existed. Everything she'd once known was long gone.

Just like Bastien.

And that almost broke her into tears, but by sheer force of will she caught herself and shoved her emotions back down.

No doubt her suppressed feelings for Bastien were what had caused her vision. She'd learned just last night that he'd been killed two years ago. That he'd died alone at the hands of a ruthless League assassin.

That news had done more damage to her heart than she'd have ever thought possible. Stupidly, she'd believed herself to be over him. To have put that part of her past to rest years ago, and come to terms with it.

She couldn't have been more wrong.

Not since the death of her parents had anything hurt so much. All the regrets she had mounted to the point they were virtually debilitating.

I should have told Bastien the truth when I had the chance. . . .

Why did I keep such a secret from him? Why didn't I marry him when he asked me?

Don't think about it.

With a ragged breath, she pushed herself up. "What happened?"

"We took a hit on our way out. Fera's working on it. At least they didn't knock out the drive."

Ember narrowed her gaze at the way Jay said that. "What *did* they knock out?"

"Life support."

"Oh goodie! Just what we can do without!"

Jay laughed. "Yeah, I know. I swear, if we get out of this and make it home, I'm grabbing my kids and my husband, and we're grounded for a while. I'm done with these risks. I don't care how much cred we're making."

Ember couldn't blame her for the sentiment. But it only worked for those who had family they could get to.

For her? It was a burning shot to her heart, as it reminded her that she had no one waiting at the Cyperian StarStation base to welcome her return.

She'd been forced by a madman to give up her family in order to keep them safe. She didn't even know where her sisters were. Ember couldn't afford to. Barnabas had wasted no effort trying to run her down and end her. To end everyone she loved.

It was what had made her Tavali. They kept her moving.

And alive.

Jay adjusted the band around her insanely bright, fluorescent red hair. In total contradiction to the Gorturnum Tavali rule book that specified an all-black battlesuit whenever they were flying missions, Jay wore one of yellow and red. But then, given that her sister was their vice admiral and the second-highest-ranking member of their Nation, she could get away with a lot of things no one else could.

The lights came up, signaling that their engineer had succeeded in saving their lives.

Again.

Jay let out an audible breath of relief. "All right, ladies," she said over the intercom for every one on their all female crew. "We're going home, and after this near-death experience, I'm taking time off. Those of you who don't want to take liberty, submit your names to my sister on our return and she'll reassign you to active crews. But after this . . . I'm done for a bit."

She paused to study Ember. "You all right, Major?"

Ember rubbed at the lump on her head and winced, wishing she could be with her loved ones. Especially a certain male someone. "Yeah, I'm fine."

Yet they both knew she was lying. She hadn't been okay in a long, long time.

Jay patted her on the arm before she headed for the helm.

Ember had never been a covetous person, but right then as she listened to the excited pirate Tavali crew beginning to make plans for their extended vacations with their loved ones, she felt so alone and isolated. She envied them.

Had she said yes that night to Bastien as she should have, she'd have been married, too, and living a life with her husband and children.

Crossing her arms over her chest, she pretended for just a second that she had Bastien with her again. Stupid, she knew. She'd kill Bastien if he were here.

Beat him until he bled for being so reckless and stupid as to not have seen Barnabas's treachery. For such a worldly, surly bastard, Bas had always been incredibly innocent. Always seen the best in people. That was what she loved most about him. He'd given everyone the benefit of the doubt.

Even the ones who didn't deserve it.

And in all these years, she'd never found anyone who'd treated her with the love and regard he had. No one had respected her more or given her such devotion.

How could I have been so blind? In her own way, she'd been even more naïve than he had.

It was too easy to take things for granted when they were right in front of your face. Especially when they were people. She'd assumed he'd always be here. That love like his would be easy to find again. Her parents had loved like that. Tasi and Cin did. . . . How stupid she was.

She'd allowed her own fears to override her joy, and her ability to see how much she relied on him. Cut his heart out when he offered it to her, and she knew it. Then instead of trying to save what they'd had, she'd ruthlessly ignored his attempts to reconcile and shut him out more. She'd let her fears, anger, and hurt get in the way of her happiness.

Now it was too late.

Bastien's dead.

Swallowing against the pain and grief that threatened to knock her down, she rubbed at the locket that held the last bit of him she had. And wished for things she knew could never be again.

While their high admiral kept them officially out of the Sentella–League War, Trajen couldn't keep his crews out of danger. The League didn't differentiate between the Nations. To them, one Tavali was all Tavali.

Of course, that was the Tavalian code. Still, this was a long way from being over. She'd left one war behind only to fall headfirst into another.

Only this time, she had no idea what she was fighting for.

Bastien drew up short as he saw the carnage in front of him. He'd been aware of the invaders near his home for days now. A huge-ass Andarion warrior with a teen male and a human female had come in first. Bastien had been trying his best to figure out why the two Andarions had a young human woman with them.

At least until the other blond human female had been dropped off. She'd made straight for them.

Then he'd assumed they must be a family on some kind of screwed-up vacation. Though why anyone would want to take a break in this fected heat and desolate desert, he couldn't imagine.

But then, Andarions were a screwed-up race with some peculiar ideas on comfort that he couldn't even begin to fathom. He'd marked this new group off as harmless and had left them alone, only checking their location from time to time to make sure they didn't come near his base.

Until he'd seen and heard the firefight that'd resulted in enough bodies to make a League assassin cream his pants.

The dead were Bolodorians from the looks of their craft and uniforms. A group of incas—freelance assassins. Lowlife scum who made his flesh crawl. But for once, they hadn't been interested in him or his bounty. They appeared to have been exclusively after the Andarion family.

Something verified as he watched the warrior searching the twenty-five bodies he'd taken down with minimal effort and heard a radio go off on one of them.

"Hiller? You there, copy?"

The warrior paused to listen, then picked up the link closest to him. "Yeah."

Bastien was impressed. Took balls to answer an ene-my's comm. Kudos to the beast.

"Did you get him? I don't hear no more fighting."

"Yeah," he repeated.

"Fucking awesome. Don't forget to bag the head with the DNA sample. We get twice the payout for it. See you in a few."

Yeah, the Andarion didn't seem to share that sentiment since it was his head they were calling for. Bastien couldn't blame him for that. It'd wreck his day too. Look on the Andarion's face said he was pissed off to be their target. And that if he laid hands to any more of these guys, he would be about as charitable as Bastien should he ever be lucky enough to get his ex-wife's neck in his hands.

Intending to wait until the Andarion finished and moved on so that Bastien could search the bodies for sup-plies, he continued to watch the warrior through the scope of his sniper's rifle.

As the Andarion moved out of his viewer range, Bastien stepped in closer, making sure not to lose sight of him.

The moment he did, the Andarion jerked his blaster out and aimed it straight at his head.

"Don't," Bastien growled, switching his targeting la-ser on with his thumb to warn the Andarion that he was already aimed at the warrior's heart.

Assured mutual destruction.

The Andarion didn't flinch or move as he kept his own dot clearly centered between Bastien's eyes. If he wasn't wearing his shooting goggles, that light would have burned out his vision and left him blind. "One twitch, hu-man, and I promise you'll be dead before I will."

Bastien refused to back down or let his words rattle him. Honestly? He'd heard worse threats from his mother for leaving the toilet seat up in her personal bathroom.

So he kept his own dot right where the Andarion's heart was. But he also knew that a lengthy standoff would give the Andarion's family time to move in behind him. Better to defuse the situation and let him know Bastien wasn't a threat than risk an injury.

With his left hand held up, he moved slowly forward. "Ditto."

The Andarion scowled as he raked a look over Bastien's ragged clothing that said he'd figured out Bastien was alone and not in much position to be a big threat to him.

Other than the blaster he held.

He could only imagine what the Andarion must think. Bastien's clothes were worn out. And though he had his hair tied back, away from his eyes, it was long and ragged from where he'd been keeping it cut with a blunt knife. He always meant to request shears from Jullien or Unira, but somehow he forgot about it whenever he talked to them. Those brief breaks in loneliness made him forget a lot of things.

His cheek itched, reminding him of how scraggly his beard was, too. Yeah, he probably looked like a reject from some psych ward.

After a few seconds, a slow smile of appreciation spread across the Andarion's face. "So are we going to stand here all day, weapons drawn? I'm game if you are."

His humor caught Bastien off guard. He relaxed a tiny degree, as the Andarion's demeanor and manner reminded him a lot of his old friend Fain Hauk. Only a mighty War Hauk could be this relaxed and nonchalant with a blaster trained on him.

Or an idiot.

That led him back to his War Hauk analogy as they were made up of equal parts of stupid and courageous.

But he didn't miss the way the Andarion watched his

eyes carefully, as if to see whether or not Bastien intended to attack him. That alone told him just how skilled a killer this gargantuan male was.

Which meant he'd kill Bastien if he sensed a threat.

With no choice, Bastien did something he hadn't done in a long time.

He trusted his gut and lowered his weapon.

Yet not so much that he couldn't get a well-placed shot off should the Andarion make a move he didn't like.

"Look, I'm just here to scavenge before the others arrive. You do your thing, I do mine, and we part ways."

The Andarion nodded. "You're Kirovarian?"

That set off every alarm in Bastien's body. He took aim at his heart again. "How do you know that?"

The warrior holstered his weapon with a nonchalance that said he had no intention of attacking. "Your accent. So what was your rank, soldier?"

Yeah, he was an astute bastard. Deciding the best course of action would be to attempt a friendly encounter, Bastien finally put his own weapon away. "What kind of Andarion knows humans so well?"

"I was schooled with humans."

Bullshit! Bastien knew that *never* happened. He brought his weapon up, intending to kill him where he stood. But before he could pull the trigger, the Andarion disarmed him with lightning speed.

Bastien attacked.

The Andarion deflected the blow and returned it with one that would have incapacitated him had it made contact. Luckily, Bastien dodged just in time. But before he could counter with another strike, the Andarion twirled, and delivered a staggering fist to his jaw that rang his bell for days. Worse, the oversized bastard head-butted him then flipped him to the ground.

Stunned and dazed, Bastien waited for the Andarion to finally put him out of his never-ending misery.

He didn't.

Instead, the Andarion stared at Bastien's stomach, where his shirt had lifted to betray the brand that cut through Bastien's soul and dignity every time he saw it.

His Ravin mark.

The Andarion immediately held his hands up and backed off. "I'm not here to hunt or kill you, friend."

Yeah, right.

And yet, he could have easily killed him a second ago and had chosen not to. Bastien wasn't sure why as he glared at the beast. "You're League, aren't you? Isn't that why you're here?"

The Andarion scratched his chin with the back of his hand. "Used to be, and was discharged years ago. If I wasn't, I'd have killed you already. These days, I'm Sentella only." He gestured toward the weapons on the ground that were left behind from his victims. "Walk with peace, brother. Take your supplies and go. I won't stop or track you."

Still not sure he could trust him not to shoot him the minute he turned his back, Bastien wiped at the blood on his lips, then pushed himself to his feet. One thing was sure, he wanted more distance between them.

Like the gutter rat he'd been forced to become, Bastien scurried over to the other side to watch the muscled mountain. He still had the traditional Andarion warrior's braids that fell to the middle of his back. And even though he was dressed in civilian gear, there was no doubt this warrior had taken a lot of lives.

Something evidenced as he viciously cut off one of the heads of the men who'd been sent to kill him and then put it in the container they'd brought to house his. Brutal and yet poetic.

Bastien would have done the same.

As the Andarion started for his airbee, Bastien called out to him. "I was captain first rank. Gyron Force."

The expression on the Andarion's face as he turned back to rake him with another look said that he knew who and what Gyron Force was. The elite of the elite for the Kirovarian armada and infantry. Less than one percent of one percent of their soldiers qualified to wear their uniforms.

Hell, even Bastien's dad had been proud the day he earned rank among them. His uncle had stood in total disbelief . . . along with his older brother, who'd never been able to pass the tests to get in.

"I'm Hauk," the Andarion finally said.

Hauk . . . yeah, he looked a lot like Fain. Fought like the vicious beast, too. They had to be related.

"Bastien Cabarro." He licked at the blood on his lips as he narrowed his gaze on Hauk. "You really Sentella?"

Hauk slid his hand toward his blaster again, as if he was now afraid Bastien might go for *his* back. Made sense given the bounty that was attached to the heads of their membership. Even before the war that had broken out, The League had hated The Sentella. A rival organization, The Sents had made their living by saving and rescuing innocent League targets and putting them in places where The League couldn't find them.

The higher-ups in The League tended to take issue with anyone who defied them.

"Yeah."

"You guys really declare war on The League?"

Hauk relaxed a degree as he heard the hatred Bastien had been unable to remove from his words. "Definitely."

"Then can you get this fucking chip out of me?" If anyone could, surely it would be a Sentella member.

"Absolutely. How long have you been implanted?"

Bastien curled his lip as a whole new wave of pissed off went through him. "Almost eight full minsid years."

Hauk let out a low whistle of appreciation that Bastien had lived so long. Because they were tagged and hunted so viciously, they couldn't risk being in any civilian population. Relegated to hellholes like this one, many ended up taking their own lives just to stop their suffering. It was physically and psychologically grueling to be hunted like an animal. And Bastien had considered the easy way out more than once. Only the need to avenge his family had kept him going.

As his brother had so often said, he was too damn spiteful to die. And no one ever got the better of him.

Hauk bit his lip, exposing a hint of his long fangs. "Damn long time to be on the run."

"What can I say? I'm a stubborn bastard, fueled by venom and vengeance." Sighing, Bastien finally relaxed as he approached Hauk. "So is that your family you're traveling with?"

Hauk drew his blaster and pinned it right between Bastien's eyes again. "What do you know of them?"

Bastien held his hands up, for the first time without fear. "Nothing. I saw your camp a few days ago. Being hunted, I make it a point to check out anyone who lands here. I figured you were on a hiking trip of some sort, so I left you alone and went away. Seems to be some kind of Andarion thing around here. But usually it's only two Andarions at a time, and they leave after a few weeks. Though why you guys want to vacation here, I cannot imagine. You are one fucked-up species."

Snorting, Hauk holstered his blaster. "Have you been *here* the whole eight years?"

"Most of them. Once I realized the magnetic field and radiation played havoc with tracking devices, I decided Shithole Central suited me fine enough."

Hauk snorted at that. "Doesn't seem to be playing with mine. They haven't had any problems tracking me."

"Ah . . . that's why they keep hitting you. Wondered about that." Bastien frowned. "So who wants *you* dead?"

Hauk lifted the container that held his confiscated head. "That's what I'm going to find out."

Gruesome, but understandable.

Crossing his arms over his chest, Bastien nodded. "Guess being Sentella, you have a lot of friends who want to play with you."

"Yeah, but I'd rather take my ball and go home."

Bastien laughed. "Why do I doubt that?"

"Probably because I'm about to take my ball and go shove it up the ass of whoever started this."

And now Hauk reminded him a lot of his cousin Jullien. "Spoken like a true Andarion."

"Known a lot of us?"

Bastien hesitated to answer. Obviously, Hauk didn't know he was royal or related to Jullien, and he wasn't about to bring that sore topic up since The Sentella had their own bounty out on his cousin's hide. Not that he blamed them. The Sentella was led by Jullien's twin brother, who hated him over the fact that Jullien had stupidly assisted Nykyrian's bitterest enemy in his abduction of Nykyrian's wife.

Hence the condition of the base Bastien currently lived in. He'd found those data files and had been shocked by them.

Until he'd heard Jullien's side of things.

His cousin had been in a dire situation, and much like Bastien, had been left with almost no options for survival. And he loved Jullien, and owed him way too much to ever judge him for the steps he'd taken to keep himself alive.

Desperate people did desperate things.

He was just too damn grateful to have his cousin still with him.

However, he wasn't about to bring up something that could get him killed right now. So he settled on a safer Andarion topic.

"Just one." Technically true since Jullien was only half-blooded and while Unira and Vasili were Andarions, the Fyreblood race was vastly different from the Ixurians—which was what those with dark hair and skin would be considered. "Nasty-tempered bastard, but damn good in a fight." He cast an amused grin at Hauk. "Now that I think about it, he looks a lot like you."

"Yeah, well, we all look alike."

Bastien rolled his eyes at the bad stereotype that Andarions used against all humans, and it definitely didn't apply to him. "Wouldn't know. He's the only Andarion"—full-blooded Ixurian, anyway—"I've been this close to, besides you. Come to think of it, his name's also Hauk. Only it's his last name."

Hauk narrowed his gaze as if he was one breath from attacking. "Friend or foe?"

"Good friend, so if you plan to shit-talk him, you better be ready to draw again and shoot when you do so."

This time, Hauk grinned wide enough to expose razor-sharp fangs. "I never shit-talk Fain behind his back. Only to his face. Otherwise, big brother would kick my ass."

Bastien went slack-jawed as he instantly knew exactly who this was—and it was a damn good thing he hadn't brought up Jullien's name, since this particular Andarion had his grudge against his cousin. "You Dancer?"

He inclined his head to him. "I'm Dancer."

"Well, I'll be damned. Small fucking universe. The way Fain talked about you, I thought you'd be the size and age of the kid you're with. Had no idea you were so close to his age and build." Bastien held his arm out to him. At a distance that let Dancer know he really was familiar with Andarions and their culture. "I owe Fain my life. You need a point or anchor, *any* time, I'm yours."

Dancer shook his arm. "How you know my brother?"

"He used to live in my neighborhood on Kirovar. We worked out at the same gym. I was the only one who'd spar with him. After a while, we ended up as drinking buddies."

Dancer nodded. "So you must know his first mate, Durden."

Grimacing, Bastien shook his head. "Never heard him mention a Durden. Didn't know he had *any* friends, to be honest. Not that he ever talked much, but when he did, you're the only one he ever really talked about." He paused as he realized what Hauk had just done, then smirked. "So did I pass?"

"Pass what?"

"Your test to see if I'm really a friend of Fain's. Not that I blame you. Don't trust strangers as a rule, either. But I do know Fain. I even know you have burn scars on your back from a childhood accident he blames himself for. And that his ex-wife was named Omira Antaxes."

Hauk let out a slow, audible breath. "He must have been drunker than hell to tell you that."

Bastien rubbed at his neck. "Yeah. It was on what would have been their tenth anniversary. He didn't handle it well. He even told me why they divorced, and I know that if I allow *anything* to happen to you, he'll hunt me down to the ends of the universe and gut me hard."

"That I believe he would." Dancer sat back as he started the airbee. "I'm headed up to bust ass. You joining or staying?"

Suddenly feeling like his old self again, Bastien grinned as he slung his leg over the airbee beside Dancer's. "Always ready for a good fight. Especially when a mighty War Hauk's involved." He powered on the engine. "And I'm harboring a serious hard-on for anyone who hunts others for a living. I'd much rather be the predator than the prey."

"Then welcome, brother." Dancer inclined his head to him before he gunned the accelerator.

Bastien had no idea where they were going, and maybe it was stupid to join him. But it'd been too long since he'd felt like a unit, and honestly, he'd missed this.

Be careful where your loneliness takes you.

Then again, it wasn't like he had anything else to do. Until the chip was out of him, he couldn't go after Barnabas. If he left this place, he'd be dead in a week, as it would trip every League alarm he came into contact with. And those fected things were lined up every few feet.

While he liked a good battle, even he had to sleep sometime and no one would fight that many assassins without a break.

So for now, he'd stay with Dancer and work as his wingman.

Dancer led him a few ticks away and then landed the airbike before he turned it off.

Cautious and alert, Bastien pulled in beside him.

Dancer removed the safeties and locks from his weapons while Bastien swung his dirty poncho over his shoulder and secured it so that the material wouldn't get in his way during the fight.

Next, Bastien took inventory of his own weapons while

Dancer secured his braids back from his face. Dancer unwound his long brown scarf from around his neck so that he could cover his head and the lower part of his face, no doubt to disguise the fact he was Andarion. Then he pulled out a pair of opaque eyeshields. Fully concealed, he took the container he'd scavenged from the assassins and waited for Bastien.

As soon as he was ready, they crept toward the shuttle where four men waited for their comrades to return with Dancer's head.

"So what are you spending your money on?" a large, grimy man asked.

"Women," his muscular companion said with a snort. "Lots of women."

"Always looking for the next ex, eh?"

"Always."

Dancer met Bastien's gaze. "Cover me."

He scowled at him. "Want to fill me in on your plan?"

"Told you already. Bust ass."

Oh, okay. Sounded like one of Ember's more infamous battle plans. Ill-conceived and guaranteed to get him shot.

But at least with her, she'd always kissed his boo-boos and made it up to him later. And while he was hornier than hell and Dancer was extremely attractive for a man, Bastien hadn't been alone quite long enough to want to bed down with another man.

Yet.

Though another hour with Dancer, enough alcohol and darkness, and he *might* be persuaded . . .

Dancer rose to his feet and walked calmly toward the group. A breeze stirred, whipping the end of his scarf out while he entered their camp.

Two of them rose with their hands on their blasters.

"Can we help you?" the largest one asked. From the

way the others deferred to him, Bastien assumed he must be their leader. His was also the voice he'd heard on the link, asking for a status update.

Without a word, Dancer tossed the container in his hand at the man. It landed at his feet, on its side.

"What's this?"

Bastien bit back a laugh. *Be careful what you ask, buddy. You might not like the answer.*

Dancer slid his gaze to each man around him in turn. "A gift."

Curious, the mercenary assassin knelt and opened the bag, then cursed as he saw the assassin's head it contained. He scrambled for his blaster.

Faster than Bastien could move, Dancer shot his three companions, before closing the distance between them. He snatched the blaster from the man's hand and pulled it back as if he was going to hit him with the stock. "Who sent you," he ground out between clenched teeth.

"W-w-what?"

Dropping the blaster, Dancer grabbed his shirt and shook him hard. "Who. Sent. You?"

Bastien came in, weapon drawn to make sure there was no one else in hiding. "Damn, Hauk. You're a selfish bastard. I thought you were going to leave some for me."

Dancer ignored him as he lowered the scarf to expose his face. With one hand, he dragged the assassin, who was now kicking and screaming, toward their skimmer.

"I'm a Boldorian! My guild brothers will swarm all over you for this!"

Dancer snorted in contempt of the threat. "Let 'em take a fucking number. Now answer my question or I'm going to start eating pieces off your body, *human*." He pulled the knife from his belt and isolated the assassin's thumb, but not before his gaze fell to the man's forearm and a series of self-imposed marks that nauseated Bastien even more than the man's stench. Those were an accounting for all the innocent lives the bastard had taken.

Some, Bastien noted, were for kids.

"We'll start with this, I think," Hauk growled.

He screamed like a bitch.

Grimacing, Bastien sucked his breath in audibly. "You know, friend, I'd tell the Andarion what he wants to know. They're not a patient race . . . and they're always, *always* hungry."

Sweat poured down the assassin's face as he gulped. "I-I-I don't know. I just have the ID code. That's all. I swear. You can see for yourself."

Bastien took over covering him while Dancer yanked the assassin's PD off his belt and turned it on.

Dancer cursed. "Cabarro? Can you read this?" He tossed it over.

Bastien took a second to look at it. "Yeah. It's the contract for your ass. Spill-kill. Bonus for your head. Damn, Hauk. If I could spend money, I'd be tempted to end you for this amount. Fain or no Fain."

Dancer shook his head, knowing Bastien wouldn't dare. "Does it say who wants me dead?"

"Nah. He's right. Just lists an anonymous ID for payment. If this armpit of the Nine Worlds had any reception, you might be able to backtrace it. But as it is . . ."

"See! I—" The man's words ended with a sharp blast to his chest.

Dancer stepped over his body.

Bastien handed him the PD. "You're one cold son of a bitch."

Dancer jerked the assassin's sleeve back to show the catalog of kills he'd carved into his flesh as proud tribute for all the victims he'd made.

Half of them were for women and children.

"He deserved worse."

Bastien shot the body three more times.

Dancer arched a brow at his actions.

Shrugging, Bastien holstered his weapon. "He deserved worse."

"Spend a lot of time in the sun, do you?"

More than he could imagine. Bastien laughed as Dancer went inside the skimmer to see if there was anything he could use to get away from any others who might come for him.

Or better yet, if they could fly it out themselves.

Unfortunately, it was low on fuel. And as he'd suspected, it was a preprogrammed skimmer used to take the assassins to and from their outer atmosphere spaceship. Which meant there were more of them waiting for this group to return.

Great. Just great. Leave it to a Hauk to rain down assassins on the head of his Ravin ass.

Bastien barely bit back a groan at this new nightmare. *Out of the frying pan and into the fryer . . .*

An alarm sounded.

"What'd you do?" Bastien asked sardonically.

Sighing, Dancer shot the control panel that housed the signal. It went instantly silent. "Must have been wired to the mission leader's vitals. It's an alarm to the mother ship notifying the others that they're dead."

Fected awesome . . . Bastien glared at the sky, expecting the enemy to start dropping in any second, given his luck. "How many you think are up there?"

"Don't know. But they're down twenty-nine men."

"Survivors will be glad they don't have to split that wide a cut."

Dancer grunted. "Boldorians won't care about that. It's

now an honor quest for them to come get me. With reinforcements."

"Really?"

He nodded. "You scared yet?"

Bastien let out a false laugh. "I'm hunted by League assassins for fun and promotion, and you think these backwater pussies scare me? Really?"

Dancer clapped him on the back as a sign of brotherhood. "When we get that chip out of you, if you need a place, The Sentella's always looking for good people."

Yeah, but that wasn't him. "I have some long-overdue payback to shove up someone's ass first. After that? I just might accept your offer."

Dancer confiscated arms, ammunition, and a radio before pulling back. He paused long enough to check the tracking device's broadcast frequency.

"What are you doing?" Bastien asked with a frown.

"Reprogramming this to their frequency. They land, talk to each other, and I can peg them as fast as they peg me."

Impressive, but he should expect no less from a Hauk. "You *are* Fain's brother."

"Taught him everything he knows."

Bastien arched a disbelieving brow.

Dancer grinned. "About electronics. He taught me fighting . . . usually by sitting on my ass until I got big enough to make it hurt when he tried."

Like him and Quin . . . and Lil. Honestly? He'd have fought Quin twice before ever tangling once with his sister. She hit three times as hard and was four times meaner.

"Ah." Bastien grabbed food and water. "So what's the plan now?"

"Pull back. Keep them after me and away from my family until reinforcements arrive." He pinned Bastien with a hard stare. "If I die, go out with a major body count."

"My kind of plan." And the kind that used to send Ember into apoplexy. Hence one mission when she'd shot him herself before battle even began to keep him out of the fray.

Not to mention the kind of plan that used to make his mother and sister break out in hives.

Dancer took a few minutes to siphon fuel from the two airbees on board the skimmer and add it to the ones they'd ridden in with.

Bastien hesitated, then realized that he might as well tell Dancer everything about his situation. After all, he had the only safe place for them to stay in the entire desert. There was no need in being selfish with it. "If you need a good defensive place to lead them to, there's an old abandoned base not that far from here where I make my home."

"Bredeh's?"

Bastien furrowed his brow. "You know it?" That stupid question was out before he could stop it. Of course Dancer would know it. Being a part of The Sentella and one of Nyk's friends, he'd probably been in with the run that had bombed it to oblivion.

"Yeah, I do. It's where I sent my family."

Should have known . . . And strangely, he had an odd feeling of being violated, knowing that there were strangers with his personal stuff. Not that he had much, but still . . . Been a long, long time since he'd shared a place with anyone else or had to worry about someone going through his things.

"Oh. Damn. Hope they don't find my porn."

Dancer arched a brow.

"I'm kidding. I have it all locked up."

Laughing again, Dancer shook his head. "You have been alone far too long."

Bastien sobered. "Yeah, I have. It's good to be around people again."

"Not people, human."

"Not human, either, brother. Lost my humanity a long time ago when I got betrayed into this hell of a life." Bastien glanced back to where they'd left the majority of the bodies. "The caves will give us some cover, but trap us in an attack."

"Yeah. We're in the middle of the great Oksanan desert. Not a lot here, period."

"Nothing but buzzards and raiders," Bastien agreed. "Look, I know you don't want to chance leading them to your family. But I'm thinking that we can use the old transmitter at the base to signal your girlfriend's transport back from the city."

Dancer went ramrod stiff at those words. "What do you mean?"

"The blonde who joined you? I couldn't really make out her features, but she came in locally, right?"

Dancer's demeanor turned darker. "You saw her arrive?"

Bastien nodded. "She was dropped off a little ways from your camp a few days ago. . . . You look like you had *no* idea."

Dancer didn't comment on that. "What all did you see?"

Bastien shrugged nonchalantly. "It was a small transport. Looked like it came out of one of the distant cities here. Didn't appear space-worthy. It lacked shielding and . . ." His voice trailed off as he met Dancer's gaze. "Why are you so pissed now?"

His breathing labored, Dancer curled his lip. "Because I think I just handed my kids off to my worst enemy."

CHAPTER 7

Once they'd returned to Dancer's camp, Bastien hung back with the airbees while Dancer walked toward the woman as if he could kill her. Though he had no idea why Dancer was this upset, given how many days they'd been here. Bastien had assumed they were long-time friends or family.

Obviously, that assumption had been wrong. There was something else at play here that he didn't know about. 'Cause that was one seriously pissed off Andarion, and he was grateful to God he wasn't the one who'd enraged him.

Dancer cornered the woman with a feral grimace that would have caused most folks to wet themselves instantly. To the woman's credit, she didn't flinch. She stood toe-to-toe with him.

"What have you done with them?" Dancer demanded in a deep, terrifying growl.

She appeared as confused by his anger as Bastien was. "What? The kids?"

"Darice! Thia!" Dancer shouted.

The moment they came into sight, Dancer ran straight

to them and jerked them against his chest as if he'd been terrified for them. He kissed each one on the head before he turned his angry glare back to the woman.

Feeling awkward, Bastien continued to hang back, out of the range of the Andarion's fury. Whatever distemper Dancer suffered from, he wanted no part of it.

"What's going on, Uncle?" the younger blonde woman asked. "Is everything all right?"

The rage on Dancer's face was tangible. "It is now." Dancer released the kids.

As the woman turned to meet his gaze and he finally saw her features clearly and up close, Bastien felt as if he'd been sucker-punched.

Damn . . .

This was some twisted shit.

"You two know each other?" Dancer growled.

She shook her head.

That woman might not know him, but Bastien knew *that* face. He'd seen it well the night he'd taken Fain home after his drunken bender that had almost caused them both to be jailed.

"Omira Hauk?" He scowled at Dancer, trying to understand just what kind of sick, psycho mind game he'd accidentally stumbled into. "What are you doing with your brother's ex-wife?"

The fury that darkened those Andarion eyes made Bastien step back—not out of fear, but so that he would have adequate room to defend himself.

Instead of coming for him, Dancer gathered the boy and girl, and put them on the airbee he'd been riding.

As the young blonde walked past, she cast Bastien a sweet little smile that left him a lot harder than he was comfortable with, considering their obvious age difference. While she was legal, it was ethically questionable.

But then, given how long he'd been without a woman, it didn't take much to "pique" his interest.

Still, she had a nice ass. Sweet face that was balanced with just the right amount of trouble-making seductress to lure any man, young or old, who had a taste for female companionship.

Damn, he felt bad for her daddy . . .

Suddenly Bastien realized that he was eyeballing a member of Dancer's family, and if he didn't stop, he'd be gutted.

Or de-nutted.

Dancer locked gazes with Bastien. "Get them to your base. And you better not betray me."

Offended that he'd even suggest it, Bastien glowered at him. "I would *never.*"

"Good. 'Cause that blonde whose ass you're ogling happens to be the most precious and beloved daughter of Nemesis. And he has only one rule for dating her . . . don't."

The color washed straight out of Bastien's face at the mention of one of the most notorious assassins ever born. The one lethal being who made League assassins wet themselves. "Your father's Nemesis?" he asked the young woman.

She sighed heavily. "On a good day, yes. On bad ones . . . let's just say you never want to be on the same planet with him. That includes me and he adores me."

Bastien returned his attention to Dancer. "Nothing, and I mean noth-thing, will happen to them."

"Good. Because if his daughter so much as stubs her toe on your watch, he will hunt you to the end of time, even if he has to come back from hell to do it."

Yeah, that was how the stories about him went. Bastien had no reason to doubt their validity.

"I don't take threats, Hauk. But this one . . . I consider a suggestion for my continued health and well-being. Thanks for the warning." Clearing his throat, he inclined his head at them. "Follow me."

He wasted no time getting them back to his base and stashing the airbees in an outlying shed.

As they left the small building and headed for his base, he finally took a second to introduce himself. "I'm Bastien, by the way."

"Darice Hauk," the boy said, proving that he was definitely a member of Dancer's family.

"Thia Quiakides."

Bastien froze at the girl's name. "Quiakides?"

She groaned out loud. "You know my father, too?"

Bastien snorted. "Never met him, but I know who he is." They were cousins, after all. But Nykyrian had supposedly died before Bastien had been born.

With the exception of Jullien, who'd kept Nykyrian's living-state a secret for both their healths and continued well-being, no one else in the family had ever been told that Nykyrian was still alive. Not until a few months before Barnabas had killed Bastien's immediate family and had him arrested for the murders.

Then Nyk had returned to resume his rightful place in the Triosan and Andarion empires with a vengeance. And Jullien had been thrown to the assassins.

Bastian started to say something to Thia about being cousins, but self-preservation kept him from it. He'd had enough family betrayal for one lifetime. Last thing he needed was to chance any more, and he didn't know these beings at all.

Better safe than a thousand times sorry. He was through being a doe-eyed innocent and having his balls handed to him by people he trusted.

As they neared the door, Thia slowed.

Immediately alert, Bastien pulled his weapon. "You see something?"

Tears swam in her eyes. Even though it was dark, they shimmered clearly. "This is where my mother died, isn't it?"

Crap . . .

He'd been so involved with his own concerns and pain, he hadn't even considered that. This had to be utterly devastating for her, especially given her tender age. Probably a decade or so younger than him, she was just entering adulthood, which meant she'd been a kid when her mother died.

Having lost his own family, he knew exactly how soul-wrecking this was for her. He couldn't imagine having to go through that loss at the age she'd have been.

Luckily, he caught himself before the words "don't think about it" slipped out of his stupid mouth. She wasn't a soldier. Wasn't used to compartmentalizing her pain. That alone had saved his sanity, though there were times when he didn't think he was sane anymore. Even more times when he was convinced of it.

But sane or not, he wasn't an insensitive jackass.

"I'm sorry, Thia."

With an admirable sniff, she pulled herself together. "I loved my mama, Bastien. I miss her a lot."

"Yeah, I get that. I still talk to mine in my head, every day." He pulled out his link and showed her the family photo that'd been taken during his last really happy memory. It was what he'd been holding on to through all this hell that had become his life. "I'd give anything to see my mother again. Tell her I wish I hadn't been such an ass when I was a teenager. Tell my dad that I wish I hadn't been such an ass, period."

She laughed at that. "Who's the dark-haired woman you have your arms around?"

His throat tightened at her question. "Ember."

"Pretty name. Your wife?"

Shaking his head, he clicked his link off and tried not to think about how many times a day he pulled that photo up to look at Ember and imagine other things he definitely didn't want to discuss with someone else. "Nah. I was never that lucky." He draped his arm around Thia's shoulders. "C'mon, I'll make you some tea."

"Tea?" Darice whined like a champ. "Gah! Do all humans drink that crap?"

"Be nice. I've got some Pleteigne for you, kid."

He perked up instantly at the mention of the sugary energy drink that was a favorite junk food on Andaria. The first time Jullien had brought it in, Bastien had panicked since the word translated to "human blood." But it was so named for the red juice that came out of a fruit that bore an odd human shape to it. Apparently, it was a delicacy in their empire.

"Pleteigne? How you get that here, human?"

"I have Andarion connections. My bud brings it to me whenever he happens this way. I got a case left from the last time he visited. Don't know how y'all drink that regularly. One can and I'm wired for days."

"'Cause you're human," Darice said proudly, puffing his chest out.

"For the record," Thia whispered to him, "if you shoot or preferably kill Darice, I'll tell Uncle Hauk it was an accident."

Releasing her, Bastien laughed. This was what he loved most whenever Jullien stopped in. Familial bantering and busting chops.

Unfortunately, he was so focused on them that he didn't realize his alarm had been tripped.

Not until he turned the dim lights on and met the angry faces of a band of Boldorians who were hiding inside his home.

Weapons drawn.

Ah, minsid hell . . .

Had he been alone, he'd have chanced their aim against his reflexes. But since more of the smelly beasts came in behind them, he thought better of it. Neither Thia nor Darice seemed particularly trained.

"Hands up!"

Bastien obeyed. "Do it, kids."

At least he knew Dancer would be coming in soon. If he could keep them distracted and their attention on him and away from the equipment, it would allow Dancer to get the drop on them.

As one of them came forward to pat him down and his hand trailed a bit too close to his cock, Bastien sucked his breath in sharply. "Hey, hey! Dinner first! No groping till you feed me! Don't know what you've heard, but I'm not a cheap date!"

That got him a rifle butt against the back of his head.

Son of a . . .

The force of the blow dropped him to his knees and almost rendered him unconscious. Only sheer force of will kept him semi-alert. But the ringing in his ears was quite special.

When they came forward to take Thia, she flipped the first one to the ground. Throat-punched the second one. And would have made it to the door had Darice not kicked his opponent into her and knocked her down.

Proving Bastien right with his earlier assessment of their skill level. While Thia had been trained in hand-to-hand, they weren't trained to fight as a unit. Damn shame, that. With Thia's skill, they would have stood a chance of escape.

Instead, they cuffed his hands and dragged him away.

Bastien glared at their captors. "You'd best not hurt the kids. You don't want to know who their parents are."

"The Andarion we're tracking."

"No. They're kidnapped Sentella children. The blonde belongs to Nemesis. The Andarion boy is his nephew. You harm them and he'll hunt you to the ends of the universe to gut you bare-handed."

"What about you?"

Bastien twisted so that he could grin into the older man's wrinkled face. "I'm just the idiot protecting them."

He ran Bastien's head into the desk. "Well then, you won't mind telling us about the Andarion we're after. And about this base . . ."

Was the *knættr* on something? You never asked a younger sibling anything about anyone. Bastien's older brother and sister had tutored him early on and well about the one basic sibling principle—*snitches get stitches*.

"Don't know nothing about the Andarion you're tracking. Ain't telling you shit about Shinola."

The grimy man stepped back to make room for one of his colleagues who could give Dancer a run for his money on gargantuan size. "We'll see how long that stubbornness lasts."

Bastien lost all track of time, as well as what it felt like not to be in excruciating pain. But as bad as this beating was, it paled in comparison to the torture sessions he'd gone through while in League custody. Hell, there had been times then when he'd considered confessing to killing his family just to get them to stop.

But he didn't have that urge tonight. Mostly because he knew that Dancer would arrive eventually.

Though why the bastard was dragging his ass, he couldn't even begin to fathom.

And then he heard it. . . .

Granted, he thought he was hallucinating at first. Good bet given the ringing that had yet to cease in his ears.

But there was no mistaking the next shout that came from upstairs. "Hauk!" a Bolodorian called out.

"What?" Dancer answered.

"Surrender or we're going to kill them all! Piece by piece, until their screams echo in your ears!"

Dancer laughed at the threat. "You do that and I will eat you, piece by fucking piece. The three of them are the *only* thing keeping you alive right now. Release them and we'll let you live. It's your choice on how you leave this place. On your feet or feet first. You have thirty seconds to decide."

Bastien let out a relieved breath. Finally . . .

It'd be over soon.

Or so he thought.

One of the assassins came in to take Thia. Bastien went for him, but that didn't last. Weakened by the beatings, he couldn't get his body to do what he needed it to.

He hit the deck hard. *Get up, you worthless piece of shit! Get on your feet!*

It was no use. Instead of rising, he felt the world go black.

Bastien wasn't sure how long he'd been out, but when he came to, both Dancer and his woman were in the room. Thia was holding on to Dancer like a lifeline while Sumi untied Darice.

The kid didn't move at all. Though unlike Bastien, he didn't appear to be harmed.

"Darice? Are you in shock?"

He blinked slowly as he scanned the room full of bodies and then looked to his uncle. It appeared as if he couldn't comprehend what Dancer had done. He frowned at Sumi. "But he works in IT."

She laughed at Darice's confusion. "He doesn't work IT, sweetie." Ruffling his hair, she cut Darice loose and went to check on Bastien.

He closed his eyes as she touched him and savored the gentleness she showed him. He hadn't felt the hand of any woman, other than the Andarion high priestess, on his body in years. And while he was a reprobate and Unira still attractive even at her advanced age, he wasn't willing to chance Andarion hell by making a pass at her.

If their Tophet was anything like their real world, he'd take the Kirovarian version of damnation any day over that.

"Is he alive?" Dancer asked.

"Yeah, but they beat him terribly."

Thia looked up at Dancer. "He refused to tell them anything about you or the base."

"Damn right," Bastien breathed, then groaned as he rolled himself over. Hissing, he grimaced. "Bastards hit like kindergarten girls. I think one of them even pulled my hair and said I had cooties."

Snorting, Dancer set Thia down next to Bastien. "I'm going to call for an evac." He placed every one of his weapons down beside them, except for his two personal blasters. He changed out their cartridges before he tucked them into his holsters. "Anything moves, shoot it with extreme prejudice."

Sumi dropped her gaze to Dancer's side and leg where he was bleeding profusely. "We need to tend those."

"Call first. I'll be back in a few."

"You're a stubborn beast, Dancer Hauk!" she called as he made his way to the door.

He turned back to grin at her. "You forgot to add sexy to that list."

"Nah, that might go to your big fat head!"

Laughing, he vanished into the hallway.

Darice still looked shell-shocked. "How did he move like that?"

Thia rolled her eyes. "Uncle Hauk *is* a war hero, Darice. One of the best of his breed."

Still lying on his back, Bastien turned his head toward Thia as he finally realized who Dancer had to be in The Sentella lineup. There was only one of those legendary warriors who could come into this base and wreak the destruction Dancer had. "He's Akuma, isn't he?"

Thia gave him a blank stare. "Don't know what you're talking about."

"Yeah, you do. But that's all right. He told me he was Sentella. Only one being I've heard of who's almost seven feet tall and fights like that. Damn." He laughed bitterly as he replayed their meeting through his head. "And here I offered to help *him*." His maniacal laughter ended with a sharp groan as pain tore through him with poison-laced talons.

Sumi moved to help him with his wounds as best she could. "Thank you, by the way."

Bastien scowled at her. "For what? Getting my ass kicked or bleeding on the floor?"

She jerked her chin toward the kids. "Keeping them safe."

Bastien quirked his lips as he considered it. Honestly? He'd enjoyed everything but the torture. "It's good to play hero again. Forgot how much I missed it."

Sucking his breath in sharply as she touched the cut

on his forehead, he growled at her. "Then again, this shit sucks! Gah, what was I thinking?"

Sumi ruffled his hair, then went to mind the other two while Dancer took his time with whatever he was doing.

Bastien rolled over and dragged himself to where he kept a few medical supplies. Sadly, he was out of pain-killers due to an injury he'd had a few weeks ago when he fell while trying to repair the roof. He'd sent a notice to Jullien to bring more on his next trip through, but no reply had come.

That wasn't unusual. Sometimes his cousin would be traveling dark and arrive before he had a chance to tell Bastien he was coming.

So he grabbed a bottled water and sat down to wait while Sumi chewed her nail and paced the room.

After a few minutes, Dancer returned. By the slowness of his movements, it was obvious he felt about as wonderful as Bastien did. With a smile, he touched Sumi's chin, then looked to Bastien. "Anything in this place you need?"

"Not really. Why?"

"We need to get going. Boldorians are pack bastards. In case they put out a beacon during this last round, I think it best we vacate."

Probably a good idea. Dancer was right about that. Where there was one, there were three hundred. Like cockroaches.

Bastien stood then fell back down when his legs buckled. "Well, ain't this a bitch? Could have sworn I was further from the floor than this a second ago."

Dancer snorted. He held his hand out and pulled Bastien to his feet against the protestations of Bastien's entire body.

They both grimaced in unison. He stepped away from Bastien. "Darice, help the man."

Darice did so without complaint.

Bastien took the shoulder he offered, and together they headed for the door.

Dancer paused to check on Thia. "You okay, *kisa*?"

It took Bastien a moment to mentally translate the Andarion word for *little sister*.

Her arms folded over her chest, she had a strange look in her eyes as she swept her gaze around the building. "Do you know where my mother died?"

Dancer winced at her question the same way Bastien had earlier. "Don't, baby."

Tears welled in her eyes as she glanced up at him. "Kiara won't ever talk about it. My father, either. I just want to know if she suffered much."

Pulling her into his arms, Dancer cradled her head with his hand. "No, baby, she didn't."

By the light in Dancer's stralen eyes, Bastien knew he was lying to the girl. But he admired him for not hurting her with the truth. And he understood exactly how Thia felt. He wondered the same thing about his own parents every day. Had they seen it coming?

Worse? He knew the answer about his siblings and their families. No matter how hard he tried, he couldn't purge the sight of either Quin or Lil from his mind. Nor the sound of the blaster that ended their lives.

It would haunt him forever.

Why, with all his training, couldn't he have stopped it?

Dancer placed a kiss to Thia's forehead. "Aksel owns enough of your soul. Don't let him take any more from you. He's not worth one molecule of your tears."

She hugged him then. "Thank you. For everything."

He nodded. "Love you, Thee."

"You, too." She kissed his cheek before she followed after them.

While they waited on Dancer and Sumi, Bastien siphoned the fuel from the airbee with the lowest tank into the next lowest one, knowing that it was the only hope they had of reaching what little civilization this backwater planet had.

Dancer came outside with Sumi to join them and handed Bastien a bag of additional weapons. "Did you get your things?"

He assumed Dancer meant his emergency bug-out pack. "Yeah."

"Good." Dancer pulled out a small handheld control, then pressed it. An instant later, the entire building blew apart.

Stunned and pissed, Bastien gaped indignantly as he watched what little he owned go up in a fierce explosion. "My porn! You Andarion bastard! You didn't tell me you were going to blow my shit up!" There was stuff in there he would have backed up and kept!

Stuff he needed to track his uncle.

Dancer cut a dry stare toward him. "Be glad I let *you* get out first."

Sighing, Bastien rolled his eyes. There was no need in attacking him over it or staying angry. It was done now and he had no place else to go. "You *are* Fain's brother. Just like him . . . bastard. All right, so what are we doing?"

"I'm taking the four of you to the Point, then coming back for Illyse. I'll be on the move until the others get here." He handed Bastien one of the trackers that was set to his TD. "Give this to Thia's father and they'll find me."

Bastien was confused until he realized that Illyse must be the name of the lorina they'd been traveling with. What with all the crap that had happened, he'd completely forgotten about the large black battle feline. Good thing Dancer had remembered.

Sumi moved to stand in front of Dancer. "I'm not leaving you. You're wounded."

"Let's argue about this later. We need to get out of here in case some of the Boldorians are around to see the explosion."

Bastien could tell she wanted to argue, but knew he was right. Safety first.

Sumi took the first airbee. Thia climbed on the back of hers. Bastien pulled himself on another, and Hauk took the third. Darice went to sit behind his uncle. When he wrapped his arms around Dancer's waist, Bastien saw the satisfied smile on Dancer's face. Obviously, the boy meant a lot to him. He patted Darice's arms then took off.

They followed him to a small oasis at the base of Mount Grenalyn. In spite of the desert climate, it was strangely lush and green, with a rapid stream that ran through it. In the early days of his fun-filled vacation here, this had been where Bastien came for fresh water and to bathe.

At least until he'd gotten the water running through the base again. Cold though it was . . .

Dancer parked and helped Darice off as they joined him. When Dancer started to leave them, Sumi caught his arm and held him in place. "You are hurt and bleeding. If you think for one second that I'm going to stand here and watch you leave without those wounds being tended, you're . . . even more insane than I think you are. And I *will* follow you."

Laying his hand against her cheek, he stroked her chin with his thumb. "I refuse to endanger you."

"You know, Dancer. Heroic is one thing. Moronic is quite another." She turned his airbee off. "Now get your ass over there, soldier, and sit!" She pointed to where Bastien was standing near Thia as she unpacked supplies. "And let me see how bad you're hurt. Then we'll revisit this whole death quest you seem to have."

Those orders choked Bastien as they reminded him so much of how Ember used to treat him. How much she used to love him.

Before he'd screwed up so badly.

Just change out the names and insults and it might as well be one of their old infamous arguments.

No one will ever love me like that again.

That was the hardest part about coming to terms with his current situation. And it wasn't melancholy or moroseness. He'd never trust himself to love anyone else the way he'd loved her.

Never be that open with anyone else ever again.

That innocent, trusting part of him had gone to the graves with his family. What was left now was more animal than man. Yeah, he could pass as a sentient creature. Use the right utensil at meals. But in his heart, he knew the truth.

Bastien Cabarro was dead.

He was only a wraith of the man who'd once believed in the goodness of others. The man who'd believed in justice and honesty.

Universe wasn't like that. It was harsh and unfair.

It sucked and didn't care for anyone. And he was done with it all.

Dancer shook his head at her. "You are so bossy. I'd eat anyone else who talked to me like this."

"Promises, promises. Now move!"

Yeah, that's exactly what Ember would have said.

Blinking back the sudden moisture in his eyes as he tried not to think about her, Bastien cleared his throat.

Hauk obeyed Sumi's orders, with a slow petulance that said he was only agreeing to make her happy. Bastien had been there, too. A woman had no idea how much control she had over a man when he loved her. There was nothing they wouldn't do to make their woman happy.

To see her smile . . .

It was what they lived for.

Growling low in his throat, Dancer slung his leg over the airbee and allowed her to lead him to a softer area near the water.

Lying down, Dancer stared up at the side of the mountain with a dark expression Bastien couldn't fathom. But it was obvious some demon was tormenting him.

Sumi sat down next to him and opened his shirt. She gasped at the sight of the wound across his ribs. "Dancer!"

He didn't speak as she cleaned it and continued fussing at him over it. And that too gutted Bastien.

How sick was it that he missed listening to his mother, sister, and Ember yell at him over his reckless disregard for his life? It'd been way too long since he was in the full-time care of someone who loved him.

She sat back and frowned at how many wounds lined his torso and arms. "You really need an MT, Dancer."

He squeezed her hand comfortingly. "I'll be all right."

She shook her head. "You're not invincible."

"Damn near."

She rolled her eyes at his arrogance. "Didn't at least one of them miss when they shot at you?"

He laughed then grimaced. "Yeah, I always wanted to be that hero in a movie where no one can shoot straight except me. Never happens. I seem to always walk into the school of award-winning sharpshooters."

Bastien knew that dream, as he had the same luck Dancer did. Never failed that he walked or landed right in the middle of the top graduates of some sick sniper academy.

In fact, that was what had caused his wingman before Ember to bug out of his company. One too many close encounters with death.

Dancer dropped his hand to the injury she had on her biceps. "You okay?"

"Told you. Flesh wound. Throbs, but I can handle it."

He smiled. "My tough *mia*."

Those words came out slurred as Dancer slowly drifted off to sleep.

Pursing her lips, she left him to come check on Bastien. His gut tightened immediately at her approach. For more than one reason.

The last thing he wanted was to have an Andarion male's female touching him. One thing he knew about their culture—they were insanely jealous and no one touched their women or children without permission.

So he tried to brush her aside.

Yet as with Dancer, she was insistent.

Bastien grimaced at her. "I've had worse from bar fights. Trust me. Beatings I can take."

"You sure?"

Bastien nodded. "Hand me a cloth and I'm fine."

She hesitated.

Glancing over to Dancer, he gave her a sardonic grin. "Sumi, I learned a long time ago, you don't touch or get touched by an Andarion's female. They get really hostile over it, and I'm not physically able to keep Hauk from killing me right now. So no offense, let's maintain at least a five-foot no-touch zone. 'Kay?"

She scoffed as she handed him the foil package that held an antiseptic cloth. "He wouldn't beat you, Bastien."

Yeah, right. Definitely not worth the bet.

"Not gonna chance it. In case it's escaped your notice, your male is a huge motherfucker. And I've had enough ass beating to tide me over for at least a month. . . . Maybe longer."

Shaking her head at him, she went to check on Thia.

Bastien lay for hours in silence, pretending to sleep. It was easier than being awake and interacting with a family. Because the way they teased and fought reminded him of everything that was forever lost to him, and it cut in a way he hadn't realized he'd been spared from. All this time, he'd cursed his Ravin status.

Right now, he was beginning to think it'd been a blessing. Over the years, he'd been focused on surviving. Finding food, and shelter. Making sure the perimeter was secured. He hadn't thought much about anything else. Even the times when he allowed himself to wallow had been few and far between. Some new threat or necessity had always cropped up to pull his thoughts to immediate survival.

It was so much easier to live that way than face the extreme loneliness he felt when he was around others.

A part of him was tempted to stay behind and rot here, but he couldn't do that. Not until he fulfilled the promise he'd made to his parents and siblings.

He wouldn't die or rest until he'd paid Barnabas back everything that was owed to him.

Everything.

And in spite of his trying to feign sleep, Sumi, Thia, and Darice pulled him into their circle. Before he knew it, they were trading old stories like long-lost friends.

In fact, Bastien was in the middle of one about Fain when Dancer finally woke up.

The laughter died on Sumi's face as her gaze met Hauk's. She got up immediately and rushed to his side. "How do you feel?"

"Like a guy who made a pass at Thia and Nyk saw it."

Laughing, Bastien grinned at Thia, who appeared less than pleased by his description. Obviously her father's overprotectiveness was a source of great irritation.

Sumi rolled her eyes. "You have one heck of a shiner. Who was tall enough in that fight to hit your face?"

"He wasn't. But the board in the bastard's hands gave him reach."

Bastien laughed again. He'd been in that fight a few times himself. A few of those times, against Fain.

Snorting at his humor, Sumi pulled out a bottle of water and then helped him to sip it.

"How long have I been out?" Dancer asked.

"A few hours."

He cursed. "I need to get going."

"No, you don't."

"Sumi . . ."

"Don't argue with me. I'm putting my foot down, Dancer. But if you attempt to leave, I'll be putting it up your ass."

He laughed then groaned.

Thia and Darice moved to stand behind her. She shoved at Darice. "Told you he wasn't dead."

"I knew from the snore he wasn't dead. I said he was *dying*."

Bastien brought over a small plate of food and one of the roots he'd managed to dig up that could take the edge off the pain. "If you took the punches I did, I know it'll be hard to chew, but . . . that root will minimize the pain."

"Thanks." Dancer set the plate down beside Sumi.

"C'mon, guys," Bastien said as he caught the gleam in Dancer's eyes and knew exactly where his thoughts were going and what the two of them would soon be doing. "Let's give them some quiet time."

Darice hesitated before he followed Bastien and Thia back to the small fire.

Hauk winced as he tried to chew the meat. Bastien was right. Eating was rough. "I need to go back for Illyse."

"We already took care of it." She gestured to the fire where the lorina was curled up and sleeping. "Bastien said you owe him a good night of drinking for the scratches she gave him."

Bastien ignored them as best he could while he entertained the kids and did his damnedest not to think about how incredibly long it'd been since the last time he had sex with someone else.

Thrāix was wrong.

The porn and sports networks did *not* alleviate that ache in the least little bit. Only a woman could ease this pain.

After a few minutes, Darice excused himself to take a bush break.

Thia slid closer to Bastien. "You're royal blooded, aren't you?"

Her question caught him off guard. "Pardon?"

"I can tell. Even though you're . . . a bit rough at the moment, you move like someone who's had royal manners and decorum beat into him from the cradle."

She was terribly astute. "Yeah, I was."

"What happened?"

"What always happens. Somebody gets greedy. Someone else gets stupid. Next thing you know, you put the wrong person at your back and you've got a knife sliding through your ribs."

"You sound like my father."

Given that they shared family, it made sense. The Triosans were famous for offing each other. Jullien had been right all those years ago with his warning. Damn shame he hadn't listened. Or thought to apply it to the Cabarro side.

As Thia excused herself, Bastien pulled his link out and turned it on. Dancer had called for a Sentella evacuation, and promised him that they could get The League tracing chip out of him.

If they could . . .

He glanced down at Ember's gorgeous face where she was staring up at him with the brightest laugh. Her green eyes twinkled. If he closed his eyes, he could still feel her hand on his face. Smell the faint trace of her perfume whenever he buried his lips in the valley between her breasts. Feel her hands tugging at his hair while he made love to her until they were both sweaty and spent.

Damn, how he missed her. His body hardened even more as his memories of her surged with vicious biting images that drove him to the brink of insanity until he feared he'd go crazy from testosterone poisoning. He wanted her back so badly he could taste her already.

Don't even think about contacting her.

She was most likely married with a couple of kids by now. Worse? She'd tell Alura he was alive—bypassing the records Jullien had forged that said he was dead so that Barnabas and the others would lax their guard and give him an advantage for taking them down. If Alura ever learned Jullien's report was false, she would run to his enemies with the news.

And yet a part of him was willing to risk it. That was the part of him that had always gotten him into trouble.

That part of him that loved Ember without reservation.

I'm not going to be stupid this time.

He'd get off this rock and get on with what needed to be done. His father had been right. It was time to start thinking with the head on his shoulders.

* * *

By the next morning, Bastien was only moving because of the roots he'd found. As soon as he heard Dancer stirring, he knew the Andarion would be in every bit as much pain as he was. So to be neighborly, he carried a root over to him.

Dancer glared at his approach.

Bastien grinned at the death he saw in Dancer's eyes. "Not enough root in the universe, eh?"

"Be glad my weapons are too far to reach or I'd shoot you."

With a groan of his own, Bastien sat down beside him. "Not a morning person, are you?"

"Fuck you."

Bastien laughed. "You're not my type and I'm not quite *that* desperate." He flicked playfully at Dancer's ear. "Though I have to say that you are awfully pretty for a male. If I were ever tempted, it'd probably be by someone as cute as you."

Dancer bared his fangs to him at the same time Sumi came over with a plate for each of them.

"Our fierce protectors." Her eyes danced with mirth. "You two don't look like you could take on a sleeping lizard this morning."

Dancer mustered a lopsided grin. "I have to say that I definitely felt better last night."

She blushed profusely.

Which made Dancer blush, too, as they all felt awkward over what the two of them had done last night.

Darice came running up to break the tension. "I saw a sparn this morning. Isn't this where they nest?"

Dancer hesitated. "Dari—"

"Can't I go with Thia while we wait?"

He shook his head. "That's a bad idea. Thia's no better at climbing than you are. I wouldn't trust the two of you at an indoor gym alone."

Darice's face swelled up immediately. "We're so close! It's not fair that I can't get my Endurance feather!"

Dancer's expression was every bit as despondent that he was having to say no. With his brow furrowed, he rubbed at his ribs as if he was actually considering taking the climb with his nephew.

Bastien was aghast. While Andarions were tough, that went straight into the realm of stupendously stupid.

Sumi looked up at the cliff in front of them. "What kind of climb are we talking about? Can it be done in one day?"

Dancer hesitated before he answered. "The main approach is just over there." He pointed to her left. "It's twelve pitches to the summit. Mostly face climbing with some corners and headwalls. There's a couple of gendarmes where sparns nest, so you shouldn't have to go all the way to the summit to get the feathers. The only hazard really is loose rock, and I wouldn't trust any existing anchors that you might find along the way." He locked gazes with her. "It's easily done in a day, barring an accident. . . . What are you thinking?"

"That I take him."

They all stared at her.

"What?" she asked in an offended tone. "League trained, folks. Head of my class. Before that, I was a xenobotanist. Been on many vertical expeditions in some frightening places. I can climb a mountain . . . building . . . dead body . . ." She cast a playful grin to Dancer. "Surly Andarions . . . no problem."

Dancer turned green and for a minute, Bastien thought he might hurl.

"Please, Dancer?" Darice begged. "Please! Please! Please! I'll do anything if you say yes! I'll even wash your boots. Sharpen your sword. Be your personal slave."

Dancer glanced to Sumi.

"You know I won't let anything happen to him."

Darice went down on his knees, crawling toward Dancer and begging as if he were in absolute agony. "Please, Uncle Dancer, please!"

With an irritated sigh, he nodded. "But!" He held his hand up to his overly excited nephew. "You lip off to her and she's to bring you right back down here. You understand me, Darice?"

"I'll be good. I promise! I love you, Dancer!" Whooping in delight, he shot to his feet and ran off to get ready.

Hauk pushed himself up with an even louder groan.

"You okay?"

He nodded at Sumi's concerned question. "I want to double-check the climbing gear."

"All right, Grandma."

"I also have the pitches diagrammed."

"That'll be helpful. Anything else?"

He pulled her against him and pressed his cheek to hers. "Don't get hurt."

Sumi smiled. "I won't let anything happen to Darice."

"Not just him."

"I know." She kissed his cheek before she pulled back. "Thia? You going with us?"

The look of horror on her face was priceless and comical. "Oh hell no. Peeing off the side of a mountain, listening to Darice moan and complain . . . I'd rather bring a date home to meet my dad—that would at least be entertaining until I had to scrub the blood out of my clothes." She gestured toward Bastien. "Think I'll hang at base camp and watch over the two males who don't whine like babies."

Sumi laughed. "All right."

While Sumi and Darice changed, Hauk checked the ropes, anchors, biners, harnesses, cams, hexes, nuts, slings, and belay devices, and packed them each a day sack.

When they returned, he and Bastien took a moment to help them gear up and double-check everything again.

Darice curled his lip. "Do I have to wear a full-body harness? Really? Dancer, I'm not a baby."

"If you invert on the climb, you'll thank me."

He made a sound of utter disgust in the back of his throat. And again when Dancer made sure everything was fastened properly to his sling. "Gah, Dancer. Really? I've been climbing since I was three. Stop, already!"

"Don't get arrogant. I had a lot more hours than you in a harness when I fell over four hundred feet, and your father had even more. Humor me."

Darice froze to stare at him. "What really happened on that climb?"

Dancer's eyes darkened with sadness. "The anchors and belay failed."

"Who was lead?"

"Your father."

Tears filled Darice's eyes. "Is that why you cut the rope?"

Bastien caught his slack jaw before it dropped as he realized that Darice was the son of Keris Hauk, who'd been killed right here.

For a moment, he thought he was the one who was going to hurl as he remembered the guilt and pain Fain carried over that event. The death of his older brother and near loss of his younger brother that fate-filled day was something Fain had never gotten over.

Until now, Bastien hadn't made the connection, and his respect for Dancer coming here again for his nephew increased exponentially. Damn, Dancer had to hate this place with a passion. And he had to love Darice even more.

Dancer winced. "I didn't cut the rope, Darice. I didn't have my hands free to do it."

He scowled. "I don't understand."

Dancer clenched his teeth. "We fell because your father hit me before I could finish tying in to the belay station. I slipped and the anchors failed until we were down to only one. I was inverted, attempting to right myself and hold on with one hand, while I was trying to steady Keris with the other." He showed Darice the scars he had from the rope burns. "My knot was coming undone and the last anchor was slipping. We both knew what was about to happen. Even so, I didn't stop trying to hold on for both of us. Next thing I knew, Keris pulled out his knife and sliced through the rope before I could stop him so that at least one of us would survive."

Darice fingered the scars on Hauk's hands. "You really didn't cut it."

"I would have died before I cut my brother loose."

Bastien had felt the same way about Quin. While they might have fought more than they ever got along, he'd have gladly died so that Quin could live. Every breath he took knowing it came at the expense of his brother and sister was absolute hell. The only thing worse than the grief was the guilt. If he lived to be a thousand years old, he'd never understand why he'd been spared his death sentence.

Surely the gods had intended him to be here for some higher purpose. Other than to torture him with the horror of it all. He refused to believe he'd been spared because of random luck.

He had to buy into that in order to get up in the morning

and not blow his brains out. Right or wrong, he firmly believed he was here to see justice met. For his family. There
could be no other reason that made sense.

Bastien met Dancer's gaze and they both knew that in
this pain and misery, they were bonded brothers. Each one
trying to find his way while lost in the guilted hell of their
pasts.

Darice wrapped his hands around his uncle's scars.
"You were my age when it happened."

"A few months older."

He threw himself into Dancer's arms. "I won't fall,
Uncle Dancer."

"I know you won't, Dare. And don't let Sumi fall, either."

Darice inclined his head to him. "I'll bring you back a
feather since you didn't get one when you came."

Dancer ruffled his hair. "Deal." He handed Darice his
climbing helmet.

Sumi offered Dancer a bittersweet smile as he met her
gaze. "We'll be very safe. I just need to get him a feather
to prove he made the climb and return here, correct?"

He nodded. "Remember, the sparn will attack if she
thinks you're going after her nest."

"Don't worry. You rest and we'll be back before you
can even miss us."

Dancer scoffed at her words. "Not possible. I miss you
already."

Thia came running to hand her bright pink helmet to
Sumi, and a pair of sport sunglasses. "Good luck. Try not
to strangle Darice."

Darice glared at her as he fastened his helmet on.

Bastien bit back a grin. For them to not be siblings,
the two acted as if they'd shared a room since birth. And
he could see the love they had for one another beneath

those barbs they traded. If anyone threatened Darice, Thia would be the first one to gut them.

"Thanks, Thia. You'll take good care of the guys while I'm gone, right?" Sumi fastened her helmet before Dancer rechecked her harness and sling.

She sighed heavily, but said nothing about his paranoia.

"Absolutely. Be safe." Thia kissed her cheek then moved to stand beside Dancer.

Sumi inclined her head to them and clapped Darice on the arm. "Ready, champ?"

"I'm your belay slave, *mu tara. Acrena tu.*"

"He said *after you*," Thia translated.

"Thanks." She led the way to the approach.

Dancer watched as Sumi and Darice began the climb.

Thia put her arm around his waist while he watched them. "It'll be fine, Uncle Hauk. You'll see."

He smiled down at her.

Bastien distracted himself with checking and rebandaging his injuries. Damn, he missed his family. What he wouldn't give to scandalize them one more time. To hear his sister's strident voice as she called for his parents to "sanction" him for abusing her dignity. Or Quin to ride his ass for being an embarrassment to their gene pool.

"One day, Bas, you're going to have kids. Are these really the stories you want floating around whenever you try to discipline them?"

"Well, Sa, I would behave, but at my age I hear you were neck-deep in a whorehouse, inciting riots."

Grinding his teeth against the agony in his heart, Bastien turned his back on the others.

Once they were out of sight, Dancer finally returned to sit and watch them through the scope in Sumi's rifle.

Bastien shook his head at the Andarion's actions. But then, he'd be even worse with his woman and nephew.

While Dancer watched, Thia went to gather rocks for her little brothers who'd been left at home. Apparently, that was the memento they wanted from the trip.

"So who was the first mother hen? You or Fain?"

He dropped the scope to glare at Bastien. "Meaning?"

"You two are so much alike. It's actually scary."

Dancer didn't comment. And as Sumi and Darice vanished completely from his sight, he cocked his head. "What was that?"

Bastien scratched at his chin, wishing he had a decent razor. "What?"

"That sound?"

"I don't hear anything."

Thia stood. "I do. . . . Someone's coming."

Dancer moved to draw his blaster, but before he could, three darts went into his chest.

Bastien went for his. Like Dancer, he was hit before he could reach his weapons. The paralytic was fast and vicious. Within a few heartbeats, everything went black.

CHAPTER 8

Bastien came awake with a foul curse to find himself inside a steel cage with Dancer and two other human men he'd never seen before.

And of course, Dancer appeared to be in the middle of a fight with a human female who stood outside the cage holding a long electrified pole. Two similarly dressed women were behind her.

"See." She balanced the pole on her shoulder and swept her gaze over the other two women. "And we have a problem. Andarions eat humans. Raw. Leave him in that cage and he'll devour the others."

Bastien laughed at the thought as the two men behind him began to whimper and whine like babies.

Dancer ignored them. "Let me go and I'll leave here without any drama."

The blonde woman tsked at him. "It doesn't work that way, cutie. You have too big a bounty on your head. Eat the others if you must. You're worth a lot more than they are."

Bastien arched a brow at her nonchalant offer. Fabulous. They were assassins as well as slavers. Just what they needed. Only good news was that they hadn't realized Bastien was worth as much, if not more, than Dancer.

Dancer glared at the women. "I *will* get out of here, and when I do—"

"Don't make me kill you, Andarion. While you have one hell of a bounty on your head, I'm thinking there are a lot of people who'd pay a fortune to have an Andarion slave." She raked his body with a hungry smirk. "Now be a really good boy and I might send you off with a smile on your face."

He exposed his fangs to her. "You're really going to let me eat your heart?"

She scoffed. "Watch them, Pheara!"

Dancer grabbed the bars over his head and used his entire body weight to kick at the door again.

Bastien cringed and braced himself for impact as he realized what Dancer intended.

The other two women took three more steps back.

Eyes wide, the woman named Pheara gulped. "I don't think that's going to hold him, Telise."

"If he kicks it open, blast the shit out of him. Price-wise, given the scars and wounds already on him, it won't matter if he's banged up a bit more."

Dancer took that insult with a roar. He pressed his face between the bars to glare at Telise. "When I get out of here, I'm going to feast on your organs."

She pressed the prod to his stomach and blasted him.

Dancer growled and somehow managed to stay on his feet, glaring at her.

That succeeded in putting fear in the *harita*'s eyes.

Unsettled, she stepped back and turned toward her friends. She handed the prod to the smaller of the two. "If he gets out, open fire and call for backup."

Oh yeah, 'cause *that* always worked. Especially against an Andarion.

Dancer fanged them again. "Hey!" he called to the two who eyed him like the vicious predator he was. "There was a woman with me. Where is she?"

Pheara cleared her throat. "We took her weapons and left her where she fell. Why? Is she yours?"

"My niece, and if any harm comes to her, I swear by every god who protects Andaria that I will rain down a hell on you so severe you will beg me for the mercy of death." He kicked the door again.

They backed up.

"I'm going for more guards." Pheara took off running, leaving the other woman to watch them with a bug-eyed stare that would be hysterical if Bastien wasn't so enraged.

Dancer turned toward the men behind him. They shrank away from him as if terrified he really would eat one of them. Dancer grimaced at the typical human reaction to his kind.

Bastien shook his head at their unwarranted fear. "Don't worry. We fed him earlier. He's not hungry. Right, Hauk?"

He glared sullenly at them all. "Feeling a bit peckish, suddenly."

That only frightened them more.

Bastien sighed at his irascible companion. Must be an Andarion thing. Fain was the same way, and Jullien set the universe's record for the shortest fuse—as most likely to agitate any situation, anywhere, anytime.

Returning to the door, Dancer eyed the woman with menace. When he went to kick it again, Bastien stopped him. "Why don't we try something a little less violent and more productive, my large Andarion friend?"

Dancer scoffed. "Blood. Mayhem. Violence. That's my go-to happy place."

His too, but right now that seemed like a profoundly bad and highly unproductive idea that might get one or both of them tranqued again. And given how badly Bastien's head hurt, he wasn't keen on taking another hit of their sleeping juice. "How 'bout we try to find a new one?"

"Such as?"

He plucked a wire out of his cuff that he kept for just such rare occasions. "Picking the lock."

"I'd rather kick it open."

"You would." Bastien snorted. "How 'bout we save it for beating on our captors?"

Ignoring him, Hauk kicked the door again.

Bastien jumped back as he saw the dart come flying toward them. It struck Dancer in his arm.

And was quickly followed by three more.

To his credit, Dancer glared at the women who joined the first one. He fought against the drug's effects with everything he had, but in the end, he blacked out.

Bastien tsked at him. "And that's why I said don't do it. Don't envy you the headache you'll be having when you wake up . . . dumbass."

Dancer came to again, cursing life and everyone in it. Most of all, he cursed the irritated smirk on Bastien's face as he eyed him from where he lay on the ground beside him.

"Told you not to kick that door, didn't I?"

Dancer ignored his sarcastic taunt. But the expression on his face said he wanted to make Bastien eat his own teeth.

He tried to move, only to discover that he, like Bastien, was in the middle of their camp, on his belly and hogtied. All courtesy of the little fit the Andarion had thrown. They'd also chained their hands to their feet behind their backs.

If I get out of this alive, Hauk, I'm so going to kick your ass.

With a lot of help.

Growling, Dancer tried to break free.

Bastien rolled his eyes. Like that was going to work . . . and like he hadn't already had his own hissy fit and learned it was a bad idea. Hence their current undignified situation. "Calm down, Hauk. All you're going to do is hurt yourself."

He glared at Bastien. "If you want to see exactly how angry someone can get, tell them to calm down when they're already pissed off!" Bellowing, he tried his best to break free.

Bastien arched a brow at his insistence on being stupid. "Is that helping? I just gotta know."

"When I get loose, Cabarro, your ass is the first one I'm kicking."

"Oh good. Hope you get out soon. Been a while since I had a good ass-kicking." Bastien made a kissy face at him.

"Says the man who's so bruised, he looks like a two-year-old banana."

"Now that's just mean and hurtful."

"Telise! He's awake again."

She moved forward and kicked Dancer in the face.

Bastien cringed at that particular brand of imbecile. "I wouldn't do that," he warned. "Don't motivate the Andarion for murder. It ain't going to work out well for any of us. 'Specially me, since mine's the first ass he's planning to come after. Let's all calm down, people."

Dancer licked at the blood on his lips as he grimaced at the *harita* through his braids.

"Learned anything yet?" she asked him.

He spat the blood out of his mouth. "Other than those pants make your ass look fat?"

Bastien had to bite back a laugh. Ah, man, the Andarion wanted to die painfully.

She kicked him hard in the ribs.

That was actually kinder than Bastien had expected given the severity of *that* insult. 'Cause he knew what his sister would have done had he ever made the mistake of saying *that* to her and he didn't even want to contemplate what Ember would have done to him.

Suddenly, a blast of color shot within an inch of Telise's face. "Touch him again and the next one goes right between your eyes."

Sumi! Thank the gods. Someone with a brain Dancer would finally listen to.

Telise reached for her blaster.

Sumi let fly a shot straight into her shoulder. "Hands up or lose your head."

Telise glared at her. "You don't know who you're dealing with."

"Neither do you." Sumi held her hand up to show the brand on her wrist that told them all she was a trained League assassin.

Bastien's jaw dropped as he realized he'd been helping his enemies.

Again.

Fuck me. . . .

And with *that* revelation, he vaguely recalled her mentioning that she was League trained before she took off with Darice for their little adventure up the mountain, but with his thoughts on Ember, it'd blown right past his attention.

Now, too late, he remembered that vital detail. Shit! That kind of carelessness could cost him his head.

He was lucky Sumi hadn't already gutted him.

"Unless you've got another League assassin in your camp, I suggest you free them, or I *will* bathe in the blood of every whore here."

Bastien saw one of the others coming up behind Sumi. With the expert training that marked all her breed, she spun and shot the woman, then caught another one he hadn't seen at all.

And her blaster wasn't set to stun. She killed them both without flinching.

I'm so screwed. Bastien saw his future and knew he wouldn't make it out of this alive.

Sumi now had both weapons drawn as she surveyed the women. "Anyone else want to die today?" she called out to them. "Please! I'm so in the mood for it." She turned back to Telise. "What about you, *harita*?"

Glaring at her, Telise reached into her pocket. Instead of keys, she drew a dagger and moved for Dancer.

She was dead before she took more than a step.

When one of them started running for cover, an explosion rocked the camp and drove the woman to the ground.

Sumi tsked. "I have charges set all over this place. Enough to blow us all to the outer atmosphere. Don't push me, people. Now who wants to be my friend and free my male for me?"

Pheara came forward with the keys. She kept her hands out so that Sumi wouldn't mistake her intentions. "We weren't going to hurt him."

Sumi stalked forward. "Then why's he bleeding?"

She swallowed hard. "Telise did that. We . . . we had nothing to do with it. Just take him and go." She freed Dancer, then Bastien, and stepped back.

Dancer pushed himself to his feet and retrieved Telise's blaster from her body.

Sumi's gaze skimmed him from head to toe. "You okay, baby?"

He shot two of the women with a stun blast. "Better now."

"Bastien?"

Not sure why she hadn't taken him into custody, or killed him, he wiped at the blood on his wrists. "All good. At least until Hauk keeps his promise to beat my ass."

Or Sumi decided to get a rank advancement by taking his scalp.

Sumi turned back to Pheara. "Where are our weapons?"

Pheara gestured toward Telise's tent. "In there."

"I'll get them," Bastien offered. The sooner he had a means to protect himself, the better he'd feel.

Moving so that her back was against Dancer's, Sumi kept her gaze on the women until Bastien came back and belted his holster around his hips.

He tossed Dancer's weapons to him, and made sure to keep his senses alert to what Sumi was doing and where she was positioned. He was not about to go down without a fight. Ever.

And given how Hauk felt about his woman, Bastien would most likely have to take them both out to save his own ass.

"Before we leave, I want to do something." Dancer went to Pheara and jerked the keys from her hand. "Is this the biofeed bypass?"

"Yeah."

He met Sumi's curious gaze. "Round the women up and follow me."

"You heard him. *Haritas* on parade. Let's go." Sumi

and Bastien, making sure to keep Sumi in front of him, followed Dancer to the cage where the other two men were being held.

Dancer opened the door and released them before he made the six remaining women file inside it. He locked the door and tossed the keys to one of the men. "Happy birthday."

And with that, Dancer draped his arm over Sumi's shoulders so that she could lead him away while Bastien stayed to the rear. While Dancer might trust an assassin at his back, Bastien wasn't about to, now that he knew who and what she was.

That being said, though, she didn't seem concerned about him at all. Maybe Dancer hadn't told her he was Ravin and maybe she didn't know.

Even so, Bastien had no intention of dropping his guard now that he knew who and what she really was. He had no desire to die. Today, at least.

"Where are the kids?" Dancer asked.

"Armed to their teeth and hiding with Illyse."

Dancer nodded. "Good."

Sumi smiled until she noticed Dancer wasn't completely with them. He'd started swaying a bit and looked unsteady on his feet. "Dancer?"

He tightened his grip on her before he kissed the top of her head. "I'm all right."

"You don't look good." She pressed the back of her hand against his cheek. "You're very clammy."

"They drugged him," Bastien said from behind them. He figured it was just a matter of time before Dancer went down again.

"With what?"

Bastien shrugged. "Really didn't get a chance to ask what they were using, or for any other recipe, either. But

I would assume something strong enough to take down a huge-ass Andarion."

Hauk ignored him while he tugged her forward. "Thank you, by the way."

"For what?"

He gave her a shaky smile. "I'm usually the one doing the rescuing. It's been a long time since anyone's pulled my ass out of the fire." His words slurred an instant before he sank to his knees.

Shit . . .

If he went down, it would be a massive bitch to handle his weight.

"Dancer!" She knelt by his side.

He held on to her, but didn't seem to be able to speak.

Bastien glanced over his shoulder, hoping they weren't being followed, then met her gaze. "We need to get out of here before they give pursuit. You take one arm and I'll grab the other."

And God help them both, 'cause this bastard weighed a ton.

He reached for Dancer.

Suddenly, a deep, growling male voice came out of nowhere. "Hands up or die."

Sumi bit her lip in indecision. Bastien saw the same desire to fight their latest attackers in her eyes that he held. But they didn't know who or what they were facing now.

Or how many.

A flash of color narrowly missed her face. She glanced around, but couldn't see anyone, any more than he could. Their attackers were using some kind of cloaking device.

Bastien cringed as his worst fear manifested. This group of assassins was much higher-tech than the previous ones. Most likely, they were League and had yet to realize she was one of them.

He ran every scenario he could think through his mind.

All ended with him dead, maimed, or captured.

If only he had some way of knowing how many were there and where they were located.

Without those two things . . .

He was screwed.

Slowly, Sumi held her hands up and put her body between Dancer and Bastien, and where that one shot had originated.

Bastien frowned at her actions. Why would she protect *him*?

"Look," Sumi said calmly, "we don't have much. Take whatever you want. Just be quick about it. We need to tend our friend. He's badly hurt."

Bastien felt the burn of a stun blast. *Mother fussing at a son!* His nervous system fried, he dropped and took Dancer with him.

With a gasp, Sumi turned to help them.

Something flickered on the other side of Dancer.

Sumi launched herself at that small betrayal of an attacker.

Until she was lifted off her feet by someone standing behind her.

"No!" she screamed, trying to break free of the man's hold. "He's unconscious. He's no threat to you. Please, just take our supplies and go!" Shrieking in anger, she picked all her weight off her feet.

The man holding her didn't even flinch or stumble.

Damn, he was strong.

Bastien tried to fight, too, as he felt the blaster's effects weakening, but he was cuffed so fast, it was terrifying. No one had ever been able to do that to him—other than Ember, when he was naked and cooperating. He growled unintelligible threats and spewed Kirovarian profanity at them.

"Please!" Sumi begged. "We just want to help our friend."

Another shimmer appeared next to Dancer as the soldier turned his cloaking device off to show an unmarked black battlesuit.

Not League, but that didn't make for something better by a long shot.

The soldier shrugged off his backpack and removed his helm to reveal a man with long dark hair tied back into a ponytail. His dark Ritadarion eyes were ringed with black eyeliner, and he had the mannerisms of someone used to taking lives and saving them.

Sumi swallowed hard. "Syn?"

The Ritadarion scowled at her. "I don't know you."

She looked over her shoulder. "Nykyrian? Are you the one holding me?"

Syn opened his pack. "How do you know us?"

"Dancer."

"Are you Sumi?" That was the voice that had originally threatened them when they stopped.

"Yes."

He released her immediately and decloaked. He gestured to Bastien, who was fighting against the cuffs that held him. "Is that one Bastien?"

"He is."

Another man, who was standing beside where Bastien lay on the ground, decloaked. Kneeling down, he uncuffed Bastien's hands. "Sorry about that."

Glaring his displeasure, but grateful that the stun blast had been mild, Bastien cursed him and his parentage as he rubbed his wrists.

Amused by the insults, the man pulled off his helmet. His short red hair held the royal harone of the Caronese emperor, and it was a face Bastien knew well, as they'd once gone to school together.

Darling Cruel.

The prick who'd started The Sentella's war with The League. That meant the still-helmeted man next to Sumi was definitely Nykyrian.

Bastien took a moment to survey the man who was both a living legend and his unknown cousin. Equal in height to Jullien, he was a bit leaner.

But no less badass judging by that I'll-kick-your-ass-and-mean-it stance that seemed as ingrained as breathing. No wonder Thia didn't date.

Yeah, *that* would be worse, and even more intimidating than meeting Ember's father and mother for the first time.

Bastien's gut knotted at *that* fun memory. It was never a good idea to date the daughter of someone trained to kill and hide bodies.

Never mind *two* such parents. The only thing more frightening than Ember's father had been her Riot Squad mother, whose reputation for cold-blooded ruthless military prowess was second only to Nykyrian's.

Sumi ran to Dancer and knelt beside him. "He said they drugged him with something while they held him. He was poisoned two days ago from a Partini blade and he has several injuries from other attacks."

Damn, Dancer was having a worse time than Bastien was.

Syn gaped in disbelief. "What the hell did you do to him?"

Sumi glared indignantly. "I've kept him alive."

Nykyrian pulled his helmet off and held it under one

arm. His white-blond hair was cut stylishly short and slicked back. Like Jullien before he'd gone stralen, he had green, human eyes and his face was covered with scars. A face that was so similar to Aros's it made Bastien wonder how no one had ever made the connection they were father and son. You'd have to be blind to miss it.

"Where's my daughter and Darice?"

Sumi jerked her chin toward the mountain range. "They're hiding near camp, with Illyse. There's a cave just to the south of the climbing approach."

Inclining his head to her, Nykyrian spoke into a link that was attached to his ear. "Jayne? We've secured Hauk. The kids should be near the base camp that we found earlier. I'm leaving Syn and Darling here with Sumi and Bastien. I need you for support while I go after Thia. Everyone else, stay where you are at camp and make sure no one goes near my kid. If they do, make them bleed hard." He headed off at a dead run for a cloaked airbike.

Impressed, Bastien continued to glare at Darling. "Are we good yet? Or do I have to don my ass-kicking boots and leave imprints some place you're not going to like?"

Darling glanced to Sumi. "Don't know. Are we good?"

Before she could answer, Dancer blinked his eyes open. "Sumi?" he whispered hoarsely.

Leaning over him, she placed her hand on his cheek. "Right here, baby."

Darling and Syn exchanged a shocked, exaggerated gape as Syn pulled out a light and checked Dancer's eyes.

With a savage hiss, Dancer shoved the light away. "Put that away or I'm going to ram it someplace both you and Shahara will curse me for."

"Dancer," she chided. "Let him tend you."

He started to grimace then pressed his lips together. "I hate that damn light. It burns."

Now it was Darling's turn to pull Dancer's eyelid back to see his eye.

Dancer grimaced and punched at him.

Laughing, Darling took it in stride. "You look like hell, buddy."

"You ain't no beauty queen, either. Asshole."

Darling grinned in bitter amusement. "You better take a nicer tone. I walked out on my wife and son to be here for you to insult me."

Dancer frowned at him as he rubbed at his eye in a very adorable boyish fashion. "Zarya had the baby?"

"Last night. About half an hour before Nyk called to say you were in trouble."

Dancer scratched at his head. "Sorry."

"Don't be. About time I get to save you, and don't think I'm not holding your impeccably inconsiderate timing over your head for the rest of eternity. You will be paying for this, that I promise. By the way, Zarya wanted me to tell you that you better get back home and see your nephew or she'll hunt your hulking ass down and skin it."

Sumi touched Syn's hand to get his attention while he evaluated Dancer's condition. "Someone planted a tracking device in Dancer's back. We've had incas coming after him for days."

Nodding, he tilted Dancer's head toward him. "You with me, buddy?"

With an irritable grimace, he slapped at Syn in a way that reminded Bastien of a little kid with a playmate who was annoying him. "I'm thirsty."

Syn pulled a bag out of his pack and handed it to Darling, who held it up while Syn prepared the IV.

When Syn stuck the needle in, Dancer hissed and started for him.

Sumi caught his fist. "Dancer, play nice with the doctor who might not want to help you if you clock him."

He calmed instantly and nuzzled his face against her knee. When she went to brush his braids from his cheek, he took her hand and laced her fingers with his.

Bastien had to look away as that tenderness reminded him of memories he couldn't afford.

Until he heard the sharp click of a blaster from behind Sumi.

Syn didn't react at all. "Put it away, Jayne. She's a friendly."

"You sure?"

He gave her a droll stare. "I've never known Hauk to cuddle an enemy. You? I mean, he is weird and all, but he's usually consistent with his surly demeanor."

Jayne decloaked and moved forward to join them. "What happened to him?" She pulled her helmet off to show Bastien one hell of an attractive woman. Long-legged. Brunette. She reminded him of Ember's sister Kindel, except she was a bit taller, and her dark hair was straight.

There was also something about her that reminded him more of the Andarions than humans. Yet she didn't have any of the telltale markers that normally defined those born of their Ixurian race.

Syn sighed heavily. "He's got enough toxins in his system that if he were human he'd be dead ten times over. Thank the gods Andarions are tough bastards."

"Is he going to be okay?" Sumi breathed.

Syn finally met her gaze. The anger there dissipated into kindness. "Yeah. I think so. Unless something has happened to Thia, in which case we'll be scraping up his guts as soon as Nyk returns."

Jayne continued to glare at her. "Who the hell are *you*, human?"

"Jaynie," Dancer said weakly, "be nice to my girl or I'll turn her loose on your hide. Trust me, I think she can take you."

Jayne scoffed as she squatted down beside Hauk and touched his shoulder. "What happened to your eyes?"

A knowing smile curved Syn's lips. "I think Hauk got around to taking your advice, Jayne."

"What advice?"

Syn glanced at Sumi, then laughed. "I'll tell you later."

Bastien laughed at the fact that Dancer must have gone stralen on this trip, judging by the way they were acting.

Darling frowned as he finally looked over at Bastien, who'd opted to sit quietly and bleed as unobtrusively as possible while Syn tended Dancer. "Do I know you? You look really familiar."

Considering how many years they'd gone to school together, he should know, but then Darling had always been preoccupied by other things—like survival. And, too, Bastien was a couple of years older than him, so they hadn't been in any classes together. He was actually closer to Darling's older brother's age than Darling's.

So Bastien wouldn't judge him for not recalling him from their school days together. Not to mention, Bastien didn't look like himself right now, covered in grime with a shitty haircut and the kind of beard normally worn by people hovered over a flaming barrel for warmth.

Even so, he started to blow it off with a joke, but then opted for truth as he stretched out on the ground. With a smile, he brought up the last time they'd been together. "Summit meeting. Years ago. I was with my father. You were with your uncle."

Recognition lit Darling's eyes. "You're the one who decked Nylan's son when he spat in my food."

"Don't remember that, particularly, but it sounds like something I'd do. Hate that rank bastard."

Darling shifted to study Bastien's ragged condition. "You're one of the Kirovarian princes."

"Was."

"Holy shit. I thought you were all dead." Darling met Jayne's gaze. "He's one of Nyk's paternal cousins, who was deposed about a decade ago."

Suddenly, Syn grabbed Sumi's wrist and shoved her sleeve back to expose her League brand. He drew his blaster faster than she could blink and held it to her jaw.

Dancer knocked it away. "Stop it!"

"She's a League assassin."

"Yeah, I know. Kyr sent her after me. Remind me to order him flowers and a thank-you card later."

Syn, Darling, and Jayne exchanged a scowl that was probably quite similar to the one Bastien felt on his own face.

"You know?" Jayne asked.

Dancer sat up slowly.

"Whoa, buddy." Syn held him back. "You need to stay down until we get a lift here for you."

Dancer hesitated before he stretched out again, only this time, he put his head in Sumi's lap. "Jaynie? Darling? Don't let anyone hurt my *mia*. Or I'll take it out of both your asses."

Darling arched his brows. "Look, bud, I know you're drugged out of your mind, but you are aware that Sumi's human, right?"

Dancer shoved at Darling. "Don't insult my female by putting her in the same class as *you*."

Jayne arched a brow. "How much crap have you given him, Syn?"

"That ain't my drug, baby. That's called l-o-v-e."

Jayne scoffed. "Hauk? Love? Lorina shit."

"It's true. That's why his eyes are red," Darling said to her. "Can't hide or deny *that*."

Syn injected something into the IV.

Dancer shoved at him. "Why did you do that?"

"You need to rest."

Dancer grabbed the front of Darling's battlesuit. "Keep Sumi safe for me. Don't let anyone harm her. Swear . . ." He passed out.

Sumi caught him against her and laid him down gently.

They all three stared at her as if she was a three-headed Gourish snake.

"What?"

Without answering her, Syn moved to check on Bastien.

Darling continued to hold Dancer's IV.

"Jayne?" Syn called. "On my twelve, babe."

She came over to him, leaving Sumi alone with Darling while she knelt down to assist Syn.

Bastien held his breath, trying really hard not to breathe in her perfume. "Hard" being the operative word he was also trying to not think about.

Damn his body. And damn him for having gone so long without a woman that being this close to one was practically killing him.

Trying to distract himself any way he could, Bastien focused on what Darling and Sumi were talking about.

"So what did you name your son?" she asked.

"Cezar."

"Congratulations. I know Dancer will be thrilled to meet him."

Darling shook his head. "And he lets you call him Dancer, too . . . damn. He really must love you."

"It's a beautiful name," she said defensively.

He scoffed. "Says the woman who didn't have to go to school or into League training with it. Take it from someone named Darling, it's been a constant source of agony for him the whole of his life."

Sumi paled. "I-I didn't mean to hurt him with it."

Darling covered her hand with his. "Trust me, given the way you say it, he doesn't mind. If he did, he'd stop you. Tolerance is *not* one of his virtues."

Bastien would definitely agree with that statement. He had yet to meet an Andarion with much tolerance for anything.

"Little Sumi?"

Bastien's jaw went slack at the unexpected appearance of Fain Hauk. St. Jake . . . it'd been a long time, but his old friend looked good. Healthy. A lot more mentally stable than he'd been back in the day.

Fain was a huge beast of a creature—even larger than Dancer. And like his younger brother, he had traditional Andarion warrior braids, too, except a portion of his had been bleached white and he was dressed in Tavali gear with one of their masks hanging loose around his neck.

Bastien frowned as he vaguely recalled seeing some of their gear with Fain back in the day. Weird that he'd never thought to ask Fain about it, nor had he assumed Fain to be a member of their outlawed guild since it was a death sentence in most empires to be caught with any Tavali markings, Canting, or gear.

Including Kirovar.

But unlike Jullien, who was part of the Tavali Gorturnum Nation and had a black bug-looking Canting, Fain had a solid red sleeve badge, which meant he was a Rogue pilot. Someone who owed neither tithe nor allegiance to any single Tavali Nation.

Bastien dipped his gaze to see that even after all these years, Fain still wore Galene's engagement ring around his pinkie. While he might have married Omira, Galene Batur was the one female alive who'd always owned Fain's heart.

Like Bastien with Ember. She would always be the one who'd gotten away. The one he regretted losing.

Sumi turned around slowly.

And the pain on Fain's painted face was tangible. He stared at her as if she were a ghost whose sole purpose was to haunt him.

Darling glanced back and forth between them. "You two know each other?"

"I was married to her older sister." Fain blinked as if finally getting a handle on the fact that she wasn't Omira and that she meant him no harm.

Jayne smacked her hand against her own forehead. "That's why she looks so familiar. I knew I recognized her from somewhere. Stupid me. I was thinking bounty sheets, not Fain's wife."

Fain's gaze dropped to Dancer's head in Sumi's lap. In that moment, Dancer blinked his eyes open as if he felt his brother's presence. Guilt and anguish marked his features as he realized how this must look to Fain.

Moving forward, Fain dropped to his knees next to Dancer. "Hey, *drey*. You still with me?"

Dancer scowled. "I'm sorry."

"For what?" Fain asked in a shocked tone.

He glanced at Sumi then back to Fain. "I never meant to hurt you."

Fain cupped Dancer's head in his hands. "Dancer . . . this doesn't hurt me." He gave him a sincere smile. "You deserve to be happy, *kiran*. It's all I've ever wanted for you." He dropped his hand to Dancer's then he took Sumi's into his other hand and joined them together. "Don't let my past darken or taint *your* future. I love both my *kisa* and *kiran*. I always have."

Even so, Bastien saw the ragged torment in Fain's eyes. It was a pain he knew all too well himself.

"I'd rather you hit me, *drey*."

Fain laughed at Dancer's words. "You're too weak at the moment. Few days . . . I'll be happy to beat you down."

He playfully slapped his brother's face. "You suck as a brother. I want my money back."

Fain snorted. "Could be worse. I'm stuck with *you*."

Bastien bit his lip to stifle the unexpected tears those words wrought inside him. And the guilt and self-recrimination they awoke. How many times had he yelled at his brother and called him every insult he knew in six languages?

He'd stupidly thought he hated Quin—so much that he'd blown off their last holiday together because he'd refused to sit through another dinner with Quin eyeballing him and judging him as lacking. For that matter, he'd barely stomached Lil most days. He'd looked for any excuse to avoid being around them, wishing he was anywhere else other than in their company.

Until they were gone.

Now . . . he'd give anything to see them and apologize. Trade every bit of his future life if he could go back to one single memory and relive it with them as a whole family.

Even a fight.

Why hadn't I gone to that stupid holiday dinner when Øda asked me?

How could they be gone now? Why was he still here without them? For that pain alone, he wanted to beat his uncle until nothing was left of him. Barnabas should have killed him, too. Should have never left a single breath in his body.

Without a word, Syn returned to them. He let out an irritated sigh as he checked Dancer's IV. "How much do I have to give you to keep you unconscious? Damn Andarion metabolism. Stay down, beast!"

He fanged Syn then looked at Fain. "Kill him."

"I would, but his wife would tear me up. And no offense, she scares me. You really don't."

Ignoring them, Syn added more medicine to the IV as a skimmer appeared. A small team of medics ran off the craft with lifts for Dancer and Bastien.

It was only then that Fain glanced in his direction. His jaw went slack as instant recognition lit his white eyes. "Bas!" he said with a laugh. "And here I thought you dead. Should have known better."

Bastien gave Fain a droll, offended stare as they placed him on the lift. "Your brother damn near finished what *you* started. Luckily, I'm like a cockroach. Hard to kill."

Shaking his head, Fain patted him on his arm. "It's good to see you again, *drey*. Thank you for fighting with my brother for me."

"Only for you, *drey*. Only for you."

The medics rushed Bastien into the skimmer, then took him to a massive interstellar ship and to a medical bay that was as impressive as the best-equipped hospital.

There were people everywhere.

Never had Bastien felt lonelier. How weird that he was more isolated here than he'd been while alone in his desert base. At least there, it wasn't as obvious that he had no one. But for some reason, having people nearby who didn't give a shit about him hurt a whole hell of a lot more.

Tears welled in his eyes as he remembered a time when he'd been flippant about being the center of attention. Dismissive of his family's overbearing love.

"Hey," Syn said as he finally came in and checked the IV they'd started in Bastien's arm. "I'm going to put you under and get that tracking device out of you, if that's okay?"

He had to ask?

"You get that out of me, Doc, and I'll kiss you for it."

Syn grinned at him. "Don't let my wife catch you. She's insanely jealous." He put his hand on Bastien's shoulder. "Just relax. We'll have you up to running speed real soon."

Nodding, Bastien closed his eyes and waited for the drug to take effect.

Syn watched as his patient drifted off, then checked his vitals. In spite of his unkempt condition, malnutrition, and slight dehydration, Bastien was remarkably fit. Injuries notwithstanding.

But hell, anyone spending time with Hauk was going to come away wounded. The bastard could find trouble lurking in a nunnery.

As he left the room to prepare for surgery, he found Nykyrian waiting for him in the hallway. "What's up?"

"Came to check on Bastien."

"He'll be fine." Syn scowled as he caught the shadow in Nyk's green eyes. The two of them had been friends for a long time. Wingmen for so long that Syn could finish any sentence Nyk started. "You don't trust him?"

"I don't know him. Hauk said he found some items in the base that had come from Jullien."

"Jullien. . . . Your brother?"

He nodded, and there was no way to miss the burning hatred in that cold expression. "If they've partnered up . . ."

"I don't think he's partnered with anyone, Nyk. He's in bad shape. Been alone and scrounging for a long time. Trust me, I know the signs." He'd been a gutter rat himself and lived among the sewers, barely surviving until Nyk had saved his life.

Nykyrian rubbed at his neck. "Still . . . my father said that the evidence against Bastien was substantial. Aside from eyewitness testimony, he was found covered in my aunt's blood. His prints all over the murder weapon."

"You gotta know he didn't do it, though. No one would have shot up his family and stayed there, waiting to be arrested for it. He's not *that* stupid. If he were, he'd have never survived on his own."

Nykyrian crossed his arms over his chest. "You're right. The testimony came from his uncle who inherited the throne in his stead. And his ex-wife, who got a divorce *and* Bastien's property, money, and titles out of it."

"Follow the creds." Syn sucked his breath in sharply. "Um, yeah . . . he definitely didn't do it." Having been accused in a corrupt legal system, Syn knew a setup when he heard one. "They framed that boy."

"My father refuses to believe it, though."

"Why?" Syn was aghast.

"He knew them all. Said Bastien was a spoiled brat who needed a good ass-beating most days."

Syn scoffed. "I live in fear of what he'd have said about *us*, back in the day."

"So you do trust Bastien, then?"

Syn shrugged. "Trust is a stretch. Like you, I have serious mental issues with that whole concept. But Hauk did, and Bastien got him out of there, even though he had nothing to gain, really."

Nyk nodded slowly as he continued to think it over. "Keep an eye on him and let me know when he wakes up."

* * *

Bastien came awake with a start in a cold, sterile room. For a moment, he was terrified as he thought himself back in League custody. With a curse, he sat up and started to rip the IV and monitors off.

Then he saw Aros in the corner, eyeing him as if he were filth.

Bastien's heart retreated from his throat as he remembered what had happened. That he was in Sentella custody. Not League. He was technically safe. But given the way his uncle was staring at him, that state might not be a lasting one.

"You've no idea how much it angers me that they removed your death sentence from you, boy."

Scowling, Bastien tried to understand what Aros meant. "I thought you begged the Overseer for clemency in my case?"

Aros screwed his face up as if the very thought nauseated him. "I would *never* have done such. I wanted to see you hung for what you did to my sister and her family."

Yeah, 'cause they weren't his family, too.

Bastien glared at him. "Then why did you send the petition to Alia Mureaux on my behalf?"

"I never sent anything to her about *you*."

Bastien's jaw went slack as he realized what had happened.

Jullien. There was no other explanation. That little bastard loved to forge paperwork. He was the only one who'd have had the skill, knowledge, and balls to pretend to be his father, and to send that in without the Triosan emperor knowing, and no one else in the Trigon Court realizing it was a forgery.

He was also the only one who'd never bought into the lies. Not once.

Leave it to Julie. But then, that was how he was. Never sought credit for any good deed, because if he was ever caught doing one, it was met with extreme suspicion from everyone around him. So he kept to the dark recesses where he couldn't be seen—a shadow dweller like Bastien.

Pet hate, indeed . . .

Forget Syn. Jullien was the only man he wanted to kiss right now.

But since he wasn't here, he pinned a gimlet stare on Aros. "If you think me guilty, why are you here, Uncle?"

With a grim expression, Aros stood up. "I wanted to look you in the eye and tell you personally that I hope you get exactly what you deserve."

Those words fell like blows against his soul. Gut punches he could have done without. So much for being home.

Yet that was okay. They also fueled his own fury and determination. Because the one thing about Bastien Cabarro, he was a scrappy son of a bitch and nothing motivated him more than condemnation and obstacles.

Over. Under. Around or through. There was always a way to get what you wanted. To get what you needed.

Let no one stand in your way, son. Especially not yourself.

His father's favorite saying.

The need for vengeance, and to make them all eat their unjust convictions against him, swelled inside him. Rising from the bed, Bastien slowly peeled the monitors off.

Then he pulled out the IV.

"For your sake, Uncle, you better pray that I don't. Because if I do get what I deserve, I will be emperor of the Kirovarian empire. And when I am, your crown is the first one I'm coming after. . . ." He raked a repugnant stare down his body. "Funny, really, I only came back for the head of one uncle, but after this . . . two heads mounted on my wall will be all the sweeter."

CHAPTER 9

"You're sure you won't stay? At least a little longer?"

Standing in the Sentella landing bay, Bastien hesitated—Nyk's question meant a lot to him. Every member of their high command was there to see him on his way. "Thanks, but I have to see this through."

Syn sighed while Jayne pouted. Even Dancer and Fain appeared to be on the verge of tears. "We've grown attached to you. Not often I find someone more sarcastic than me."

Dancer concurred. "Yeah, you're like that fungus in the bathroom that no matter how hard you try to scrub it off, keeps coming back. Till you're forced to live with it."

Laughing, Darling nodded. "We hate to see you go."

"Appreciate it." *I think.*

But in spite of the missions he'd flown with them over the last few weeks, they weren't his tribe. And he had a date to keep. "I've waited a long time for justice. It's time I see it met."

Syn nodded. "You need us, call immediately."

"Thanks."

Dancer caught his arm as he started to leave. That personal contact wouldn't mean anything coming from a human, but for an Andarion to make such a gesture was significant. It meant he considered Bastien family. "I owe my daughter's safety to you, Cabarro. And my life, and Sumi's. Night or day, you call."

He inclined his head to Dancer and clapped him on the back. "It was my honor to see Kalea returned to you and her mother. No family should be separated."

"Which is why you need to stay with us." Jayne winked at him. "You're one of us now."

Bastien laughed before he returned his attention to Nykyrian. "I'll return the fighter to you as soon as I can."

"It's yours, *drey*. Least we could do given what we owe you." Nyk's expression turned even grimmer than it'd been before. "Sorry about my father and how he treated you."

"It's all good."

Aros hadn't told Nykyrian that Bastien had threatened him. Most likely because he didn't think it a real threat.

Then again, it wasn't.

It'd been a promise.

But first he had another to keep. "I'll be in touch."

Their good-byes followed him as he climbed aboard the fighter and prepared for launch.

After pulling his helmet on, he took a moment to glance back at Nyk, Darling, Syn, Fain, Dancer, and Jayne, who was waving at him.

It'd been tempting to accept their help for this, but the last thing he wanted was to drag their nations into another war while they were already fighting against The League. They had their own battles.

This was his.

If he failed, he didn't want to destroy anyone else's family in the process. Especially not after getting to know them. A sad smile tugged at his lips as he saw Sumi and Kalea in his mind. They'd met him for a farewell breakfast.

Kalea had broken into tears at the thought of Uncle Bas-Bas leaving. He could still feel the warmth of her wet hug. It really had been his honor to help them rescue the little girl from League custody.

Now grateful for this send-off, he inclined his head to them and signaled control before he launched.

He was headed for Jullien. Another reason he'd been unable to accept their offers of aid. The one time he'd brought up Jullien's name, Nyk had almost torn his head off.

He's a bastard and a snake. I wouldn't trust him for shit! If I ever meet him again, I'll hand him his testicles and laugh while he bleeds out at my feet.

While extreme, that threat wouldn't mean much coming out of the mouth of the average person. Coming from the mouth of one of the most lethal assassins ever trained by The League . . .

It was as much a promise as the words Bastien had delivered to Barnabas.

So for now, he wouldn't even attempt to cross-pollinate those two. Nykyrian obviously needed more time to forgive his brother.

Few more decades, at least.

After breaking atmosphere, Bastien let his thoughts wander to where they always went when left unchecked.

Ember. Against all common sense, he'd tried to trace her from the Sentella's computers, but there had been no records for her over the last few years. Her sisters either. Only Alura showed up.

His gut drew taut in fear that something bad had happened to them during Barnabas's takeover. Had Ember married, there would have been something to mark it.

But the last movements he could find on her were about a year after he'd been made Ravin. The Gyron Force logs had her and her sisters and mother listed as MIA.

Yet he knew better. KIA would be most likely. Because if she were still alive, she'd have returned to duty.

Unshed tears choked him at the thought of her dying in the field with her sisters by her side. If Barnabas had been behind it, then he would gut him with his bare hands.

Closing his eyes, he could still feel her touch on his flesh. Hear her laughter in his ear as he made love to her for hours on end.

Going home without her there would be excruciating. In fact, he could still remember the first time she'd taken him to meet her parents.

"Are *you* nervous? Captain Ghost Gadget?"

He'd given her a droll stare. "Of course I'm nervous. Never met parents before. At least not intentionally."

She'd scowled at him. "Meaning?"

He'd flashed his most charming grin at her. "Well . . . there was this one time when Dad came home early while I was at university. Wouldn't have been so bad had he not been one of my professors."

"Oh my God! Bas, tell me you weren't?"

"What? Naked? Of course I was. Her, too. Needless to say, flunked that class."

Her laughter had ended in a sympathetic groan. "Well, keep it in your pants, flyboy. I've already warned them about you."

"Meaning?" he asked, using her favorite phrase she had anytime she wanted more information on the given topic.

"Oh, c'mon. Like you don't know."

"Know what?"

"That you're the friend everyone has to explain before they meet you and then apologize for afterward."

"Oh gee, thank you."

Bastien smiled at the bittersweet memory. Ember had been the only person he'd ever met who could make him laugh while she insulted him. Tell him to go to hell and make him look forward to the trip.

You were ever a woman of multiple, unique talents.

And he would love her forever.

She was still on his mind when he finally reached the main Gort base and asked the hostile controller for permission to land. Obviously not something they granted out of routine procedure like most bases. And judging by the amount of time between their communications, it must be taking an act of the gods for them to clear him.

Eternity passed before the woman returned with the permission he needed to land in their North Bay. There was no missing the shocked disbelief in her voice as she told him he'd been approved.

Wow, Jules . . . paranoid much?

Then again, he couldn't blame him, given the number of beings out to end his life.

As soon as Bastien landed, he spotted Jullien waiting for him with a man and woman he didn't know. Hard to miss his cousin's gargantuan ass, even among the huge Fyreblood Andarions who called this place home. Only their species could make Bastien feel like a middle-schooler, since they dwarfed him. It was weird not to be among the tallest in a group.

But they put his genetics to shame.

Bastien removed his helmet and jumped to the deck, then made his way over. He pulled Jullien in for a brotherly hug.

Jullien laughed when he saw that while Bastien had trimmed his beard down to shadowed whiskers, he'd kept his long hair and wore it pulled back into a messy ponytail. "What is this?" He tugged playfully at it.

Bastien shrugged. "A reminder that I'm no longer civilized, and I have no intention of ever again playing by anyone's rule book."

"I understand. And I take it by your presence here that you're no longer tagged?"

"No," he said gratefully. "Syn Wade pulled it out of me. Finally."

Jullien's jaw dropped in shock. "Really?"

Nodding, Bastien clapped him on the arm. "Really long story short, they ended up on Oksana with The League hot on their ass, and I got caught in the cross fire. After a lot of bruising and damage and a couple of near-fatal catastrophes, it ended well for me." His gaze went to the exceptionally beautiful and pregnant female standing beside his cousin.

Even without an introduction, he had no doubt that this was Jullien's wife—the Gorturnum Tavali's vice admiral. Her white-blond hair was identical to Vasili's and her silvery-white eyes and fangs definitely marked her as one of the rare Andarion Fyrebloods who'd been exiled from their empire by Jullien's grandmother.

Jullien stepped back. "My much better half, Ushara. Shara, my cousin Bastien."

He inclined his head and bowed respectfully to her. *"Imprä turu, Ger Tarra Samari."*

She gaped at Bastien's formal Andarion greeting. "You speak Andarion?"

Straightening, Bastien winked at Jullien. "Not really. Just a few key phrases here and there that Julie taught me when we were kids."

"Impressive, nonetheless." Ushara gestured to the tall, dark-haired man beside her. "And this is Trajen."

Surprised that the high admiral of the Gorturnum Tavali would deign to be here, Bastien didn't miss the way those dark eyes probed everything about him.

Yeah, nothing got past this man. He had the mark of a well-trained soldier who'd been through hell and lived to tell about it. There was also a refinement to him that said he'd been noble born. That innate grace and bearing that seemed to come from their genes.

Bastien held his hand out to him. "Pleasure to meet you."

Trajen hesitated before he shook his hand. "And you . . . Highness."

Bastien shivered. "Please, don't. I was never all that into the pomp and ceremony, anyway. It's just Bastien or Bas. Asshole, if you really must."

"Ah God, there are two of you in this universe," Trajen muttered as he passed a knowing stare toward Jullien that said he and Bastien were far too alike. "So what brings you here?"

"To beg a favor from my favorite cousin, which I know I shouldn't. But . . ." He flashed another grin at Jullien. "Dancer Hauk blew up my base without warning."

Jullien gaped at that unexpected disclosure. "Pardon?"

Nodding, he sighed at the memory. "The whole bloody damn thing. I got nothing left. Not even my porn collection Thrāix gave me. And I need that database I shared with you, if you don't mind."

Jullien gave him an equally gimlet stare. "You're going after Barnabas?"

"Hell yeah. He killed my family. Be damned if I'm going to let him sit on my father's throne in peace. I don't care who rules, just so long as it's not him or any bastard he spawned."

Jullien dropped his gaze to the Alliance patches on the sleeve of Bastien's borrowed Sentella uniform. They had designed a new badge that stood for the empires who'd aligned themselves with Darling and Nykyrian to war against The League. It was basically The League insignia with a giant X through it. He had to give them credit. Nyk and crew were a ballsy lot.

"The Sentella helping you?"

"They offered me a position with them. I'm not interested in that. All I took was the clothes on my back and the ship, which I intend to return once this is over—provided I don't die. My mistress is Vengeance, and she's the only one I'm cuddling up to for now."

He knew if anyone could relate, Jullien definitely understood the sentiment. "I'll get you a copy of the database. Is there anything else you need?"

"No. Just the files on the family. Once I have those dossiers, I'll be out of your hair. Sorry I dropped in unannounced." His gaze went to Ushara's distended belly. "Congrats, by the way. I didn't realize you had another one on the way. Is Vasili excited, or afraid of having more spiders he has to hide his things from?"

As soon as the question was out of his mouth, Bastien caught the startled look from Jullien as he remembered that they *had* told him about the baby.

Damn. How could he have forgotten that? But then when you lived a life where the vast majority of your conversations took place with imaginary people in your head, you tended to forget what was real, what was memories, and what you fabricated to keep yourself from going bat-shit crazy. There were some of them so real, that he swore they'd happened, only to learn that it was nothing more than his mind struggling to make sense of his forced isolation.

Ushara gaped. "You know Vas?"

"He's made a few stops with his father on my rock to drop off food and ammo."

She tsked at Jullien. "Someone's been keeping secret missions from me."

"Only to protect Bastien. I didn't want any logs of that particular landing, or anyone wondering why we kept going to the desert for no apparent reason. Just in case."

And that was why he loved and trusted his cousin.

"Makes sense." She smiled at Bastien. "Why don't you stay for dinner, then? Meet the girls and say hi to Vasili? I'm sure he'd love to see you."

Bastien would love to as well, but . . . he looked to Jullien. His cousin was nothing if not a private beast. "I don't want to intrude."

"Just don't flush my head down the toilet, and we're good."

Bastien burst out laughing at the mention of what Lil used to do to Jullien when they were kids and she'd get aggravated at him. "Gah! You think you had it bad? I was the one who lived with her. *And* Quin. Plus, she ended up as my wingman. How the hell I survived my childhood without being drowned, I do not know. Can you imagine how much better a human I'd be if I hadn't suffered severe oxygen dep and brain trauma as a child?"

Trajen laughed, then spoke to Jullien. "I see now why you like him." He held his hand out to Bastien. "It was a pleasure to meet you, Bas. I've got a lot of things I need to take care of, so I'm heading out, but I'll make sure and clear you for any future visits you want to make here. Consider yourself welcome anytime. I know Jules would appreciate having some family around who doesn't want to hang him or screw him over."

Yeah . . . he wasn't the only one.

As Trajen left with Ushara, Jullien led Bastien through their bay and to the residential area of their base.

Bastien glanced back over his shoulder. "You're a lucky male, Jullien."

"Believe me, I know. I'd be dead had she not saved my life . . . in more ways than one." He paused to glance sideways at Bastien. "How's my brother?"

"Good. Aside from the stress of the war, but he hides that well." Bastien noticed that he didn't ask after his parents—both of whom had been on Bastien's rescue flight when Nykyrian had picked him up on Oksana. "I saw your father."

Jullien's stralen eyes darkened. "Couldn't care less."

"Yeah, don't blame you there. No love lost here for him, either. He didn't have much to say to me that bears repeating."

"Sorry."

Bastien shrugged. "As you once said, we black sheep need to stick together."

As soon as Jullien opened the door to his condo, an ear-splitting shriek sounded.

"Paka's home!"

Two small, dark-headed blurs came running to assault Jullien. One launched herself into his arms while the other latched onto his leg and squeezed it tight. Laughing, Jullien held his twin daughters. He kissed the cheek of the one in his arms. "Viv, meet your cousin Bastien."

"Hi, Bastien!"

"Nice meeting you, Viv."

The one on Jullien's leg looked up at Bastien with a fierce frown.

Bastien knelt down to hold his hand out to her. "You must be Mira."

Mira left her father's leg to pull at Bastien's lips so that she could inspect his teeth. "But if you're Paka's family, why don't you gots fangs, too?"

"And black hair?" Viv chimed in as Jullien set her down. "Don't all Ixurianir have black hair?" She slapped her hands to her face as if completely exasperated. "I'm so confuzzled."

Laughing, Jullien picked her up again and kissed her cheek. "My paka's human, and he's the older brother of Bastien's mother, who is also human. So a lot of folks on Andaria, and in some other places, don't consider me Andarion."

Bastien nodded. "Yeah, and I'm completely human. Sadly, I have no Andarion blood in my veins at all."

Mira sighed heavily before she patted Bastien's cheek in sympathy. "I am very sad for you. But we loves you anyway, *kýzi*. Even though you gots no fangs."

Laughing, he smiled at her. "Thank you, Mira. I deeply appreciate that." He ruffled her hair and flashed a grin at Ushara, who'd just come through the door to witness her daughters' reaction to him. "They are precious. I can't believe anything so sweet came from Julie's surly, irritable hide."

Jullien snorted as he went to the kitchen to get them drinks while Vasili gave Bastien a bashful, welcoming hug. "Thanks a lot."

"Well, you have to admit, you were *never this* cute." Stepping away from Vas, he tickled Mira until she squealed and jumped from his arms to run to her brother for protection.

"Neither were you."

"True. I was too busy being the baby brat. A job I relished quite seriously." He took the ale from Jullien's hand and lifted it for a swig. "You remember that god-awful summer camp when Barnabas was trying to make us run the obstacle course?"

"Remember? Hell, my dignity's still on that wall, pinned next to my left testicle."

Bastien laughed as he turned toward Ushara and Vasili to explain the scenario for their benefit. "My uncle's a total scabbing prick. I loved my dad, but he had some weird parenting techniques, which included occasional weekend maneuvers, and summers every year spent at Camp Hernia for a full six-week program of survival training. And poor Julie got roped in one year when you were what? Thirteen?"

"Fourteen. I was supposed to have been on my Andarion Indari."

"Indari?" Bastien scowled.

He took a drink of ale, then explained the term for Bastien. "It's an Andarion coming-of-age ceremony where an elder of the family takes a younger one on a quest to teach them how to survive on their own. The youngster goes out a kid and supposedly returns as a capable adult, ready to take their place in Andarion society."

"Ah . . . *Endurance*." That was the word Dancer had used for it—which made sense. It would be the Universal translation for the Andarion term Indari, and Dancer wouldn't have known that Bastien had any exposure to the Andarion language.

Which made him wonder something as he made a peculiar connection. "Is *Indari* and *Andaria* related linguistically?"

Jullien saluted him with his bottle. "Impressed that you caught that. Most don't. But yeah. Andari was the ancient word for endure."

"Says a lot about your maternal race, *drey*."

"Don't it though." Jullien scratched at the scar on his neck his grandmother had given him as a boy.

Wanting to quickly change the subject, Bastien returned them to the previous topic. "So how'd you end up on Kirovar for your Endurance?"

"Because I was half human and fat, none of my Andarion relatives wanted the embarrassment of being seen with me when I failed the family quest. So my aunt shuffled me off to my father, who promptly sent me to yours, who then shunted me to your uncle. Fun times."

Yeah . . .

"Indeed."

Ushara paused in her dinner preparations. Bastien caught the glint in her eyes that said she thought as much of Jullien's parents as he did.

They were scum.

But Jullien didn't seem to care as he winked at her and Vas, who was suddenly interested in the story.

"So there we were," Jullien continued the story. "The hottest summer in Kirovarian history, on maneuvers with these massively heavy backpacks Barnabas had loaded with heat-absorbing rocks, where it was eight hundred degrees in the shade. Not that there was any shade to be found on that course, mind you."

"He's not exaggerating. It was so hot, it melted my granola bar."

Vas scowled. "How do you melt a granola bar?"

"Exactly!" Bastien said with a laugh. "I swear the heels of my boots melted off."

"Yeah, and unlike Bas and his siblings, I was overweight, with atrophied muscles from a period of—" He paused as he glanced to Vasili. "—confinement, and I wasn't used to their atmosphere. At all. It's a lot thinner than what we have on Andaria, with different gravity and allergens. So I'm disoriented, choking and wheezing, and doubled over, puking."

Screwing his face up at the memory, Bastien nodded. "Not a pretty sight. I don't know what they'd fed your paka, but it was gross. My brother and sister stood there yelling at poor Julie because my uncle's threatening to make us run extra laps if he doesn't get back on the course and finish it. And I give him credit, he's on his hands and knees, trying his damnedest to push himself to his feet. Hell, he's even crawling in an effort to get to the end. I'd never seen anyone so determined to get up in my life, but it's just not happening. He's choking and sweating so badly that I'm expecting Julie to die any minute."

"So," Jullien says, interrupting him. "In true Bastien form—and keeping in mind that he's only seven at the time—he yanks off his helmet, throws his backpack down, and lies on the ground, using the helmet for a pillow, and says to them, and I quote verbatim, 'Later, bitches. I'm done for the day. Y'all can carry me home or call for a lift. Either way, I ain't moving from here. My ass is too precious for this abuse.'"

Ushara gasped. "How did *that* go over?"

Bastien snorted as his ass twitched in response to the memory. "Like sacrificing a fluffy kitten on a high holiday. My uncle set my precious ass on fire. But it got the attention off poor Julie."

"Yeah, but you bought yourself a world of hurt that day."

Bastien shrugged nonchalantly. "You weren't there when my mother saw the ass bruises after we got home. I promise you, what he did to me pales in comparison to her reaction on him when she saw them. But for my father's lightning-quick reflexes, I'd be shy a few cousins.

I actually owe *you*. Because of that particular fun adventure, I didn't have to go back to summer camp until I was a teenager. And I went with bodyguards my mother had ordered to shoot my uncle if he, or anyone else, so much as raised an eyebrow to me." He grinned at Ushara. "As I said, my ass was quite precious."

Jullien laughed. "Your mother was something else. Until Shara, I'd never seen anyone so protective of her young. I'm amazed she ever allowed you to join the military."

"Again, you missed the fireworks. Holy Jacob . . . she actually tried to shoot *me* to get me out of it."

"I would say bullshit, but knowing your mother . . . it sounds about right."

Ushara gaped. "Seriously?"

Bastien sobered as he remembered the vicious fight he'd caused for his mother and father after boosting a transport that had belonged to a friend's parents.

"He's going into the military, Lia! He needs discipline and you won't let me give him any! You cradle and coddle the boy like he's still in nappies. I've even seen you cut his meat up when it's served to him . . . and that was just last night!"

"I swear to the gods, Newie, if my baby gets hurt because of your selfish stupidity and rampant insistence on this folly, your balls are the first set I'm coming after!"

That was as close to profanity as his mother had ever come. 'Course that was his special talent. Driving his saintly mother to curse and his stoic teetotaler father to drink.

Bastien cleared his throat. "Yeah, my mother loved us. We definitely lucked out when it came to parents. They didn't deserve what Barnabas did to them, and I won't rest until I make this right."

Jullien reached for a handful of the carrots Ushara had just cubed. "You going after the throne?"

Bastien glanced over to where the twins were playing on the floor. They were so innocent of the horrors of the world. How he wished he could keep all children that way.

And it made him long for the days when he'd played with his brother and sister like that.

"I don't know. I was never supposed to be ruler. . . . Third born. It should *never* have come to me. I was supposed to be the fun-loving playboy of the family, who screwed up and gave the others something scandalous to talk about at cocktail parties."

Swallowing, he locked gazes with Jullien. "How did you handle the guilt when everyone thought Nyk was dead?"

"Didn't. Like you said, I never wanted the throne. But after a few years, when I realized that my mother wasn't going to sober up and have more children, and that my father had no intention of remarrying or fathering another heir, I threw myself into school to learn as much about politics, history, and diplomacy as I could. Not because I cared. Just felt like I owed it to my brother's memory to be the ruler I thought he'd have been."

Bastien frowned as he considered those words. All this time, he'd felt guilty. But this was a new perspective. "Never thought of it that way."

"That's because you were supposed to be the playboy. I was the spare."

He laughed and clapped Jullien on the back before they carried dinner to the table.

They bantered through a relaxed, laughter-filled meal the likes of which Bastien had never thought to have again. Here, unlike his time with Nykyrian and The Sentella, he didn't feel like an outsider or lonely.

This felt like home. Jullien's family felt like his.

For the first time, he was tempted to forego his vengeance and stay with Jullien.

If only he could. . . .

Sadly, his conscience would never allow him peace if he let this go.

After dinner, he helped Ushara clean up while Jullien put the girls to bed and Vasili went to play online with his maternal cousins.

The normality of it all was almost more than he could handle. But beneath that was something he hadn't felt in a long time.

Jullien had been written off by the world. By all their families. Yet here, among an outlaw Nation, he had the very things Bastien would have sold his soul for.

Love. Peace.

Family.

"Ushara?"

She paused in her cleaning to glance up at Bastien. "Yes?"

"Thank you."

"I'm not quite sure what you're thanking me for, but you're welcome."

He put away the glasses before he gave her a hard stare. "You give me hope, and that's something I haven't had in a long time."

She sealed the last of their leftovers into a tub and put them away. "What do you mean?"

"Unlike Jullien, I had a great childhood. The kind every kid ought to have. It's why I never understood how Aros could be so nice to us and then such a douche to his own son." Or how his uncle could turn on him so fast over Barnabas's lies, when Aros should have known better. "I still don't really understand what crawled up his ass and grew there. Julie wasn't a bad kid. Just a lonely one who grew up intimately acquainted with a treacherous side of others that I was blissfully unaware of. I grew up in a world that if someone, even my uncle, did me harm, it was only because they cared about me and were trying to teach me a valuable life lesson and that it was for my own good."

"You were naïve."

"Blessedly so. Sheltered, even though I didn't know it. So when it all came crashing down on me, and those I thought were my family and friends turned out to be enemies . . . I lost all faith. In everything. But this—" He gestured at the pictures of their family on the wall. "—it helps more than you'll ever know. It restores some of the faith I'd lost. I'm glad you saw in Julie what I've always known."

She smiled at him. "I can't imagine my life any other way." Rubbing his arm, she motioned for him to follow her down the hall to the girls' room, where she cracked the door open so that he could see their bedtime ritual.

On top of the covers, Jullien lay on the queen-sized bed the girls shared with his ankles crossed, propped against a stack of stuffed animals. The twins were tucked under each of his arms, beneath the covers, and draped on his chest while he read to them.

Bastien gaped at the sight of his fierce Andarion cousin so gentle.

His deep voice as he mimicked the characters made the girls giggle. "And then the lorina tackled her sister and went *rawr*!" With a guttural sound effect, he grabbed Mira and tickled her until she squealed, then he turned and did the same to Viv.

"Jules," Ushara said chidingly, "you're supposed to be putting them down, not winding them up."

Eyes wide, he gasped at the girls. "You got me into trouble again with mama."

They giggled and snuggled deeper into his side as he returned to reading the story.

Ushara closed the door and headed back toward the living room.

Bastien lingered a moment longer to collect his thoughts before he rejoined her. "That's what I mean, Ushara. I wish you could see what a miracle *that* is." He gestured toward the hall with his thumb. "Julie didn't learn that from his parents. I've never known him to be so open and happy as he's been since he found you."

Embarrassed, she cleared her throat and changed the subject. "So you were with his brother before you came here?"

"Yeah."

"What's he like?"

Bastien shrugged. "I barely know Nykyrian, really. He was assumed dead my whole childhood. I was twenty-six when he returned and was reinstated as heir."

Anger darkened her vision. "And you didn't help Jullien when they threw him out?"

"I tried. Believe me. But you have to remember that it was only three months after Jullien was disinherited that my entire family was slaughtered and I was convicted for it and sentenced to being a Ravin. In retrospect, my father did him a favor. Had Julie been on Kirovar, he'd have been murdered, too."

She sucked her breath in sharply. "I didn't realize that happened so close together."

Bastien nodded. "So no, I never had a chance to get to know Nyk. At all. Not until a few weeks ago, when they showed up on Oksana. He seems decent enough. But I don't have the war stories with him that I share with Julie.

Nyk never had to suffer through one of our grandfather's interminable parties."

She laughed. "So I've heard."

"I'll bet you have. To the day he died, my brother Quin counted Julie among his heroes for having the nerve to do that."

"Are we back to the pool pissing?"

Bastien turned at Jullien's question. "I could always count on you to make things interesting."

Jullien rolled his eyes. "Let's not go there." He pulled his jacket out of the closet. "I have the files you need stored on my ship. You want to stay here or come with me?"

"As much as I enjoy your wife's company, I'll come with you and give her a break from my boorishness."

"You're anything but a chore to put up with. And you're welcome here anytime."

"Thank you, Ger Tarra." Bastien took a minute to say good-bye to Vasili, who actually hugged him. "Take care, sport."

"You, too."

And with that, Bastien trailed Jullien back through the station.

They hadn't gone far when Bastien brought up something that had been on his mind all night. "Thank you."

"For dinner? You're more than welcome."

"No. For saving my life."

Jullien practically stumbled. "Don't know what you mean."

"Yeah, you do. It wasn't Aros who sent that missive to the Overseer that kept her from executing me. I know it was you."

Red crept over Jullien's features. "I wish I could have done more."

"I'm stunned you did that much, given you were being hunted at the time. How did you manage?"

Jullien shrugged. "Made it my priority. I was on Ritadaria when I saw the trial coverage. I knew they'd convict you based on the bullshit I saw, and that my father, true to his assholishness, wouldn't do anything to stop it. So I did what I could."

Bastien pulled him in for a hug. "Again, thank you."

"You sure about that? 'Cause after seeing that hell you called home . . .'"

Laughing, Bastien shoved him away. "You were always an ass."

"Yeah, uh-huh." Jullien went to get the files.

When Bastien started to leave, Jullien stopped him. "Before you go, you want to loosen up some? Make sure you're ready for this?"

"What do you mean?"

"When was the last time you trained?"

Longer ago than he cared to think about. "I'm in my prime. Don't need no training."

Jullien snorted at his feigned accent. "I don't know. You're looking a little worn out."

Bastien gaped. "I don't want to hear it from someone as old as you are!"

"Old? Hah! That's it!"

Next thing Bastien knew, they were in a ring, sparring, as a crowd gathered around them to watch it.

He lost track of the time as they laughed and beat each other, all the while urging one another to hit harder and move faster.

Hot and sweaty, he saw Jullien get distracted. So he moved in for the kill.

Before he could blink, Jullien whipped around, grabbed him, and slammed him to the mat, then kissed his cheek.

"We have to stop now." He jerked his chin toward Ushara, who stood off to the side, hands on hips, glaring at them.

Bastien looked over and laughed. "Ah, crap. Now I'm the one who got you into trouble with your female."

Grinning roguishly, Jullien got up and offered Bastien his hand to help him to his feet. Both of them were bruised, sweating, and bleeding. Yet neither cared.

It'd been a good match and one Bastien had needed more than he realized.

Ushara shook her head as they neared her. "Really? This is how you wanted to say good-bye to each other?"

Jullien rubbed sheepishly at his neck while Bastien went for towels. "We were just going to practice a bit. Then we got a little carried away."

"A *little*?" She glanced at the blood all over the mat, which looked as if someone had been murdered there and their body dragged away to be hidden.

Trajen emerged from the dispersing crowd to join them. "I'm impressed with you both."

Bastien handed a towel to Jullien before he wiped at the sweat and blood on his stomach where he still bore his League Ravin mark. "Yeah, I had no idea Julie could do all that. I'd love to see him and Fain Hauk go at it. Julie's the only one I've ever fought who could drag my ass around a mat as much as Fain did."

"War Hauk Fain?" Jullien scowled.

Bastien cringed as he realized what he'd let slip. But he wasn't about to lie to his cousin for anything. "Yeah. I used to train with him when he lived on Kirovar."

Jullien wiped his face. "I had no idea you knew him."

"Small universe, right? I figured you two probably knew each other, since he and his brother went to your school when you were kids, but given how Anatoles feel about War Hauks, and War Hauks feel about Anatoles, and the long-standing feud between your lineages, I knew to never, *ever* mention to him or his brother that we were related or knew each other in *any* capacity. Andarions are a *highly* territorial and volatile species." Not to mention the story Aros had once told him about Jullien and Dancer.

Honestly, he didn't know what to believe there, but he was sure there was a lot more to the story than Aros had given him. Because nothing and no one could ever diminish Jullien in his mind, especially after his kindness to Bastien over the last couple of years.

As far as he was concerned, Jullien was a saint.

Jullien nodded at Bastien. "Good call, kyzi. They'd have killed you."

"Exactly." Bastien wiped at his face and shoulders. "Sorry about this, Ushara. Please don't harm my cousin. It was all my fault."

"Hardly. I'm the one who started it."

When they began to argue over blame, Ushara stopped them. "It's fine." She gently wiped at the blood on Jullien's lip. "I'm glad that your arm's working so well. But you shouldn't be stressing it so soon."

"I wasn't using it too much. I don't have precise control over it yet, and I didn't want to kill him."

Ushara sighed in bitter amusement. "So, Bas, since it's now so late, are you staying until morning?"

How he wished he could, but . . . "Nah, I was going to head on. Since I got Julie into trouble, don't want to risk wearing out any more of my welcome."

Jullien dried his hair. "Where are you headed?"

"Starken for supplies and more intel. Then I'm after Barnabas."

Ushara scowled at his words. "Alone?"

He nodded. "I don't have anyone else I trust, really.

Don't want a stranger at my back. Not about to drag Julie or Fain into this. So if I fall, it's only on my ass. And there's no one to really grieve over it."

Ushara wrinkled her nose. "Why don't you hit the showers before you leave?"

"What?" Bastien asked in an offended tone. "You saying I stink?"

Trajen snorted. "Well, you did just spend two hours beating the utter hell out of my field admiral. You both smell like something rotted and dead. How Ushara can stand being this close to either of you while pregnant, I have no idea."

Bastien laughed. "Fine. I can take a hint." He headed for the locker room.

As soon as he was gone, Ushara dug out her link.

Jullien scowled at her. "What are you doing?"

"Hailing someone. Obviously."

Jullien met Trajen's gaze. A cold feeling went through his gut at her unexpected vague answer. He was usually the evasive ass, not her. "Who?"

She ignored his question. "Hey, this is Admiral Samari. I know you requested reassignment yesterday and that we were meeting about it tomorrow. Believe it or not, something interesting came up tonight. It's an outside mission. For Kirovar, but it's something I think you might be interested in." She paused to listen. "Yeah. You want to meet us in the North Bay in a few minutes?" A smile curved her lips. "Great. I'll see you then."

Trajen growled low in his throat. "Do you know what you're doing?"

"Yes."

Completely confounded as his powers failed him, Jullien turned toward Trajen. "Could someone clue *me* in?"

Ushara tucked her link away. "Jay has grounded herself

for a few months. She wants to spend more time with her kids, and let her husband do the runs. So some of her crew has requested temporary reassignments."

"Okay . . ."

"I'm thinking one of them would make a perfect point for Bastien."

While Jullien appreciated the thought, he knew that wouldn't play well with his cousin. Bas was even more paranoid than he was. And with good reason. Once you'd been through the kind of betrayal they'd suffered, it tended to stay with you.

"Shara . . . Bas isn't going to put someone at his back he doesn't know."

"Yeah, but she has Gyron Force training. He has to respect that."

It wouldn't matter. In fact, that could be worse. If they knew each other, it could even anger Bas.

Jullien pulled his shirt on and groaned out loud. "Trajen, tell her what a bad idea this is. For all we know, they could be enemies."

"I don't think so," Ushara insisted. "She left Kirovar and joined The Tavali because of the overthrow."

"What was her rank?"

"Major."

Trajen crossed his arms over his chest. "Let them meet. See if they get along."

He made it sound easy, but Jullien knew better. He also knew better than to argue with the two of them. They invariably won. Trajen because he wouldn't give in. Ushara because she fought dirty.

Jullien tossed the towel in a bin. "Fine. I don't want him to do this alone anyway."

Bastien came out of the shower with a weird feeling in

his gut. Something wasn't right. He didn't know what, but something in the air had changed.

By the time they were in the North Bay, his skin was crawling as if it were alive.

Was some hidden instinct trying to tell him to forego this trip?

Jullien tried again to get him to stay, at least for the night. "You sure you want to do this? You know you're welcome to stay as long as you want."

Bastien clapped him on the back. "And you make it tempting. But I have to do this. I owe it to my family."

"I understand. If you need anything else . . ."

Bastien cast a playful grin at Ushara. "Really appreciate it, but I won't take you from your family. They need you more than I do." He held his hand out to Jullien. "You take care, *drey*."

"And you."

He inclined his head to Ushara, then shook Trajen's hand.

Ember couldn't breathe as she entered the North Bay. At first, she thought she was hallucinating. But there was no mistaking the man who'd haunted her, night and day, since the first moment she'd first met his reckless hide. That tall, lean, and ripped body that made her mouth water and body hum . . .

Only one badass warrior stood like that. Cocksure and approachable. Serious and fun-loving. A total contradiction that had to be experienced to be understood.

Tears welled in her eyes as she heard his deep, rumbling cadence of a refined Kirovarian accent. No longer the highly polished aristocrat she'd fallen in love with, this Bastien held an even more dangerous edge to him. One that said he wouldn't hesitate to take a life. And it wasn't just the long brown hair with creamy blond highlights he had pulled back from his sculpted face. Or that shadowed jawline that sported a few days' growth of whiskers—something the polished Bastien of old would *never* have tolerated.

No, this stranger was more barbarian than visir.

More villain than hero. *Damn you to hell. . . .*

Suddenly, a voice cut through the bay that left Bastien stunned completely numb.

"Bastien Cabarro . . . you lousy, worthless piece of human shit!"

No . . .

The color fled from his cheeks as he stepped away from Trajen and turned to see the absolute last person he'd ever dreamed of seeing again.

Dressed in the Hadean Corps officer uniform that was preferred by the police division of the Tavali Nation, it was Ember. . . .

And she was as devastating to him today as she'd been the moment he'd first seen her trying to get to her trapped sister. Only thing missing was the smudge of dirt across her cheek and the panic in her fiery green eyes.

He couldn't breathe as every hormone in his body went into overdrive and left him hard and aching, and completely unable to think straight. She still had that familiar military swagger that was ingrained in any Gyron Force officer. And she stalked toward Bastien like she fully intended to gut him.

With a rusted-out nail file.

Bastien didn't move or speak. He just stood there, gaping at the slender, auburn-haired Tavali who meant everything to him.

She stopped in front of him, hands on hips. "Have you *nothing* to say to me?"

Yeah, but he didn't know where to begin, so he spoke the first idiotic sentence that came to his blood-drained mind. "I thought you were dead?"

Sneering at his answer, she grabbed his jacket and jerked him forward. Instead of racking him, as Bastien fully expected, she gave him a kiss that blistered his lips and left him harder than he'd ever been in his life. Growling, he fisted his hands in her uniform and pulled her closer to him, reveling in her lush curves that fit against his body to absolute perfection. It was as if the gods had created her specifically for him alone. Nothing in the universe could please him more, except finding a private corner so that he could sate the need he had to taste every inch of her.

Wide-eyed, Ushara glanced at Trajen, then Jullien. "I think they know each other."

With a stifled smile, Jullien ran his thumb over his bottom lip. "Uh, yeah, I'm going to bet on that, too. Either that, or the greetings on Kirovar have vastly improved since the last time I visited."

His entire body electrified, Bastien finally came up for air. Not that he wanted to. Indeed, his only thought now was stripping her uniform off and showing her exactly how much he'd missed her.

Or better yet, ripping it off with his teeth.

Cupping her face in his hands, he stared down at her, grateful to every god on Kirovar that she was alive and well. He brushed his thumb across her swollen lips and smiled, intending to tell her that he loved her.

Until she kneed him in the groin. Hard. "That's for marrying my sister, you feckless bastard!"

Hissing in pain, Bastien limped away from her, clutching

at his abused groin. He glared at her and cursed. Oh yeah, that sucked every bit of tender feeling out of him.

In that moment, he wanted to kill her!

"You broke up with *me*! Remember?"

Unrepentant, she curled her lip. "I said I wanted some time to think about where we were heading. That wasn't an invitation for you to go bang my sister five minutes later."

Was she fucking kidding? That was *not* how it happened. "I didn't just go 'bang' your sister. And it damn sure was more than five minutes later." Straightening, he tried to level his breathing. "She asked *me* out. Then I asked *you* and *you* said *you* didn't care what, and I directly quote, or *who* I did."

"I. *Lied*," she snapped between gritted teeth. "Holy Jake! You were my wingman. You were supposed to be able to read my expressions and know me better than that!"

Bastien held his hands up. "Not Trisani, Ember. Don't read minds. You told me you wanted us to be friends, and your sister said you only went out with me because you didn't want to turn me down and hurt my feelings, since we were partners. How was I to know?"

Raking him with a glare, she made a sound of supreme disgust. "Gah! You were always so dense!" She turned toward Ushara. "Is he my assignment?"

"Uh—" She glanced about nervously. "—yes? But I'm going to assume you want to pass on it."

Ember narrowed her gaze on Bastien. "You going after your uncle?"

"Of course."

"Then I'm in."

Bastien snorted at the very thought, which terrified him. "Uh, yeah, no. I don't think so. Especially not after *this*." He gestured toward his abused groin. "I don't need the cold-cocking. Trust me. Life's done it enough."

"Don't even, Cabarro. You won't last ten seconds without us in this fight. You want vengeance. So do we."

"Us?"

"Riot Squad. We all got left for dead."

Ushara glanced between them. "Riot Squad?"

"Special tactical unit of Gyron Force," Bastien explained. "Commanded by her mother." He returned his attention to Ember. "Did all of you make it out?"

She shook her head. "You're not the only one who lost that day Barnabas took the throne."

"I'm sorry."

"Yeah, well, we all got wounds to lick. So am I in? Or you running suicide?"

Refusing to let her go again while she was this close to him—even if it meant having to be racked every time she thought of Alura, Bastien picked up the bag she'd dropped by his feet and slung it over his back. "Don't drag your ass, Wildstar. I won't tolerate slack."

"I don't want to hear it, GG. I outrank you."

"GG?" Jullien asked Ember.

"Ghost Gadget. So named for the way he always found the right tool whenever we needed to blow something up in battle. Or could repair anything mechanical or electrical that broke down."

Ushara passed an amused smile to Jullien. "Like *you*."

Jullien didn't comment. "And Wildstar?"

"Based off my last name. Wyldestarrin."

"Yeah. Not even," Bastien scoffed. "So dubbed for her temperament and the fact that during training, she set fire to a fellow classmate's airbee when she caught him cheating on her." A pattern that had been hers until they broke up. Somehow he'd been spared that part of her fury. The only thing of his she'd ever set fire to had been his hormones.

Ember narrowed her gaze on him. "Something *you* should have kept in mind. Huh?"

"I didn't cheat on you. *You* broke up with me. How many times do I have to repeat that?"

"Asshole!" Shaking her head, she rolled her eyes. "I take it yours is the Sentella fighter?"

"Yes. Are we going to fight the whole way?"

"Probably."

"Oh dear gods . . ." Bastien whimpered all the way to the ship.

Without a backward glance, she climbed onboard, giving him a prime view of her ass that was just cruel.

By the time Bastien had joined her in the cockpit, he was in all kinds of pain. Something not helped by the fact that it was so tight a fit, she was basically in his lap. He stowed her gear and made ready to launch.

"What? You couldn't afford a bigger ship?"

He ignored her obvious dig. "Wasn't expecting company."

Then the scent of her body hit him. Closing his eyes, he could barely focus on anything else as he imagined what he really wanted to do right then.

And it wasn't fly the damn ship.

Until her link buzzed.

"I need to launch," he reminded her, not wanting to hear the sound of one of her sister's voices right then. Their added condemnation was the last thing he needed. His ego had been kicked enough for one night.

She checked the number, then shot a lethal glare at him over her shoulder. "It'll wait a few." She tapped her ear. "Hey, baby, is everything okay?"

Those words slapped him hard and furiously.

Until he realized it wasn't a man's voice on the other end of her call. Or her sister's.

It belonged to a young boy. "Hey, Ma! Do you have a few minutes?"

"For you, precious, always. How was school today?"

"Do I have to keep going? Isn't there a law against torture or something?"

"Not for school kids, sorry. That's just par for the course."

He made a sound of supreme annoyance. "I miss you, Mama. When you coming to see me?"

"As soon as I can. Promise."

"Okay," he said petulantly, then sighed heavily—as if the world were coming to an end. "Well, Aunt Cin says I have to go do homework and not bother you. But that she'll call you later. Love you, Ma!"

"You, too, doodles." She made a kissing noise at him as he cut the connection.

His gut tight over the fact that the love of his life had a child with someone else, Bastien struggled to not let the hurt he felt show. But it was hard. Practically impossible as images of her in bed with another guy ate him raw.

While he'd known life wasn't fair, this was a kick to his stones he really could have done without.

Trying to be a bigger man than that, he took a deep breath and leveled his tone. "Is your husband all right with you flying out on this mission?"

With me.

She shot a furious glare at him, over her shoulder. "I don't have a husband, jackass."

For reasons he didn't want to think about, that made him feel better. A *lot* better. "Divorced?"

"Never married."

He wanted to shout out in happiness. But that would

definitely make him the jackass she'd proclaimed him to be. So with as much dignity as he could muster—which wasn't much—he launched them.

After they were safely away, he tried to let the obviously sore topic go.

He couldn't. Curiosity ate him and sank its nasty talons in deep. So deep that he couldn't think about anything else. "What happened to your son's father?"

That only seemed to irritate her more. "My baby has a name. Florian."

Florian? Bastien mouthed the horrific name in mockery, grateful she couldn't see his actions. Truly *that* was the only thing he could think that was worse than the awful name his mother had saddled *him* with.

Clearing his throat, he tried to tell himself not to say anything. To stay out of something that was none of his business.

He couldn't.

For the kid's sake, he had to speak up. "Florian? I can't believe his father let you get away with that god-awful monstrosity."

She let out a fierce, angry growl. "His father wasn't around when he was born."

"Where was he?"

Ember sat there, silently fuming, as a million caustic responses played through her head. A part of her wanted to cut him to the bone, but as he reached around her to control the ship and she saw the scars on his hands and arms from all the years he'd had to fight hard for his survival, she bit them back.

Worse? The scent of him filled her head and the warmth of his body cocooned her. And all the years she'd missed him slammed into her with such ferocity that it was all she could do not to turn around, strip his clothes from him and hold him skin-to-skin.

Don't, Em. Let it go.

For too long, she'd thought him dead. There was no reason to hurt him more.

"Ember?"

A tear slid down her cheek at the sound of her name on his lips. Yet it wasn't just that, it was the tenderness underlying that deep, fierce rumble. No one had ever said her name the way he did.

It carried the weight of his love and concern.

She wiped the tear away before he saw it. "He left me."

Bastien fell silent as he remembered the guy he'd beat the hell out of on her behalf. From the sound of the kid's voice and his approximate age, that would be around the same time. He most likely was the father. It would explain the conversation he'd overheard between her and her sister.

Which made him all the gladder he'd trounced the bastard.

"I'm sorry. For everything."

Those words had the opposite effect than what he intended. Instead of cheering her, she burst into racking sobs the likes of which he'd never witnessed from her before.

Switching on autopilot, he gathered her into his arms. "Ember? What's wrong?"

"I hate you!" she screamed before she started slapping at his hands. Not in a painful way, because he'd seen her actually lay a man low with a single punch, so he knew she wasn't really hitting him. This was more what an angry mother would give to a child reaching for sweets at dinnertime.

"Stop it!" he snapped, losing patience with her. "What's gotten into you?"

"What's gotten into me?" She drew a trembling breath and yanked off her helmet so that she could wipe unhampered at her eyes. "Oh, that's rich! Well, let me tell you what got into me, mate. 'Cause I've been dying to tell you for *years*! You want to know about Florian's father? He was a bastard son of a bitch! A prick! A dick who ran off and got himself convicted of murdering his family and left me alone to deal with his psychotic uncle. Another bastard son of a bitch I was terrified, day and night, would find us and kill my son for the blood that runs in his veins. Just like he did his father's family and my parents!"

She turned the link on and shoved it into his face. "Florian's *your* son, Bastien."

CHAPTER 10

Bastien sat there, stunned, as he stared into the face of his son. He would deny it as impossible, but there was no way. The kid looked just like he had at that age. Same dark blond hair that had a tendency to appear brown, depending on the light. Same hazel eyes. He even had the same small cleft in his chin.

If not for the modern clothing, he'd swear it was a picture of either him or Quin.

"I don't understand."

Ember laughed hysterically. "Those prenatal photos Alura gave you? They were mine, Bastien. Alura told Barnabas I was pregnant and he stole the medical files to fool you. That *was* your child, and he didn't die—not even when he almost set the house on fire when he was six. Though I felt like killing him for it. However, the only thing you had wrong was the name of the mother."

Bastien felt ill as he thought back and remembered the times he'd heard Ember being sick and had attributed it to her being upset by his marriage to Alura. To the fact that he'd noticed she was gaining weight back then, but hadn't dared to ask about it as his mother and sister had tutored him well on the fact that no man who valued his life, or balls, ever commented on a woman's fluctuating weight.

"Why didn't you tell me?"

She clicked the link off, but Bastien gently took it from her so that he could see more pictures of his son. "I'd just found out I was pregnant the night you asked me to marry you, after you were almost killed and your father threatened us both. I was still reeling from the shock of it all when you sprung the other on me. All I kept thinking was that your parents would force me out of the military the minute they found out I was pregnant, especially if we were married."

He wanted to deny it, but she was right. His mother wouldn't have stood for it and his father would have done whatever his mother demanded.

"How did Alura know?"

Her lips trembled. The expression on her face said it was from anger. "I don't know, but when she found out I was going to tell you about Florian, she ran ahead of me and told you *she* was pregnant—literally a matter of hours before I'd planned to. I was just waiting for the party to end before I said anything. . . ."

Because Ember, unlike Alura, would have never embarrassed him in front of his family, or caused more harm to his tarnished reputation with a public scandal.

"She knew I'd marry you immediately."

Ember nodded. "And I knew your parents would take me into custody if they learned of it."

For the baby's safety.

Bastien felt ill over the thought of her going through all that alone. He hated the fact that she'd kept it from him. "Did you tell anyone else?"

"Cin and Kindel knew within an hour of the test coming back positive. It was why I switched wingmen. I was terrified you'd catch on given how sick I was during the first trimester."

It'd never entered his mind that she might be pregnant. In spite of all the paternity suits he'd been hit with, he'd never impregnated anyone else. Since they'd been using two different forms of birth control. . . .

He'd stupidly assumed she'd done it only to get back at him or to punish him.

"Is that why you avoided me after my proposal?"

Ember licked her lips. "I was afraid I'd tell you. And you've never been able to keep a secret."

That was true enough. He told on himself even when he didn't mean to.

Bastien stared at the boy who was a stranger to him as he flipped through her pictures. "You've had him in hiding all this time?"

She nodded. "I didn't dare risk his life. My mother and father covered up my leave so that I could have him in secret. I stayed with him as much as I could when he was an infant, but once you were arrested, in spite of what my dad thought, I knew we were on borrowed time. It wasn't long after your arrest that I learned my medical files had been hacked by Barnabas. I had no doubt since Rian was the last surviving heir of the direct ruling family that your uncle would be coming for us, so Tasi took Rian to live with her family."

Bastien was aghast. "Her *outlaw* family?"

She arched a brow at his indignant tone.

"Yeah, okay, so I'm an outlaw, too." As was Jullien. "But I'm not a member of the Dread Reckoning. I didn't *choose* to be on this side of the law. I was thrown here against my wishes. Tasi's family has never chosen to be otherwise."

The Dread Reckoning was a lawless bunch of rene-gades and miscreants. While Tavali were organized and had strict laws they were bound by, the DR had nothing that came close to resembling a legal code. Or even a code of decency. Theirs was a society of derelicts and a free-for-all when it came to following rules.

Even their own.

"They're not as bad as you think."

Yeah, right. He didn't believe that for a heartbeat. "Then why are you Tavali?"

"It was the only way I could keep working and have some semblance of safety for Rian. Since Tavali and the DR hate each other so much, no one would ever look for my child to be among my number one rival organizaton."

She had a point. But he still didn't like it.

"Does he know about me?"

"I would never have deprived him of that. He's known all his life who his father is and why he has to remain hidden."

Those words meant a lot more to him than she could imagine. She could have easily told their son nothing about him. The fact that she hadn't kept him a secret from Florian . . .

"Thank you."

Ember went stiff as Bastien wrapped his arms around her and held her close. Even more disturbing, he laid his head on her shoulder like he used to do when they dated. As if he were cherishing the moment with her, and she was the lifeline he needed to stay afloat.

"Can you ever forgive me for hurting you?" His whis-pered words were like a shout in the silence.

Biting her lip, she ran her fingers down his scarred forearm. "A part of me wants to."

"And the other?"

"Wants to beat you till you bleed."

She could feel his smile against her shoulder. "I'll be happy to strip myself naked and let you spank me all you want, especially if you're naked, too."

A groan came out before she could stop it. "I see you're still twisted."

"Only around your pinkie. You always had control of me when no one else did."

"Yeah . . . that's why you slept with my sister, right?"

He went ramrod stiff and pulled away so fast it sent a chill over her body. All humor and sweetness evaporated as his mood took a sinister bend.

"What?" she teased. "No cute comeback?"

"Not really." There was no mistaking *that* tone.

Ember turned to stare at him in the darkness. He was hiding something. She knew that ominous aura intimately. "What aren't you saying?"

Pain played across his features before he sighed quietly. "I didn't."

"Didn't what?"

"Sleep with Alura that first time."

Her jaw went slack. "What?"

A tic started in his cheek as he refused to meet her gaze. "She was proud to tell me *all* about it the day they branded me Ravin. Looked me right in the eyes and spilled the whole story on how she'd drugged me in the bar, got me home to her place, and stripped my clothes off so that in the morning I'd think we had been together. At first, they were going to blackmail me for creds if I didn't call her for another date. Then she concocted the pregnancy, knowing that my parents would force a marriage if I didn't propose on my own."

Ember cursed in her head as she realized what her sister had done. That bitch! "She heard us."

"Heard what?"

"Me and Kindel, when we were first talking about plans for the baby." Tears choked her as it dawned on her that none of this had been his fault. Alura had connived against them both.

From the beginning.

And if she ever laid hands to her sister again, she'd choke the life out of her for it. "Those are almost verbatim my words as to why I didn't want to tell you I was pregnant."

He let out a fierce growl. "We both played into their hands."

"No," she choked. "My fears did. I should have believed in you, Bas."

"And I should have been sober that night she came to the bar and tried to cheer me up after our fun encounter in the landing bay. But I let it get to me."

"I shouldn't have attacked you like that. I'm so sorry."

He snorted. "Yeah, you should be." In spite of the harshness of his words, there was a teasing note that took the edge off them and let her know he wasn't being serious. "That dinner date with Alura was the worst night ever. Honestly, I had no interest in her. We didn't even make it through the second course before I took her home and left her there—without so much as a peck on the cheek."

A part of her wanted to deny the truth of that, but she knew him well enough to recognize the fact he wasn't lying. Not to mention abandoning dates like that was one of the things he was famous for.

If he learned a woman was out with him for no other reason than he was a visir or if she showed more interest in his money or family than him, date over. There had even been well-publicized cases of him leaving and his security detail being sent in to escort his dates home.

Bastien didn't play with people's emotions.

Except for hers.

"Why did you ever go on that date?"

He laughed bitterly. "You were supposed to pitch a fit when I called that night to ask your permission, and tell me no. Show some emotion that there was hope for us. Instead, you gave me permission to date and, or, screw your sister. Those words cut me to the bone. So I thought I'd go to dinner, spend a few hours with her to agitate you, and be done with it all. But Alura got on my nerves so badly by the time we arrived at the restaurant that had she been anyone other than your sister, I'd have taken her straight home. In the end, after we were married and I came to the conclusion she hated me, I figured it was divine retribution for me trying to hurt you when I should have just been patient and given you the time you asked for."

"Why weren't you?"

"Damn, Ember. How can you ask that? We were practically living together. You had more stuff in my barracks cell than I did. Then I come back from PT after suffering through my brother's reaming over my pouting about you to find that you'd cleaned out all my stuff and had me transferred over to my zusa's division. I felt gutted. In the blink of an eye, you were gone from my life and I didn't know why, or what I'd done to push you away."

Bastien broke off as he relived that moment when he'd faced the corporal. It was like Ember had never existed. Like he didn't matter enough to her for her to waste a moment of her time to explain to him what he'd done that was so awful. She was just gone from his life. He'd felt violated.

Worse, he'd felt abandoned.

"You wouldn't even throw me a bone. After months with nothing from you, and after Alura had told me that you'd never really been interested in me—had only gone out because you were afraid of what I'd do to you and your family if you didn't and you wanted to hurt her for the fact that you'd caught her sleeping with your ex . . . I figured she must be right. How else could you leave like that, without so much as a backward glance?"

Ember winced as she heard the pain in his deep voice. Damn Alura for knowing both their vulnerabilities. Her sister had put her lies right where they could do the most damage. "Can you ever forgive me?"

"Forgive you? Ember, you're the only thing that got me through this nightmare."

Leaning back against him, she closed her eyes and tried to come to terms with all the deceptions and years that had separated them.

Because she was an idiot.

"So where does this leave us?"

Bastien's grip on her tightened. "I don't know. But now that you've told me about Florian, I can't let you fight with me. I won't take his mother from him."

"I won't let you fight alone, and if you don't stop Barnabas and clear your name, we have no future anyway. He'll kill Florian if he ever finds him."

Bastien winced at the truth. Barnabas was crazy and had even killed his brother, Jackson, when he feared Jackson might turn against him after the slaughter and expose him.

Not to mention that with Bastien's conviction still in place, Florian was the rightful heir of Kirovar and should be on the throne. They could legitimately overthrow Barnabas, and his uncle knew it.

It was a miracle and said a lot about Ember's exceptional skills that she'd been able to keep their son alive and safe all these years. Especially given how normal he'd sounded when they talked. Like any other child in the universe.

Instead, Florian should be in the palaces where Bastien had grown up. He should be spoiled rotten to his little core.

I screwed up everyone's life. . . .

Sighing from the guilt of it all, Bastien wished he could go back in time and slap the absolute shit out of himself. "How did this become our lives, Em? All I wanted was to be holed up on some beach, drinking, and making love to you till I happily died of old age, in my sleep."

Ember laughed at the mere thought of that as Bastien's life. "You were *never* that man, Bastien. Since the day I met you, you've had your balls to the wall and one foot in the grave. It's why your mother was so afraid for you. She knew you were suicidal."

Yet for Ember, he'd have settled down. He'd been willing to give up his career to marry her. He'd even faced down her parents to date her.

A smile tugged at her lips as she remembered the first time her father and Bastien had faced off.

"Captain?" Her father had sneered at Bastien's patch, and left off the impressive part of Bastien's status.

"First rank," Bastien had corrected in a move that was as stupid as it was audacious.

Her father had arched a brow at that. "You getting lippy with me, soldier?"

"No, sir. My lips are reserved solely for your daughter."

Her father had started for his throat. But her mother had caught him before he could kill Bastien. "Brandon . . . calm down." Then she'd turned to face Bastien with an evil glint in her eyes. "Are you trying to insult us?"

"No, ma'am. Just really nervous. Sadly, whenever I'm nervous, I get stupid, and things come out of my mouth that even I cringe over."

Her father had finally laughed. "Well, at least he's honest."

"I am that, Commander. Again, stupidly so. And when it comes to Ember, I have a special level of moron that's reserved solely for her."

"What's that supposed to mean?"

Bastien had shrugged. "That I'd jump into a decaying hole on fire during a massive bombing run and risk a building coming down on me to keep her safe and to protect whatever she loves."

Clapping him on the back, her father had handed him an ale. "Good man. For that, I'll let you live."

Ember had never known anyone to charm her parents, before or after Bastien. Out of all their daughters' boyfriends, he was the only one they'd ever liked. Him and Tasi the only two that her parents had welcomed in as their own.

Like it or not, he is family. Through their son, she would be forever tied to him.

With that thought on her mind, she leaned forward to reset his nav system.

"What are you doing?"

"Before you take off after Barnabas, don't you want to meet your son?"

"More than anything."

"That's what I'm doing."

Bastien stared at her in complete disbelief that she was willing to do this. That she'd actually given him a son and hadn't abandoned their child. It would have been so easy to give him up and free herself. Instead, she'd risked her life and that of her family to keep his son safe.

That was why he loved her so.

I'm a father. . . .

And with that thought came a whole new fear. "Can I ask a favor?"

"I'm not having sex with you in a fighter. You can forget it, buddy, right now. You're not that cute in a flightsuit."

He laughed at her droll tone. "Technically you've already done that. Years ago. Many times. So I am that cute in *and out* of a flightsuit. But that wasn't what I was going to ask."

She dipped her gaze down to his groin, which was painfully swollen and woefully obvious. "No?"

He shook his head. "Can we not tell Florian that I'm his father?"

"Why?"

"In case I die, I don't want him to have to cope with the pain of it. I'd rather just be a passing stranger he meets and never thinks about again."

Ember choked at his words and the thoughtfulness. Bastien had always been that way—except for when he'd accepted Alura's invitation to dinner.

You can't hold that against him.

Well, she could. Yet in all fairness to him, he had called her first, and had she not been such a bitch when he asked about it, he wouldn't have done it. So as much as she'd like to pin it all on his shoulders, she really couldn't.

She shared as much blame in the fiasco as he did. Unlike the other men in her past, he hadn't acted behind her back. He'd done everything above board. It'd always been one of his more endearing qualities.

And against her common sense, she leaned back in his arms so that she could touch the dimple on his chin that their son shared. In fact, they shared a lot of traits, which was strange given that they'd never met. "He knows what you look like, Bas."

"How?"

How? Really? All he had to do was look in a mirror. The child was a clone of his father—which had been extremely painful for her at times. They even had the same warped sense of humor, and the need to lip off at the worst possible time. It'd given her a whole new respect for Bastien's parents and the fact that they hadn't drowned him as a child.

She smirked at him. "I gave him a photo of you, long ago. He keeps it in his room, next to his bed. And every night after he says his prayers where he asks the gods to watch over you, he kisses it goodnight and talks to you until he falls asleep."

Raw torment shadowed his eyes before he reached to redo the settings.

Ember stopped him. "Don't. Let him meet you. Just once. It's all he's ever wanted. You both need this, especially if you're bent on suicide."

Bastien wasn't so sure about that, because as she said, he didn't think he'd make it out of this alive, but he didn't want to argue with her anymore. He'd done that enough for ten lifetimes.

Honestly, he just wanted to be inside her. To make love to her until the universe ceased to exist.

And every heartbeat that passed with her squeezed in front of him was its own version of hell.

"I should have taken a bigger ship."

Ember smiled at the deepness of his tone. "That'll teach you to be practical."

She stared at how tense his grip was on the controls. "How long has it been?"

"Since?"

"You had sex?"

Was she serious? "With someone else?"

She squeaked at the question. "Of course. Why would I ask about solo practice?"

His cock jerked at the mere mention of the word as disgust filled him. "Hell, I don't know."

Scowling, she leaned back so that she could meet his gaze through his crash helmet as she had yet to put hers back on. "What do you mean you don't know? You were there, weren't you?"

He snorted at the ridiculous question that she should know the answer to. "I'm Ravin, Em. If anyone sees the mark on my stomach, they'll know that I'm wanted. Can't take the risk."

"Are you telling me that you haven't been with anyone since Alura divorced you?"

"Since long before that."

Both her eyebrows shot up. "Pardon?"

"You have to know that we didn't have an amicable marriage." And their divorce had been spectacularly violent, given that her parting gift to him had been a death sentence.

"No . . . Alura never said anything other than how happy she was and how much you loved her."

In her dreams only . . .

"Happy because I seldom went to where she lived and she had all the creds she could spend. We consummated the marriage and then I tried to make the marriage work, but . . ."

"But what?"

"I called her Ember one night early on, and she basically banned me from her bed."

"You're kidding!"

He shook his head as a particularly nasty memory over Alura's violent reaction went through him. She'd assaulted him like a pissed-off lorina, and left him with bleeding welts on his neck, arms, and chest. "She was convinced you and I were cheating to get back at her." He slid his sleeve up so that she could see the four deep scars on his forearm. "That was from one of her more stellar tantrums. She'd scratch and bite every time I got near her. So I learned to stay away for fear she was going to cry rape or something worse."

Ember flinched as she realized something worse had definitely happened. She'd accused him of murder and seen him innocently convicted of it. "Why didn't you divorce her, then?"

"To what end? You were done with me. Last thing I wanted was to listen to my family tell me how disappointed they were that I couldn't even manage to hold on to my pleb wife for more than a year. Quin was married almost fifteen years. Lil nine. And theirs had been political marriages, assigned to them by my father. They'd have barbecued me had I filed for divorce. Especially my mother. She was traditional Ikarian."

"Meaning?"

"A Triosan religion where no one gets divorced. Ever. It's why my uncle Aros never married. He wanted Cairie as his wife, and if he couldn't have her, he didn't want to spend the rest of his life locked into a loveless marriage with someone else. He kept waiting for her to abdicate her throne and live with him."

That made her feel terrible for both of them. "I am so glad I'm not royal."

Bastien tsked at her. "Ah, baby, you're wrong about that."

"Why? Because I had your son?"

He shook his head. "You were always a monidara to me," he said, using the Kirovarian term for empress.

Ember hated the effect those words had on her. The weepy feeling they awoke. She'd forgotten how sweet her irascible captain could be.

Just like his son.

"I hate you so much, Bastien."

"Most people do . . . Andarions, too."

Bastien quirked an eyebrow as she switched on autopilot and then turned around in the seat to squat on her knees, between his. "What are you doing?"

Ember pulled his helmet off, without answering. The expression on his face was comical. He looked as if he expected her to slap him.

Instead, she loosened his hair until it fell free from its restraint over his shoulders and she could run her fingers through it. A tiny smile played at the edges of those lush, masculine lips.

"You look so feral with this hair."

"I am feral."

"No." She toyed with the soft strands, reveling in the way they slid across her palm. "You're still that man who jumped into a hole to play hero. The lunatic who scaled a building without the proper gear because you thought I'd been captured."

"Yeah, I should have got more intel before I jumped the gun on that one."

It wouldn't have mattered. Rash was his middle name. Careless.

Most of all, loving.

Ember traced his lips with her fingers as her memories ran loose. He'd been so scared for her. By the time she heard what had happened, he'd rescued six of their soldiers. "You did get an accommodation and medal out of it."

She wrapped her legs around his waist.

He sucked his breath in sharply as the center of her body collided with his groin. "Don't toy with me, Ember. This is cruel."

"I'm not toying with you." She slowly unfastened his flight suit. The new scars on his torso tugged at her heart. But nothing prepared her for the horrific Ravin brand that ran from the center of his chest to his pubic bone. That had to have been excruciating. She couldn't imagine how much it must have burned.

And then they'd turned him loose with it, still raw and bleeding, to fight for his life.

Damn them for that!

Wincing, she ran her hand over the additional scars that fell in horrific lines across both of his sides. She couldn't imagine what had caused those. "What did they do to you?"

His heart pounded under her fingertips as his hazel gaze burned into her. "They tried to make me confess to killing my family."

And no one could make Bastien Cabarro say or do anything he didn't want to. "You were ever the most aggravating man alive."

He leaned his head back as she nibbled at his jaw.

Ember savored the taste of him and forced herself not to sink her teeth into his flesh and draw blood as she remembered him at his wedding. . . .

To her sister.

How could she be so angry and hungry for him at the same time?

But the truth was she hadn't been near another man in so long she could barely recall the name of her last boyfriend. Most men fled the moment they heard she had a son.

The rest, the minute they met her insane family. Indeed, her sisters scared off everyone.

Bastien had taken their open hostility toward him as a personal challenge. One by one, he'd targeted her sisters until he made them like him.

She still didn't know how he'd managed. Especially Brand. She hated everyone.

But not Bastien.

His hands trembled as he opened her jacket and shirt until he could touch her breasts. The heated look in his eyes stole her breath. The raw hunger there was tangible. And when he dipped his head down to taste her, she growled at how good his mouth felt against her flesh. She cupped his face in her hands, relishing the sensation of his prickly whiskers scraping her palms.

How she'd missed him. And when he dipped his hand down to gently finger her she cried out in bliss.

He pulled back to stare down at her. "You're right. I hate this fighter, because right now, I really want to taste you."

Laughing, she shrugged her top off, then the two of them struggled with her pants. "Agreed. Next time, a bigger ship. How did we do this before?"

"Like this." He slid her pants down until she was naked in his lap.

"Just so you know, Bas, if you get a call, I'm going to kill you."

He snorted at her threat. "Don't worry. I can promise you there's no way I'll answer. Besides, I don't have anyone who would bother."

Those words saddened her because she knew he wasn't joking. Bastien had always been a loner. That had been her greatest surprise about him when they first started dating. Because of the hatchet job reporters had done against him where they ran with unverified rumors, she'd thought him a monster party animal who had dozens of friends around him at all times.

But he'd been burned so many times by people cozying up to him due to his fame and money, just so that they could be in the papers or have stories to tell to others, he'd been highly cautious about so-called friendships. Very few got past his defenses and were allowed to see the side of him that she'd known.

And that she'd cherished most.

He'd been hers alone.

Bastien sucked his breath in at how good it felt to hold Ember again. To have her hands and body sliding against his. It'd been so long since he last had any sort of tenderness. Had the scent of a woman on his skin . . .

It took everything he had not to rush this. And at the same time, he wanted to take as long as possible to savor every bit of it. Her scent. Her touch. Her taste. He wanted to brand all of it into his memory so that if she threw him away again, he'd have something to hold on to. Fresh memories that weren't faded by time.

Closing his eyes, he groaned as she nibbled her way down his throat. In all his life, no one had ever touched him the way she did. Not just his skin. She penetrated all the way to his soul.

And when she finally slid herself onto him, he almost came instantly. It took everything he had to stay in check.

"You okay, baby?"

Biting his lip, he nodded. "Seeing stars."

She laughed as she slowly rode him.

Bastien lifted his hips, driving himself even deeper into her body. Every molecule was on fire as pleasure dug its heels into him. This was where he wanted to stay for eternity.

And when she sank her nails into his back and kissed his lips, he couldn't contain himself anymore. He came in a blinding wave.

Luckily she followed with him.

Breathless, he held her, waiting for his heart rate to slow. "I thought I was in trouble, there, for a minute."

She lifted his chin until their gazes locked. "You almost were. But I would have forgiven you . . . this time."

"That's not what I want you to forgive me for, *Elskamun*."

Ember choked on a sob at his use of her old nickname that he'd given her years ago.

He dropped his gaze to the stretch marks on her abdomen that were left behind from birthing their son. "I wish I could have been with you."

"You didn't miss much. I cursed you the entire time. And your parents and ancestors."

Grinning, he leaned to kiss her belly. "I'm warning you now that if I survive taking down Barnabas, I'm going to ask you to marry me again."

"Bas—"

He broke her words off with another kiss. "It's okay, *Elskamun*. You can say no, but you can't stop me from asking."

She started to speak, but the alarms on the fighter went off. "What's that?"

Bastien scowled at the panel. "Shit! Someone has their cannons locked on us. That's their targeting system. We're about to be blasted."

CHAPTER 11

Squeaking at the fact that she was still naked and they were under attack, Ember grabbed at her clothes and hurriedly dressed.

Bastien attempted to reach his controls to engage, but because of her movements, it was impossible. In fact, she accidentally elbowed him in the eye as he tried. Cursing, he covered it as it watered uncontrollably.

"Sorry!" Her heart hammered in panic.

"Drop your shields, Sentella. Give us your mission parameters. Now!"

The light in Bastien's eyes said that he was about to tell them where to shove their orders.

But she knew that deep, irritating voice. At least she thought she did.

Ember caught his hands as he reached for the communications and pulled them away from the controls. Making sure to keep the video off, she turned on hailing.

"Badger? Is that you?"

Static answered at first. It stretched out until she was ready to let Bastien blast them in case she was wrong.

Until she finally heard a hesitant answer. "Wildstar?" he asked in disbelief.

Grateful that voice did indeed belong to her Badger, she breathed a sigh of relief. "Yeah, knock off the target locks. What are you doing this far out?"

"Making a run and headed home. Why are you on-board a Sentella fighter?"

"Headed to see my boy. This was the only ride available."

As typical, Badger wasn't quick to accept her answers. "Why am I showing two people, then?"

"I have a friend with me."

"Friend have a name?" That man was ever suspicious. He never took anything at face value. Not that she blamed him, given his past. She had trust issues herself, but he took them to a whole new level of ridiculous.

"G. G."

"G. G. Sentella?"

Dear Lord, Badger was worse than a dog after its favorite bone. Hence the call sign they'd dubbed him with. He could have easily been employed as a League interrogator.

"No, he borrowed the ship."

"Borrowed, or stole?"

Ember bit back a groan at his endless inquisition. Seriously, they all wanted to beat him at times when he started doing this. But then, when you wanted to annoy someone, he was definitely the man to call, for he did it well. And with panache.

Worse?

He actually enjoyed watching people's temples begin to throb.

"Own," Bastien said to her.

Ember didn't bother repeating that to Badger, as it would raise his suspicion levels even more. "Borrowed. And no, he doesn't have a blaster trained on me. There's no need in being alarmed. Drop your weapons. It's all good here."

"Then why's there no video?"

Bastien quirked a playful smile. "Yeah, Wildstar. Why's there no video?"

"Shut up, both of you! Badger, stop being a *knættr*. I swear to the gods . . . it has to be genetic!"

"What?" Bastien and Badger asked simultaneously, thus proving her point.

Ember barely caught her slip before she exposed something she knew would piss Badger off to no end. They needed to get on the ground before that bomb was detonated.

Closing her shirt as quickly as she could, she turned around in the seat and took over communications.

"Take the lead, Badge. Get us home."

"Fine. Do your sisters know you're headed in?"

"Cutting the comm, now." She flipped it off and let out a frustrated sigh.

One not helped as she realized how tense Bastien was. "What's wrong with *you*?"

He fell into that horrible quiet that only came whenever he was seething about something. "Badger your boyfriend?"

Was he serious? She couldn't believe he'd even ask that. Let alone be so pissy about it.

How dare he!

"You better be glad you have your helmet back on. Otherwise, I'd be tempted to slap you for that."

"Why?"

"Obviously, I don't have a boyfriend. If I had, I wouldn't

have just had sex with you! Saint Jake, Bastien! That's your territory, *not* mine!"

He bristled at that. "I've never in my life cheated on someone! You know that better than *any*one!"

She did, and it was a sore topic for him, as he'd been accused of it repeatedly. Not just by the press, but by his own family. And apparently Alura, too. It was what had made them so good together. Her worst fear had been a cheating boyfriend, and he would never cheat because he couldn't stand being blamed for it.

Not to mention, he'd seen the damage cheating had caused for his parents. And while he'd loved his father, that had always been a very, very touchy subject for them. In fact, Bastien had been arrested in his late teens for assaulting his father when he'd first learned of it—it was what had caused him to be sent into the military.

After Bastien had lifted a skimmer that belonged to a friend's parents, his father had shown up with his mistress to bail Bastien out. His mother thought Bastien's enlistment had resulted from the theft.

Neither of them had ever told her the real reason. His father because he'd always lied to her about his affairs. Bastien because he'd have sooner died in war than hurt his mother in any way. Which made no sense, as his death would have been the worst tragedy of all for her.

But Bastien's thoughts had only been on sparing his mother's feelings, any way he could. It was why he'd always been her favorite child.

Ember sighed. "Sorry." She sighed as she thought over everything she'd learned about him. "Did my sister really accuse you of having an affair with me?"

He growled low in his throat. "*You*. My sister. Hell, she'd even speculated I was sleeping with the pool boy."

She burst out laughing at the thought. "Seriously?"

"Oh yeah. She was convinced I was chasing everything that moved. Female. Male. Fluffy bunnies. Even pack animals. If it breathed, she accused me of jumping into bed with it."

She shook her head at Alura's stupidity. "Again, sorry."

"It's all right. Besides, I aggravated her suspicions out of principle."

"Meaning?"

He laughed evilly. "During one of her more stellar tirades, I asked if she'd mind me having a three-way with Cinder and Tasi."

Oh, that had to have been rich. Ember could hear the screams in her mind. "You didn't!"

By the sound of his voice, she knew he was still grinning. "You know me better than to ask that question."

Of course she did.

And of course, he did. It was a vintage Bastien move. Why just aggravate a situation when you could annihilate it and bomb it up a few levels?

"Your mouth has always gotten you into more shit, Cabarro."

"I know. Can't help myself. I have this moment of reason where my inner sense tells me to bite my tongue. Then my 'fuck-it list' kicks in and I'm doomed." He cleared his throat. "By the way, your jacket's not fastened properly. You might want to fix that before we land."

Looking down, she cursed as she realized he was right. "Thank you for noticing."

"There's nothing about you I don't notice."

Her brow shot north as she felt him growing hard against her hip again. "You cannot be ready for another go 'round. Surely . . ."

"*Elskamun*, you have *no* idea. All I have to do is catch

a whiff of your scent and I swear I could hammer in a nail with what you cause down there."

"Hammer a nail? I might test that theory later."

"Again, don't tease me."

Oh yeah, there was no missing the way his voice deepened. Or how much she'd missed japing with him like this.

Ember fell silent while they followed after Badger, and noted what Bastien was doing. "He won't turn you in, you know."

"Pardon?"

She inclined her head to where he was entering notes into the fighter's system. "That's why you're logging his serial on the ship and its markings, is it not?"

When Bastien answered, he kept his tone flat and even. "Doing my due diligence. Wanted to know what and who I was dealing with."

"He's DR. What more do you need to know?"

"What he is to you."

She leaned back so that she could stare up into Bastien's face. He had the shield lightened on his helmet so that she could smirk at the suspicion in his eyes. "He's a pesky little brother who's like a father to your son, so play nice even if he is a member of the outlawed Dread Reckoning."

Bastien ground his teeth as a fierce wave of jealousy went through him over those words. "Father?"

"Don't even get that look on your face, Bastien Cabarro. He's Tasi's cousin, who was orphaned young and raised like her brother, and they were very kind to take Rian in for me. We owe them a debt of gratitude."

But the surly expression on his face said the only thing he wanted to give Badger was a kick in the ass.

"You will love him when you meet him."

"Doubtful."

She tsked at him. "Careful with those absolutes . . . they have a nasty way of coming back to bite you."

He scoffed at her words and remained churlish until they landed on the small outpost where the leader of the Dread Reckoning made her home—or at least as close to a leader as the DR came. Which wasn't saying much. It basically meant Tasi's mother was the nastiest of them all.

Inside the fortified bay, Ember climbed out of the fighter first.

Bastien was much slower, especially once he saw Badger heading for her. Dressed in his all-black Armstitch suit, Badger was almost as handsome as Bastien. But he lacked that je ne sais quoi that Bastien had mastered from the cradle. Something about Cabarro was infectious and charismatic.

And she was grateful every day that their son had inherited that trait from his father. Even if it did lead the boy astray from time to time.

Just like Bastien.

Eerily quiet as he tagged along behind her, Bastien had that tenseness to his body like a coiled spring while he approached Badger. It usually heralded an ass-beating for whatever male had caused it.

Wanting to head it off, fast, before it exploded into something deadly, Ember gave Badger a hug and whipped his helmet off so that she could kiss his dark, whiskered cheek.

Bastien froze the moment he made eye contact with the young man. His breath left him as if he'd been sucker-punched. And that's exactly what it felt like as he stared into eyes that were an identical match for his.

And his father's.

More than that, while Badger's features were similar enough to Bastien's, they were *identical* to Quin's. It was like staring into the face of his brother's twin, especially since Quin hadn't been much older than this kid when Barnabas had murdered him.

Ember stepped back. "Iskander Zeki, meet Bastien Cabarro."

Fuck me . . .

Zeki . . . he should have known. That had been the unmarried name of the bitch his father had run around with for *years*. The same woman who'd been with his father when Bastien was arrested his last year of university.

Even now, he could see her standing behind his father in that sterile office when he'd shown up to bail him out. Never in his life had he been angrier.

And this was their offspring. . . .

Recognition flared in Badger's eyes a moment before he let fly an audible curse that matched the silent one in Bastien's head, and started away from them.

"Badger!" Ember barked as she pulled him to a stop. "Don't you dare leave here."

"I've got nothing to say to *them,* and you of all people know it."

"Bastien had nothing to do with your father's actions. It was Newell's choice to walk away from you when you were a child. And right now, neither of you has enough family left for you to be assholes to the only brother you have."

Indecision played across Iskander's dark brow. It was an expression so close to the one Quin had whenever he was perplexed or undecided that it sent a chill down Bastien's spine.

There was no doubt in his mind that they were brothers, just as she'd said.

Unbelievable.

This was the last thing he'd expected, and it ranked right up there with his unknown son. What other surprises did Ember have in store for him? At this point, he was getting punch drunk from being slapped in the head with them.

Stunned and unsure of how to proceed, Bastien stepped forward. "I don't know what went on between you and my fath—"

"*Our* father," Iskander corrected between clenched teeth. "Though he wasn't much of one to me, for damn sure. I never saw him again after my mother died."

Bastien held his hands up. "I meant no slight with that. Slip of the tongue, mate. I would *never* insult you that way."

Iskander scoffed and rolled his eyes.

Damn, he was hostile. But then Bastien did the math in his head . . . Odile had died during his first year in the military. Given Iskander's present age . . . A bad feeling went through him. "How old were you when she passed away?"

"You mean when she was murdered and I was left as an orphan? Seven. Barely."

No wonder he was pissed off. Bastien couldn't blame him, and he didn't understand how his father could have done that to him. So much for all the lectures his dad had given *him* on taking responsibility.

There was no way he'd have *ever* abandoned a child of his.

"Icky! Mama!"

Bastien scowled at that high-pitched squeal that was followed by the sound of a heavy, slapping footfall of a boy around the age of nine who came running across the bay like a frazzled blur. It wasn't until he launched himself into Ember's arms that Bastien realized the boy hadn't said "Icky Mama," but rather had been calling out to Iskander and Ember.

Disbelief filled him for the second time since he landed as he stared at the small, dark blond boy whose hazel eyes matched his and Badger's.

It'd been one thing to see his son in pictures. In the flesh . . .

Bastien had no grip on this moment. Dropping his helmet to the ground, he went to the boy and Ember, and wrapped his arms around the two of them and held them tight. All he wanted to do was keep them there for the rest of eternity.

Ember couldn't breathe due to Bastien's crushing embrace. Still, she sank her hand into his unbound hair and held him while he kept Florian wedged between their bodies.

"I. Can't. Breathe!" Florian growled as he struggled for freedom like a fish that had been dumped on land.

Bastien refused to let them go.

"Mama! Help! I'm being molested! Stranger danger! This is making me uncomfortable!"

She laughed at her son's misery. He was so tall now that the top of his head reached her chin, but he barely reached mid-chest on Bastien. "He's your father, Ri. Give him a moment to hold you."

Florian stopped moving instantly as his jaw went slack. He leaned his head back to stare up at Bastien. "Papa?"

Bastien cupped Florian's head in his hands. The anguish and love on those chiseled features brought tears to her eyes and reminded her of his face when he'd learned his family was dead. That restrained agony that wrung her heart. This was the man she'd fallen in love with. Irritating. Hostile. Reckless. Capable.

But most of all, he was loving to the depths of his soul. Bastien never did anything halfway.

He loved as he lived. With a breakneck speed that was impossible to keep up with.

His lips trembling, he smiled proudly. "Hi, Florian."

Florian looked from Bastien to her and back again. "Mom never told me you were gigantic."

Bastien laughed. "Not as big as my Andarion friends or my cousins, but I was taller than my brother."

Iskander scoffed. "Not as tall as I am. Nor as muscled. And *I'm* the youngest."

Ember slapped him playfully on his hard, muscled abdomen. "Now, now, no jealousy!"

"I was just saying . . ."

She rolled her eyes at that Cabarro competitive spirit.

Bastien ignored them as he tried to think of something to say to his son. Love, pride, disbelief, and fear tangled inside him, leaving him speechless.

What did someone say to a half-grown kid they didn't know they had?

"It's an honor to meet you." Even Bastien cringed at the stupidity of *that* statement. *Why don't you ask his age and remind him of all the years you've missed while you're at it?*

Great intro . . . moron.

Florian laughed. Then he reached up to touch the cleft in Bastien's chin. "Everyone says I take after you. I do, don't I?"

"God, I hope not." Bastien grinned. "'Cause if you do, your mother has a whole other reason for wanting me dead."

Her features softened. "You have no idea. Curse you at least three to four dozen times a day."

"Oh my God! Bastien!" That shriek was even more ear-piercing.

Turning, he saw Tasi, Cin, and Brand as they came running.

And grabbed him into hugs so fierce, they almost knocked him over. It was like being dragged under by a riptide.

But he loved it too much to complain.

"We thought you were dead!" Tasi balled her hand in his hair and held him close as she rained kisses over his face.

"I saw The League report where you'd been killed!" Brand pulled Tasi away so that she could hug him.

He laughed at the unexpected exuberance. It was more than he'd ever hoped to experience from them. Honestly, he'd expected them to hate him as much as everyone else did. "My cousin Jullien did that for me so that they'd stop hunting me."

Cin leaned against his back, making him the middle of their sandwich. Which reminded him of what he'd suggested to Alura that had sent her spiraling into a special level of pissed off she probably had yet to come down from.

Florian made a rude noise. "Not so fun when you're the one getting squished, is it?"

Bastien laughed. "I disagree. This is awesome! Sign me up and leave me here."

Pursing his lips, he glanced over to Ember. "You failed to tell me my father was mental."

Iskander laughed at that. "I could have told you, kid."

"And speaking of . . ." Tasi glanced to Ember. "By the two of you being here, I'm assuming this isn't a social call."

"No." Bastien stepped back so that he could touch his

son. "I'm going after Barnabas. We're here to meet Florian and then I'm going to finish this."

Iskander's eyes widened at those words. For the first time, he looked at Bastien with something other than contempt. "Brother! Good friend, buddy, oh pal of mine! You are my new best friend. Where you go, I go."

Bastien took another step away from him at those peculiar words. "What kind of distemper do *you* have?"

"The same one you do. Barnabas Cabarro. He killed my mother too, and he damn near killed me. You're going after him . . . I plan to help."

"You know that this is most likely a one-way trip."

Iskander shrugged. "So long as he goes with me to the grave, I can die with that."

Florian gasped at his words. "No. No, you can't! Neither of you can die." He turned to Ember. "Mom! Stop them!"

How she wished. Sadly, she'd never been able to stop either of them from being stupid.

Bastien opened his mouth to reassure him, but before he could, an alarm sounded. He grimaced at Ember.

Suddenly, there was a voice over an intercom. "League ships are sighted and heading in. Battle stations!" Then it switched over to an air raid siren.

Confused, Bastien watched as members of the Dread Reckoning came out of the hallways at a dead run to prep their ships for a scramble. "I'm not tagged anymore. How are they . . ." His voice trailed off as a sick feeling went through him. "Anyone have a scanner?"

"For what?" Tasi asked.

"The ship. I think it could be tagged."

Ember arched her brow. "What are you thinking?"

"Nykyrian mentioned that he thought they might have

a spy in The Sentella who's working with The League. I'm wondering if they tagged the ship."

"Yeah, it is." Iskander showed him the readings on his link. "It's hotter than a dwarf star."

"Oh, it gets worse." Tasi pulled her link out of her ear and turned it to speaker.

They heard The League commander addressing Tasi's mother, who was the leader of the DR.

"While we don't condone the Dread Reckoning, we are willing to overlook your unsanctioned, criminal base of operations. But only if you hand over the felon we're after."

"And who is that?"

"Bastien Cabarro. Return him to us and we'll leave peacefully. Protect him or allow him to get away and we'll level your base and leave no survivors."

CHAPTER 12

Bastien cursed at the confirmation of a spy. "There you go. As far as The League knows, I'm dead and buried. My file showed termination two years ago. Only people who knew I was still around were in The Sentella."

Minus the guard he'd told when they rescued Kalea Hauk. But that had been weeks ago. Had the guard filed a report outing him, The Sentella would have picked it up and warned him to run. No one got past Syn Wade's alerts or bypassed them.

No one. He was the best tech in the Nine Worlds.

Not to mention, The Sentella had their own crew of spies who would have instantly relayed that intel.

This definitely came from the suspected spy Nykyrian had warned him about.

And with the thought of his hidden enemy, his old familiar battle calm came over him. There was one way to stop this and protect what he loved.

"Where's a comm link?" he asked them.

Ember went cold at that tone of voice she knew a little too well. Bastien had a battle plan. And while his plans were always innovative, they were usually highly risky, and often explosive.

If not downright stupid.

"What are you thinking, Cabarro?"

That old charming grin that had melted her heart more than once split his face. "Not sure I want to disclose it at this time, Major."

Yeah, stupid for the win.

Her stomach knotted to a sickening level at the thought of what he might do. "Don't even."

But Tasi, who had no idea what level of carelessness Bastien was capable of, handed her link over to him.

Ember cursed her silently.

Bastien turned to Badger. "Load my fighter with enough explosives to detonate whatever they have. *Tonde!*"

Her jaw dropping, Ember arched a brow at that last order, which was the Kirovarian military term for *tel-ass*.

"Bastien . . ."

And still the irritating beast ignored her as he activated the link. "Put me on with The League MCO."

She gaped even wider as he demanded to speak to the mission's commanding officer. Was he out of his Kirovarian mind? *This cannot be good.* Bastien and commanding officers didn't mix. And she said that as one of his former commanding officers.

A bad feeling went through her. And Rian must have felt it too, because he came to stand beside her so that he could whisper, "What's he doing, Ma?"

"No idea. Now you see why I tell you not to act like your father?"

Rian ignored her.

Just like Bastien.

When the MCO picked up, Bastien didn't flinch or show any emotion whatsoever. "Hello, Dumbass . . . back your troops off this station. I'm coming out and turning myself in. But only *if* you withdraw."

"No!" she gasped before she could stop herself. Surely he wasn't planning to commit suicide. .

But to protect them, he might. Bastien had a fanatical need to do the wrong thing for the right reasons. And with a son to protect, his suicidal level would be ratcheted up even more.

Bastien turned on the mute and glared at her. "Do you mind not interfering with my noble act of extreme stupidity, Major? Please?" Then he turned the mute off so that he could continue his conversation with The League. "Yeah, I'm on my way as soon as you pull back. I'll be in my fighter. You can't miss it. Sentella ship. Has The League flag with a big X going through it on a black field. Will need clearance to land it, though."

Holding on to Rian, she ground her teeth, wanting to thrash Bastien. If he thought for one minute that she was going to allow him to do this, he was even more delusional than normal! Which was saying something.

And still Bastien ignored her as he made plans to die.

Her sisters were all gaping, too. But they didn't speak until he had the coordinates and cut the link.

He blinked innocently at all of them while Ember made a sound of supreme disgust in the back of her throat. "What are you thinking, Bas?"

With a devilish wink, he headed straight for his fighter. "Not thinking at all. According to you and my father, I never do."

"Bas! I'm not letting you do this!"

He gave her a coy glance. "Does this mean I'm forgiven?"

"No, it means you're an idiot!"

He tsked at her vim. "You know, that's what I missed most all the years we were apart. Your unfailing support and sweet-talk. It humbles me."

"Don't be an ass."

"See! That's what I'm talking about. No one else could ever insult me the way you do. And I still have one testicle left you haven't kicked."

"Mom?"

Only then did Bastien take pity on them. "Don't worry, champ. I've got this." Without a word, he jogged to the fighter and shot up the ladder, but instead of getting inside it to launch, he opened the engine bay.

Following after him, Ember frowned as she watched him work on who knew what. Though as she saw him scrambling about she began to have some idea of what he intended.

Yet there was one major problem. . . .

"You know, they'll scan for life forms. If you send it up on autopilot, they'll detonate it before it can cause harm."

"That would be true in most cases."

"Meaning?"

"That I've had years and years alone to hone my skills and plot my revenge. They've no idea what they're dealing with. But I'm about to set them up for some hostile lessons."

Brand scratched at her ear as she watched him working. "You think he can do it?"

Ember shrugged. "We didn't call him Ghost Gadget without cause."

"True."

Still, she did have doubts.

Pulling away from her, Rian ran to climb up the fighter behind his father. She started to grab him, but Bastien reached down to help him move to stand by his side so that they could work on it together.

The sight of them like that . . . of Bastien's patience with their son as he explained to him what he was doing and why . . . it made her strangely weepy.

"So this will work?" Rian asked.

"It should. Or it'll piss them off and they'll kill us." Bastien pulled out his link and handed it to their son. "Please, hold the light so that I can see a little better."

"Okay. And for the record, I don't want to die."

"For the record, I don't intend to let you. I'd never hear the end of it from your mom. And she really scares me most days."

Rian glanced at her, then whispered, "She scares me, too."

Ember sighed as that tweaked her heart, in a psychotic kind of way. Bastien made it so hard to stay angry at him. But then that was nothing new. The entire time they'd dated, she'd been on the verge of wanting to choke the life out of his body and then he'd surprise her with an act so incredibly kind or thoughtful that she'd instantly forget her rage.

His mother had complained of the same thing. And so had Lil. In fact, she could hear his sister's voice in her head to this day—*"It's the only reason I didn't drown him while he was still in nappies. . . ."*

"So what are you doing now?" Rian asked excitedly.

"This is the heater for the ship. If we scramble things about, it'll heat up the seat and make it appear as if there's someone in it."

"You can do that?" Rian gaped.

"Sure can. Then we need to rig the drive so that it can pilot out on remote. And the sensors so that they'll think they see a phantom body in the seat."

"That's awesome. How will you land it?"

"Won't have to. SOP for The League is they'll tractor beam the ship in. They won't chance my ramming their facility out of suicidal tendencies." Bastien flashed a charming grin down at her. "Of which I have many, according to your mother."

"Wow . . . how do you know all this?"

"Studied hard in school."

Rian screwed his face up at his father. "Not what Mama says."

This time, Bastien glanced down to her and smirked. "What lies has she been telling on me?"

"She says you're where I get my slackness from. That you charmed your way through school and negotiated grades with your teachers like you were running for political office. You never studied for anything, other than how to avoid responsiblity."

Bastien feigned being offended. "Why she tell you that?"

He shrugged. "Don't know."

Bastien grimaced down at Ember. "Why you tell my boy those stories?"

" 'Cause he's little Bastien, all the way. Just look at him. He's not your son so much as your clone."

Rian was digging around the engine, toying with various belts. Just the way Bastien tinkered whenever he had a new toy. He looked up with a charming smile that was identical to the one his father used whenever he got caught doing something he wasn't supposed to.

Bastien grinned proudly.

Ember groaned and then had to smile at the two of them and the trouble she was in while facing their combined force.

Cin wrapped her arms around her. "I like seeing you with that expression on your face."

She leaned back against her sister. "It's not happiness. I'm imagining creative places to hide Bastien's body should my child be harmed."

Brand laughed.

Until Badger returned, with Kindel in tow, hauling enough explosives that it made her sick to her stomach. Ember couldn't believe how much he'd found.

Or how quickly.

Good Jake, you are Bastien's brother.

How had their family ever survived to become rulers of anything?

Bastien forced Rian down the ladder and away from the ship while they wired the explosives.

Against the child's protests, she had Brand take him home so that if something went wrong—like she maimed his father over this "brilliant" plan, he wouldn't be here to witness it.

Or worse, get caught in the blast range.

Crossing her arms over her chest, she watched the men running around to rig the explosives. Bastien was a little too cavalier with the highly volatile compound for her tastes. As was Badger. "Are you sure you know what you're doing?"

"Not at all," Bastien said with a laugh. He scowled at Badger. "Is it the red and green wires you're not supposed to cross?"

"Um, yeah. So please don't forget that. Especially while I'm in range."

Bastien nodded. "I guess this would be a bad time to tell you I'm color blind?"

Badger turned stark white. "Are you effing kidding?"

"He's joking, Xander." Ember laughed.

Bastien flashed that evil grin. "You feel more alive now, though, right?"

The expression on Badger's face said that he wanted a place to hide Bastien's body now. "I swear I'm going to murder you."

Bastien laughed again as he finished wiring the ship.

Once they'd jumped down, Bastien scowled at the remote. "Boy, I hope I didn't fuck up those connections."

It was her turn to go pale. "Meaning?"

"You might want to stand back a few miles while I do this."

"Bastien . . ."

He calmly flipped the switch. "Oh hey, it's all right. I'll be damned. Works. That's a first!"

Xander screwed his face up. "He always like this?"

"Yes," she growled. "You should have been in the field with him."

"I'm surprised his own troops didn't shoot him . . . in the back . . . of the head."

"They tried," Kindel said with a laugh. "Bastard moves fast for an aristos."

Meanwhile Bastien continued to chuckle at them while he launched the ship. "Time for that spectacular enema."

A few minutes later, they heard The League commander telling Bastien to drop shields.

Bastien's face lost color. "Ah, minsid hell, I forgot that part. . . ."

"Ha, ha," Badger mocked. "You're not funny, Cabarro."

"He's not joking this time." Ember stepped forward. "What do we do?"

Bastien glanced around at all of them. "Run!"

"Not without you."

He grimaced at her. "You don't even like me."

"I know. But it would traumatize my son if I let you die right now."

"Great." Bastien started to argue, but there wasn't time.

He met Badger's gaze. "Don't scramble fighters. Withdraw everyone into whatever bomb shelters you have. *Tonde!*"

Issuing orders, everyone evacuated in expectation of a League assault.

Ember took Bastien's hand and ran toward the condos where her sisters lived with Rian. There would be shelters there.

They heard the fighter detonation over their links.

It was followed by sirens blaring to warn them of an impending strike.

"Cabarro!" The League MCO shouted. "You've damned them all by your actions!"

Bastien cursed under his breath.

An instant later, bombs fell against the station, jarring them off their feet.

Bastien grabbed Ember and threw her under a reinforced beam as another shock wave went through the building and brought down sections of the roof and walls around them. "You always rocked my world. Nice to know things haven't changed."

She moaned at his cheesy lines. "Not the time."

Suddenly, there was a massive strike against the base. One that lit up the sky like a nuclear device had detonated. The wave from it was so fierce that it knocked all of them from their feet.

The whistling sound of engines and bombings deafened her.

Amidst the smoking debris, Bastien rose slowly and helped her up.

Terrified of what was going on, Ember grabbed him and held fast. She let the scent of his skin ground her. But most of all, it was his strong arms and the slow gentle beating of his heart that soothed her.

That was one of the things she'd missed most about him. His calmness when everything was falling apart. Nothing ever rattled him. Not even a bombing run. It was just like the day they met when he'd jumped headfirst in after Alura.

His gaze warm, he kissed her forehead and gave her a light squeeze to reassure her. "It'll be fine, Ember. I'll die before I allow them to harm you or Florian."

She fisted her hand in his hair and let his whiskers scrape against her cheek. Tears filled her eyes as she realized that they might not make it out this time. And if they died, she didn't want him to go not knowing the truth of how she felt for him.

How she'd always felt about him. He'd lived too long doubting her and that was her fault.

No more.

"I still love you, Bastien."

"I know." He pulled back with a playful grin. "How could you ever stop loving all this sexiness?"

Snorting, she wanted to beat him for his facetious humor, which she didn't appreciate right now. But it did succeed in making her laugh. "You're a beast!"

Bastien winked at her. "But I'm *your* beast."

And he wished he believed the lies he was spewing for her benefit. The truth, however, was that he had no idea what was going on or how to help her or her people out of this disaster. *How could I have brought this down on them?* He should have remembered that damn shield. . . .

"How many fighters can we scramble?" he asked her.

"You said not to."

"Circumstances have changed my mind."

She bit her lip as she considered it. "I don't know. Not my base." She looked around for her sisters, but they seemed to have vanished during the attack.

Until Kindel popped up from the rubble on her left. "Ember? Do you know the call sign Merksaker?"

She shook her head.

Kindel tapped her link. "Blast him out."

"Wait!" Bastien stopped her. "Give me the digits."

"Hold on that order," Kindel said quickly, then handed him her earpiece so that he could hear the pilot.

"Drake? That you?"

"Yeah . . . can you tell these lunatics to back it down a notch?"

"You alone?"

"Here with Jari. On Kimmerian business. We were sent as your backup."

By that, Bastien knew Drake didn't want him to let the others know he was the Caronese prince or that Safir was a former League assassin. "Gotcha, *drey*." He glanced over to Kindel. "They're friendly. Can we not blast them out of the sky?"

She relayed the orders on Cin's link while Bastien returned to the call. "Who sent you?"

"Was the least we could do after everything you've done for our families. Since they were all tied up with official business, Saf and I decided we couldn't let you do this alone. We picked up your tail after you left the Gort base and were planning to hang back until your League friends showed. Nice fireworks, by the way. Learned from Darling?"

"Hauk, actually."

"Nice." Drake laughed.

And their presence here touched him a lot more than he would have thought. "By the way, I appreciate you coming."

"Think nothing of it. It's what families do."

"Hey, I don't mean to interrupt," Safir Jari said, cutting in. "But as the resident League expert here, I can tell all of you that our friends will be sending reinforcements. A lot of them with a ton of warheads. We need to evac that base immediately. If you don't have a safe place, we need to locate one that can jam them from identifying life-forms."

Bastien turned toward Ember.

She looked to Kindel.

"I'll get it started."

"We'll need a ship," Bastien reminded her. "You know, mine kind of exploded."

Ember groaned at the reminder.

Drake laughed in his ear. "I have a small ship that can seat five. You want me to take passengers?"

Bastien didn't hesitate to accept. "Yeah. Thanks."

"Let me get clearance and I'll be down in a few."

As soon as he cut the transmission, Ember gave him a peeved glare. "You trust him?"

"With my life." Coming from him, that was the highest testament.

"You're sure? What if they're the ones who led The League here? Isn't Saf Jari the younger brother of Kyr Zemin? *The* League prime commander?"

She had a point. "He is, but Kyr captured and tortured him because he helped their brother Maris, who is the best friend of Drake's brother. Then Kyr had him stripped of his League rank and declared a traitor. Given that, I don't think Saf is likely to be working with them."

"But you said they had a spy. . . ."

"I did. However, Saf would be too easy a target to spot and suspect. Kyr's more devious than that."

Ember wasn't so sure, but they did need to get out of here as soon as possible. So when Florian returned to the bay with her sisters, she sent him off with Kindel for the base evacuation. Just in case. The last thing she wanted was to take a chance with her child staying with her when he'd be safer with Kindel, since she and the others were planning to head for battle.

She and Bastien went with Drake.

Ember pulled up short the moment she saw the youngest Caronese prince. Unlike his brother Darling who had short red hair, Drake's was jet black and as long as Bastien's. He also bore that same innate regal aura undercut by strict military training that said he tolerated no fools and would sooner kick ass than kiss it. Yeah, this wasn't a typical aristo or politician.

Drakari Cruel was no one's puppet or pawn.

Dressed in an elite Kimmerian assassin's uniform, he greeted Bastien like a brother. But his blue eyes glowed with suspicion as they narrowed on her.

"Ember Wyldestarrin, meet Drake Cruel."

She had the impression that he could read her soul with that slow, probing stare. "Your Highness."

A friendly smile lightened his dark demeanor. "Please, no formalities. I don't want to hear that unless I'm at court, and even then it gets on my nerves." He shut and locked his ramp, then gestured for her to follow him. "Come, my lady. Make yourself at home."

As they headed for the flight deck, he shook his head at Bastien. "What is it with uncles? Fucking bastards, all. I'd say to kill them, but being one myself . . . I don't want to die."

"Well, I assume you've no intention of killing off your nephew for his throne."

"Minsid no to that. He's adorable. Plan to teach him everything I know to make Darling crazy. Payback's a bitch. Besides, I had a chance to take the Caronese throne. Don't want no part of *that*."

She didn't miss the sadness in Bastien's eyes. He'd never wanted to inherit either. Especially not over the bodies of his family.

Wanting to cheer him, she quickly changed the subject. "Nice ship."

"Thank you. Designed her myself. Kimmerian code, all the way."

"Rather unusual occupation for a prince."

Drake flashed her a charming grin. "We had an unusual upbringing." He paused to touch his link. "Merksaker, here." He listened for several minutes. "Aye, Lady DR. We can pull the rear. If you'll send the coordinates, Saf and I will make sure no one follows. *Saker Mara*, out."

"Saker Mara?" Ember asked with a frown.

"Name of my ship. It's Caronese for *Outlaw Nightmare*."

"Ah . . . and Merksaker?"

"Dark outlaw." He waited for them to strap in before he launched and followed the rest of the Dread Reckoning toward their remotest outpost, where they retreated any time things got hot for them.

Once they were clear of escape velocity, Drake turned to smirk at Bastien. "When was the last time you slept?"

"Not sure."

"No offense, it shows." He checked his headings. "We've got a while. Why don't you and Ember head to the crew quarters, shower, and take a nap. Eat. If you need a change of clothes, I'll unlock the door to my room. Take whatever you need and don't worry about it. My sister's room is the last one on the left. She's a little taller than Ember, but she should have something in there that she can change into, too. Believe me, Ana won't miss anything. Woman has more clothes than a department store."

"Thanks, *drey*."

"Any time."

Bastien unbuckled himself and headed for the back with Ember one step behind.

As they walked in silence, she couldn't help noticing just how gorgeous he was. But as Drake had noticed, he was tired. She could tell by his slow, methodical movements.

"You okay, Bas?"

"Been a heck of a day."

It had indeed.

When they reached the first room, Bastien turned around and gave her a kiss so hot that it left her breathless.

"Been dying to do that. And I would kill to make love to you, but I have got to have a nap."

She laughed. "You have been running on empty."

"You have no idea." He gave her one more searing kiss before he pulled himself away and went to literally flop on the bunk.

Ember laughed at his actions.

He didn't even bother to remove his boots. Feeling sorry for him, she moved to disrobe him while he lay there like a corpse. At first it reminded her of undressing Rian when he was too tired to bother, but as she uncovered more of his delectable body, all thoughts of their son fled her mind.

Bastien had always possessed one of the best physiques she'd ever seen on any male. He still did. Every sleek, hard muscle of his body was clearly defined and honed like steel. It beckoned her with a hunger that was undeniable.

Unable to resist it, she quickly stripped and slid herself into bed beside him and snuggled up against his warm, bare flesh.

He let out a contented sigh, but he was already asleep.

Smiling, she took her time playing with his hair and listening to him breathe. Took her time running her hand down his muscled arm and ribs and buttocks. When she reached the short hairs at the center of his body, she started to leave him alone, but that had also been one of her favorite things to caress. And it'd been too long since she last had him like this.

At least any place other than in her dreams.

Before she could stop herself, she sank her fingers into the crisp mat and ran her fingernails through it. He grew hard instantly. And yet he didn't wake. Which told her exactly how exhausted he was. In the past, he'd have awakened instantly and been inside her within a few minutes. Foreplay be damned.

One of his more irritating habits. But it'd been one that she'd decided she could live with as it'd always proven to her how much he desired her. How much he loved her.

Her humor over that died as her gaze dipped to the Ravin mark that marred his abdomen. The injustice of it all enraged her to a level that made her want to kill everyone involved with what had been done to his parents and hers.

Wrongfully convicted. She'd spent hours over the years trying to imagine the horror he'd lived through having seen his family slaughtered, and then having been arrested and sentenced for it.

How could Alura do that to him?

Ember had never understood, and still didn't. There was nothing in the universe that could compel her to harm someone that way.

Sure there is.

You'd do it to save your son.

But only for that reason. Alura had had none whatsoever. None. It'd been heartless and cruel. Especially after

Bastien had given up his happiness with Ember to marry Alura over a lie that she knew would destroy them both internally.

How selfish could one human being be? But then her sister had always been that way. She'd always held her needs out as greater than those of the rest of them. A congenital birth defect.

I swear, Alura, if I ever get my hands on you, I will strangle you for this.

Her days of protecting her sister were over.

Bastien slept for two full days. He didn't stir until they were landing on the Dread Reckoning outpost. Even then, Ember had to practically inject him with adrenaline to wake him.

Like a languid cat, he opened his eyes and stretched. "Where am I?"

"We landed about half an hour ago. . . . I've been trying to wake you."

"No wonder I have to go so badly." He flashed a grin before he rushed from the bed.

She laughed as she waited for him to return.

And waited.

By the time he came back, she realized he'd taken a quick shower first.

He flashed that devilish grin at her. "I was rather ripe."

"No comment."

Stretching, he yawned. "Where's Drake?"

"They went into the main hailing room to talk to Tasi's mom. Apparently, he's known her for a while, but she didn't realize who he was until now. And had never given her his call sign before."

"Good thing or bad thing?"

"Appears good."

Bastien let out a relieved breath. They could use·some good.

And speaking of . . . He swept a hungry gaze over her lush body. She'd always made him hungry.

Hard.

He didn't know what it was about her, but damn. An image of her long dark hair in his lap really didn't help the mood, either.

"I know that expression." She tsked at him. "We can't. Rian's waiting for you."

"I know. And I need to make plans with Drake and Saf. Which I meant to do instead of sleep the entire trip."

"You must have been exhausted."

He nodded. "Been a long time since I had someplace really safe to sleep."

"Safe because of me or Drake?"

"You." His eyes darkened. "Definitely you."

"So you trust me?"

His gaze turned warm as he began to slowly kiss his way around her neck. "I've always trusted you, Ember. You were the one who lacked faith in me."

She looked away, letting him know he'd struck the truth with that comment.

But before he could pursue it, Drake came on board.

"Ember?"

Bastien pulled away from her with a frustrated hiss.

"Yeah?"

"You're Hadean Corps, right?" Drake asked from outside, in the hallway.

"I am."

He opened the door to see them, and grinned at Bastien. "Nice to see the dead has risen."

Bastien rolled his eyes.

Ignoring him, Drake returned his attention to Ember.

"I'm intercepting some strange Tavali stuff, and I can't get ahold of my brother, Ryn. But I swear I heard his mother's name mentioned and it concerns me. Can you take a listen and see what you think?"

"Absolutely."

She and Bastien followed him off the ship and outside to the primitive base that had once been a mining facility. But it'd petered out centuries before and been abandoned. Since no one had come here and it seldom showed on maps, the DR had decided it was a great place to use for emergencies.

Like now.

The old shed appeared abandoned on the outside. But inside, it was crisp and clean, outfitted with the latest technology. She tried not to let her thoughts wander to how good Bastien smelled when freshly bathed as they went to the comm room where Cin and Kindel were waiting.

At first, she couldn't understand the thick accents of the speakers over the channel. It wasn't Gorturnum. But the longer she listened, the more she began to understand.

Finally, she deciphered it.

Drake had been right. It was about Hermione Dane and it did involve the Tavali.

She felt the color drain from her face as she met his concerned gaze. "They're planning to bomb Hermione and kill your brother, Ryn."

CHAPTER 13

Drake went ramrod stiff at Ember's declaration that the message he'd stumbled on was the plot for Hermione Dane's murder. "What?"

She nodded. "Sounds like they're going to try for it in two days."

"You're sure?"

She squinted as she continued to listen. "The accents are thick, but yeah, I'll stand by that. It sounds like a major strike they're planning against all of The Sentella."

Drake cursed. "I have to find my brother and warn him."

"And Darling," Bastien reminded him.

"Yeah. And Darling," he agreed. "Definitely Darling." He bit his lip. "You're one hundred percent sure about this?"

"Absolutely."

"Then may the gods be with us."

But as the days went by, it began to feel like they weren't. While they were able to save Hermione's life, The League made a devastating run against the Porturnum Tavali StarStation, they hijacked a Caronese freighter that had been carrying medical supplies to orphans, hit the

Wasturnum West Fleet that was being led by Drake's sister-in-law, and bombed the Andarion palace to the ground.

Their casualties included Drake's sister-in-law, Mack Hinto-Dane. Nykyrian's family—wife, children, and parents. Drake's older brother Darling and his wife and son. Syn Wade's wife and son, along with his sister-in-law, and basically the families of the entire Sentella High Command.

Even Saf's nephew and brother-in-law went down with the palace.

And Jullien and Thrāix.

None of them had been left unscarred by the waves of attacks against them.

Bastien reeled from the pain. It was too much to contemplate. He couldn't breathe. Couldn't function or plot.

Neither could Drake. Their anguished grief rendered them useless.

Ember had never seen Bastien like this as they sat in the living room of Kindel's small cottage. It was as if he were reliving the death of his parents and siblings, only worse. He had latched on to Rian and wouldn't let him go.

"Should we call someone?" Cin whispered as she watched him with a worried frown.

"Yeah, like a priest?" Ash wasn't joking.

Chewing her nail, Ember debated what she could do to help him. "I don't know."

Bastien finally wiped at his eyes and shook his head. "This is bullshit!" He met Drake's gaze. "Jullien isn't dead. Not with Thrāix by his side. I know better."

Drake scowled. "What are you saying?"

"I know my cousin. He's a gutter rat, like me. You don't go through what we've been through and die like this. You just don't." He kissed Rian's head and stood. "Where's a link?"

Kindel handed him hers.

Bastien tried Nykyrian and couldn't get through. So next he called Ushara. She picked up immediately. Silent tears fell down his cheeks. "Shara, I just heard."

"Shh, Bas. It's not what you think."

His heartbeat sped up as he felt some hope. "The Dagger still flies?"

"Yes. Until I lay hands on its hilt. But yes, the Dagger has sworn to return to its sheath where it belongs, along with the rest of the forks and spoons. They're a little bent, but whole."

He let out a half laugh as she threatened to kill Jullien when he got home with the others. "And Kere?" he asked, using Darling's Sentella call sign.

"You can't stop the god of death. You know that."

His breath left him in a loud rush at the confirmation that everyone had survived. And that he had understood her code for what it was. Thank the gods that for once, they were merciful. "Tell Nyk that we're coming in, to watch for us. We'll be loaded for League."

"Be safe and careful. I don't need another scare like the one I just had or else I'll be in early labor."

"No worries." He cut the transmission and returned the link to Kindel. "Darling's alive and so's Jullien."

Drake shot to his feet. "What the minsid hell! I'm going to gut him!"

Bastien snorted at his fury. "And this after you were crying over losing him three seconds ago?"

"Yeah, 'cause they'd crowned me emperor. I don't want that shit! You know how much responsibility comes with a throne? No, thank you!" He shuddered. "I can barely tolerate being prince."

But Ember saw through his bluster. Drake adored his older brother and the relief in his eyes was tangible. "So what's the plan, Captain?" she asked Bastien.

"I'm planning to lend a hand with their rescue efforts."

"Count me in."

"And us," her sisters each agreed.

Bastien nodded. "They'll need every hand for a few days."

Drake let out a ragged breath. "Just when we were about to strike at your uncle. I swear that bastard has nine lives."

"A temporary reprieve. We secure our families and then in a week, we go for him. His defenses'll be down. With all this, they'll think The League is in a position of strength and that The Sentella is weak. It actually works in our favor. He won't be expecting anything right now."

Drake nodded.

Bastien and Ember said a reluctant good-bye to Florian before they and Drake rallied Kimmerian and Dread Reckoning forces to lead them toward the Porturnum Station and join The Sentella forces there.

Whatever Nyk and his crew needed, they'd do.

As they prepared their launch, Ember couldn't shake the familiar feeling of being back in action with Bastien. It was just like old times.

More than that, it felt right and natural. This was where she was meant to be.

As a girl, she'd never understood how her parents could work together as a military unit. Especially given the way they fought so much at home.

But with Bastien, it made total sense. They were in synch. She knew what he was thinking without him speaking.

He did the same with her. More than that, she took

strength from having him by her side. Such as now, as they prepared to launch. He stood next to her on the bridge with his hand on the small of her back while she worked. An insignificant lingering touch to steady himself while he entered data and she checked their systems.

It was automatic. He wasn't even aware that he did it. Yet the scent of his skin permeated her head and left her drunk and calm at the same time.

"Coordinates?" he asked in that smooth drawl.

She sent them over.

He entered them, then paused. A slow smile spread over his face. "You know, when you look at me like that, it makes me want to carry you off to the corner."

"Look at you how?"

"Like you're already tasting me."

Heat scorched her cheeks. "You're imagining it."

"Am I?"

She cleared her throat. "Yes."

"Am I?" he repeated in a more teasing tone as he pressed his body closer to hers.

Iskander cleared his throat over the intercom. "You two do know that you're live, right?"

"Oh shit!" Bastien cut the mic. Now he was glowing even more than she was.

"Yeah," Iskander said slowly. "My thoughts are a little more colorful. Dude, that's my sister."

"I'm your brother."

"Blood only. I actually like Ember."

"Gee, Badger, thanks," Bastien said drily.

"Ah, now, don't pout. You're slowly growing on me."

Snorting at his dry tone, Bastien launched and took control of the Kimmerian troops and the few Dread Reckoning who'd signed on for the venture. Even though Ember and her sisters outranked him, they let him take over since he was known to The Sentella and they weren't. Not to mention, neither the DR nor Tavali were legal organizations with a lot of protection.

They'd learned long ago to keep their heads down or lose them.

But instead of rendezvousing with the Gort Tavali, they were sent to provide backup for the Andarions who were struggling to get control back from Nyk's and Jullien's insane grandmother. Apparently, she'd rushed in after the bombing, declared everyone dead, Nykyrian a traitor, and had reseized her throne.

Ember sat in the navigator's chair as she scanned the other ships around them. "How do you think this war will end?"

Bastien sighed. "I don't know. My father always said it'd come. That it was long overdue. The League started out as a noble idea, but as with all things, people corrupted it. The idea of a single police force for everyone . . . just doesn't work."

"The Sentella seems to balance it."

"Because they're fighting The League. Anytime you have one group with all the guns and training . . . you have tyranny. Nature of the beast. It's why all things in nature are dual. Good and evil. Hot and cold. Positive and negative."

"Then shouldn't that be those trained and those not?"

He snorted at her. "That's not balance. That's inequality. Like a twelve-year-old girl trying to defend herself against a nineteen-year-old man. It's not physically possible and she's at the mercy of his morality. It works, provided he *has* morality. When he doesn't . . . she's his victim." He sighed. "Moderation and balance. Do no harm. Respect all life. That's what my father taught me. Damn shame Barnabas didn't learn that."

Bastien frowned as he met her gaze. "But then I can't reconcile how my father treated Jullien . . . or Xander. I mean, really. He harmed them both. Greatly. Badger was as much his son as I am. As Quin was. And Badger needed our sa a lot more than we did."

"People aren't perfect."

"I know. It's what I keep telling myself. But I just wish I understood."

Now that they were launched, Ember went over to hold him. "I'm glad you don't. It's what makes you different."

Bastien closed his eyes as her hand brushed against his scalp. Double-checking the comm, he made sure no one could see or hear them and turned on the autopilot.

"What are you doing?"

He pulled her into his lap to hold her close. "Right now, holding you. In the next few minutes, I plan to be inside you."

She sucked her breath in sharply. "You're incorrigible."

"But you're not saying no."

"I know." It'd been too long for her too. She needed him as much as he needed her.

She kissed his lips.

When she lifted her head, she saw the dark look in his eyes. "What's wrong?"

"Nothing. Just thinking of what you asked. If we lose this war, we'll all be put to death."

"I won't let them have you."

"And I won't let them take you or Florian."

"Then don't look so sad." She reached down between their bodies to undo his pants. The moment she touched him, he let out a deep hiss.

Ember smiled. This was what she'd always loved most. The power she had over him whenever he was like this.

He might be stronger and much larger, but he was hers to command at will.

And they both knew it.

He was hers. He'd always been hers.

Every day they were together, it was getting harder to think of not having him around. Harder to remember how she'd made it without him.

Smiling, she watched him undo her shirt before he slid his hot hand over her flesh. There was magic in his touch. How a man so brutal could be so tender, she'd never understand. And yet he had patience and kindness in a way few did.

Her thoughts wandered as he slowly tongued her breasts, and she remembered finding her picture among his meager gear. It and a photo of his parents and siblings had been the only personal items he'd kept during his exile. When she'd asked him about it, he'd been completely unapologetic.

It's what got me through.

And he was what currently saved her sanity. His son had been what had kept her going through everything else.

She owed him her life. Rian had given her focus. He'd given her purpose.

Most of all, he'd given her unconditional love.

"Don't ever leave me again, Bas."

He pulled back to gently cup her breast. "I'm not going anywhere, *Elskamun*. I'm right here."

Nodding, she slid herself onto him. They both moaned in pleasure.

Bastien watched as she rode him slowly. He still couldn't believe that she was back in his life. Every day he woke up, he expected her to leave again. Every minute, he held his breath, expecting her to banish him back to the darkness without her.

It was why he tried to cherish every heartbeat he had with her and Florian. He was tired of fate or whatever ripping him out of their lives. Jullien had said the same thing to him about Ushara and his kids when he'd lived on Oksana.

He'd been unable to relate to his cousin at the time. But he fully understood now.

That was the hardest thing about loving. That fear of loss. Especially after she'd already cut his heart out once and fed it to him. Trusting her again was so much harder than he'd ever imagined.

And yet he couldn't stay away. No matter how hard he tried to protect himself.

He loved her. Against all common sense and self-preservation. Really, it wasn't fair.

But then, nothing in life was. And right now, he didn't want to be anywhere else except inside her. Staring into her beautiful eyes while she made love to him.

And when she came in his arms, he smiled, then joined her there.

With a contented sigh, she collapsed against him and laid her head on his shoulder. That action stunned him, as she'd never done such before.

"You okay, *Elskamun*?"

"Petrified."

The fact that she'd admit it . . . "I'm not going to let anything happen to you."

"I wish you'd say the same about yourself, Bas. That's what scares me. I have a bad feeling that won't go away. Every day it grows worse." Tears glistened in her eyes. "I was holding my mother when she died. She looked at me, choked, and was gone." A sob racked her. "I don't ever want to live through that again, Bas. I couldn't take it if I lost you again."

"I'm sorry."

"Why does it have to be so hard?"

"I don't know, Em. My father used to say that life tries us all without prejudice or mercy."

"But why?"

"No idea. I just know that we're all veterans of a fucked-up world. No one gets out without their scars. Some of us just hide them better than others."

She nodded, then kissed him. "I'm sorry for the ones I gave you."

"You were trying to protect yourself. I get it."

"But it doesn't make it right."

"Nor does it make it wrong. It just is, my lady."

Ember shook her head and held him. And as she lay there, she prayed for the knot in her gut to loosen. For her premonition to be wrong.

Bastien had suffered enough. She'd buried enough of her family.

She refused to bury him, too. And yet the vision remained.

It was Bastien lying in his casket.

CHAPTER 14

It took them longer than expected to route The League and Andarions and get Jullien home. Bastien was more than frustrated as it seemed that the gods of Kirovar wanted the injustice to stand and for Barnabas to rule on a stolen throne.

But it did allow him more time with Ember and Rian, and to plan an attack that would work. So he savored his every minute with her and made sure to double-check everything so as not to risk her or her sisters.

Now they were back at the Gort base to celebrate the birth of Jullien's son Vidar. And what a strange gathering of a motley band they were, too.

"Congratulations!" Bastien clapped Thrāix on the back as he held his infant son, Admon Simon Eteocles Sparda, in his arms. "You really planning to call him Sphinx?"

The expression on Thrāix's face said that he'd gone a few months without a bowel movement. "Not by choice. But Mary outranks me in all things, so . . ."

Bastien laughed. He well understood that. "Beats Florian," he whispered.

Thrāix burst out laughing. Sobering, he tucked the

sleeping infant under his chin. "I'm just glad I made it back and that Mary's here, with him."

Yeah. It'd been close. Thrāix had been trapped in the bombed Andarion palace with Jullien and Darling, and Mary had been captured by their enemies for a short time, and assumed dead. They were both lucky to have survived their ordeals.

Bastien clapped him on the back. "So you gonna pull a Caillen and retire?" After the palace had gone down on his wife, children, and sisters, Caillen had decided that he was through fighting. He'd handed in his resignation to The Sentella and retreated with them to the main Exterian palace, where he intended to wait out the rest of the war.

Thrāix gave him a wry stare. "Please," he said drily. "Mary would never let me go that long without babysitting Jullien." Because Mary's sister was Ushara, and so she sent her husband along to ensure that Jullien didn't do anything completely stupid—like Bastien would do.

Unira came over to them and smiled. "So, Bastien . . . when will I be performing a wedding ceremony for you?" She cut a meaningful gaze to Ember.

Little did she know what a kick to his stones that was. "Not up to me, Holy Mother. I'm willing. The bride has better sense than to tie herself to the likes of my worthless hide."

She tsked. "Well, I'm here anytime you two change your minds."

Bastien stepped back as another herd of Ushara and Mary's relatives swarmed Thrāix and the baby. He couldn't believe how many months had gone by as they fought The League and he tried to find a chance to get at Barnabas.

It was as if some unholy power protected him.

Sighing, he retreated to a corner where he could watch Ember holding Jullien's newborn son, Vidar. And that brought its own ache to his chest as she cooed and made the baby laugh. He'd have given anything to see her playing with his child like that.

His gaze went to Florian, who was in the corner with Vasili, gaming. The two of them had hit it off immediately.

And as he glanced about, Bastien wanted to be content with what he had. He wanted to let it go and forget the past.

He couldn't.

I can't live knowing Barnabas is alive and they're not.

It was that simple. His uncle had bought his happiness at the expense of Bastien's entire family. Because while he was grateful to be here with his new family, he was all too aware of the members who weren't here.

And why.

Quin should have his son with Florian. And they should be gaming. Lil should be nagging him about Ember. His mother should be fussing about his attire. His father over his lackadaisical attitude and long hair.

No, he owed it to them. He couldn't let himself forget that.

Trajen, Jullien's boss and the leader of the Gorturnum Nation, came over to him. "Breathe."

Bastien shook his head at the Trisani pirate as he took an ale from Trajen's hand. "I am breathing."

"Well, if it helps, The Sentella have been calling for you."

"Have they?"

"Check your link."

Bastien did, and Trajen was right. "Damn, boy, you got some scary powers."

"Yeah, I know."

As Bastien moved to return the call, Trajen drifted over to Thrāix.

It was a recorded message from Syn with intel Bastien had been waiting on. A slow smile curved his lips.

"Ach, now, if that's not a frightening look. I'm shivering in me boots!"

Bastien smiled even wider as he recognized the smooth, deep cadence of a familiar voice. Jory Hinto. He had been the Jup that day on Oksana when Jullien had first returned to Bastien's life. And since the day Jullien had introduced them, they'd become fast friends, as it was impossible not to adore Jupiter Hinto.

He turned toward the Tavali pirate with a smirk.

"Don't you be cutting them eyes at me like that, cade. I'm just here to corrupt and entertain."

Bastien laughed. "Jory, you asshole. What are you doing here?"

"Ach, now, was invited. I'm assuming you were too. Besides, it's not me you need to be fretting, me Kirovarian brother. It's your maither over there, sitting on us all."

"My mother?"

He jerked his chin toward the door, where a new group had just come in. "Fain Hauk."

Bastien laughed again, especially as he noted Fain and his wife Galene interacting with Ember and her sisters. But his laughter died the instant it dawned on him that they were all Tavali here and The Tavali were the natural enemies of the Dread Reckoning.

Ah minsid hell . . .

Clearing his throat, he glanced back to Jory. "They're friendly, but they're DR. Please don't kill them."

"Well, you're asking a lot. Good thing I still love you. And that Fain is too happy about his own new grandbaby to be in a slaughtering mood." With a wink, Jory headed over to see Sphinx.

"Who's Jory?" Ember asked as she came up behind Bastien.

"Jory Woods Hinto. Son of Gadgehe Hinto."

Ember choked as she instantly recognized *that* name. "Gadgehe . . . as in the HAP of the Septurnum Nation?"

"Affirmative. Also Jory as in the brother-in-law of the VA of the Wasturnums, and the ambassador of the entire Tavali joint Nations. Not someone you want to shoot at." He smiled down at Ember. "By the way, you should always ask Jory if he's hauling Precious Cargo."

"Into battle or the party?" She screwed her face up at him, not understanding the reference. "Why would he do that?"

"He'll know what it means."

Ember arched her brow as she tried to decipher his cryptic words. "How so?"

Bastien laughed evilly. "It would mean that Ryn Dane is with him."

She gaped at *that* name. Not only was he the above-mentioned ambassador and Wasturnum VA, he was also the older half-brother of Darling and Drake Cruel, both of whom would be extremely upset should anything happen to him. No wonder they called the man Precious Cargo—an apropos call sign, indeed. "Anyone else we need to make sure we don't hurt?"

"Probably." Bastien stretched out the word. "If Fain, Ryn, and Jory are here, it's a real good bet they're hauling Chayden Aniwaya with them, as Jory seldom goes anywhere without Chay following. Those two are thick as thieves."

"And Chayden would be?"

"A prince of the Qill empire. Beloved brother of the

Exeterian and Garvon princess. Which means she would have sent their prince and heir, Caillen, to guard her brother. Or Caillen's here just to bust heads and have fun because he makes me look sane."

"I thought he retired."

"That's what he claims, but I'll believe it when I see it, and as I said, Desideria isn't going to let her brother be hurt."

Ember let out an aggravated sigh. "Is there anyone you *don't* know?"

He sobered instantly. "My son."

Guilt cut through her at his unexpected reminder as Bastien went over to talk to Vasili and Florian.

Ember stayed back to gather her dignity over what she'd intentionally done to the one person she should never have hurt. Bastien would have stood by her through the fires of hell. And she'd cut him adrift out of fear. Fear of his father. Fear of her own emotions and fear of his uncle.

How could she have been so stupid?

Kindel moved to stand by her side. "You okay?"

"I don't know."

Kindel laughed. "You've never known. Mind some advice?"

She passed a droll grimace at her older sister. "Of course I do. I hate your advice."

"Because it's usually right, and in this case, it's extremely true."

As much as she hated to admit it, Kindel wasn't wrong about that. Damn her for it. "Fine. What is it?"

"Get out of the way of your happiness."

"How so?"

Kindel jerked her chin to where Bastien was smiling and greeting an extremely attractive auburn-haired man dressed in the red uniform of a Wasturnum Tavali. One who bore the same noble bearing and regal refinement that was innate to Bastien. "You overthink *every*thing! You panicked the night he asked you to marry him, and rather than tell him why, you ran. Stop running. Stop thinking. Just feel and do."

"Said no one ever in the history of the United Systems. That is the worst advice ever, big sister."

Kindel pointed to where Bastien was now hugging Fain Hauk and greeting the others. "You have been in love with that man since the night he called you in the hospital and asked you out for dinner. Do you remember what you said to me?"

"Not at all."

"That Bastien was the only man who ever met you and Alura at the same time and then chose *you*. And that he was sexier than hell."

"And the craziest lunatic ever born!" She definitely remembered saying that part.

Kindel ignored her outburst as she continued. "Why do you think Alura did what she did to you and Bastien?"

That was easy. She was a selfish bitch, but most of all . . . "She wanted to be a visira."

"In part. But mostly, it was to get back at Bastien for daring to love you and not her." With a gimlet stare, Kindel folded her arms over her chest. "You know why she testified against him?"

And that was an even easier question to answer. "To save her own ass." It was what Alura was best at.

"No." Fury glinted in Kindel's eyes. "Back then, she talked to me. Told me everything. Originally, she had planned to hide while Barnabas did his coup. What changed her mind, you ask? Bastien overheard *you* talking to Cinder about your breakup with Cedric. You remember that?"

"Vaguely." He'd been an unimportant rebound. But it had cut her to the bone when he broke up with her after he found out about Rian. He'd been furious to learn she had a child and hadn't disclosed it to him on their first date.

"Well, you can ask Cin to verify this. While talking to you, she turned around and saw Bastien's face. He looked as if he'd been gutted. At first, she thought he was feeling sorry for himself. Until she heard later that he'd gone to Cedric and beat the utter shit out of him for hurting you."

Ember's jaw went slack. "You're kidding me."

Kindel shook her head. "He made you cry so Bastien made him weep. When Alura found out who Bastien assaulted and he refused to tell her why, she put it together and was furious that he was still defending you. That he still loved you enough to care and go to jail for you. So she went to Barnabas and told him she'd do whatever he wanted to get back at her husband . . . because he loved *you*, his ex-girlfriend, more than he loved her, his wife."

Yeah, that sounded like something her sister would do. No one hurt Alura's feelings with impunity. "Does Bas know?"

"I have no idea. But I thought you ought to, given what it cost him."

She was right. And now she felt all the worse about it. "Thank you, Kiki."

Leaving her sister, Ember headed for Bastien, who was laughing with a tall, dark-haired Qill who must be the Chayden Bastien had mentioned earlier. By his Tavali patch, she saw he was a Rogue pilot.

"Psycho Bunny?" she asked as soon as she saw the name on his patch.

He laughed good-naturedly over his call sign. "Chayden Aniwaya . . . although, Psycho Bunny is much easier to pronounce."

Bastien clapped him on the back, letting her know they were close, too. "They were just explaining to me how they blew our League friends out of the sky."

"Yeah," Jupiter said with a wicked grin. "You missed one hell of a great dogfight, Cabarro. You should have been there, cade."

"Well, my ship was, during one fight . . . without me."

Now it was Fain's turn to laugh. "You know, when I first heard that story from Drake, I thought you were in it, till I realized you're not *quite* that crazy. How much explosive did you load on it?"

"I was hoping enough to take them all out. Epic fail to that."

Ryn, who was even in height with Bastien, shook his auburn head. "You've been hanging out with my little brother too long. I thought only Darling was that reckless with explosives."

"Really?" Bastien asked drily. "'Cause Dancer Hauk was the one who blew my base to smithereens. I'm still pissed about that."

Fain snorted. "You? I still can't believe my brother did that, given how much he hates explosives and explosions. Says it all about how worried he must have been."

"Given the fact that we were responsible for Nyk's beloved daughter at the time? I'd risk the explosion, too."

"Truth to that." Chayden laughed. "You weren't there when I helped escort Thia here for her new assignment. I don't think any of us breathed until we were clear of Sentella-controlled space and made sure Nyk wasn't trailing after us, target-locked."

"Speaking of being target-locked . . ." Fain glanced around the group. "Has Ryn told you?"

"What?"

"We've got intel on Barnabas from Syn. We're all planning to go with you to fight him."

Bastien gaped. "Suddenly, I feel so loved." Then he grinned, but only for a second, until it melted into a frown. "I can't believe you'd risk your lives for me and mine."

Ryn snorted. "You didn't think we were going to let you fight alone?"

"Um, yeah." Bastien inclined his head to Ryn. "Don't you have a baby to tend?"

"Not yet. And it was either I come to back Jory in this fight, or Mack would have come. So I docked her with my mom and flew right out as I don't want my pregnant wife doing something profoundly stupid while protecting her lunatic brother."

Bastien snorted at the mention of Ryn's headstrong wife. "Gutsy."

"Yeah, not really. Mack and my mom scare me, they get along so well. I keep waiting to get booted out of the family."

"That's 'cause you married your mom."

Fain and Jory turned to glare at Chayden for his comment.

"What?" Chayden said innocently. "Oh, c'mon! I cannot possibly be the only one who's noticed that Mack and Hermione are basically the same person. They look alike. Dress alike. Even move alike."

Jory slapped him hard in the stomach, then between gritted teeth said in a loud whisper, "We don't talk about *that*! Ach, cade, are you insane?"

"They are nothing alike!" Ryn insisted.

But Ember could tell by the expression on Bastien's face, as well as the others', that Ryn was being willfully obtuse about it.

How much could they favor?

Before she could ask for clarification, Cin and Tasi brought Rian out to them.

"Do we really have to leave now?" Rian asked.

Ember ruffled his hair. "Sorry, baby. We have to get back to our base."

All of the men fell quiet as they noticed the fact that Rian was Bastien's clone. It was actually comical the way they glanced between them.

"Yeah," Bastien said after a second. "I know. And yes, he's my son. Florian, meet Chayden, Jory, Ryn, and Fain."

His jaw dropped at the massive size of Fain. "Are you an Andarion?" And before he could answer, Rian hurriedly added, "You know you look just like the Iron Hammer! He's an Andarion Ring fighter."

Fain grinned, exposing his fangs. "Yeah, I know. Talyn's *my* son."

"Really?"

"Yeah," Fain said proudly. "You ever want an autograph, just let me know." Then he glanced back to Bastien. "Love your kid. He's adorable, now pick a ship before we all get into a fight over you."

Bastien laughed at the thought. "Whose is largest?"

"Jory's."

Bastien turned to Ember. "Looks like I'll be taking the aptly named *Ship of Fools*."

"All right." Fain stepped back to leave.

"But my ship's prettier!" Chayden pouted.

Fain growled at him. "There is something profoundly wrong with you, human."

"Yes"—Chayden slid his gaze to Fain—"and he's standing on my left."

Fain shoved him away from him.

Ignoring them, Bastien said goodnight to Florian

before Ember's sisters took his son to wait for them in the bay.

As they headed out, Ryn pulled Bastien to the side. "Syn also came across some data while gathering those files you asked about that he wanted me to give to you personally."

Bastien paused at the odd note in his voice. "What?"

Ember returned to listen.

A dark shadow haunted Ryn's blue eyes as Jory stopped by his side. "Go ahead, cade. 'Tis something he'll want to hear."

Still Ryn hesitated.

Ember knew Bastien dreaded the words. But both of them were completely unprepared for the bomb he dropped on top of them.

"Your brother, Quin? He's still alive."

CHAPTER 15

Bastien couldn't breathe as Ryn's words slapped him. Hard. Unable to comprehend them, he shook his head. "No. I saw my brother die. In front of me."

Ryn's expression darkened. "And I swear to you that he's alive. We would *never* play with you that way. There's not a one of us who hasn't been through hell for their family. And of all people, Syn isn't the one to take the death of a sibling lightly."

No, he wasn't. It was common knowledge that he'd lost his sister to suicide. So no, he'd never toy with anyone about such a somber topic.

"He's sure it's Quin?"

Ryn nodded. "You and Ember come with me and I'll explain it."

Bastien hated to let his son go back home without them, but if his brother was alive, he needed to find him.

Sick to his stomach, he went to where Florian waited by the door.

"I know." He flashed a grin at them. "Rian, go with Aunt Cin. Be good. Brush your teeth. Do your homework."

Ember cupped his cheeks and kissed him. "Love you, precious."

"You, too. Be careful."

Bastien held his hand out. "When this is over, you and me, bud . . . long camping trip. No one else. Male bonding. Uninterrupted. Lots of porn."

"Bastien!" Ember snapped at him.

Florian smiled. "Promise?"

"Absolutely . . . minus the porn, though, as I don't want your mom to hurt us." He hugged his son. "And a Cabarro never breaks his word."

"That's what Mom says."

Bastien held him a little longer even though he knew time was of the essence. It was hard to let go. But he had no choice.

Kissing the top of his son's head, he forced himself to do the last thing he wanted.

He released him to Cin's care. "Thank you."

She hugged Bastien. "Don't worry. We adore little Bastien as much as we do big Bastien. It was Alura we voted out of the family."

He laughed. "I always loved all of you. Really missed you."

Cin kissed his cheek and hugged him. "We missed you, too, little brother. And just so you know, Tasi and I told Alura that we'd take you up on that threesome any time you wanted."

He burst out laughing until he realized that his son might have heard her. A quick check told him that Florian was thankfully out of range. "You're lucky you didn't find yourself in jail alongside me."

That sobered her. "No. We found ourselves left for dead and under assault by the Eudorans and under friendly fire.

Trust me, there's no love for Alura among us anymore. She killed it the day she betrayed us all for your uncle. Go kick her ass, with our compliments."

"Don't worry," Ashley said as she came up behind Bastien. "I plan to cut her head off and hand it over to all of you to play ball with before everything is said and done. Just like our ancestors did."

Bastien had to do a double take since they were both dressed up for the party. When they were in battle clothes, it was easy to forget how much Ashley and Cin favored. When they were dressed up and not standing side by side, it was hard to tell them apart. He'd gotten into trouble a couple of times for mistaking them. Which he'd felt terrible about until Tasi had told him that she'd accidentally groped Ash by mistake a time or two herself, for the same reason.

With a curt nod to her sister, Ash and Cin took Florian out, and Bastien and Ember followed Ryn to get the details he had.

Ryn led them to the North Bay, where he'd docked his ship. Without a word, they went to the flight deck. Ryn's first officer, Yra, materialized in front of them, ready to shed blood. Though not very tall, the blue-skinned, red-eyed Starken was tougher than nails and more than capable to take down an entire League hit squad.

Until she saw Ryn. Then she relaxed into a smirk. "One day, Ambassador, I'm going to shoot you, thinking you're here to steal your own ship. When are you going to start warning me?"

"Probably one day after you shoot me for not doing it."

She rolled her eyes.

Bastien laughed. "Your crew is a little paranoid, Dane."

"And with reason."

"How so?"

"It's how he met his wife," Yra said drily. "She took our entire shipment while he had his pants down."

"I really wish you'd quit telling everyone that story!" Ryn snapped.

"Why? Mack tells it more than I do."

Grumbling, Ryn went to his con to power up the ship to basic maintenance level. "I curse the day I chose to surround myself with lippy women."

"Yeah, 'cause mouthy men are so much better."

He snorted at Bastien. "Good point."

Bastien swept a hot look over Ember. "And they're not nearly as much fun to ogle."

"Now that's sexual harassment," Ryn reminded him.

"Not if you do it right." Bastien grinned.

Ember sighed. "I'd be offended if I thought for one second he was serious. But I know he's joking. I've never been around anyone more respectful than Bastien."

Ryn laughed as he brought up a map and files. They hovered in the air in front of Bastien. "This is the prison where Syn found him. Apparently, he was only wounded during the coup, and hauled here while you were taken into custody."

Bastien's jaw dropped as he saw the old abandoned prison that had been condemned by his great-grandfather. "Are you sure?"

Ryn shrugged. "Wade doesn't normally make those mistakes." He pulled up more files for Bastien. "Syn's theory is that Quin was to be held so long as you were on the run, in case you came home. He's a pawn Barnabas plans to use against you."

"Can we get to him?"

"That will be tricky. It's a treacherous area of Kirovar and he's down in a hole. Wade said it appears they drop food in to him from time to time. But mostly he's left there to wallow."

He glanced over at Ember. "I'm an expert climber and I've been rappelling my whole life. I can get to him."

Ember nodded in agreement. "I can testify to that."

"All right, then. Operation Suicide. Tell me what you need and we'll scramble."

Bastien should have specified a body double as a parameter for this mission. Damn, it was tight, squeezing down to get to where Syn had said they were keeping his brother. Forget rappelling, this was caving, with them having to drill their way down at times.

"I take it you're also a caver?"

He smiled up at Ember, who was apparently determined to make their son an orphan, as she kept joining him for his suicide runs. "Little bit. Usually with Quin. Lil never had much taste for it."

"I can see why," Xander groused. "Not my idea of fun."

Ryn snorted at him as he continued to dig down. "Stop whining. This isn't so bad. Besides, you never know when the skills will come in handy."

"Like now." Bastien returned to chiseling.

"Exactly."

By the time they reached the bottom, they were exhausted and covered in dirt and grime.

Grimacing, Bastien scratched at his neck and adjusted the light on his helmet. "I'd stay upwind of me if I were you," he warned Ember.

With a gentle tsk, she kissed his cheek. "Your smell doesn't offend me."

He grinned at that. Until he caught a sound off to his left. They drew blasters.

It stopped.

"Quin? That you?"

No one answered.

Bastien walked closer to where the noise had originated. His heart pounding, he tried to peer into the darkness. "We should have brought an Andarion."

Ryn snorted. "We'd have had to blast to get the opening large enough for their body mass."

That was true, but they didn't need a lot of light to see.

"Quin?" Bastien tried again. "You here?"

A whistle rent the air. One he was all too familiar with.

This time, Bastien ducked and twisted out of the way as the paralytic dart shot toward him. It landed harmlessly in the wall.

He lunged at the shooter.

It was a tiny woman. Hissing, she sank her teeth into his hand so hard, she let blood.

Bastien cursed.

"Let her go!"

His heart stopped at that deep, dark voice. A voice he'd never thought to hear again. "Quin?"

Turning his head, he expected to find his ever elegant, impeccably groomed brother. But the man there bore little resemblance to the Kirovarian heir. Dressed in rags, Quin looked worse than Bastien had on Oksana. His brown hair was long and shaggy—and his grimy face had been painted with symbols.

Bastien's jaw went slack. "It's Bastien, *theren*. I mean you no harm." He let go of the woman, who scrambled to Quin's side.

It was only then that Bastien saw she was in the beginning stages of a pregnancy.

Quin still had his blaster trained on Bastien. "What are you doing here?"

"I came to get you free." Bastien held his hands out so that his brother wouldn't mistake his intentions.

"No! You're here to kill me."

When he went to shoot, Ember disarmed him. She flipped Quin to the ground while Ryn and Xander covered the woman. "Don't you dare harm him. Not after everything he's gone through to get to *you*!"

"Ember?" Quin scowled up at her.

"Yeah." She jerked her chin toward Bastien. "Your *theren* was convicted for your murder. You want to explain how it is you're alive and breathing?"

Rage and pain mixed in his eyes with such force it was tangible. A tic started in his jaw. "Barnabas," he growled. "I woke up down here, alone. He told me that Bastien was on my throne."

Bastien opened his coveralls to show his Ravin mark. "Here's a big fucking surprise. He lied."

That drained the anger out of Quin. "You were really convicted?"

"Yeah. For killing all of you. I've been hunted for almost a decade. Thank you for that. You bastard! All you had to do was climb up out of here and you could have told someone the truth!"

"Told who? They'd have killed me."

Bastien scoffed bitterly. "You could have tried, *theren*. Did you?"

"To what end? Everyone but you was dead."

When Bastien lifted his blaster to shoot him for that statement, Ember disarmed him. "Stop it! Remember how upset you were when you thought him dead?"

"Yeah, well, I got over it. Now I remember why I couldn't stand him when he was alive."

Sighing, she shook her head. "We never could leave the two of you alone in a room. I swear." But with that determined glint in her eye that made Bastien's gut tighten, she turned on Quin. "You're both coming with us. We will exonerate your brother, and then if you want to return to live down here, feel free. First, we kill Barnabas and restore Bastien's freedom. Then I don't give a shit what you do."

Bastien wrapped his arm around her and kissed her head. "My baby."

She elbowed him hard. "Don't call me baby."

Coughing, he wheezed from the blow. "Okay . . . forgot how much you hated that. Will *never* forget again."

"Good. Now, let's get out of here."

The woman gestured at Quin.

He shook his head. "He's my brother I told you about."

She gestured again and Quin laughed.

"Yeah, something like that." Sobering, he faced them. "Bastien, this is my wife, Myrna. She was a political activist Barnabas threw down here to die . . . after he cut her tongue out."

Bastien winced. "I'm so sorry."

She gestured at him. While he recognized some of the signs she used, most were her own concoctions.

So Quin translated. "She says it's a pleasure to meet you, and wants to know if you're really planning to kill Barnabas."

"It's why we're here." Bastien gestured to Ember. "This is my wingman, Ember Wyldestarrin. Ryn Dane, and our half brother, Iskander Zeki or Xander as he prefers to be called."

Myrna gasped as she finally looked at Iskander. Then she glanced back and forth between them and gestured wildly.

"Yeah," Bastien said. "They look like father and son."

Quin gaped.

When he started to speak, Bastien cut him off. "He's our *theren*, Quin. An incredible warrior and pilot. And a good man. Treat him better than you ever treated me."

The fire went out slowly in Quin's eyes before he did the one thing he'd never, ever done before. He backed down to Bastien and nodded.

Xander stood slack-jawed until Ember reached up and closed his mouth. "Did he just compliment me?"

"I think you're growing on him." She smiled.

"I think hell just froze over."

Snorting, Bastien and Ryn began looking for a passable way out. But it became obvious why Quin had given up. There was no easy route to the surface.

Not that that had ever deterred Bastien. Over. Under. Around. Or through. He always found a way. And he had too big a debt to settle. High motivation for not staying down here.

As they slowly and carefully made their way up, he tried to understand Quin's mind-set. But then, he'd never understood his brother. Unlike Quin, he'd have never been able to live this close and not strike out.

And Quin had lost a lot more than Bastien had that night. It made no sense.

"People are different, Bassie. You shouldn't judge them by what you would and wouldn't do. What seems easy to you is impossible to someone else. And that's what you should always remember and fear. For too often our prisons are the glass walls that we've fashioned for ourselves with the excuses we've made for why something is impossible when it's not. And we're held back by nothing more than the phantoms of our minds. Shadows that scatter whenever they meet the light."

His mother's words had never seemed more true than they did right now. She was right. Quin wasn't him. It was why they'd always fought. If someone said turn, Quin would go right and Bastien left. It was just how they were.

But that didn't mean that Bastien didn't love his brother. End of the day, he'd kill or die for him, and that was what he couldn't lose sight of.

Or let Quin's acerbic tongue make him forget.

They were brothers. And together, they would all get out of this.

Iskander patiently helped Ember and Bastien up. "I can tell by the light in your eyes that you have a new appreciation for me, GG."

Bastien snorted. "Don't push it, Badger. But yeah, you are cute and fluffy."

And though it took them a couple of hours, they did make it to the top.

Bastien spread out on the ground and pulled Ember down over his body. "I'm just going to stay here for a few hours. Ryn . . . go get the ship and pick us up."

"Ha, ha, ha. Not even. That would require I move, and I don't think I can, either."

Xander rolled his eyes. "What a bunch of old men I got saddled with. Fine. I'll go get it. Y'all stay here and whine."

But the moment he stood up, a shot rang out. It hit him dead in the chest and knocked him to the ground.

CHAPTER 16

Bastien ran to Iskander to check his vitals while Ryn covered them. Choking and wheezing, Xander was bleeding profusely.

His eyes telegraphed his agony.

For the first time, Bastien realized how right Ember had been. This *was* his brother. The fact that they were half-blooded didn't matter for shit. Especially right now.

In fact, he liked Badger a hell of a lot more than Quin. At least he got along with him. He could put him at his back and trust him to protect it. And somehow over the last few months the sneaky little bastard had carved a sacred place in his heart and life. Yeah, Badger was a smart-ass, and crabby . . . a lot like Bastien.

But none of that mattered.

"I've got you, *blyt theren*. Hold on. Don't you dare die on me."

Xander met his gaze. "Are you high?"

Bastien cracked a grin. "Love you, too. And if you die, I'm going to hell so that I beat your ass for it. You hear me?"

He nodded.

"Bas! We've got to move!"

He wrapped his arms around Iskander while Ember took his blaster and offered cover fire for them. As fast as he could, he carried his brother to Ryn's ship, trusting in Ryn to see to Quin and Myrna.

As soon as they were onboard, Ember went to help Ryn with preflight checks. Bastien took Iskander to the infirmary and tended him as best he could.

"Man, I should have paid closer attention in those field dressing classes."

Iskander coughed again. "Yeah. I've seen the scars on your body. You should have."

"You hassling me? Seriously? In your condition?"

"Can't help it. I take after my older brother."

Bastien paused to meet his gaze. It was the first time Xander had said that with any kind of affection in his tone. "Family?"

Iskander nodded and held his hand out toward him. "Family."

Bastien took his hand and held it. "I'll never leave you, *blyt theren*."

"That, I believe. You're too stupid to have any self-preservation."

"I wouldn't need any if my little brother could learn to not walk into a sniper's kill zone."

They were still trading insults when Ember came to check on them after launch.

She paused in the open doorway to take in the sight of her beautiful man with the warrior who'd stepped in to be a role model for her son, even though he wasn't that much older. Because Xander had known how hard it was to not have a father around when he was young, he'd made sure that Florian never missed out.

It warmed her heart and soul to see the two men who were so important to her getting along.

To see them finally as brothers.

Her eyes teared at the sight. "I take it he's okay?"

"Unless I reconsider stabbing him, he'll live."

Iskander tossed a wadded-up piece of gauze at Bastien. "What hit me?"

"League. They're everywhere. What the hell?"

"It's war."

Ryn snorted as he turned on the monitor. "It's more than that. I'm thinking we're tagged. They're following us, so I need all of you to lock in. It's about to get hairy."

"Where's Quin?"

Ryn turned the camera to show him and Myrna buckled into seats on the bridge. "Taken care of. Now batten down. Precious cargo at the helm."

Iskander rolled from the bunk. Bastien helped him out to the hallway, where crew chairs were anchored to the wall. He buckled him in and checked Ember's belt before he took his own seat. He'd barely fastened the harness before Ryn banked a hard starboard.

His crew opened fire on their pursuers.

"Damn, that man can fly." Bastien passed an amused stare to Ember.

She nodded. "It's in his blood. And if you think he's something, you should see his mother in battle. There's a reason they dubbed her Kirren as a call sign."

If her abilities were anything like her son's, he could imagine. The Kirren were mythological birds of prey from Qillaq folklore. It was said their gods would unleash them against their enemies and that no one could stand against them. They flew in with a flash of lightning and a scream of thunder, with tails on fire, raining down their acid breath until nothing was left except smoldering remains.

From what Bastien had heard about how Hermione reacted against anyone who threatened her only child, that sounded about right.

However, at the moment, they were being hammered.

Bastien glanced to Iskander. "You hanging in there, kid?"

He nodded, but appeared a little green and wan.

Bastien reached out for Ember's hand. "You with me?"

"To hell and back."

He smiled at what she used to say back before Alura had driven a wedge between them. And it gave him hope.

"You know, Ember, in my life I've only loved three women."

"Three?" she choked indignantly. "Really?"

"Really. My mother. My sister, and you."

Ember blinked as a wave of tender love for him tightened her throat. "Oh."

"And I failed all three of you. But if we make it out of this alive, will you please, for the love of the gods, finally marry me?"

She laughed at the anguish in his tone. "Yes, Bastien, pain in my ass that you are. I will definitely marry you, so don't go and get killed this time."

"Icky? You heard her, right? You're my witness?"

"I heard, and I will make sure she abides by it, if Ryn doesn't kill us with his flying."

"Good man."

But Ryn was certainly trying. Worse, they were taking direct hits.

Suddenly, a buzzing started. Bastien thought it was an alarm until he heard Ryn's voice over the intercom. "Um, hey baby. Little busy right now. Can I call you and Mom back in a few?"

"Ach! Are you under fire, me Wassie loon?"

"Little bit, yeah."

"And where's me worthless brother who's supposed to be a-watching your back?"

"Not here. Need to focus. Love you."

"And you." Mack cut the link.

Wow, that was some accent she had, and here he'd thought Jupiter's was thick.

He winked at Ember. "Wouldn't want to be Jory when he gets that call, eh?"

She laughed, then groaned.

A shot blasted them and broke through the shields. The ship began to whistle in that unique way that meant they were venting atmosphere.

Shit . . .

If it went out, they wouldn't last any time. And with the way the ship was careening, they couldn't reach the hardsuits.

This was getting scary.

"Everyone harnessed?" Ryn asked over the intercom.

"Yeah."

"Good. I'm going to have to set her down. Hard. Brace!"

Ember turned pale. "Are we near a planet?"

"Hope so." No one wanted to set down on an asteroid while leaking life support.

Her grip tightened on his hand.

Bastien didn't say a word. He was too busy holding his breath as they dodged more fire.

By the time they hit a planet, even Ryn was cursing as most everything had begun short-circuiting. Which meant they hit the ground so hard, it rattled every bone in their bodies. Parts of the ceiling came free and crashed down around them.

Bastien smelled the burning wires and fuel.

Shit! They were going up in flames. His heart hammering, he moved to check on Iskander. "Can you move?"

He nodded. "Get to Ember."

Bastien left him to check on her.

She was unconscious. Worse? Her harness had been damaged on impact and wouldn't release. He pulled out his knife and began to saw on the straps. But because they were made to be fireproof and impact proof, they didn't give.

The smoke thickened. His eyes burned and blurred his sight. Choking on the fumes, he tried the release again. It was still jammed.

Damn it!

Fire crackled and popped. His ears buzzed from his elevated blood pressure and he tasted bile as his panic rose up to choke him. "Come on, baby," he breathed. "Don't you dare leave me. You can't do that to Florian. He'd never forgive you for making me his only parent. I'll screw him up on my own. You know I will. I'm grossly incompetent. I'll be feeding him sweets for breakfast. Letting him wear things you'd kill us both for. He'd never have a bedtime and we'd both be surfing for porn together."

"Don't you dare corrupt my baby!"

He smiled at her irate tone. "Knew that'd revive you better than smelling salts."

She grimaced at him. "You always know just what to say to piss me off."

"That I do." He kissed her lips as a section of the ship fell down around them.

Finally the belt came free.

Scooping her up in his arms, he ran as fast as he could.

He'd barely reached the door when the ship blew apart and sent a shock wave that pitched him forward, onto the burning grass.

Bastien covered her with his body and prayed nothing rained down on her.

Ember groaned as pain throbbed through every last bit of her body. It wasn't helped by Bastien's unholy weight on top of her, but she understood why he was there.

"Are you okay?" she asked him.

He nodded.

Thank the gods.

She had no idea what she'd do if she lost him again.

Bastien rose slowly, then helped her up. Iskander was sitting a few feet away, along with Ryn, Quin, and Myrna, and Ryn's crew.

"We lose anyone?" Bastien asked.

"No, thank the gods." Ryn let out a tired breath. "But the *Cruel Victory* is toast."

Yra patted him on the back. "You better call your mother and wife or they'll be headed this way as soon as their alarms sound."

Cursing, he reached for his link to obey her.

Quin held his wife as he surveyed the damage. His face was pale and haunted. As if reliving a nightmare.

"You all right?"

He shook his head at Bastien's question. "I don't want any part of this, ever again."

Bastien gaped at him. "What the fuck is your problem?"

Quin shot to his feet to confront him. "What's my problem? Everyone in my family was murdered! I have nothing left. What's the point of fighting? There will only be someone else who comes along and tries to take it."

Bastien did the one thing he'd never done in his entire life.

He backhanded his brother. "Fuck. You. Quin. You piece of shit! After all the lectures you gave me about being responsible? About growing up and not being self-absorbed? You dare sit there on the grave of our parents and let our people suffer under the hands of a madman?"

Stunned and furious, he gestured to Myrna. "Look at what Barnabas did to your wife. You think she's the only one he's harmed? He killed Ember's parents and ours. We are Cabarros, you worthless dung-licking dog! You get up and you fight for your people. Your wife! Your child! That is what we do. That is who we are!" He shook his head. "I can't believe I ever looked up to you. That our father held you out to me as the paragon of virtue by which I was always found lacking."

Quin curled his lip. "Open your eyes, Bastien. We're two people. What can we do?"

"Barnabas was one. And if you want to see what one man can do . . . watch me."

Iskander rose. "I'm with you, brother."

Ember blocked his path. "What are you planning?"

"Death. Mayhem. Massive dismemberment."

She didn't move for an entire minute. He was expecting her full argument.

Instead, she nodded. "Let's go."

Iskander scowled at them. "Out of curiosity . . . our ship is over there in flames. So how are you planning to get there? Mindhike?"

Bastien let out an irritated sigh. "You know, I'd be much more pissed off if I didn't feel like having to tolerate you is some kind of karmic debt I've earned."

Ember laughed. "We can hail my sisters."

"All hail the Wildstars."

She popped Bastien's butt. "You're not funny."

"I don't know," Iskander said. "That was pretty good. Wish I'd thought of it."

But all joking aside, Bastien knew things had changed.

And he was done playing.

Bastien was grateful Kindel had put her foot down and insisted that Iskander stay out of the fight. He just wished that she and the others had backed him with keeping Ember out of it, too.

While he liked having her at his back, he would rather not risk Florian's mother.

He paused onboard Cin's ship as they neared Kirovar and drew closer to the palace where Bastien would either fulfill his promise to kill his uncle.

Or die trying.

He turned toward his favorite sister-in-law. "Tasi?"

"Yeah?"

"You still have your priestess license?"

"I do."

"Then marry us before we do this."

Ember's brows shot north. "Pardon?"

"I asked and you accepted. If this goes wrong, and I go down, I want to make sure that no one questions Florian's place as an heir of this empire. It's to protect you both."

Ember's throat went dry at his kindness. Nodding, she agreed. "I always imagined a more formal affair."

He grinned. "Save me from my routine stupidity. Get me out alive, and I'll throw you the biggest damn wedding in the history of the Nine Worlds."

"I don't need that, but something between the level of Nykyrian's and Caillen's will do."

Since Nyk had eloped in a deserted hangar bay with

only criminals to witness it, and Caillen's had been record setting, that left a lot of room for negotiation. "Whatever you want, it'll be yours."

She sobered instantly. "I just want you."

Bastien kissed her. "And I, you."

"Well," Tasi said with a smirk. "You two are married. That was easy. Nice vows. All I need is to declare you as two united hearts before the gods. May you live in peace and remember to hold each other sacred, and yourselves solely one to the other." She drew a circle in the air around each of them and then united it. "There you go. Happy union."

Cin held up her link. "Bas, fingerprint here."

He let it scan his print.

"Now you, sis."

Ember followed suit.

Cin pressed the send. "Paperwork filed. The marriage will hit the system within an hour."

Bastien kissed her. "All right, Major Cabarro. Let's go kick ass."

She cleared her throat. "That's Visira Ember."

He laughed. "Technically, it's monidara."

"Pardon?"

"My brother abdicated. You heard him. As soon as I take Barnie's ass and mount it on my wall, you'll be Her Most Excellent Ember, High Monidara Cabarro."

Ember shook her head as that reality slapped her hard. "Um . . . is it too late to ask for a divorce?"

"Only the monidar can grant it. And I have no intention of doing so. Now . . ." He turned toward Kindel and took the Gyron axe off her belt as they landed in the port just inside the main city with paperwork Syn Wade had forged for them.

She frowned at Bastien's actions. "What are you doing?"

"I swore to bury my Gyron axe in Barnabas's head. Since I don't have one, Kindel's will have to do."

And with that, he lowered the battle shield on his helm and led the way from the landing bay to the palace.

Lacking the easy confidence he exuded, Ember followed with her sisters in tow. How he managed to make this look so easy, she had no idea.

But he was right, no one questioned their presence or the validity of their uniforms that The Sentella had provided for them. They appeared as all the other palace guards. And as Bastien had always said, *act like you know what you're doing, no one questions it.* They didn't even garner a second look.

As if testing his theory, Bastien walked room by room through the elegant Kirovarian palace that had been his home. And Ember tried not to think of the parties she'd attended here where his mother, sister, and Quin had made her feel horrible.

Made her feel lacking and unwanted.

No, that wasn't true. She'd allowed them to make her feel that way. Bastien had never seen her as less. Had never treated her as anything other than his monidara.

Her sister was right. She should never have allowed her own doubts and insecurities to come between them. His family hadn't run her off.

She had.

Bastien could sense Ember's nervousness on this mission. Brand's too. But Kindel, Ash, and Cin were rock steady. Tasi fell between them. She was a bit of both.

His only aggravation came at the fact that he had yet to find Barnabas.

Where was that bastard hiding?

They entered the courtyard where his cousins were playing a chasing game of some kind.

Bastien paused to watch them. Barnabas's granddaugh
ters. Cala would be nine now . . . right around his son's
age. The other two were younger and would have been
born after his exile.

That sent a wave of fury through him that his cousin
Neville, had been allowed to continue on with his life in
happy bliss. Spawning children and living in luxury.

Through the blood of Bastien's family.

His vision turned dark as he left the children in peace
and headed away from them, back into the palace toward
the bedrooms. It was the only place left that Barnabas
could be.

And he wasn't there alone.

The moment he entered the master bedchambers, Bas
tien ground his teeth at the sight of a girl who couldn't be
any older than fourteen. She was in tears.

Half-dressed, Barnabas turned on them with a growl.
"What is this? I didn't request security!"

Bastien glanced over his shoulder to Brand.

She immediately locked the door behind them.

Barnabas went pale. "Open that door!"

Bastien tsked at him. "You know the hardest part about
finding you? The eight palaces my father frequented . . .
you changed up when the emperor occupied them." He
pulled his helmet off.

Barnabas's eyes narrowed threateningly. "You! You
don't scare me! You were never anything more than your
mother's pampered brat."

Bastien nodded. "I was that. And I cherished every mo
ment of it." He waited until Cin had the girl out of harm's
way and isolated in a corner. "You should have never got
ten greedy, Uncle."

"None of you deserved to rule. And none of you will!"
He lunged at Bastien.

Bastien caught him with his fist. And he'd intended to continue it with his fists, until Barnabas pulled a blaster from his boot.

He grabbed Tasi and held it to her head.

Ember gasped.

Bastien went cold. A part of him was pissed that he'd allowed Barnabas to get the drop on them.

It wouldn't happen again.

"You don't want to hurt her," Bastien warned.

"You don't order me around." He glanced about frantically. "All of you! Out of my way!"

Bastien nodded at them to obey. "I'm not the same boy I was, Barnie."

"Don't you dare call me that!"

Bastien held his hands up. "Fine. Asshole works better for me, anyway."

A palace alarm sounded.

"You know what that is?" Barnabas laughed. "It's all of you heading for your executions!"

He was wrong. It was the countdown on his life. But the bastard was too stupid to realize it.

Bastien shook his head. "Do you remember what I said to the Overseer?"

"It doesn't matter."

His guards began pounding on the door with a battering ram.

Barnabas smiled even wider. "They'll be through it in a minute, and when they are, you'll all be arrested."

"What are we doing?" Kindel asked in a panicked tone. "Shouldn't we be running?"

"No," Ember said calmly. "They'll catch us. Just wait here." She gave him a knowing look that said she knew exactly what he was thinking and doing and that she was behind him completely.

"For what?" Cin held a hysterical note in her voice.

"You'll see." Ember smiled.

"What I see is all kinds of crazy!" Brand glared at Ember. "Do something with your husband!"

Ember screwed her face up as she watched Bastien closely. He had a plan. She didn't know what, but she trusted him. "It's okay."

"Not okay," Ash said with a note of panic in her tone.

And still Bastien was completely calm.

Even when the door splintered and guards poured into the room to surround them.

"Arrest them!" Barnabas shoved Tasi toward the guard nearest him.

The instant he did, Bastien let fly his axe, faster than anyone could blink.

Faster than a single guard could shoot.

With unerring aim, it embedded straight between Barnabas's eyes.

Tasi shrieked as his blood splattered all over her.

The guards took aim for Bastien.

"Drop it!" he snarled at them. His regal Cabarro tone was filled with so much inherited command that they obeyed instinctively.

He glared at them. "Now you will bow before your monidar. Long reign His Royal Eminence Bastien, High Monidar Cabarro!"

They hesitated.

Until Ember's sisters took up the chant and bowed to him. The others followed suit immediately.

Bastien held his hand out to her. "My monidara?"

That title sent a chill down her spine. And she had no idea how to address him in turn.

But she took his hand.

He tucked it into the crook of his elbow, then turned toward the captain of his uncle's guards. "Get the body out. Call housekeeping and have this room cleaned and fumigated." He jerked his chin toward the girl. "Call her parents and make sure she's returned to them safely. I'll have my attorneys contact them in the morning. Round up the rest of the former tyrant's family and bring them to the throne room. If Neville so much as sneezes, kill him with impunity. And find the bitch Alura Cabarro."

With those words, he led Ember and her sisters to the throne room.

Every step of the way, she kept waiting for someone to stop them.

They didn't. In her heart, she knew that he was their leader. Rightfully so.

Still, this was terrifying.

More so because he was under a League death sentence.

As soon as they entered the throne room, Kindel cast her gaze around the enormous, gilded walls that were decorated with thousands of formal portraits of Bastien's ancestors. "Uh . . . is it just me or was this too easy?"

Bastien let out an evil laugh. "Day's not over, love. League will order me arrested as soon as this is reported, and Neville will report it immediately."

"Then why are we here?" Cin asked, wide-eyed. "Shouldn't we be fortifying our positions? Arming ourselves? Running?"

Bastien headed to the computer nearest him. "So that I can send *this* over the official network. . . ." He played the file he'd videoed of his brother's outburst that showed Quin was alive and that Barnabas had been the one to orchestrate the murders of their family. "Once the

Overseer sees that, she'll open a formal inquiry. I should be absolved and my Ravin status removed. But only if Neville is dead."

They heard shots fired.

Ember and her sisters drew their blasters.

Bastien didn't.

"What was that?" Brand asked after a few minutes when no one came to arrest them.

"Neville being the idiot. So we no longer have to worry about him testifying."

A few minutes later, a guard came and verified that indeed, Neville had fought against them and had been shot and killed.

"Does this mean we're good?" Ember asked hopefully.

"We're good," Bastien lied. He still had doubts, but he wasn't about to let her know that. Not until he had his son's future secured, and Xander's.

And most of all, Ember's.

One thing was certain. He'd either won a throne today. Or ended his life.

Yeah, his father had been right. He was forever a reckless gambler with one foot in the grave. But as he looked to Ember, he knew that she was his one anchor in life. And that whenever those suicidal tendencies kicked in, she was the only force in the universe capable of pulling him back from it.

She was and would always be his lifeline.

EPILOGUE

In full emperor's robes, Bastien entered the throne room with Ember by his side. This was the day they'd been waiting for and dreading.

Kyr Zemin, the League prime commander, stood there, waiting with his crew and the Overseer.

Ember's hand trembled in his, but she showed no other sign of her nervousness.

And Bastien showed no emotions whatsoever as he met Alia's cold gaze.

"Well?" he prompted.

"You kept your word," Alia said with a light note in her voice. "I will give you that."

Bastien didn't find any humor in her words. "And how do you find now, Overseer?"

"Everything you said has been proven. I've ordered Prime Commander Zemin to remove your name as a Ravin. You're free, Emperor. Congratulations."

Congratulations? Was she fucking kidding, after everything they'd put him through?

He wanted to bury the axe in *her* skull.

But he caught himself and, as he'd promised Ember,

he inclined his respectfully head to the Overseer, even though it galled him through and through. "Thank you, my lady."

Kyr stepped forward. "Now that you've been exonerated of killing your family, I'm here to accept your loyalty oath to The League and the United Systems."

Yeah, right.

Bastien sucked his breath in sharply. "Mmm . . . sorry, Kyr. 'Fraid I can't do that, punkin."

His jaw went slack and the scar around his eyepatch turned whiter. "Pardon?"

Bastien moved to shield Ember with his body and pulled his blaster on Kyr. "Consider yourself arrested by order of the Alliance."

Kyr's one eye flared. He lunged at Bastien, but Bastien caught him and countered the strike. It took him several minutes, but he finally subdued the prime commander and cuffed him.

"This war ends. Today. I've buried enough people I love. I'm not burying any more."

Kyr laughed. "You've no idea what you're doing, Cabarro. You've just made the worst mistake of your life."

"No. I just ended a war that never should have started." He shoved Kyr into the hands of his guards. "Take him to lockup while I call Nykyrian Quiakides to let him know we have Kyr waiting for him."

Alia went pale. "What of me?"

"That's for the Alliance to decide. . . . I hope your son has more mercy on you than you had on him when he stood before your judgement." Bastien jerked his chin at his captain. "Take her."

Ember didn't breathe until they were gone. "I can't believe that worked."

"I told you it would. Now, if you'll excuse me, I have a call to make."

Ember bit her lip as she watched her gorgeous husband head for his war room. She still couldn't believe the last few weeks. So much had happened that it all seemed like a dream most days.

"Alødara?"

She turned at the hesitant sound of her secretary's voice. "Yes?"

"You have an old friend outside who wants to meet with you, but she won't give me her name."

Ember wished she could say that was weird, but since her coronation, old friends had been turning up everywhere. Wanting money, favors . . .

Souvenirs.

It gave her a whole new respect for how normal Bastien had always been, given the attention he'd been exposed to from birth.

With a heavy sigh, she went to her receiving room, expecting to find an old school chum.

But when the petite blonde turned around, all the air left her lungs.

It was Alura.

"What are you doing here?"

Alura raked her with a snotty glare. "So you won after all."

Ember screwed her face up. "This wasn't about winning. My God, Alura! Bastien's a person. And I'm your zusa!"

"None of you ever treated me like family. You were all so jealous of me. My beauty and the fact that I was sasa's favorite."

"Is that why you had him killed?"

She hissed at Ember. "I tried to help him. Tried to warn him. He wouldn't listen!"

Yeah, right. Alura never served anyone but herself. Even now, she was impeccably dressed and it was obvious that she'd suffered no hardship while in hiding.

"Why are you here?"

"Tell Bastien I'm dead. Get him off my back. You owe me that much."

Was she insane? "I don't owe you anything!" Other than maybe a severe ass-whipping.

"I'm your zusa!"

"Yeah. And as you said, you never acted like it. You lied and took my husband from me. You knew I was pregnant and you stole even that! And you think I owe you?"

Alura hissed. "You're such a bitch. Fine. But don't say I didn't warn you."

"Warn me about what?"

She didn't answer. Instead, she headed for the door.

And ran straight into Bastien.

His eyes flared with instant recognition. But before he could reach for her, she turned and ran in the opposite direction with an ear-piercing scream.

Bastien exchanged a fierce frown with Ember as Alura headed for the balcony. There was no place for her to go.

Unless . . .

They both had the exact bad feeling at the same time.

Running together, they reached the doors just as Alura jumped over the edge and plunged to the street below. Traffic screeched to a halt and horns blared.

When she started to look over the edge, Bastien took her arm and pulled her back. "Don't."

Instead, he glanced to the scene below.

"Is she . . ." Ember couldn't get the word past the painful knot in her throat.

"Yeah. She's dead. I'm so sorry, Ember."

Ember burst into tears.

Bastien held her close and let her cry. He wished he could feel the same, but every time he tried to feel bad for Alura, he saw an image of his mother and sister lying dead and couldn't. In his mind, she'd deserved a far worse fate.

But he wouldn't begrudge Ember her grief.

Or her love. Family was family. Even when they hurt you. Even when it was done intentionally. Though he'd never understand why some were born so broken they couldn't be fixed. Why some people could only find happiness by lashing out at others and ruining their lives.

All he could do was be grateful that he wasn't counted among their numbers. Life wasn't about misery. It wasn't about spreading pain.

His father had always said that life was a balance. Good and bad. The goal was to make sure that when you left the world, you left it with the scales shifted as much to the good column as you could.

And so he made himself remember the times with Alura when she hadn't sought to hurt them.

Forgiveness was the only way to heal. And the only way to make sure her poison didn't spread was to forget that she'd ever planted it.

In the end, that was the only way to deal with such creatures. Give them no fertilizer to grow their evil. Let it die with them. Let them pass from the world with no memory that they'd ever walked it.

So he would think no more of their bitter, pain-filled past. Only the future that was Ember and Rian.

And the new life that was growing inside her.

"Bastien?"

Kissing Ember's head, he looked up at Xander's call from inside the room. "Yeah?"

"I hate to bother you."

He rubbed Ember's arm as sirens began to blare from the streets outside. "We know. We saw her jump."

Xander winced. "Not that tragedy. Another one. Kyr."

His stomach tightened as bile rose up in his throat. *Please, gods, no.* "What about him?"

"He just escaped custody."

Bastien cursed as he realized that the war wasn't over. Rather it'd just taken a more sinister bend.

And this time when Kyr returned, he'd be out for all of them. . . .

BONUS STORY

Jullien couldn't have been more stunned had his fraternal twin brother demanded a testicle from him. At least *that* he'd have expected, given the past animosity between them that had resulted in years of the two of them trying to kill each other. He was actually surprised Nykyrian hadn't gelded him before now with a rusted-out spoon.

But this . . .

This was one fucked-up turn of events he'd have never conceived in his most vivid nightmare. Or drugged-out delusion. Obviously the gods were seriously bored and had chosen him for their daily amusements.

Standing in Nykyrian's Triosan office, he arched a brow and tried to keep a straight face as he did his best to wrap his head around his brother's shocking question. "You're sure about this?"

"It's what she wants." Nykyrian swallowed hard as he rose from his desk and slowly approached him. The pain-filled sincerity in those green, human eyes stunned Jullien, as his assassin-trained twin so seldom showed any emotion whatsoever. It just wasn't in Nyk.

Or him, either, for that matter.

And those eyes weakened him even more. Eyes that were so similar to Jullien's and at the same time, served to alienate them both from their birth mother's Andarion culture that hated all things human.

That mutual tragedy was the one tie that bound them and allowed the two of them to put their own mistrust of each other in the past and build a shaky alliance. While they had a long way to go before they were whole with each other, they were slowly making strides to at least become friendly for once.

And that was the biggest miracle of all.

For both of them.

Jullien scratched at his dark beard. "You know, you could ask Ryn to train her." The Tavali ambassador Ryn Dane and Nykyrian went way back. Unlike his bitter, mistrustful feelings for Jullien, Nyk had always trusted and respected Ryn. That would be the much more logical choice for a matter this delicate.

Nyk shook his head. "She doesn't want Ryn. He's not family. And given that his wife is about to birth his son, he'll be distracted and preoccupied with them, as opposed to her safety. Besides, Thia asked specifically for *you* to train her."

Ouch. Talk about wanting to coldcock your dad—and Jullien was definitely an authority on *that* particular topic, as he'd lived his entire youth trying to piss off both his progenitors.

His niece's request must have stung his brother to the marrow of his bones. "Teenage rebellion?"

Nyk snorted at his suggestion. "No, she's not *you*."

Double ouch there. Not that he'd hold it against Nyk. His brother was right, after all.

Jullien was forever a contentious ass, first and foremost. How his wife, Ushara, could stomach him, he had no idea.

There were entire days when even Jullien didn't want to be around himself.

Nyk let out a ragged sigh. "I fear she feels out of place with my other children. Kiara and I have done everything we can to make her feel loved and welcome. But . . . we just can't seem to get through to her. No matter what we do, she still feels like a stepchild."

Jullien ached for his brother. The love Nyk bore his eldest daughter was evident in every line of anguish on his face and in the deep timbre of his voice as he spoke. And Jullien knew from their shared near-death experience that Kiara felt the same about Thia. She couldn't love the girl any more if she'd birthed her.

For himself, he was lucky that his eldest son, Vasili, didn't view him as a stepfather, but rather accepted him as if Jullien were Vas's natural father. And in turn, Jullien loved Vas just as much as he loved the children he'd fathered with Ushara.

It was a shame that Thia couldn't find that same peace with her stepmother that Vas had found with him. And as Nyk had said, he knew it wasn't from a lack of effort on Kiara's part.

Or Nyk's.

He'd seen their love of Thia firsthand. Yet Thia still felt out of place with them. No one knew why.

But if he could help them in any way . . .

"I will guard her like my own."

That finally succeeded in making his brother smile. Or at least as close to it as Nykyrian could manage. A lopsided grin that was more frightening than friendly.

For most people, anyway.

Jullien wasn't most.

Nyk cleared his throat. "That's why I'm entrusting her to you, little brother. I've seen your psychosis where your children are concerned." Crossing his arms over his chest, he smirked. "You still putting Vidar down to nap on your chest instead of his crib?"

"Absolutely." Jullien grinned proudly at something everyone mocked him over. "And to sleep. No way in Tophet I'd trust my infant to rest in his own room. Not after all the shit that I've seen and what was done to us. My girls and Vas are lucky I let *them* have their own beds."

And Vasili was eighteen.

His girls would be starting school in the fall. They'd only graduated to their own beds because Ushara had insisted on it. And had used her unfair wiles against him that he couldn't resist.

He grew hard just thinking about *that* particular fight. It was the only one in his life he'd been happy to lose.

Nykyrian laughed as if he knew where Jullien's thoughts had gone. "That's why I know you're the Tavalian for the job of keeping my girl safe for me." He held his hand out to Jullien.

The moment he took it, Nyk jerked him closer for a brotherly hug.

Jullien closed his eyes, savoring the novelty of it. Though neither of them would ever say the words, they both regretted the years of bitterness that had driven an awkward wedge between them.

But they were getting better.

Slowly.

While still not brothers per se, they were no longer enemies, and were learning that they could reach out to each other without getting slapped for it.

In time, they both hoped to become the family they'd never been.

Clearing his throat gruffly, Nyk clapped him hard on the back and stepped away. "She's in her rooms."

Jullien's gut clenched involuntarily at those words, as he remembered the vicious slap he'd felt when he'd first learned that Thia had been given his old quarters in the Andarion palace after he'd been ruthlessly disinherited. A palace that had been leveled by their own grandmother in an attempt to kill Nykyrian and his family—after putting a brutal hit out on Jullien's life.

But for Jullien and his Tavali brethren, the bitch would have succeeded.

Thankfully, they'd all survived, and now his brother had moved his family into their birth father's palace on Triosa. A palace where Jullien had been made to feel about as welcome as a lethal STD in a whorehouse.

So given that, he well understood Thia's feelings of isolation and not belonging. Of wanting to escape this hell as fast as possible. But to be fair to Nyk, his brother was a good and decent father.

Unlike theirs.

Yeah, there was nothing here he missed at all. The sooner he could leave and get back to his Gorturnum base, and more importantly the family that loved him, the happier he'd be.

And as they entered the east wing, Jullien saw that Thia's current rooms were the ones that had belonged to an aunt who'd finally married. Not that he begrudged his niece her place in the royal family. Never would he slight any of his nieces or nephews anything. Rather, he hated his parents for their lack of regard where he was concerned.

Hence his years of teenage rebellion.

But that was another story and the last thing he wanted to think about.

At the end of the hallway, Nyk knocked on the door and waited for Thia's bored, irritated voice to bid them enter. Rolling his eyes at Jullien, Nykyrian opened the door.

Jullien wasn't expecting the sudden ear-piercing shriek that greeted them.

"Basha Dagger!" Nykyrian's twin sons came running so fast, he barely caught them before they leapt against a part of his anatomy that would have rendered him on the ground in agony.

He smiled at his rambunctious nephews, who jumped all over his body in an attempt to tackle and hug him. "Hey, Terry and Tier. How are my boys?"

Laughing, they wrapped their spindly bodies around his and squeezed tight. Now he fully understood Vas's complaints about his sisters whenever they attempted to scale his body.

After sliding off Jullien's back, Taryn looked down the hallway behind Jullien. "Did you bring Viv and Mira?"

"Vas?" Tiernan added as he clapped his hands in hopeful excitement and did what would also double as an I-need-to-go-to-the-bathroom-Dad dance.

"Sorry, my glorious Fetchyns. It's just me this trip."

Tiernan pouted, but Taryn smiled even wider as he showed Jullien his arm where he still sported Jullien's Tavali patch on his sleeve. "You haven't forgotten, right, Basha Dagger? When I'm growed up, I'm going to be on your crew like kyzu Vasi!"

Jullien barely caught himself before he corrected Taryn's Andarion. "Kyzu" was the female term for a cousin. Vasili would have a fit over that mistake. "Kyzi" was the word the boy wanted. But if Nyk wasn't teaching them proper Andarion, then be damned if he would. "Absolutely, Terry."

Thia tsked at her brothers as she pushed her way past them. "You two need to learn a little restraint." She leaned forward to kiss Jullien's cheek. "What brings you here, Basha?"

He frowned at Nykyrian.

"I didn't tell her I was calling you. Thought you'd want the honor of it, since the final decision about it is entirely yours."

Jullien hesitated. While that was true, he wasn't used to this kind of trust or respect from his birth family. It actually scared him. "Your paka said that you wanted to sign on with The Tavali?"

Her jaw went slack an instant before tears welled in her eyes. "Really?"

Nyk's own eyes moistened. His angst-filled expression probably mirrored the same one Jullien had worn the day he'd decided to let his own son follow him into battle. To this day, he got sick to his stomach every time he glanced over to see Vasili on his ship whenever they came under fire.

"If it's truly what you want, Thia, I won't stop you."

Her joyous shriek made a mockery of her brothers' and caused Jullien to visibly cringe from it. And like her brothers, she threw herself against him so unexpectedly that he barely caught her before they fell to the floor.

"Oh my God! Oh my God! Oh my God!" she repeated fast and furiously. "Love you, Daddy!" She released Jullien, then jumped up to kiss Nykyrian before she dashed into her room to begin frantically pulling clothes from her closet and throwing them on the bed and floor.

Jullien scowled at her exuberant packing. "Should I tell her now or later that The Tavali have a strict dress code and everything she's tossing about is futile?"

Nykyrian grimaced as he stroked his light whiskers. "You can try. She never listens to me."

"Can I go, too, Uncle Basha?"

Smiling at the redundant terms, Jullien picked Taryn up and squeezed him gently. "I'd love to take you, Terry, but I don't think your paka could handle letting go of two babies at once. Your mum, either."

Nykyrian pulled Tiernan into his arms while his younger twin protested it. "Definitely not. Still not sure I won't yet stun Thia and carry her back to her room when she starts to leave."

"Daddy!" Tiernan fussed. "You're crushing me!"

"Sorry."

The tears in Nyk's eyes made Jullien's throat tighten.

"I felt the same way when we dropped Vasili off at university. Ushara cried for a week, and hugged the twins so hard that they're still scarred from it."

Nyk cupped his son's head and kissed the dark curls before he set Tiernan down. "How did you deal with it?"

"Talked to him nine times a day—until he threatened to get a new line and not let us have the frequency. . . . You know I'll bring her straight back if you need me to."

Clearing his throat, Nykyrian wiped at his eyes, then took Taryn from Jullien. "Thank you for doing this. I owe you, little brother."

"Not really." Jullien winked at him. "Given our gruesome past, taking care of your daughter for you is the least I can do."

Thia came running up to him. "Got everything packed. When do we leave?"

"As soon as your father can stand to let you go without shooting one of us."

Nyk ground his teeth, then nodded. "She can go now if she wants."

Taryn's gaze shimmered from his tears. "Thia's leaving?"

That finally shattered her happiness as she knelt down

by his side. "I'm only a call away, Terry. Day or night. And I'll be back every holiday and birthday. Okay?"

Sniffing, he nodded. "You better. I'll miss you."

"Me, too," Tiernan said, wiping at his eyes with a chubby fist.

Jullien turned to find Kiara in the hallway with her youngest daughter asleep in her arms. Out of Nyk's six kids, Zarina was the only one who looked Andarion. The rest could easily pass as fully human.

"Thia's really leaving?" A tear slid down Kiara's cheek.

Thia nodded bashfully. "I'll be back."

And still the tears fell down her face unchecked. Her gaze anguished, she stared up at Nykyrian. "That's it, then. You're right. We're chaining the rest to their beds until after we die."

Thia let out a tired sigh. "Great. My siblings will hate me forever . . . and speaking of—Let me go say good-bye to Adron and Jayce. I'll be right back."

Kiara's gaze followed after her, then she turned to glare at Jullien. "Take her out of here and I'll kill you myself."

He choked at her uncharacteristic threat.

Nykyrian pulled her into his arms and kissed her cheek. "Now, now, Ki, don't threaten him for doing something I asked him to do."

She nodded, and glanced back to Jullien. "You will watch over her?"

"Like I do my own."

Sniffing and laughing, she stepped away from Nyk to give Jullien a kiss. "If she needs anything, call us. We can get to her immediately."

"I will. And don't worry. Ushara's already made a room for her. And Nadya's looking forward to having an older sister-cousin. She was making a welcome banner for Thia with her sisters and my twins when I left."

Thia came dancing out of her brothers' room to grab Jullien's hand. "I'm ready!"

God, how he envied her that enthusiasm that came from venturing into the world with a safety net that would cushion her should she stumble. It was something he'd never known.

Nyk either.

They'd been thrown to the wolves to fend for themselves when they'd barely been out of their nappies. No one had ever given a single shit what happened to either of them. It was what made the two of them so insanely protective of their children.

Jullien glanced between his brother and Kiara. "Are you two ready?"

"Not at all." Nyk winced as he took Zarina from Kiara as if it was the only way he could trust himself to not grab or shoot Thia to keep her there.

"Me, either."

Jullien well understood. "You two stay here and pretend she's going off with friends. It'll be easier."

Kiara yanked Thia into her arms and wailed in the poor girl's ear. "I love you, baby!"

"Love you, too," Thia choked out. For the first time, Jullien saw grief in her eyes and knew that Thia did love them.

But she was old enough now to try and find her own way in the world.

She released Thia to Nyk's embrace. He lifted her completely off her feet with one arm. "Stay safe. Don't make me kill my brother."

"I will and I won't."

And with that, he released her to Jullien's care.

Jullien said a quick good-bye, took Thia's bags from

her hands, and then he and Thia headed for the main entrance of the palace.

He hesitated as they descended the stairs. "You sure about this? You're not going to try and kick open the door when we go to launch, right?"

She laughed. "I'm good. Thank you, Basha Jules."

"My pleasure. As long as you don't get me killed." Jullien winked teasingly at her.

Until they turned the corner toward the exit and came face-to-face with his father.

Tall, blond, and handsome, Aros was an almost identical copy of Nyk, except he lacked the facial scarring Nyk had from his brutal childhood and battles.

Scowling, his father glanced between them. "Is something wrong? Are we under attack again? I was just told that Nyk had granted you clearance to land."

Yeah, because Jullien knew better than to make the request to his father, who'd banned him from landing privileges here more than a decade before—after his father had disinherited him and abandoned him to every assassin in the Nine Worlds who'd been hunting Jullien for his grandmother's thrill-kill warrant. He was so used to his father coldly rebuffing him that he'd long ago stopped reaching out to him in any way.

But Thia didn't know anything about their bloody history, and the last thing he wanted was to taint her relationship with her only surviving grandfather. "Basha Jules is going to train me to be a Tavali."

Aros looked even less enthused about her leaving than Nyk as he met Jullien's gaze. "You weren't planning to tell me you were here?"

Not really. And why should he? Not like his father hadn't banned him from all Triosan territories.

And Jullien's birthright.

Jullien tried his best to ignore the sick feeling in his stomach he got whenever he spoke to his father—like someone had just kicked him in the stones. "Didn't see the need for it, any more than I thought you'd grant me docking privileges if you knew it was me trying to land here."

A harsh dig at his father, but then considering the last time Jullien had requested those privileges he'd been bleeding out from an attack assassins had made on him, and his father had coldly denied the request, it was a well-earned one as far as Jullien was concerned.

"I see." His father cleared his throat, then turned back to Thia. "Stay in touch, my precious little one. We'll all miss you."

She kissed her grandfather on the cheek before Jullien began to lead her away.

"Jullien?"

His gut tightening even more, he paused at his father's call to look at him.

"Take care of yourself and your family."

Like you really give a shit what happens to me, old man.

"I intend to." With that, he left, hating the fact he hadn't been able to make a clean exit. Damn it. Last thing he'd wanted was to see either parent.

Their total lack of care for him while he'd been a kid and cold attitudes toward him as a teen and adult had left him with a bitter hole that could only partially heal so long as he stayed far away from them. The moment they came around, those old wounds ripped open anew, and he despised the fact that they still got under his skin and hurt him.

Why couldn't he put their past to rest? Why did it have to continue to burn so much? So often?

"Are you okay, Basha Dagger?"

He smiled at Thia's warm concern. "Always. Just don't do anything that makes your father kill me," he repeated.

She laughed. "Is Vasili on board?"

"No, sorry. He's studying for the first Tavali exam he has next week so that he can go for his Hazard in the fall. And his pilot's license."

She gaped. "He's that close to becoming a Canted citizen?"

Jullien smiled as he opened the ramp on his ship. "He is."

"You must be proud."

"Honestly? Scared shitless. Last thing I want is for him to be able to request a transfer to another crew."

"You think he'll do that?"

Jullien scratched at his beard. "You know how you're fleeing your father's cloying grasp to join The Tavali because you feel stifled by his overprotective ways?"

"Yeah."

"Let's just say I make your paka look careless with his progeny."

"Oh dear God!"

"Exactly."

"And I suspect ole Jules here will be even worse with *you*."

Thia let out a shriek as she heard Chayden Aniwaya's voice as they entered the flight deck where he was waiting for them. "Chay-Chay Poo Bear!" She ran to hug him.

Bemused, Jullien locked gazes with his first mate and brother-in-law Thrāix, who'd flown in with him and Chayden. "Chay-Chay Poo Bear?" he repeated.

"Don't even start, Dagger," Chayden warned. "My girl can call me whatever she wants. But you two better not."

Thrāix snorted. "Word to the gods, I will *never* call

you Chay-Chay Poo Bear. Especially if there's anyone else around to hear it."

Laughing, Thia moved to kiss Thrāix's cheek. "Basha Tray! How's Sphinx?"

"Growing way too fast for my peace of mind."

"Please! He's barely two months old." Jullien shook his head. "I don't want to hear it, since my girls are now school age. I swear, I blinked and they're ready to start piloting lessons."

"They're not *quite* that old." Thrāix shoved at Jullien. "And speaking of babies, Thia . . . have you heard Dagger's latest news?"

"About Vidar?" she asked. Which made sense since Vidar was Jullien's youngest child.

Chayden snorted. "Sort of."

She screwed her face up at his cryptic response. "What's that mean?"

Jullien turned bright red as Thrāix answered for him. "He's going to have a little brother."

"Pardon?" She gaped.

Jullien cleared his throat as he shifted uncomfortably. "Ushara's pregnant again."

Both of Thia's eyebrows shot up. Not that he blamed her. He'd had the same reaction when Ushara had told him. While he'd been thrilled with the news and was overjoyed to have another baby on the way, he was worried about his wife's health.

But it was what Ushara had wanted. And she'd insisted that she was fine to be pregnant so soon again after Vidar's birth. He, however, was terrified for her.

"Vidar's not even on solid food, is he?" she asked.

Starting the ship, Jullien sighed and rubbed at his forehead. "No. We were using birth control, but . . ."

"Only abstinence is one hundred percent foolproof, Andarion. Didn't you learn anything useful in school?" Thrāix laughed. "We've all been giving Jules hell over it. Feel free to pile on with us."

She tsked at them. "I think it's sweet. Besides, it's not his fault. Everyone knows that Andarions redefine the term 'fertile.'" Winking, she moved to hug Jullien in his chair. "Congratulations, Basha. I always wanted to have siblings close to my own age. Can't wait to meet the newest addition."

A dark shadow fell behind Thrāix's eyes at her innocent comment. Jullien felt for the man. Thrāix's siblings had all been killed during the hostile war that had left his entire race on the brink of extinction.

But Thia had no idea, since it was something Thrāix only spoke about whenever he was extremely drunk, or his wife pried details out of his wounded soul.

Chayden flashed his famous cocky grin. "I still say that if Thrāix is right and this one's a boy, too, we ought to revoke Dagger's naming privileges. Vidarri Samari." He choked. "Poor kid's going to strangle you the day he realizes his name's a nursery rhyme."

Jullien glared at him. "Shut it, Qill. Least we can pronounce his name. What was your last name again? Any Who Yippee Yah?"

"Ah-nah-WAH-yah," Chayden pronounced slowly and in a surly tone, since he took issue with the fact that no one off his home world knew how to spell or say his name. "You're such an ass."

Yes, he was. Chayden should have *never* let him know he had a weakness when it came to his own name. Jullien was a little brother, after all. Irritating others came with that birthright.

Laughing, he glanced at his niece. "If you'll strap in, we'll launch."

Thia ran so fast to her seat that Jullien felt bad for his brother. He prayed his own children were never so eager to leave his company. While Vas's bitching about being left behind whenever Jullien deemed a mission too dangerous for him could wear thin at times, he'd take that over Thia's eager break for freedom any day.

Hours later, Jullien docked them on the Cyperian StarStation that was the Gorturnum home base. He took a minute to marvel at the fact that here on this remote outpost of Tavali outlaws and pirates lay the only true home he'd ever known. Yeah, he'd grown up in palaces, but none of them had ever been nearly as beautiful as this metal-and-glass structure that floated serenely far away from the court life he'd been groomed for.

This fabricated structure placed here by Tavali pirates centuries ago was truly the only peace he'd ever known. Best of all, this was where his real family was waiting.

The sight of their eager faces in the North Bay brought a smile to his lips and a deep warmth to his heart. Even though he'd been flying missions from here for years, he could always count on Ushara to greet him with their children and extended relatives in tow. The only times she missed was when she was with him or some intergalactic threat kept her locked in her office. Then her relatives would be here in her stead, welcoming him as if he were their real son.

After a lifetime of suffering a family that didn't care where he was concerned, he still couldn't believe this was real. That she was really his wife. She had no idea how much it meant to him to see all of them there.

Or maybe she did.

Either way, her thoughtfulness was just one of many reasons he loved her and couldn't imagine returning to a life where she wasn't the best part of his day.

As soon as they had everything locked down, he opened the ramp and cleared Chayden and Thrāix to leave.

Thrāix used his Trisani powers to teleport from the ship to where his wife and son were waiting next to Jullien's.

Thia gaped at him. "I didn't think the Trisani used their powers around others."

Jullien smiled. "Normally they don't. But we're all family here. And if I had that particular set of skills, I'd use them to get to my wife and kids, too."

Chayden grabbed her gear to carry it for her. "Take it to your place?" he asked Jullien.

"Yeah. Thanks."

Thia pouted. "Is there any chance I could get my own apartment or flat?"

Jullien burst out laughing. "Remember, I make your paka look careless. I won't even let Vas live alone."

"Am I going to regret this?"

"Probably," Jullien snorted. "Most beings regret being around me, sooner rather than later." He winked at her. "But as my new Crew Cock, I own you and am responsible for everything you do."

Chayden shook his head. "Don't take it personally. Your uncle's insane."

Jullien snorted. "You know, *Psycho Bunny,* she's not the one you need to worry about taking that personally. I'm the one who's currently armed."

"Yeah, but you love me."

Jullien rolled his eyes as he left the ship and was swarmed by his daughters and nieces. He knelt on the ground so that they could each have a turn at hugging him.

Thia hesitated at the sight of the banners that welcomed her to their Nation.

Jullien watched her while he returned jubilant hugs and kisses. He stood up to kiss Ushara and take his infant son from her arms so that she could greet Thia.

Thrāix's wife—Ushara's youngest sister, Mary—came over to him. "You want me to babysit while you get Thia settled?"

Jullien wrinkled his nose at her. "Appreciate the offer, kisa, but I haven't seen my boys or girls in days." He cradled Vidar under his chin so that he could hold him with one arm while he cupped his daughter Mira's head with his hand. Any time he returned, Mira always clung to his leg for two to three days. It was amazing to him how well he'd learned to walk with her as a symbiotic life form attached there. She was even standing on his boot so that she could stay in place while he moved.

Mary rose up on her toes to give him a kiss. "Love you, *drey*. Remember that I offered." She flounced off to return to Thrāix, who was as eager to get her home as Jullien was to be alone with Ushara.

But that would be hours away—after the kids were all settled.

His adoptive mother, Unira, approached, laughing. "Want me to hold Vidar for you, precious?"

He cracked a shy smile. "Nah, Mata. You know I live for this."

Rubbing his back, his mother kissed his cheek, then went to greet Thia and welcome her to their family. As a high priestess, she had the warmest heart of anyone Jullien had ever met.

Except maybe Ushara.

As soon as Unira spoke to her, tears welled in Thia's

eyes. An instant later, she caught a sob and dashed off toward the work area.

Stunned, the entire crowd turned to stare at him like he'd been the cause of it.

Every bit as surprised, Jullien finally handed his son to his mother, then picked up Mira. "Paka needs to see to Thia, bug. Can you stay with your mum for a minute?"

"Okies, Paka."

Ushara bit her lip. "Should I go?"

"I'd love to toss this at you, but I better do it since I'm her blood basha. Be right back."

He used his extrasensory powers to find Thia inside the ladies' room. Her sobs would have been evident even without his heightened Andarion hearing.

Shit. It figured she'd find the one place he couldn't follow.

Clearing his throat, he knocked on the door. "Thia?"

The sobs lowered, but remained constant.

Jullien sighed in irritation. "If anyone other than my niece is in there, speak up, 'cause I'm coming in!"

He paused for an answer, then reached for the controls. Before he could open it, Thia did.

Her eyes glistened as her lips quivered. Damn, he'd never been able to stand seeing a female cry. Cupping her cheek, he gently wiped her tears away. "You miss your paka?"

With a ragged breath, she shook her head. "Sorry, Basha. I just . . . I wasn't expecting them to be so nice and welcoming."

He laughed at her words. "Yeah, the one thing about the Altaans . . . anything worth doing is worth *over*doing. You want me to scatter them?"

Sniffing, she licked her lips before she spoke again. "Can I ask you something? Will you be honest?"

Almost afraid of that question, he nodded. "You can ask anything. But I warn you that I'm terribly blunt. Shara gets onto me all the time for it."

"I'm good with that. My dad refuses to answer most questions. It's like interrogating a hostile war criminal. He just stares at me like an alien lifeform . . . and my step-mother is so polite it's irritating. I swear she dances away from topics she doesn't like even better than she dances onstage."

"Well, no worries there. I definitely don't fall into that latter category. No one has *ever* called me polite."

Wiping at her eyes, she offered him a bashful smile. "I know some of the background with you and my grand-mother. And Aunt Tylie and Grandpa Aros. But I wanted to know if you ever felt out of place while you lived with them?"

"Only every minute of every single day."

Sniffing, she dabbed more at her eyes. "That's why I wanted to come stay with you. You're the only one who doesn't tell me how lucky I am and how great my parents are. That I should show more gratitude toward them all. I mean, I know they love me, and they are great most of the time, but I'm tired of being treated like I'm some frag-ile object that they're afraid is going to crack if they say or do the wrong thing. I just want to find someplace where I belong."

"I can definitely relate to that. And I promise you, no one here will treat you like you're fragile. Tavali pull their own weight."

To his further shock, she walked herself into his arms. "Thank you for letting me come here. I hope I didn't offend them."

"Nah, trust me, precious, that wasn't offensive. They tolerate my contentious ass and I'm hard to get along with on my best days."

She laughed. "You really don't mind training me?"

"We're family, Thia. You'll always be welcomed wherever I am. And once you're Tavali, you'll never be without a home."